More praise for
The Trials of Tiffany Trott . . .

"[A] picaresque tale of a single woman's quest for the man of her dreams." —*The Independent* (London)

"Tiffany has a sense of humor as she ploughs her way through a succession of disastrous dates."
—*Literary Review*

"There's something about our Tiffany that gets under your skin and really makes you care whether or not she bags her man." —*Options*

"Takes a humorous look at the ever-growing singles scene, and the dilemma of the successful older (thirty-something) woman trying and failing to have it all."
—*Dillo* *Review*

The Trials of Tiffany Trott

Isabel Wolff

AN ONYX BOOK

ONYX
Published by New American Library, a division of
Penguin Putnam Inc., 375 Hudson Street, New York, New York 10014, U.S.A.
Penguin Books Ltd, 27 Wrights Lane, London W8 5TZ, England
Penguin Books Australia Ltd, Ringwood, Victoria, Australia
Penguin Books Canada Ltd, 10 Alcorn Avenue, Toronto, Ontario, Canada M4V 3B2
Penguin Books (N.Z.) Ltd, 182–190 Wairau Road, Auckland 10, New Zealand

Penguin Books Ltd, Registered Offices:
Harmondsworth, Middlesex, England

Published by Onyx, an imprint of New American Library, a division of Penguin Putnam Inc.
Originally published in Great Britain by HarperCollins*Publishers*.

First Onyx Printing, August 1999
10 9 8 7 6 5 4 3 2 1

PUBLISHER'S NOTE
This is a work of fiction. Names, characters, places, and incidents either are the product of
the author's imagination or are used fictitiously, and any resemblance to actual persons,
living or dead, events, or locales is entirely coincidental.

For my parents.

And in memory of my brother
Simon Paul Wolff
The funniest person I ever knew.

ACKNOWLEDGMENTS

Many people helped me get this book off the ground, and I would like to thank them from the bottom of my heart. I am grateful, above all, to Clare Conville, probably the best agent in the world; to Amanda Denning for being my willing partner in crime—or rather fun; to Eric Bailey and Kate Summerscale for helping me dream Tiffany up; to Rachel Hore for her editorial guidance, and to the talented team at HarperCollins; I am also indebted to Kim Macroddan and Lynn Gardner for their ideas and constant support; to Elizabeth Mellen for expert advice on babies and art; to Louise Clairmonte who was there through thin and thin; to Marjaana Vanska and Marian Covington of the Chelsea and Westminster Hospital; to Lauren Brink and Edip Adanir of the Ritz; to the staff of the Chelsea Arts Club for letting me snoop; to William Hanham for showing me round Albany; and to Richard Beswick for the brass band. For translations I would like to thank Lindis Hallan, Cristina Lerner, Cristina Di Rienzo and Takako Prentis. I am very grateful, too, to Marian McCarthy for her generous enthusiasm, and I am profoundly thankful, as ever, to Matthew Wolff and all my family.

May

OK. Champagne—tick; Cheesy Wotsits—tick; flowers—tick; balloons—tick; streamers—tick; cake—tick; candles—tick—oh God, oh God, where are the candleholders? Blast—I haven't got thirty-seven, I've only got, um . . . eighteen, nineteen, *twenty*. Blast. *Blast*. Where's that list gone? Oh here it is. Right. Where was I? Oh yes . . . candleholders . . . Twiglets—tick; Hula Hoops—tick; assorted mixed nuts—tick; nosh—tick. Oh gosh. Nosh. Rather a lot of that. I mean, how are we going to get through 150 prawn toasts, 200 devils-on-horse-back, 350 cocktail sausages glazed with honey and tarragon, 180 oak-smoked salmon appetizers and 223 spinach and cheese miniroulades? *How* exactly are six people expected to eat all that? Plus the ninety-five chocolate éclairs? Just six of us. Half a dozen. Or precisely twelve percent of the original invitation list. Bit of a disappointment, and I'd had such high hopes for this evening. I'd had the sitting room decorated specially. Terribly pretty Osborne and Little wallpaper and a hand-gilded chandelier. But then I felt like pushing the boat out a bit this year. Going the whole hog. After all, I've got something to celebrate—a Very Serious Relationship with a *really* nice bloke. Alex. My boyfriend. My chap. *So* nice. Lovely in fact. Really, *really* lovely. And there are still quite a few people who haven't met him, and I really wanted to have this party for him as much as for me. And now it's going to be a damp firecracker. But that's the really annoying thing about entertaining, isn't it?

The way people cancel at the last minute, when you've already done all the shopping. Unfortunately I've had quite a lot of cancellations—forty-four actually—which means my big bash for fifty is now going to be rather a discreet little affair. This means it is most unlikely to make the society pages of the *Highbury and Islington Express*. Blast. But then all my friends are having crises with their babysitters, or their nannies have resigned, or their offspring are off-color or their husbands are unhappy. It's such a bore when the majority of one's pals are married and family pressures take precedence over fun. For example, Angus and Alison canceled this morning because Jack's got "potty trouble"—did she really have to be quite so graphic about it?

"I'm terribly worried, it's gone all sort of greeny-yellowy-orangey," she said.

"Thank you for sharing that with me," I replied crisply. Actually, I didn't say that at all, I simply said, "*Poor* little thing, what a *terrible* shame. Anyway, *thanks* for letting me know." Then at lunchtime Jane and Peter blew me out because their au pair's run off with the boy next door, and even Lizzie—my best and oldest friend—even Lizzie can't come.

"*Sorry,* darling," she said when she called me yesterday morning. "I'm, really *really* sorry, but I'd *totally* forgotten it's school vacation, and I want to take the girls away."

"Oh, well, never mind," I said, philosophically. "Where are you going?"

"Birdwatching in Botswana. The Okavango's divine at this time of year."

Crikey—some vacation treat, I thought, beats a day out at the zoo.

"I've just managed to pick up a last-minute package with Cox and Kings," she said, audibly drawing on a cigarette. "We're flying to Gabarone tonight."

"Is Martin going with you?" I inquired.

"Don't be *silly,* Tiff," she said with a loud snort. "He's *work-*

ing." Of course. Silly me. Poor Martin. And then Rachel phoned last night to say she couldn't face the party because she's got terrible morning sickness ("But my party's in the *evening*," I pointed out); and two hours later Daisy rang to say she's got funny pains in her lower abdomen and daren't come out because it's probably the baby arriving early. Then this morning Robert phoned to say his mother-in-law's ill, so *they* can't come, and then Felicity rang to say that Thomas is teething and won't stop blubbering and so that's it—now we are six. Six singles, as it happens: Sally, Kit, Catherine, Frances, Emma, me and, of course, Alex. My boyfriend. My chap. I may not have a husband but at least I've got a bloke. Which is more than can be said for my other single women friends. Poor things. Must be *so* depressing for them. Being single. At our age. Dreadful. And incomprehensible—after all, they're so eligible. And so attractive. Especially Sally. She's really gorgeous. And she's loaded. But even Sally finds it hard to meet decent blokes. Luckily for me I've got Alex. Phew. And it's serious. Actually I've been going out with him for quite a long time now—eight months, three weeks and five days. In fact, well, put it this way—I've just taken out a subscription to *Brides and Setting Up Home*.

I'd like to say it was an unforgettable party. And in some ways it was. It started quite promisingly. Sally arrived first, at seven-thirty, which amazed me as she works twenty-nine hours a day in the City, and OK I know she earns a fortune—I mean her half-yearly bonus is probably twice my annual income—but even so, she's *so* generous with it—she'd bought me a Hermès scarf. Wow! You don't spot many of those around here. That should bring the area up a bit. I can see the headline in the local paper now: HERMÈS SCARF SPOTTED IN UNFASHIONABLE END OF ISLINGTON. HOUSE PRICES HIT NEW HIGH.

"It was duty free," she said with a grin, "I got thirty percent off it at Kennedy Airport. Oh Tiffany, you've decorated in here—it looks lovely!" She removed her pale-pink cashmere cardigan, revealing slender, lightly tanned arms.

"God, I've had an awful day," she said, slumping into the sofa. "The dollar dropped ten cents in half an hour this afternoon. It was panic stations. Sheer bloody hell."

I always find it hard to visualize Sally at work, yelling into her phone in a testosterone-swamped City dealing-room, screaming, "Sell! Sell! Sell!" at the top of her voice. That's what she does, not every day, but quite often, and it's hard to imagine because she's as delicate and fragile-looking as a porcelain doll. Unlike Frances, who arrived next. Now Frances is by contrast rather, well, solid. Handsome, I suppose you'd say. Impressive, distinguished-looking, like a Sheraton sideboard. She's alarmingly bright too—she got a double first in law at Oxford. I don't think this endears her much to men.

"Happy birthday, Tiffany!" she exclaimed in her booming, basso profundo voice. It's an amazing voice, deep and reedy, like a bassoon. She was looking smart in an Episode linen suit, dark of course, for court, her auburn hair cut short and sharp around her fine-boned face. Anyway, she'd brought me this lovely book, *Face Facts—the Everywoman Guide to Plastic Surgery.*

"That's really thoughtful of you, Frances," I said. "I'm terribly interested in all that, as you know."

"Yes, that's why I've given it to you," she said. "In order to put you off. The photos are absolutely beastly."

And then Catherine arrived, bearing a huge bunch of peonies, her fingers still stained with paint, a faint aroma of turpentine clinging to her long red hair. Catherine restores pictures, painstakingly swabbing at them with cotton buds and tiny brushes, eliminating the grime and dust of decades. Showing them in their true colors, I suppose you'd say.

"Sorry, I haven't changed, Tiff," she said. "Hope we're not too formal."

"Well no, it's just the six of us," I said. "Everyone else has cried off."

"Oh good," she said, with a glance at the dining room table, "all the more for us! Gosh those sausages look delicious!"

Catherine is very boyish. She usually wears jeans, and her lightly freckled face is always shining and scrubbed. And I have never, ever, seen her wear makeup. Not even mascara. Not even *lip gloss*. Whereas I—well, the thing I seem to use most of all these days is concealer. Industrial amounts of it actually, which I carefully apply with a garden trowel, filling in the widening fissures beneath my eyes.

Then at eight Emma turned up with a large box of Godiva chocolates. "School was a *nightmare*," she said. "I've had the most desperate lot of delinquents all day. TGIF, as they say— Happy birthday, Tiffany—my God, what a lot of food, are you expecting an army?"

"Er no, just a few regular troops, actually."

Last to arrive was Kit. "Happy birthday, Tiffany!" he said, wrapping me in an enormous hug and planting a noisy kiss on my left cheek. Thank God for Kit. I often think I should forget about Alex—where *was* Alex, I wondered—and concentrate on Kit. My mother thinks I should marry him. My father thinks I should marry him. Lizzie thinks I should marry him. *Everyone* thinks I should marry him. Why didn't I marry him? I suppose because the moment when it might have happened came and went years ago. But he's still my other half—my creative other half, that is. I do the words, and he does the pictures. He's my art director, you see. That's how we met—on the Camay account at Gurgle Gargle and Peggoty. But now he's my *knight chevalier*, my best male pal and, quite often, my colleague too. I love working with Kit. He's freelance, like me, and we still collaborate on campaigns sometimes, though what he really wants is to direct TV commercials.

"Did you get the Kiddimint job?" he asked as we sat sipping champagne in my tiny garden.

"Yes, I did," I said, picking a few late lilies of the valley to put on the dining room table. "Blow, Coward Spank want the script in three weeks. Haven't a clue what I'm going to do with it. Never done toothpaste before, let alone kids' toothpaste. They want a cartoon. I might do something with Macavity, from *Old Possum's Book of Practical Cats.*"

"You mean something like 'Use Kiddimint twice a day kids, and Macavity *won't* be there!' "

"Yes. Something along those lines. That sort of thing. If they're prepared to pay the royalties. What are you working on?"

He grinned. "I'm going to be—assistant director on a hair-spray commercial!"

"Kit, that's *fantastic.*"

"I *know.*" He could hardly conceal his joy. "Cinema and TV. *Big* budget. It should look great. Head Start hairspray. For Yel-lowspanner. We're shooting it in Pinewood, sci-fi style. We've cast this Claudia Schiffer lookalike," he continued. "She's rather scrumptious, gorgeous in fact—and the way she tosses her hair to camera is sensational! But I'm not telling Portia that," he added anxiously. "I wouldn't do anything to make her feel insecure."

Pity, I thought. It would do no harm at all for Portia—commonly known as "Porsche"—to feel less than one hundred percent confident in Kit. She walks all over him in her Manolo Blahnik stilettos, leaving a trail of bleeding holes. I don't know why he bothers. Actually, I do. After all, he's told me often enough. He bothers because he loves her and has done ever since she tottered onto the set of that vodka commercial eigh-teen months ago. Portia, you see, is a model, but she's hardly a model girlfriend. In fact, to be quite honest, she treats Kit like dirt. But he adores her. Isn't that funny? He worships her. And the more indifferent she appears, the more intense his interest becomes. But then I'm the same. I mean, I'm always *incredibly* nice to men—and what do they do? Treat me disgustingly. I don't know why. It's not as though I don't make an effort. I listen to them drone on for hours about their problems at work, and then I cook them supper. If there's a show they want to see, I'll get tickets for it, often queuing for returns. I buy them birthday cards to send to their mothers, and sew the buttons back onto their coats. And what do they do for me? Not ring when they said they would, then not even remember that they forgot to ring. And sometimes—and this is *really* annoying—they don't turn up at all. All the ones I've been keenest on have treated me like that. Isn't that strange? All except Alex, that is. Alex has always been *so* sweet. *So* considerate. *So* thoughtful. For example, he got me a really good discount on my Nina Campbell curtains and he gave me some excellent free advice about paint effects in my kitchen.

"Look, no one rag rolls anymore, Tiffany," he said. "And sponging is such, well, *vieux chapeau*. I suggest you go for a very simple colorwash in a pale tone, say eau de nil, with the barest hint of teal. That's what I've just done for Lady Garsington—I could get some mixed for you too." He also showed me how to accessorize my bathroom properly, with antique stoneware bottles and waffle-weave bath towels and lovely pebble doorknobs—no more ceramic fish and bobbly bath mats. Oh no. I've really learned *a lot* from him. I mean, what he doesn't know about cracked glazes . . . but where *was* Alex, I wondered again. He's usually as reliable as a Rolex. And then I found myself wondering what he'd got me for my birthday—probably a year's subscription to the *World of Interiors,* or something tasteful in the soft furnishings lines. He gave me a pair of wonderful velvet cushions in chrysanthemum yellow for Christmas—typically thoughtful. But that's Alex all over—really, really nice and considerate although . . . now, I don't want to sound disloyal or anything, but there is just *one* thing I'd criticize about him, and that is that he doesn't play tennis—and I love it. In fact he's not very sporty. Also, I'm not too mad on his button-right-up-to-the-neck pajamas or his habit of playing Scrabble in bed. But then, well, you can't have everything. It's all a compromise, isn't it? That's what it's all about. Taking the wider view. And it was so nice to meet someone caring and kind after my miserable time with Phillip. Phil. Commonly known as Phil Anderer. No, Alex was such a refreshing change after all that.

Suddenly Kit stood up and went and leaned against the French windows. "I'm sorry I didn't bring Portia with me," he said. A slight frown furrowed his brow. "You see, she's got one of her headaches. Didn't feel up to it. But she said she didn't mind if I came on my own. Didn't want to spoil my fun. She's very good like that. Not at all possessive. I offered to come round and look after her," he added with a rueful smile, "but she said she didn't need me. Said she could do without me."

What a surprise, I thought. From inside the dining room we could hear the popping of champagne corks and the squeak of party blowers.

"*Wahay*—let's get sloshed," I heard Frances say.

"Yeah—*let's*," said Emma. "Let's get really *plastered*. I mean it's Friday. We work bloody hard. And this is a *party*. God these canapés are good. Pass me a mini pizza, would you? I had the most horrible lot of fifth-formers today—thick as pig shit."

"Sally, please would you put your laptop away?" Frances boomed. "*Relax*. The weekend starts here."

"I'm sorry," I heard Sally reply pleadingly. "I just need to have a *quick* look at Wall Street to see how the pound closed against the dollar—won't be a sec."

"We're doing the Napoleonic wars at the moment," Emma continued. "I've just been supervising their GCSE project and one particularly thick kid managed to get a nuclear submarine into the battle of Waterloo!"

"That's unbelievable," said Frances.

"Quite," Emma replied.

I looked at Kit. His black curly hair was a little long, his face appeared tired and strained. He was fiddling thoughtfully with the stem of his champagne flute. Then he turned to me and said, "I don't know what to do, Tiff."

"About what?" I said, though of course I knew. We'd had this conversation many times before.

"About Portia," he said with a sigh.

"Same problem?" I asked.

He nodded, mutely. "She says she needs more time," he explained with a shrug. "That she's just not ready for it. Of course I don't pressure her," he added. "I'm just hoping she'll change her mind. But I'd really *love* to marry her. I'd love to settle down and have a family. This single life's a drag."

"Hear hear!" said Catherine, stepping through the French windows. "But you're a rare bird, Kit—a man who actively wants to make a commitment. My God, I'd marry you tomorrow!"

"Would you really?" he said.

"Yes. If you asked me. Why don't you ask me?" she added suddenly. "I'm sure we'd get on."

"Or me, Kit," said Sally, following behind. "I'd snap you up in a flash—you'd better watch out, Portia, I'm after your man!" She giggled winsomely, but then an expression of real regret passed across her face. "I wish all men were like you, Kit, ready to bend the knee, then girls like us wouldn't be crying into our hot chocolate every night."

"Speak for yourself," said Frances. "I'm not crying—I'm out clubbing. Much more satisfactory. And the music drowns out the loud tick tock of my biological clock."

"I can't hear mine," said Emma, "it's digital."

"Mine sounds like Big Ben," said Frances. "Except that there's no one to wind it up. But do you know," she continued, peeling a quail's egg. "I really don't care; because finally, after thirty-six years, I've realized that the vast majority of men simply aren't worth having. Anyway," she added, "who needs one? I'd rather go rollerblading in the park on a Saturday morning than go to Sainsbury's with some totally useless bloke."

"I don't think you really mean that," I said. "It's because of what you do—I mean sorting out other people's ghastly divorces all day would put anyone off marriage."

"It's not just that," said Frances. "Though after fifteen years of establishing who threw the bread knife at who in 1979 you certainly *do* get a little jaundiced. It's simply that most men are boring. Terribly, terribly boring. Except you, of course, Kit," she added quickly.

"Thanks," he said, peevishly.

"I mean why should I go to all the trouble of pinning down some bloke," Frances was still going on, "only for him to *bore* me to death!"

"Or run off with someone else," added Emma with sudden feeling. "Just like my father did."

"There just aren't any really nice, *interesting,* decent, suitable, trustworthy men," Frances concluded comprehensively. *Yes, there are,* I thought to myself smugly. *And I've got one.*

"I'm just facing facts," she said with a resigned air. "I've weighed up the evidence. And the evidence is not in our favor. So no Bland Dates for me," she added firmly. "I, for one, have decided to give wedded bliss a miss."

"Better single than badly accompanied," added Emma.

"Quite!" said Catherine.

"Three million single women can't be wrong," said Frances, who always has some handy statistic at the ready. "Anyway, why bother when over forty percent of marriages end in divorce?"

"And *why* do they end in divorce?" asked Emma with sudden vehemence. "Because it's usually the man's fault. That's why. It was certainly my father's fault," she added fiercely. "He just fancied someone else. Plain and simple. And believe me, she *was* plain and simple. But she was younger than my mother," she went on bitterly. "Mum never got over it."

"Men get far more out of marriage than women," said Frances expansively. "Sixty percent of married women admitted in a recent survey that if they could have their time over again, they would not have married their husbands."

"I'm really not enjoying this conversation much," said Kit with an exasperated sigh. "I mean it's so difficult for men these days. Women have made us all feel so . . . redundant."

"You *are* redundant," said Frances with benign ferocity. "What can a man give me that I don't already have? I've got a house, a car, a good job, two holidays a year—long-haul—a wardrobe full of designer clothes and a mantelpiece that's white with invitations. What on earth could a man add to that?"

"Grief!" said Emma rancorously.

"Ironing," said Catherine.

"Boredom," said Frances.

"Acute emotional stress," said Emma.

"Arsenal," said Catherine.

"Betrayal," said Emma.

"A baby?" said Sally.

"Oh don't be so old-fashioned," said Frances. "You don't need a man for that. How old are you now?"

"Thirty-eight."

"Well, if you're that desperate to procreate, just pop down to the sperm bank or have a one-night stand."

"Alternatively, you could arrange an intimate encounter with a turkey baster and a jam jar," added Emma, with one of her explosive laughs. "I hear they're very low maintenance and you wouldn't need to buy any sexy lingerie!"

"Or, if you're prepared to wait a few more years, you can dispense with the sperm altogether and get yourself *cloned,*" said Frances. "That day is not far off—remember Dolly the sheep?"

"I'd *love* to have a baby," said Sally. "I really would. My parents would love me to have one too—they go on about it a bit, actually. But I'd never have one on my own," she added purposefully. "Cloned, turkey-basted or otherwise."

"Why not?" said Frances. "There's no stigma these days. I'd

do it myself only I'm far too lazy. All that getting up in the middle of the night would kill me at my age."

"For God's sake, you're only thirty-six, not sixty-three!" said Catherine.

"What, precisely, are your objections to single motherhood, Sal?" Frances asked.

"Well, I just don't think it's fair on the child," she said. "And then some poor man always ends up having to pay for it, even if he never gets to see it and it wasn't even his decision to have it."

"Then the silly bugger should have been more *careful*," said Emma triumphantly.

"Well, yes. But, speaking personally—this is just my point of view, OK—I think it's unfair and I know that, well, it's something that I would *never, ever* do," Sally said. Suddenly a high warble began to emanate from her Gucci handbag. "Sorry," she said, getting out her mobile phone. "This'll be my update on the U.S. Treasury Long Bond. It's been a bit wobbly lately. Won't be a moment." She stepped back into the dining room, where we could see her pacing slowly back and forth while she talked, with evident agitation, to a colleague in New York.

"Lucky old Tiffany," said Catherine, snapping a breadstick in half. "She doesn't have to worry about all this sort of thing."

"No, she doesn't," said Emma, shivering slightly in the cooling air. "She's got a man. It's all sewn up and she's heading for a wedding." She cupped her hand to her ear. "I can hear the peal of bells already. So when's he going to pop the question, Tiff?"

"Oh gosh, well, I mean I don't . . ." Pity the sun had gone in.

"Yes. *When*?" said Frances, with another gulp of champagne. "And can I be your maid of dishonor?"

"Well, ha ha ha! Uhm—I don't know . . . er . . ." I glanced at the sky. A thick bank of cloud, gray as gunmetal, had begun to build up. Where had that come from?

"Are we all warm enough?" I asked. "And, er, who wants another parmesan and red pepper tartlet?" In fact, I was desperately trying to change the subject because, you see, I really didn't want to rub it in—I mean the fact that I had a chap, and they didn't. Because, to be quite honest, I had been sitting there, throughout that discussion, quietly thanking God for Alex. Even if he has got sloping shoulders and a rather girlish giggle which, to be perfectly frank, does make my heart sink at times. But, still, I thought, at least I don't have to contemplate self-insemination or agonize about my ovaries because a) I've got a chap and b) I know for a fact that he likes kids. He really, *really* likes them. Loves them. I mean he's *awfully* good with his niece and nephew—spoils them to bits—and I'm sure he'd be a brilliant father. He wouldn't mind changing nappies. In fact he'd probably *enjoy* it. And OK, so I know he's not perfect—in fact there are one or two other things about him that I'm really not crazy about, including his goatee beard, his outlandish taste in socks, and his thin, unmuscular thighs. But then no one's perfect. It's all about compromise, isn't it? That's what enlightened and mature people do. And Alex is really charming. Absolutely *sweet,* in fact. And certainly not the unfaithful type. Unlike Phil. In fact, when I first met Alex, he was such a gentleman it took him three months just to hold my hand. Which was rather nice. In a way. *Anyway,* I was quite sure that Alex was about to pop the question. I could tell by the vaguely nervous way in which he'd been looking at me recently. And eight months is quite long enough, isn't it? At our age? I mean, he's thirty-eight. I'm now thirty-seven. So what's the point of hanging around? Why not just, well, *get* on with it? It's not as though he's got three-ex-wives and five children to support; he's totally unencumbered—another *very* big point in his favor, incidentally.

So while the others continued arguing about the changing roles of men and women and the declining popularity of marriage, I did some mental shopping for the wedding which would be in, what . . . September? Lovely month. Or if that was too soon, December. I love the idea of a winter wedding.

Dead romantic. We could all sing "The Holly and the Ivy" by candlelight, and I could have tinsel draped over the altar and wear a captivating fur-trimmed train. Now where should I get the dress? Chelsea Design Studio? Catherine Walker? Terribly expensive, and in any case if Dad was spending that kind of money, I think Alex prefers Anthony Price. I know Alex would definitely want the flowers to come from Moyses Stevens. He's very fussy about his floral arrangements. How many guests? A couple of hundred—217 to be exact, I've already drawn up the list, actually. Well, it'll save time, won't it? And what about the honeymoon? Probably somewhere arty, like Florence. Alex would really like that. Or maybe Seville. Or Bruges. Somewhere with loads of art galleries and at least seventeen cathedrals. And . . .

"Tiffany, where *is* Alex?" Catherine asked. "It's a quarter past nine."

"Er, I don't know," I said. "Maybe he's stuck at work."

"What's he working on?" Emma inquired.

"Well, he's doing up this big house in Pimlico, it's a total wreck. Brown hessian on the walls. Formica kitchen. Exploding cauliflower carpets. He said he was going to be there all day, but . . . well, he should be here by now."

"Maybe he's had an accident," said Frances helpfully.

"God, I hope not," I said. I went inside and anxiously called his mobile phone. "Thank you for calling Vodafone 0236 112331," intoned a robotic female voice. "Please leave your message after the tone." Damn.

"Um, Alex, hi, um, it's me. Tiffany, " I said. "And I'm just wondering where you are. Um, hope you're OK. I'm a bit worried about you, actually. But perhaps you're on your way. I hope so, because it's nine-fifteen now and everyone's been here for quite a while, and to be honest it's getting a little out of hand—ha ha ha! In fact there's quite a heated debate going on about gender issues and that sort of thing and I think we need another man to balance it up a bit. So see you soon, I hope. Um. Tiffany."

"Gosh it's getting dark, isn't it?" I heard Emma say. "Ooh—was that a spot of rain?"

"Women today have *appalling* attitudes toward men," Kit was saying as everyone strolled inside, "And then you all wonder why we run a mile? It's totally unfair. You refuse to compromise. You don't want us unless we're perfect."

"No, we *don't*," they all shrieked, as they flopped onto the chairs and sofas in the sitting room.

"Yes, but are *you* perfect?" asked Kit as he lowered himself onto the chaise longue. "Ask yourselves that."

"Yes we *are*," they all shouted. "We're totally fantastic! Hadn't you noticed?"

"Er, yes," he replied gallantly.

"Well *I'd* happily compromise," said Sally, "but I hardly ever get to meet men, unsuitable or otherwise."

"But you work with *thousands* of men in the City," said Catherine enviously.

"Yes, but they never approach female colleagues because they're terrified of being sued for sexual harassment. In any case, they don't regard us as real women—to them we're just men in skirts. And then when I do meet a nice ordinary guy from outside the City, let's say a doctor or a vet," Sally continued, "they tend to run a mile because I'm so . . ." She blushed. "I'm so . . ."

"Loaded!" shrieked Frances and Emma in unison. Sally rolled her eyes.

"Oh come on, Sally!" persisted Emma. "Your luxury apartment in Chelsea Harbour, your colossal, six-figure salary, you can't hide them from us, you know. A lot of men would find that totally emasculating."

"I was going to say because I'm so *busy,* actually," said Sally. "Options traders work *horrible* hours—that's the price we pay. That's the compromise I've made. I'm at my desk by seven-thirty every morning, and I'm there for twelve hours. I can't even have lunch—a sandwich is brought to my desk. And I'm never really off the hook because I have to watch the markets round the clock. And the older I get, the harder it is. So don't envy me my cash—I think I'd rather have a life."

As I lit the candles on my cake, I mentally gave thanks for my freelance status. I work hard, but at least I can choose my own hours and I don't have to worry about exchange rates and closing prices at birthday parties—nor do I earn the kind of money which some men might find threatening.

Then, suddenly, I heard someone say, "Tiffany . . . Tiffany! Phone!" Oh good, I thought as I lit the last candle, it must be Alex. And it was.

"Happy birthday, Tiffany," he said quietly.

"Thanks!" I replied. I could hear the pattering of heavy rain on the path, and, from the sitting room, the strains of "Happy Birthday." "Alex, I've been so worried, where are you?" *Happy birthday to you . . .*

"Well, actually, to be honest, I just couldn't face it," he said. *Happy birthday to you . . .* "In fact, Tiffany . . ." *Happy birthday, dear Tiffaneeeee . . .*

". . . there's something I've really got to tell you."

Happy birthday to you!!!

June

Isn't it annoying being dumped? I mean, it's really not enjoyable at all. Getting the Big E. Being handed your cards. Especially when you're thirty-seven. Especially when you thought the bloke was about to propose. Especially when you thought that, within a matter of mere months, or possibly even weeks, you would be progressing triumphantly up the aisle to "The Arrival of the Queen of Sheba." Oh no. Being chucked was definitely not quite what I had in mind on my thirty-seventh birthday. You see, I was convinced Alex was on the point of seeking my hand in marriage—he said he had something to tell me. Instead he simply looked me in the eye the following day and said, "I just can't face it."

"Face what?" I asked suspiciously as we sat at my kitchen table. There was a silence, during which he looked uncomfortable, but calm. His rather soft, girlish lips were pursed together, his cowlick of chestnut hair brushed forward onto his brow. I do wish he wouldn't do it like that, I found myself thinking, it makes him look like Tony Blair. Then he spoke, and out it all came, in a guilty rush.

"Isimplycan'tfacethefactthatI'mstringingyoualongandwastingyourtime." *Ah.* Oh. Oh dear. He looked rather stricken, then he took a deep breath, inhaling through his aquiline nose. "You see I feel under pressure to marry you, Tiffany, and I don't want to get married, but I know that's what you'd like."

"Oh no, no, no, no, no. I'm not bothered about that at all," I said, sipping my Nescafé. "Really. I honestly hadn't given it a *thought*. I was perfectly happy to go on as we were. Marriage? Good Lord, no. It never entered my mind."

His face expressed a mixture of puzzlement and relief. "Oh. Well, I suppose I was misled by the way you kept stopping and looking in the window at Cartier and going up to the bridal department at Peter Jones and flicking through wedding stationery in WH Smith. I thought you . . . I thought you wanted . . . *anyway,* the fact is that I really can't stand the thought of marrying you, Tiffany. Nothing personal," he added quickly. "But you see, I don't want to get married to anyone. Ever."

"Why not?" I inquired, hoping that my bright, but not too brittle demeanor would mask my grievous disappointment.

"Well, I've really been thinking about it, and it's lots of things," he said. "For a start I like my own space. I've never lived with a woman. And I hate the idea of a woman . . . you know, messing up my things. And then—and this is the *main* thing—" he gave a little shudder, "the thought of children." He lowered his voice to a conspiratorial whisper. "*Babies.* To be honest the whole idea makes me feel sick. All that crying, and all that, you know, *effluent*. At both ends. I just don't think I could handle that at all."

"But you're so good with children," I pointed out accurately, while mentally congratulating myself for remaining calm. "Your nephew and niece adore you."

"Yes, but I don't see them every day. It's different. And I didn't really bother with them until they were both safely out of nappies."

"But Alex," I said slowly, "if you don't ever want to get married, why did you bother to go out with me in the first place?"

"I liked you. I mean I *do* like you, Tiffany. And you share a lot of my interests—I mean you like going to art galleries with me, and the ballet—"

"—and the theater," I interjected.

"Yes, and the theater."

"And the opera."

"Yes, and the opera."

"And contemporary dance."

"Yes, yes."

"And lunchtime talks at the Royal Academy."

"Yes, yes, I know."

"And the London Film Festival."

"Yes . . ."

"And video installations at the ICA."

"Yes, yes, all that kind of thing . . ."

"And any number of jazz venues."

"I know, I know," he said, "but I'm afraid that's as far as it goes. I'm not looking for anything else."

"Oh. Oh, I see. You just wanted a companion. A female escort. For assorted cultural pursuits."

"Well, no—I wanted friendship too. But somehow, well . . . I could just see the way things were shaping up, and I felt it was time to come clean. I'm sorry if I ruined your party," he added. "But I just couldn't face all your friends, knowing that."

"It's all right, Alex," I said, fingering the Elizabeth Bradley antique roses tapestry kit he'd brought me as a birthday present. "I really don't mind. Please don't feel bad about anything. *And especially please don't feel bad about the fact that you've just wasted eight months of my life!*" I hissed. Actually, I didn't say that at all. I just said, "I'm afraid I'll have to take you off my BT Friends and Family list."

"Of course," he said. "I understand."

"Would you like some more coffee?" I asked.

"Yes," he said, staring at his empty cup with a pained expression. "But you know, Tiffany . . ."

"Yes?"

He looked genuinely upset now. This was obviously very

tough for him. "You know I can't *bear* instant," he said. "It really offends my taste buds. I gave you some very good Algerian arabica the other day, can't we have some of that?"

"Of course we can," I agreed.

Later that day, as I sat stabbing away at the antique roses canvas with my tapestry needle, reflecting on my newly single status and on the fact that I myself could perhaps be described as an antique rose, Alex phoned. He sounded nervous and unhappy. For one mad, heady instant I thought he might have changed his mind.

"Yes?" I said.

"Tiffany, there's something else I meant to say this morning," he said. "Now, I know you're probably feeling a bit cross with me . . ."

"No, not at all," I lied.

"And I'm sorry to have let you down and everything, but I really hope you'll do me one big favor."

"Yes," I said. "If I can."

"Well, I know you're probably feeling a bit cross with me and everything . . ."

"Look, I'm *not* cross," I said crossly. "Just tell me what you want, will you, I'm trying to make a cushion cover here."

"Well, I'd rather you didn't sort of, bad-mouth me to everyone."

"No," I said wearily, "I won't. Why should I? You've been perfectly nice to me."

"And I'd especially be grateful if you didn't tell everyone about that time . . ."

"What time?"

"That time you found me, you know . . ." His voice trailed away.

"Oh. You mean the time I discovered you in my bedroom dressed in my most expensive Janet Reger?" There was an awkward silence.

"Well, yes. That time."

"Don't worry," I said. "Of course I won't tell anyone. And I won't tell them about the Laura Ashley either."

"You should tell *everyone* about that," said Lizzie when she got back from Botswana. "That'll serve him right for dumping you. Bastard. And on your birthday. Bastard."

"He's not a bastard," I pointed out accurately. "He's nice."

"He's not nice," she countered. "It's not nice to say, 'Tiffany, I really can't stand the thought of marrying you.'"

"I'm sure he *meant* it nicely," I said. "It's just unfortunate for me that he took so long to realize he's not the marrying kind."

"Too right he's not. He's a complete wimp," she said viciously. "I always thought so with his mimsy, fussy, girly pernicketiness and his suspiciously refined taste in soft furnishings. And from what you told me about"—she lowered her voice to a whisper—"*that* side of things, you'd have had more fun with a eunuch! I mean really, Tiffany, you've got more testosterone than he has." This was probably true. "I'm *glad* you're not marrying him," she added. "Mind you, the girls are going to be disappointed—damn! I'd told them they were about to be bridesmaids."

"Not yet," I said. Not ever, in fact. Because since Alex, or rather Al-*ex* dumped me, a whole month has gone by. Well, three weeks and five days to be precise. And during that time I've been turning everything over in my mind. Reviewing the situation. Mentally rewinding and then fast-forwarding the video of my romantic life. Pressing the pause button here and there, and scrutinizing key frames. And I've made this momentous, life-changing decision. It wasn't easy, but I've done it. I've given up the husband hunt. I've chewed it over, and I'm going to eschew chaps. Frances is right. It's just not worth the pain and grief. Much better to face life alone. So I am now emphatically *hors de combat*. I have pulled up the drawbridge.

The sign says DO NOT DISTURB. And I have started to like my hard little shell. The prospect of yet another Saturday night on my own at home in front of the TV no longer fills me with dread. Who needs the romantic darkness of the cinema and dinner tête-à-tête when there's a Marks and Spencer easicook-lasagne-for-one and the National Lottery Live? My newfound neutrality suits me—no gain, of course, but no pain.

Lizzie says it just won't do. "You've *got* to get out there," she said again this morning, bossily, waving her fifth Marlboro Light at me. "You're not doing anything to help yourself. You've got to *forget* about Alex, write him off *completely,* and get back on that *horse.*" I often wonder why Lizzie talks in italics. Maybe it's because she went to such a third-rate drama school. She paced up and down the kitchen and then flicked ash into the sink. "You know, Tiffany, you're like . . ." I waited for some theatrical simile to encapsulate my predicament. What would I be today? A traveler thirsting in the Sahara? A mountaineer stuck at Base Camp? A promising Monopoly player resolutely refusing to pass "Go"? A brilliant artist without a brush? "You're like someone falling asleep in the snow," she announced. "If you don't wake up, you'll freeze to death."

"I just haven't the heart for it anymore," I said. "It always leads to disaster. Anyway, I'm only thirty-seven."

"*Only* thirty-seven? Don't be ridiculous, Tiffany. There's nothing only about being thirty-seven. To all intents and purposes you are now forty, and then very, very quickly, you'll be fifty, and then you'll really be *stuffed.*"

I sometimes suspect Lizzie's only being cruel to be cruel. I don't mind her nagging me. I nag her about her smoking. But I can't quite see why my lack of a husband and progeny bothers her so much. Perhaps in her funny, crass way, she is trying to be of help. And of course she is thinking how delightful Alice and Amy would look in primrose-yellow bridesmaids' dresses, or maybe ice-blue, or possibly pale-pink with apricot hair bands, matching satin slippers and coordinating posies—she hasn't quite decided yet. Anyway, I know, I *know* that she is right. It's just that I simply can't be worked half to death anymore. It's all too much of an effort—because nice, interesting, decent men with diamond rings in their pockets don't simply drop from the trees; you have to go out and pick one, or rather knock one down with a very large stick. There are plenty of windfalls of course, but they tend to be bruised and wasp-eaten and I've had my unfair share of bad apples over the past few years. But even if I really *was* pursuing men—the very idea!—I have to face the fact that, as Lizzie keeps telling me, it all gets harder with age. And that's another thing. Whatever happened to that dewy look I used to have? And when exactly did that little line at the side of my mouth appear, not to mention the creeping crepiness in the texture of my eyelids and the tiny corrugations in my brow? NB: Get more expensive unguents PDQ.

"I'm losing my looks," I said to Mum over the phone after Lizzie had gone. "I'm really going down the pan. In fact I'm quite ancient now. Basically, I'm almost fifty. I found my first gray hair this morning."

"Did you, darling?" she replied.

"Yes. Yes I did," I said. "Which is why I'm now firmly on the shelf. I'm going off. I'm the Concealer Queen. And this is why I'm being dumped all the time and why men never, ever, *ever* ask me out."

"What about that nice Jewish accountant?" she said. "The one you met last year?"

"I didn't fancy him," I replied.

"And that television producer—you said he was quite keen."

"Possibly, but his girlfriend wasn't."

"Oh. Oh I see. Well what about that one . . . you know . . . whatsisname, the one who does something clever in computers?"

"*Dead* boring."

"And what about that solicitor you told me you'd met at the tennis club? I'm sure you said he'd called you."

"Mummy—he's got two heads."

"Oh. Well at least you can't say that no one asks you out."

"Yes I can. Because those ones don't count."

"Why not?"

"Because I'm not interested in them. In fact I'm not interested in men full stop. In any case I really don't need a husband."

"Darling, don't say that."

"No. I'm absolutely fine on my own."

"No you're not. You're miserable."

"Only because I've had the wrong attitude. The thing to do is to embrace aloneness. Take spinsterhood seriously."

"Darling, no one will take *you* seriously if you say things like that."

"No, honestly, Mum, I'll be brilliant at it. I'll really apply myself. I'll get a cat and knit blankets for the Red Cross. I'll develop a passion for cricket and crosswords—"

"You don't do crosswords, darling."

"I'll learn. And I'll man cake stalls at bring-and-buys. And I'll selflessly babysit for all my friends. I'll be the most professional spinster there's ever been—I'll probably pick up an award for it. Spinster of the Year—Tiffany Trott, brackets Miss, close brackets."

"Darling, I'm afraid this negative and unhelpful attitude won't get you anywhere."

"I'm just being realistic."

"Nihilistic, darling."

"But I'm unlikely to meet anyone new."

"Don't be silly, darling, of course you are."

"No I'm not. Because I read in the paper the other day that forty-five percent of us meet our partners through mutual friends and I've already met all my friends' friends. And twenty-one percent of us meet them through work."

"Darling, I do wish you could get a proper job again. All you do is sit on your own writing slogans all day."

"But Freelancers Have Freedom!"

"Yes, but you're not meeting any men. Except for Kit. *Why* didn't you marry Kit, Tiffany?"

"I don't want to go through all that again, Mummy. Anyway, he loves Portia."

"Don't your friends know anyone?"

"No. And when I think about the men I have met through my set they've been disastrous—especially Phillip."

"Oh *yes,*" she said meaningfully. Feckless, unfeeling Phil Anderer.

"But men!" I spat. "Who needs them? Not me. Anyway," I added, "I'm not going through all that grief again. No way. Forget it. No. Thank. You."

Two hours later, the phone rang. It was Lizzie. "Now listen to this, Tiffany," she said, audibly rustling a newspaper. "Listen very carefully."

"OK. I'm listening."

She cleared her throat theatrically. " 'Tall, Athletic, Passionate, Propertied, Sensuous Academic, thirty-six, seeks Feminine Friend to share Laughter, Love and . . . Life?' " She managed to get a melodramatic, upward inflection into the final word.

"Yes?" I said. "You read it very well. What about it?"

"It's a personal ad," she explained.

"I know."

"From the *Telegraph.*"

"Good."

"In fact it's a particularly appealing one, don't you think?"

"I suppose so."

"And you're going to reply to it, aren't you, Tiffany?"

"Yes," I said suddenly. "I am."

* * *

I also said yes when Lizzie told me that she wanted me to go on a blind date with a colleague of Martin's. Did I say no one ever introduces me to matrimonially minded males? Let me take it back right now!

"He's called Peter Fitz-Harrod," she said, when she'd finished telling me about the Tall, Athletic Academic. "He's in syndicated loans, whatever they are. I think he lends money to Mozambique. I met him at a company do last week," she explained. "He's forty-two, divorced, with two small children. He's really *quite* good-looking," she added, "and very keen to marry again."

Now I have absolutely no objections to divorced men—as long as the first wife is dead, ha ha!—so I told Lizzie she could give him my number. Then I sat down to write my reply to the Tall, Athletic Academic. I soon got stuck with my pen poised over my best-quality oyster-colored Conqueror paper. How on earth should I go about it? I mean, what the hell do people say? Do they write, "Dear Tall, Athletic, Passionate, Propertied . . . ," or, "Dear Abundantly Erotic Existentialist . . . ," or, "Dear Bewitching Brunette, fifty-seven and a half . . ."? What does protocol require? Maybe I should come clean and say, "Hallo there, my incredibly bossy best friend saw your intriguing ad and told me that if I don't reply she'll kill me." Maybe I should say, "Hi! My name's Tiffany. I think I could be your feminine friend." Feminine Friend? It sounds like a brand of tampon. Maybe I should start, "Dear Box Number ML2445219X." Maybe I should simply write, "Dear Sir . . ."

I decided to go shopping instead. There's nothing like a trip to Oxford Street on the number 73 to clear the brain, and soon I was entertaining positive thoughts about Tall, Athletic, Passionate, Propertied, etc. (think I'll just call him "Tall" for short). By the time the bus was speeding down Essex Road we'd been out to dinner twice. As it pulled away from the Angel, he'd shyly held my hand. By the time we turned into Pentonville Road, he'd come up to meet my parents. As we drove past Euston station, our engagement announcement was in *The Times,* and by the time we pulled up outside Selfridges half an hour later, we were married with two children and living in Cambridge, where he is undoubtedly professor of something terribly impressive, such as cytogenetics. Bus journeys do not normally give rise to such pleasant fantasies. Usually they remind me of the appalling problems I have with men. For example, I step happily on board the number 24, confident that I am going, say, to Hampstead. It all seems perfectly straightforward, the destination quite clear. But then, just as I'm relaxing into my book—*ding dong*! "Last Stop. All Change!" and there I am, marooned at the grottier end of Camden. And when I gently remonstrate with the bus conductor about my unexpectedly abbreviated journey, he calmly points to the front of the bus where it says, in very large letters, CAMDEN HIGH STREET ONLY. And that's what it's been like with men. I have failed to read the signs. So I have allowed them to lead me not just up the garden path, but through the front door, into the house, through the sitting room, up the stairs, and into the bedroom, before being shown out through the back door—usually with instructions to cut the grass before I leave. Unfortunately this whole process takes quite a long time, as I have learned to my great chagrin.

What a fool I am—what a damned, silly little fool. I have let selfish, commitment-shy men tie me up for too long. I have cooked my own goose and stuffed it. Perhaps I could get Tony Blair to introduce legislation, I mused, as I went over to the expensive unguents counter. I'm sure he'd oblige if I asked him to be tough on commitophobia—tough on the causes of commitophobia. Men would not be allowed to monopolize women over the age of thirty-three for more than six months without making their intentions clear. Fines would be incurred, and repeat offenders like Phillip would be sent off for institutional reform in a confetti factory. No longer would men be able to shilly-shally around with girls during what Jane Austen called our "years of danger." This would improve our lives immeasurably, I thought as I sprayed Allure onto my left wrist. One father I know, frustrated by his daughter's four-year wait for a wedding ring, simply put the engagement announcement in the paper—just like that! The boyfriend was whizzed up the aisle before you could say "Dearly Beloved." Other women of my acquaintance have waited for years, and then got dumped the minute they tried to pin the bastard down.

"I really don't think we belong together," Phillip said after we'd been together for almost three years and I had politely inquired whether my presence in his life was still required.

"In fact," he said very slowly, "I *now* realize that we're fundamentally incompatible. So it wouldn't be *right* for me to marry you. It's a great pity. But there it is."

"Yes, it is a pity," I said, as I removed my clothes from his cupboard, trying not to mess up his golfing gear. "It's a pity it's taken you so long to decide. It's a pity I didn't leave you when you admitted you'd been unfaithful. It's a pity I believed you when you said you wanted me to stay with you forever. In fact," I added through my tears, "it's a pity I met you at all. You're a good architect," I said as I left.

"Thanks," he said.

"That conservatory you did for the Frog and Firkin was brilliant."

"Thanks," he said again.

"And that loft extension in Putney was tremendous."

"I know," he said.

"But you're useless at building relationships."

A few months later, I met Alex. It all seemed so promising at first, though he was terribly shy to start with. All those chaste dates—the strain was exhausting.

"At least he's not another pathetic womanizer," said Lizzie accurately, after I'd come back un-snogged from my twenty-third date. And he was so nice—and no golf! Hurrah! And no negative comments about my clothes, either. In fact, as it turned out, he really *liked* my clothes. Especially my lingerie. And my evening wear. But then we all have our foibles, don't we? Our little peccadilloes. But now look what's happened. Curtains again. Exit boyfriend stage left. *Left.*

"Don't let them bugger you around anymore," says Lizzie. "Get *tough.*" And so now I *am* tough. If they don't propose within five minutes—that's it! Goodbye! Or possibly five weeks. In exceptional circumstances, and if they have a note from their parents, five months.

"Your pores are rather enlarged," said the white-coated crone on the expensive unguents counter as she sat me in front of a magnifying mirror. "In fact they're huge," she continued. "I'm afraid it's something that happens with age." Oh dear. If I'd known they were that big, I could have offered Phillip the use of my face for indoor putting practice.

I bought three tubes of pore-minimizer (£87.50) and a tiny tub of moisturizer—can someone please tell me why moisturizer always comes in such small pots?—and headed home. Then I read the ad again: *Tall, Athletic, Passionate, Propertied, Sensuous Academic, thirty-six, seeks Feminine Friend to share Laughter, Love and . . . Life?* Now you're talking, I thought to myself as I dashed off a letter. Just a few brief details about myself and a not-too-out-of-date passport photo—don't want to see the guy's face collapse with disappointment when we meet. I signed it just "Tiffany" with my telephone number, but no address of course—just in case he turns out to be a Tall Athletic Serial Killer. Then I sealed it. As I stuck on the stamp— first-class, natch, *don't* want him thinking I'm a cheapskate— the phone rang.

"Oh hellooooo . . ." said a slightly gravelly female voice. Who the hell was this?

"Hellooooo . . ." it said again. "Is that Tiffaneee? Tiffanneee Trott? This is Peter Fitz-Harrod." Christ, it was a bloke.

"Yes," I said, shocked. "That's me."

"Ah. Well, ha ha ha ha ha! Lizzie Bohannon gave me your number. Ha ha ha ha ha! She's told me all about you. Ha ha ha ha! You sound absolutely *splendid*. Would you like to meet me for a drink?"

June Continued

I bet Peter Fitz-Harrod's wife left him for someone else. I don't blame her in the slightest. He sounds like a total wimp. Unlike Tall Athletic.

"Lizzie, why are you setting me up with this weedy little man?" I asked her over the telephone. Actually I didn't say that. One has to be tactful with friends who are doing their level best to help one up the aisle. What I really said was, "Lizzie, what's this Peter Fitz-doobery man like? I mean it's *very* nice of you to think of me, and I do really, *really* appreciate it, but to be brutally honest, he sounds like a complete and utter jerk."

"I know the voice is a bit awful, but he's *much* better in the flesh," she said reassuringly. "He's *definitely* worth a try. *Would* I suggest him otherwise?" I was prepared to take her word for it, though I definitely preferred the sound of Tall Athletic. I bet he's got a lovely voice. All that lecturing—his students must find him mesmerizing. He should have had my letter by now. Sporty and brainy—marvelous! What enticing images this conjures: squash followed by a bit of Schopenhauer; tennis followed by the Tate; swimming while discussing Solzhenitsyn; hill-walking with a hint of Hindemith. Golf . . . hang on a mo. Not golf. Anything but golf. If he plays golf, we're through. "No, no, no, you go and play," I'd say to Phillip every Saturday morning. "You need to relax. You've got a very high-pressure job," (unlike me, of course). And by six o'clock he'd be back having played thirty-six—or was it seventy-two?—holes. And then he'd do the same on Sundays. "I had a bloody good game," he'd say, as he switched on Sky Sports. "Bloody good. Tremendous. What's for supper, Tiff?"

No, I'm putting my foot right down. Tall Athletic is not allowed to play golf. He can play tennis, cricket, croquet, football, hockey, squash, rugby, baseball, basketball, badminton, Ping-Pong, polo, Eton fives, seven-a-side rugger and darts. He can go surfboarding, rollerblading, waterskiing, rally-driving, scuba-diving, ten-pin bowling, white-water rafting and rowing. He can do heli-skiing, parascending, motocross, hang-gliding, parachuting, sky-diving and three-day-eventing, but if he plays golf—we're through. Phillip's much-married mother used to say, in her wearying, worldly-wise way, "It's good for men like Phillip to have a regular sport like golf because then at least," and here her voice would drop to a conspiratorial whisper, *"you know exactly what they're up to."* And how my heart would sink, as it always did when she gave me advice of this kind; and later on, when I finally knew, well . . . how ironic it seemed.

This evening I met Peter Fitz-Harrod for a drink. Here's what happened. We arranged a rendezvous at the Ritz at six-thirty, and I had planned my escape in the form of a phantom dinner appointment at eight-fifteen. My first blind date for more than fifteen years! What a bizarre thing to do—go to a hotel to have a drink with a man on whom I had never laid eyes before. But having laid ears on him, I wasn't that excited—just curious to see whether he was as frightful as I imagined. I had described myself to him: "fair hair," I said, deliberately avoiding the word "blonde"—he sounded quite overexcited enough as it was and I knew he wasn't my type. But I dressed carefully—nothing that Phillip would have made an appalling fuss about, just a pretty little suit and a discreet amount of makeup (no foundation—*so* ageing). As I spun through the swing doors I saw a man in a Burberry raincoat sitting by the night porter's desk. I looked at him, he looked at me, then he jumped to his feet like a crocodile leaping off the riverbank. It was him. Keen as mustard.

"Hello, ha ha ha ha ha! You must be Tiffaneee," he squeaked, offering me a clammy hand.

"How did you guess?" I asked him—the Ritz was stuffed to the rafters with thirty-something blondes.

"Well, ha ha ha ha ha! I don't know, I suppose you just look like your voice," he said.

"Thank God, *you* don't," I just managed not to say, because actually, Lizzie was right. He really wasn't too bad. About five foot ten, with curly brown hair. Blue eyes. Medium build. Discreet gray suit. Black lace-up shoes—well polished. Tasteful silver cufflinks. In fact, quite OK-looking-bordering-on-the-almost-acceptable (NB—do not, in future, judge blokes on basis of voices).

We sat in the bar and ordered drinks. A beer for him, a glass of white wine for me. "Sauvignon please, rather than Chardonnay," I instructed the waiter in my best "girl-about-town" style. Good God! I suddenly realized I was trying to impress this man. Was I interested? Well, maybe. His ghastly voice had dropped by about an octave, and the nervous machine-gun laughter had stopped. I certainly wasn't sitting there thinking, You Have Got To Be Joking! In fact, I was smiling quite a bit and I didn't have my arms defensively crossed. He was really quite nice, I thought, as I nibbled a pistachio. How could his wife have left him? What a cow. Probably led him a merry dance with a string of Latin lovers which she no doubt entertained three at a time in the marital bed, only venturing out in order to blow all his money on Gucci and Louis Vuitton. Poor chap. Obviously been through a hell of a lot. Needs to have his faith in women restored. I asked him about his work, which is scheduling loans to southern African countries. He asked me about mine.

"Oh—advertising, Go To Work On An Egg and all that!" he exclaimed enthusiastically.

"Yes, that sort of thing," I replied, without getting into the intricacies of Kiddimint.

"Vorsprung, Durch Technik!"

"Yes, that's right."

We talked about sport; he hates golf—brilliant! And he likes tennis—even better. I dropped in a strategically sensitive but not at all intrusive question about his children, whom he sees every Sunday. Then we ordered another drink. It was all going rather well. Gradually, the conversation became a little more personal. He asked me why I'm not married.

"I'm too young," I said. "My parents feel I should wait."

"Ha ha ha ha ha ha! That's very good," he said. "*Very* good. Too young! Ha ha ha ha ha ha!"

"And why did you get divorced?" I inquired. "Was it your wife's decision?"

"Oh *no*," he said. "No, it was entirely *mine*. My wife didn't want to get divorced at *all*. In fact she was *terribly unhappy* about it. Still is." Ah. I see. This took me aback. Men do not normally leave their wives unless they are in love with someone else.

"She thought we were very happily married," he continued above the tinkling of the piano. "But I didn't. She resisted the divorce for months." Suddenly I found myself feeling rather sorry for his wife. Why had he left? Maybe he *did* have an affair, though he didn't seem the type.

"I wasn't interested in anyone else," he confided. "But the problem was that I found my wife very boring." Oh! Oh dear. Boring.

"Was she very quiet, then?" I asked him as I fiddled with the stem of my wine glass.

"Oh no, she had *lots* to say," he replied. "She's not shy or introverted at all, and she's got a lot of interests. And she really *loved* being a wife and mother . . ."

Oh. Oh, I see. Except that I didn't really see at all.

"I was just *very bored* with her," he continued. "That's all I can say. Bored." Well, there are worse things to be than boring, I thought. Like unfaithful, controlling, neglectful, selfish, cruel and mean. But boring?

"She wasn't very entertaining," he explained. "And she didn't pay me enough attention. She just wasn't"—he gave an exasperated little shrug—". . . a stimulating partner."

What was she supposed to do, I found myself wondering, monocycle round the kitchen while juggling the Wedgwood and singing highlights from *Oklahoma!*?

"And also"—he leaned in a little closer—"she was really *hopeless* in bed."

Aaarrrggghhh!!! I did not want to know this. It made my stomach turn. By now I was feeling extremely sorry for Mrs. Fitz-Harrod. I wanted to go right round to her house and say, "Now you listen to me, Mrs. Fitz-Harrod, you are *well* out of it. Your ex-husband is an unchivalrous swine." Instead I glanced at my watch. "Goodness, it's five past eight, I really must get going. It's been very nice talking to you," I lied, as a frock-coated waiter brought him the bill.

"Ditto," he replied. "I'd love to see you again. We could play tennis," he added as I hailed a passing cab. "I'll call you."

"Yes. Yes. Do," I said as I got in, giving him an arctic smile. "That would be nice. Give me a ring some time. Any time." Or, preferably, never. Never would be just fine. I sped home feeling slightly depressed. And rather embarrassed, too—after all, I had only met him at Lizzie's suggestion. I'd have to tell her how ghastly he was—I should never have let her persuade me. Still, she meant well, I reflected as I walked up my garden path, pausing to snip off a couple of pink roses with my nail scissors. They'd look pretty in the kitchen and the scent would cheer me up. I mean it's not Lizzie's fault, I thought. She wasn't to know—she'd only met him once herself. But what a ghastly evening. What a ghastly, ghastly man.

I turned the key in the lock brightening considerably when I opened the door to see the answer-phone's green light winking gaily at me. My index finger hit "Play." *Beep. Beep. Beep.*

"Hello there, Tiffany," said a silky-smooth male voice. "You don't know me—yet. My name's Neville. You were kind enough to answer my ad, and I'd *love* you to give me a ring."

When you are thirty-seven, single and childless, there are certain things that people say. They say. "Don't worry, your prince will come," or "Cheer up! Your luck will change!" Or—worst of all—*"There's someone nice just around the corner."* I had been about to ban Mum from ever saying that again.

"No there *isn't* someone nice just around the corner," I usually say in reply to this well-meant, weekly cliché. "There's probably someone *nasty* just around the corner. In fact, you can bet there's a right *bastard* just around the corner who's going to get me *very* interested, waste an awful lot of time and then *bugger off,* leaving me back at square one."

"Don't worry, darling, there's someone nice just around the corner," she said to me again this morning, but this time I simply said to her, "Well Mummy, I think you might be right." Now *why* did I say that? Because Tall Athletic's just around the corner—that's why. And he really *does* sound nice. A gorgeous voice for starters—*dead* sexy. American. Or at least . . . well, it was rather embarrassing actually. Because when I realized I had a Sylvester Stallone soundalike on the other end of the line I said, "Which part of the States do you come from then?"

And there was this awkward silence for about—ooh, a minute—and then the voice said, "Actually, I'm Canadian."

Anyway, I eventually managed to persuade him not to put the phone down, and we began to chat. Now, I don't know what other people do on these occasions, but I decided not to talk to him for too long. I wanted us to have plenty to say to each other when we met. So I didn't ask him about his academic career or what he loves most about the British or anything like that, I just asked him what he meant by "Athletic." And he said—be still my beating heart!—"Ice hockey." Wow! That is *such* a macho game.

Anyway, we decided to meet at this little Italian café in Soho he knows, because he told me he was a great "Italophile." And this seemed to be true because when he rang off he said *"ciao"* instead of "bye." *"Ciao."* Just like that. Isn't that great? *"Ciao."* Yes, I *really* like the sound of him. However, there are two drawbacks: 1) he lives in Walthamstow and 2) his name is Neville. Now, Neville is not a great name. In fact it's pretty awful—on a par with, say, Kevin, Terry or Duane. But then, he's Canadian, so it's sort of OK, and of course a lot of famous Canadians do have quite weird names, don't they, like, um, famous Canadians, famous Canadians—oh yes, Margaret Atwood and Bryan Adams. And as for Neville living in Walthamstow— well I'm sure he'd relocate if we hit it off, which I really think we might.

Why oh why oh *why* do men feel the need to exaggerate their height? I mean, it's not even as though I'm particularly prejudiced in favor of tall men—I'm not. It was the "Athletic Academic" bit of Neville's ad which appealed to me because I really like clever men. Anyway, when I arrived at the Café Firenza—a bit of a dive frankly—I asked for Neville and was shown to a table at the back. I saw this bearded man sitting there—why didn't I check him for facial hair over the phone? And when he stood up to shake my hand I realized he was no more than five foot eight and three-quarters, which is *not* tall, it's medium. And medium is absolutely fine. There is nothing wrong with medium. But it is not to be confused with tall. So instead of the big, brainy lumberjack of my dreams, there was this rather slight, bearded man, with sloping shoulders, small hands and large, gray, staring eyes. My heart sank into the soles of my Patrick Cox loafers. Still, he did have a very sexy voice—unlike Peter Fitz-Harrod. He ordered the wine, in Italian. This seemed to take quite a long time for some reason, even though it was quite clear to me, from my smattering of restaurant Italian, that he was ordering a bottle of the *vino da tavola—rosso*. And then, when the waiter had gone, Neville did this funny thing. He just sat there, looking at me very intensely, saying *nothing*. Just staring. Obviously terribly shy. I smiled encouragingly at him.

"Are you feeling tense, Tiffany?" he suddenly asked me.

"Tense? Oh, no, no, no. Not at all. No."

"It's just that you *do* seem quite, well, tense. And nervous. I think you *are* tense and nervous, aren't you, Tiffany?" he persisted as the bottle of house red arrived.

"*Mille grazie,* Rodney," he said. "You see, I do have that effect on women," he continued. "I'm told I make them nervous. I can't help it," he added as he poured wine into his glass tumbler, and then mine. He looked up at me. "I seem to have this . . . *power* over women."

Neville was wearing a checked shirt with no tie, the top three buttons undone. And in the hairs on his chest was a white, pus-filled boil, like a tiny electric lightbulb. I found myself staring at it, wondering if it was about to pop. To distract myself I asked him about his academic career, and it turned out he wasn't a professor of cytogenetics. He wasn't a professor of anything. He wasn't even a lecturer. He was still a student—at thirty-six!

"Still trying to get those O levels?" I quipped as the wine kicked in.

He looked offended. "Actually, I'm doing a Ph. D."

"Wow! What's it about?" I inquired, chewing the end of a breadstick.

"It's about the influence of Breton ballads on early nineteenth-century Quebecois poetry. It's really fascinating. You know, you British really have no idea how vibrant Canadian culture is."

"On the contrary," I replied. "I've read all of Margaret Atwood's novels. They were jolly good. And I've got three Glenn Gould CDs."

"You're all so insular," he said, warming to his theme. "I mean, there were local elections in Winnipeg last week, but there was *nothing* about it in the British press. And the Quebec problem hardly gets covered at all, despite the fact that the potential breakup of the Canadian federation is an issue of enormous international concern." By this time I couldn't have cared less if Canada became the fifty-first state in the Union.

"Don't mind me," he suddenly said with a little, low laugh. "I'm very pugilistic. I like to provoke. I get in a lot of fights. I get in a lot of fights over women." He shifted in his seat, then hooked his elbows around the back of his chair. "Sometimes, I just walk out of tutorials, right in the middle of them—bang!— just like that. My Ph.D. supervisor says I'm a mixture of charm and war." Charm and war! Gosh. Charm and *bore* more like.

He looked me straight in the eye. "I'm gonna level with you, Tiffany," he said. "I'm very . . . complex. I've done a lot of drugs and I've had a lot of women. A whole string of them. It's been pretty easy for me." Why, then, the need to advertise his charms in the personal column of a national newspaper? "But I'm tired of womanizing," he added, by way of explanation. "I want kids. Lots of them. But only with the right kind of woman. Hence my ad. Now a lot of really gorgeous women have written to me, Tiffany. And one of them is going to be the mother of my children. Maybe it'll be you, though frankly I think you're a little bit old for that. But I thought your photo was cute."

Suddenly he leaned forward and said, "Guess who holds the world record to break dancing at high altitude?"

"Er, I don't know," I said. "That's rather a tricky one. Um, let me guess . . . not . . . *you*?"

He nodded slowly, with a lopsided little smile.

"Gosh!" I said. "And how often do you play ice-hockey?"

"Tiffany." He was staring at me intensely again. "Enough

about me. I want you to tell me all about yourself. You haven't told me a thing." He hadn't asked.

"I'm sorry, but I've got to go," I said. "It's half past eight, and I've got an early start tomorrow. But it's been very interesting meeting you," I said truthfully, putting down a fiver for the wine. "And, well . . ." I groped for some definitive valediction. "Good luck."

"Thanks," he said. *"Ciao."*

July

I'm going to try the small ads again! You see, I'm beginning to get the hang of it now. But no more weird, superannuated students thank you very much—Eligible Successfuls only from now on! And I must say I rather like these Twin Souls telephone ads, where you don't have to write off to some anonymous post box and then wait weeks for a reply. You just dial a number, listen to their recorded voice-mail and leave them a message of your own. It's brilliant because, let's face it, voices are pretty important. I mean, on paper a man could look fantastic, but then the "Successful City Professional, 44" could, in reality, be a "Successfuw Ci-ee Professionaw, Faweefawer." And that wouldn't do at all, would it? So these answerphone ads are jolly good. Expensive, of course. But then what's fifty pence a minute compared to my future happiness?

Anyway, having listened to—what?—forty or fifty of these earlier on today I've found one I really like: "Adventurous, Seriously Successful Managing Director, 41, 6 foot, slim, attractive, amusing, urbane, WLTM unforgettable girl in her 20s/30s who doesn't mind being spoiled a little, or even a lot." His voice was so nice—neither horribly posh, nor obviously plebeian. Smooth without being smarmy. Cultivated, but not cut glass. Perfect. Wonder why he's still single? Anyway, he can spoil me as much as he likes, and I'll spoil him right back—with interest. Of course, leaving the reply's a bit of an ordeal. I felt quite shy actually, and had to have a couple of goes at it, but then hell! We're all in the same boat here, so what's the problem? We're just people who are too busy, too dynamic, too successful, too eligible, too desirable and too *bloody attractive* to find the time to stop being . . . um . . . *alone*. So we're just being really sensible about our completely puzzling lack of a life partner and resorting to a little artifice.

"Hellooooo," I whispered into the receiver in the most Felicity Kendalish voice I could manage. "My name's Tiffany. Tiffany Trott. Now, I know you'll have heard from about seventeen million unforgettable girls in their twenties and thirties, but you don't need them — you need me! Why? Because I'm happy and busy, and I like jokes and I'm thirty-seven, single, and um . . . desperate—ha ha ha! No, but seriously . . . I'm short, blonde, on the fat side and quite jolly. Ummmm . . . so there we have it. That's me, Tiffany. Tiffany Trott. So please give me a call soon. P.S.: I hope you don't like golf. P.P.S.: Isn't this fun?"

Wow! That's it. I hope he gives me a ring—preferably one with a big diamond on it, lozenge cut. On the other hand a larger square emerald would be nice *or*—and this is dead trendy—a right knuckleduster of an aquamarine. Yes, according to this month's edition of *Brides and Setting Up Home* magazine, aquamarines are *the* stone of choice. In the meantime, there's dinner with Angus and Alison this evening. I suppose I'll be the only single woman—as usual. And *as usual* they'll have invited along some dreary, physiognomically challenged, halitotic ex-army chap for me, who will have absolutely *nothing* to say. And seeing me struggle to extract conversation out of him over the curried avocado will make Alison and Angus think how *lucky* they are to be married, and *thank God* for that Young Conservatives do in Croydon in 1982, otherwise they'd *never* have met each other and they'd have ended up sad singles too, like poor, poor Tiffany.

* * *

Got that one completely wrong. On several counts. I wasn't the only single woman—Catherine was there too, thank God. And my "date" was OK-looking-bordering-on-the-almost-acceptable. A GP in his early forties. And he certainly wasn't dreary. Oh no. He had plenty to say.

Hello, I thought to myself when we were introduced, you're a bit of all right. A damn sight better than the usual pond life they dredge up on my behalf. He was very flirty. Very animated. He giggled a lot. He drank a lot. Though, like me, he politely declined Alison's homemade cheese and peanut dip. But he looked incredibly fit and he had a lovely tan. I wasn't too keen on his stubby little mustache or the gold bracelet on his left wrist, but I really liked his natty turquoise silk embroidered waistcoat. Very unusual. Though Catherine didn't seem that impressed with him—she looked at him, then looked at me, and discreetly rolled her eyes. But personally, I rather liked the look of him.

Anyway, Angus and Alison ushered us all into the dining room, and they sat Catherine next to this accountant—now he *did* look dreary—and they put me next to the GP, who was called Sebastian. And we started to make small talk over the macaroni-cheese-stuffed eggs, and he politely asked me about my interests. And when I said tennis, he said, "What do you play—singles?" I found that awfully amusing. And then he kept going on, rather oddly I thought, about how gorgeous-looking Greg Rusedski is and how much he'd like to be on Greg's receiving end.

"Now, there's herby apple-glazed pork roast next," said Alison. "Or blue cheese chicken rolls if you're vegetarian."

Anyway, then because Abigail whatsername was pregnant—smugly rubbing her vast stomach all evening—the conversation naturally turned to babies.

"Are you hoping to have children?" Sebastian asked me, passing me the bowl of cheesy-topped vegetables.

"Well . . . yes . . . yes, I am actually," I replied, as I passed it on. I didn't really want to discuss it, to be honest, but he didn't seem to pick up on that at all.

And then he said, "How old are you?" At this point everyone suddenly started listening.

"I'm fifty-three," I quipped, to cover my annoyance at being asked.

"Gosh, I'd never have thought it," he said with a sly grin. "I thought you were only—ooh—forty." And everyone laughed, except Catherine, who looked horrified. But all the others seemed to find it *extremely* funny, especially, it seemed to me, Abigail, who's only twenty-nine. And while I sat there wondering if I have ever, *ever* in my life said anything so calculated to hurt, humiliate and demoralize another human being, he went on and on and *on* about the bloody biological clock.

"I'm sick of seeing late thirty-something and early forty-something women come bleating to me for IVF because they've never got round to having babies before," he said, adding, to me, "so I wouldn't hang around, Tiffany."

"Oh, I'm working on it," I said. "In fact I'm fairly confident of giving birth before I'm due to have my hips replaced."

"By the time women are over thirty-five it's getting critical," he said expansively, pouring himself another glass of Bulgarian Cabernet. "Perhaps you should have your eggs frozen, Tiffany." And then he went into this really long, *detailed* spiel about how women are born with all their eggs—hundreds of them—but how they gradually start to go off as we age, and how by the time we're thirty-seven plus we're practically infertile and almost guaranteed to give birth to three-headed monsters—that is if we can get pregnant at all.

"So I do advise you to get on with it," he finished, "because even if you were actively trying to start a family you might find that, at your age, it takes you ages to get pregnant."

"What about Jane Seymour?" I said, taking a sliver of peach melba cheesecake. "Twins at forty-four."

"And Annabel Goldsmith had a baby at forty-five," interjected Catherine.

"Yes," I said, "and Jerry Hall had another when she was forty-one. They were all absolutely *fine*."

"That's different," he said. "They're rich. And anyway, they'd had children before—it's much harder having your *first* baby late."

"But Madonna was thirty-eight when she had her first child," said Catherine, with an indignant little laugh.

"And Koo Stark was forty," I persisted, because, you see, I always pay close attention to stories like that in the newspapers. In fact Mum cuts them out and sends them to me—I've got quite a collection now in the "Late Motherhood" section of my index file.

"And that other woman, Liz Buttle, she was *sixty*," added Catherine vehemently. "Which means Tiffany and I have got *loads* of time left."

But Sebastian didn't seem impressed. "You know," he said, cutting into the Danish blue, "all this talk about older motherhood being fashionable—it's total baloney. This is what women like to say to make themselves feel good about it all. But the fact is that children don't want geriatric parents. It's embarrassing for them. But then the problem *is*," he added, "that if women *don't* have babies, then they run an increased risk of getting breast cancer."

Sometimes. Just sometimes, taxi drivers can be really, really nice. Especially mini-cab drivers. On the way back from Angus and Alison's—my God, a fifteen-pound fare and I hadn't even had a nice time!—I saw the driver rummaging in the glove box. Then he passed back a thick wadge of tissues.

"Thank you," I said quietly.

"Cheer up, darlin'," he said, as we sped past the Angel. "It may never happen."

"Yes," I said. "I know. That's just the problem."

* * *

Location. Location. Location. Where blokes live is critical, because the fact is—and I don't know why this should be the case—that whenever I'm going out with someone I nearly always end up going over to their place. And that's the big drawback about London, isn't it? The trek across the capital when you're romantically inclined. Take my ex-but-one Phil Anderer for example. He lived in Wimbledon! Not very convenient for me, but I didn't like to complain.

"Oh no, I don't mind the journey over at all," I used to say. "It only takes two days on the number 93 and there are so many interesting things to look at along the way." And I didn't resent the fact that he practically never came over to my place because I understood that he needed to be near the golf club and in any case, I quite agreed with him that the back end of Islington can be a *very* dangerous place. And as for Alex, well although he lived very centrally, in Fitzrovia, behind Tottenham Court Road, somehow I hardly ever went to his flat. Usually we met outside the theater, or the opera, or the ICA or the National Gallery, or St. John's, Smith Square, or Sadler's Wells, or the Jazz Café or the National Film Theatre or wherever. Anyway, I've given this issue quite a bit of thought, and I've decided that there's no way romance is going to blossom if blokes do not possess at least one of the following postcodes: N1, N4, N5, N16, W1, W2, WC2, SW1 or—in exceptional circumstances—SW3. I do hope my Adventurous, Seriously Successful, Managing Director qualifies on that front. Actually, I haven't heard a whisper. I don't think he liked my reply to his ad. Lizzie didn't like it either.

"Why on *earth* did you tell him your age?" she barked, as we worked out in her local gym. "You must be out of your *tiny mind*."

"As he's very likely to find out how old I am, I might as well be upfront about it," I said calmly, as I lay back on the bench and lifted little weights with my feet. "Anyway, there's nothing wrong with being thirty-seven. Thirty-seven's just fine. Greta Scacchi's thirty-seven," I pointed out.

"But you're not Greta Scacchi," Lizzie replied, as she pounded away on the running machine. This was true.

"Daryl Hannah's thirty-seven too," I said. "So is Kim Wilde. So is Kristin Scott Thomas."

"*Don't* talk to me about Kristin Scott Thomas," panted Lizzie, as she increased the speed. Oh dear. I'd forgotten. I'd forgotten that if it wasn't for Kristin Scott Thomas, Lizzie would be a very famous actress by now. In fact she'd be as famous as, well, Kristin Scott Thomas. But in 1986 Kristin Scott Thomas beat Lizzie to the lead role in some B movie or other, blighting Lizzie's career ever since.

"Well, I like being thirty-seven," I added. "I feel good about everything at thirty-seven, except my eggs, which are apparently going off according to a sadistic doctor I met last week. Apart from that, I'm in my prime."

"Tiffany, you are *not* in your prime, you're getting on," she said, stopping to light a cigarette. "And will you please *stop* telling these men that you're short and fat. You're not."

"I know," I said. "But if I tell them that I *am* short and fat then, when they meet me, they'll be so relieved, having had such low expectations of what I'm going to be like, that they'll instantly fancy me to bits. You see I've worked it all out."

"If you tell them you're short and fat," she said slowly, "you won't get to meet them at all. I mean why do you think this Seriously Successful hasn't called? I rest my case."

When I got home, the phone rang. "Oh, hello, is that Tiffany?" said the "Adventurous, Seriously Successful Managing Director, 41," whose voice I instantly recognized.

"Yes, it is," I said happily. "Hello!"

"Thank you *so* much for replying to my ad," he said. "It was lovely to hear from you. You're number sixteen million, nine hundred and ninety-nine thousand, by the way."

"Oh dear—a disappointing response, then."

"And how many other Twin Souls ads have you replied to?"

"Four hundred and fifty-six."

"I see. Well I think it's very sensible of you not to overdo it. And what do you do?"

"I'm an advertising copywriter."

"Oh. Go To Work On An Egg—Vorsprung Durch Technik, that kind of thing," he said.

"Yes. That sort of thing. Pick Up a Penguin."

"Don't Leave Home Without It."

"Helps You Work, Rest and Play."

"Lifts and Separates."

"Things Happen After a Badedas Bath."

"Refreshes the Parts Other Beers Cannot Reach."

"Simple. But Brilliant."

"Pure Genius," he said. "Now, tell me, are you really short and fat?"

"No, not really," I said.

"Well, that's a pity, because I like small cuddly women."

"Nor could I conceivably be described as tall and thin," I pointed out. "And are you really 'Seriously Successful'?"

"Yes, I suppose I am."

"Well, that's a pity, because on the whole I prefer life's losers and the walking wounded."

On and on we bantered. A man with a quick wit—fantastic! Better still, he got my jokes.

Unlike Phil Anderer: "You know what your problem is, don't you?" Phillip would say. "No," I'd reply, while wondering whether he was going to tell me, yet again, that it was my "abject" dress sense, or the fact that I "talked too much" or had "too many little opinions."

"What *is* my problem?" I'd say wearily. "Tell me."

"You've got *no* sense of humor . . ."

"Now, I think we should meet," said Seriously Successful after about twenty minutes of happy badinage. "Do you like the Ritz?" Do fish like water?

"Love it."

"Good. I'll book a table for two on . . . Thursday? At eight o'clock?"

"Fabbo," I said. "See you there. But hang on a mo—how will I recognize you?"

"I'll be wearing a Hermès tie," he said. "What about you?"

"I wear contact lenses."

"Good. That'll be easy then."

Wahay! I'm having dinner at the Ritz with a quite possibly gorgeous, successful, charming, and *very* amusing man, complete with outsize bank balance and impeccable taste in neckwear. Does winning the lottery feel this good?

On Thursday evening I showered, dressed carefully in an elegant little Alberta Ferretti linen suit which I've had for five years but *love,* and set off for Piccadilly on the number 38 bus. As I walked through the revolving doors of the Ritz for the second time in a fortnight, trying not to look as though I was on another blind date—and desperately hoping not to see Peter Fitz-Harrod again—I spotted a rather interesting-looking man standing at the reception. Tall, with wavy chestnut hair, fine features and chocolate-brown eyes, he wasn't conventionally handsome, but he looked very animated and alert. He was beautifully besuited in a Prince of Wales check and, as I approached, I noticed that he had his tie twisted round so the label was showing. He looked at me, raised his eyebrows inquiringly, then suddenly broke into a broad smile.

"Hallo, Tiffany Trott," he said confidently.

"Hello, Seriously Successful," I replied.

"The Effect is Shattering," he added.

"Thank you. It's Good to Talk."

"Let's eat," he said, gently taking hold of my left elbow and steering me, along the pink-and-green carpet, through the Palm Court bar, toward the restaurant. Now, I thought this instant physical contact was a little bit forward, but I didn't

mind. In fact, I rather liked it. It was nice. Seriously Successful
was obviously at home in the Ritz—the waiters all seemed to
know him. We were shown to a table on the left, near the large
gilded figures of Neptune and his Nereid. The tablecloths were
of the heaviest white damask, the china a pure turquoise blue.
A silver vase containing two Stargazer lilies scented the surrounding air. I breathed it all in. It was lovely. I looked around
at the other diners, substituting for their faces those of Noël
Coward, Nancy Mitford, Evelyn Waugh and the Aga Khan.

"There's so much history in this room, isn't there?" I said.

"Oh yes," he replied. "Edward the Seventh was a regular.
Just think, he and Alice Keppel may have dined at this very
table."

Seriously Successful ordered the wine with obvious *savoir
boire* and kept smiling at me over the top of his menu as I
perused the hors d'oeuvres. "Oak-smoked wild salmon—
£17.50." Maybe I'd have the mosaic of Devon crab, or the
toasted game salad with celeriac wafers, or the artichoke heart
with wild mushrooms and asparagus. I really couldn't decide.

"I do hope you'll have something really high-calorie," said
Seriously Successful suddenly. "I love curvy women. May I
recommend the terrine of foie gras followed by the roast rack
of lamb with a large helping of Dauphinois potatoes, and then
the double chocolate mousse —with added cream, of course."

"I'm not sure that'll be enough," I said, though the truth was
I had the butterflies and didn't know how I was going to eat
anything. I found him so damned attractive. He was very con-
servative, and yet artistic, too—a devastating combination. He
told me about his work—publishing trade magazines—and his
passion for playing the cello, which he said he practices every
morning. He also told me about his farmhouse in Sussex, and
his luxury apartment in Piccadilly —in the Albany apartments
no less.

"So the Ritz is really your local," I said as our main course
arrived.

"Yes. And Fortnum and Mason's is my corner shop," he replied. "These little stores are so useful." He grinned. I smiled back. How incredible to think that such a nice-looking, funny, generous, stylish, eligible man was still single! Amazing. What a piece of luck. Thank God I'd been brave enough to answer his ad, I thought, as I listened to the gentle clattering of silver cutlery. It was such a *sensible* thing to have done. We talked with startling ease about, well, lots of things—recent films and books, tennis technique and travel, birth signs, politics and paintings, love, life and earth. And of course advertising, which he loves. In fact he has an encyclopedic knowledge of slogans and straplines, including one or two of my own. This was highly gratifying. The evening was going brilliantly well. And then, as the waiters took away our plates after the main course, Seriously Successful removed his napkin from his lap and looked me straight in the eye. And I thought he was going to say, "Miss Trott. In vain have I struggled. It will not do. My feelings will not be repressed. You must allow me to tell you how ardently I admire and love you!" Instead, he leant forward and said, "Now Tiffany, I've got a little proposition for you."

What is wrong with men? Why do they always give me such a hard time? After all, it's not as though I've failed to make any effort with them. Have I not cooked for them and ironed their shirts, including that rather tricky bit at the base of the collar? Have I not planted their gardens and watered their window boxes? Have I not posted their letters and picked up their prescriptions and collected swatches of carpet and curtain fabric when they were having their houses done up? Have I not changed my clothes when they told me they didn't like them, and lost weight when they said I was too fat? Have I not—have I *not* trotted after them round the bloody golf course shouting, "MARVELOUS SHOT!"—even when the ball was clearly heading for the lake? So what, precisely, is the damn problem?

Why is there always some matrimony-murdering sting in the tail? Take Seriously Successful, for example. There I was at the Ritz, lost in love, mentally rehearsing his wedding speech, and naming our children (Heidi, Hildegarde, Lysander, Tarquin and Max) when Fate, with malice aforethought, sneezed in my ashtray again.

"Now, I don't want you to be shocked," said Seriously Successful, seriously. "But I've got this little proposition for you. For us, actually."

"Oh, what's that, then?" I asked airily, fiddling with my pudding fork and hoping that what he had actually meant to say was that he had in mind a little proposal for me. Propositions always sound vaguely dodgy, don't they?

He fiddled with the knot of his tie. "You see," he began hesitantly, "my wife and I . . ."

"Your *wife*?"

"Yes." He looked at me. "Wife."

"Oh." My heart did a bungee jump.

"You see she . . . Olivia. That's her name. Olivia and I . . ." He took a sip of water. He appeared to be struggling. ". . . well . . . we don't really get on. In fact, we were never really very compatible in the first place," he continued. "We've soldiered on for years, but recently we've just found it pretty intolerable. There's never been anyone else involved," he added quickly. "I wouldn't like you to think that. But it's just that our marriage is, well, a bit of a farce, really."

My hopes rose as swiftly on their elasticated rope as they had plummeted a moment before. In that case he could get divorced, couldn't he, and it would all be OK? I could still have my dream man with his lovely voice and his smart suits and his exquisite neckwear and his jokes.

"However," I heard him continue, "we are extremely unlikely to split up."

"Oh." Oh. "Why?"

"Because her father is my main backer. He lent me a considerable amount of money when I set up my company fifteen years ago."

"I see."

"I had nothing then. Except my ideas, and my energy, and my ambition. And he enabled me to make a success of it. It would have been almost impossible otherwise. And it has been, well . . ."

"Seriously Successful?" I suggested.

"Yes," he said with a little shrug. "It has. That's why I have the house in Sussex and the smart flat in town. That's why I'm wearing a Savile Row suit and handmade shoes. That's why my daughter goes to Benenden. All because Olivia's father laid the foundations for my business success."

"But if the company's done that well, couldn't you just, well, pay him back?" I ventured.

"I have," he replied. "Of course I have. With interest. But it's not as simple as that, because when he agreed to back me, he said he would only do it if I promised always to look after Olivia and never, ever leave her. That was the condition. He was very emphatic about it, and I said I would honor it. And I will. In any case," he carried on with a slight grimace, "divorce is so unpleasant, especially where children are involved. I really *don't* want to inflict that on my daughter."

"Well personally I think adultery's very unpleasant. I really don't want to inflict that on myself."

"And the reason why I put in that ad is because I'm just, well, rather lonely and love-starved really, and I wanted to find someone I can care for and . . ."

"Spoil a little or even a lot," I said dismally.

"Er. Yes. Yes. Exactly. Someone I can have fun with. And when I talked to you, and met you this evening, and was terribly attracted to you, which I am, then I knew that the person I could have fun with was you."

"What the hell makes you think I want to have *fun*?" I said. "I don't *want* any bloody *fun*. I want to get *married*."

"Well, I'm afraid I can't actually offer you marriage," he said. "Not as such. But we could still have a wonderful relationship," he added enthusiastically. "Though of course it would have to be part-time."

"Part-time? Oh I see," I said, twisting the handle of my pudding spoon. "Well, perhaps you could tell me what that would involve. I mean, how many days off would I get? And would I have any union rights? Would I get the usual benefits and sick pay, and could you guarantee me a minimum wage? And if I were to sign a contract what would happen if Britain signed up to the Social Chapter? You see I've got to think about these things."

"Don't be bitter," he said, as the waiter arrived with the pudding and cheese. "Why did you assume that I was single?"

"Because you didn't say that you *weren't,*" I said, throwing my eyes up in anguish to the clouded, *trompe l'oeil* ceiling. "Why didn't you just be done with it and say, 'Suave businessman in dead-as-dodo marriage WLTM curvy girl for fun legovers with absolutely no view to future'? Anyway, you could have told me over the phone."

"You didn't *ask.*"

"But you should have said. We talked for long enough."

"Well, OK, I didn't say because I liked the sound of you so much and I was afraid that if you knew my situation you wouldn't agree to meet me."

"Too bloody right. Being someone's side-order wasn't exactly what I had in mind."

"I don't know why you're so shocked," he said, with an air of exasperation as he buttered a Bath Oliver. "I'm offering something very . . . civilized. And let's face it, Tiffany, lots of people have these sorts of arrangements."

"Well, lots of people aren't me," I said. My throat was aching with a suppressed sob; tears pricked the back of my eyes. I glanced away from him, taking in the Marie Antoinette interior with its shining mirrored panels and gilded chandeliers. Then I looked at him again.

"You said it was a proposition. And I don't accept it. So I'm afraid you'll just have to put it to someone else." I put my napkin on the table and stood up. "I think I'll go home now. Goodbye. Thank you very much for dinner."

I walked out through the bar, aware of the happy babble of voices, and the merry chink of cut glass. My face was flaming with a combination of indignation and the humid, midsummer heat. What a bastard, I thought as I crossed Piccadilly. Who did he think he was? More important, who did he think I was? What a cad. What a . . . I flagged down the number 38 and stepped on board. Empty. Good. At least I could cry without being stared at.

"Cheer up darling," said the conductor as I sat in the front seat shielding my face with my left hand. "It may never happen."

"I know," I said, as a large, hot tear plopped onto my lap. Especially if I make a habit of dating men like Seriously Successful. What a creep. What did he take me for? I reached into my bag and pulled out my mobile phone. I'd ring Lizzie *right* now and tell her what a bastard he was. Part-time girlfriend indeed! She'd be sympathetic. I dialled her number.

"We're *so* sorry, but Lizzie and Martin aren't here at the moment," declaimed her recorded voice. "But *please do* leave us a message . . ." God, so theatrical—you'd think she was auditioning for the RSC—"and we'll get back to you *just as soon* as we can." Damn. I pressed the red button. Who could I talk to instead? I had to talk to someone. Sally. She'd dish out some sympathy. If she wasn't in New York, Tokyo, Frankfurt, Washington or Paris. *Ring ring. Ring ring.*

"Hallo," said Sally.

"Sally, it's Tiffany and I just wanted to tell you . . ."

"Tiffany! How *are* you?"

"Very pissed off actually, because see I've just been on a date, a blind date . . ."

"Gosh, that's brave."

"Yes, I suppose it is. Or rather it's not really brave, it's stupid. Because you see I met this bloke, this adventurous, seriously successful managing director . . ."

"Yes? Sounds OK. What happened?" The bus stopped in Shaftesbury Avenue, then—*ding ding!*—it moved off again.

"Well, it was all going very well," I said. "I thought he was terribly attractive, and very interesting and incredibly funny . . ."

"Oh hang on, Tiffany, I've just got to catch the business headlines on Sky . . ." Her voice returned a minute later. "It's OK, I was just checking the Dow Jones. Carry on. So what happened?" *Ding ding!*

"Well, it was going really well," I repeated. "And he seemed very interested in me, and I was certainly very interested in him and *then* . . ."

"Yes?"

"Move down inside the bus please!" *Ding ding!*

"He told me that he was *married* and was only looking for a *part-time girlfriend*. What do you think of that?"

"I think that's awful," said the elderly woman sitting behind me. I turned round and looked at her. "I hope you gave him what for," she said.

"Yes, I did actually. I was extremely insult— Sally? Are you still there?"

"Yes," she said. "How ghastly. What a creep. But didn't his ad *say* that he was married?"

"No. It *didn't* say he was married," I said dismally, as we chugged up Roseberry Avenue. "It simply said that he was looking for an unforgettable girl in her twenties or thirties to 'spoil a little or even a lot.' " A guffaw arose from behind me. What the hell was so funny? I turned round again and glared at the other passengers.

"But Tiffany, you should have known," said Sally. *Ding ding!*

"How?"

"Because an offer to 'spoil' a woman is shorthand for seeking a mistress. Like an offer to 'pamper' her, or a request for 'discretion.' You've got to learn the code if you're going to do this kind of thing."

"Well I didn't *know* that," I wailed. "I know that GSOH means Good Sense of Humor and Know VGSOH means *Very* Good Sense of Humor and that WLTM means Would Like To Meet."

"And LTR means Long Term Relationship," added Sally.

"Does it?"

"And W/E means 'well-endowed.' "

"Really? Good God! *Anyway,* I didn't know that offering to 'spoil' someone meant you already had a *wife.*"

"Everyone knows that," said the middle-aged man across the aisle from me, unhelpfully.

"Well, I didn't—OK?" I said. "Anyway Sally, Sally are you there? Hi. I'm just really, really pissed off. Seriously Success-ful? Seriously Swine-ish more like."

"What's his real name?" she asked, as we left the Angel.

"God, I don't know. I never asked," I said. "Anyway, what-ever Seriously Slimy's real name is, is *no* concern of mine. Seriously Unscrupulous . . ."

"Seriously Shallow," said the woman behind me.

"Yes."

"And Seriously Sad," she concluded.

"Quite. I mean, Sally, what on earth did he take me for?"

"Never mind, Tiffany, that *was* bad luck," she said. "But I'm sure there's someone nice just around the corner. Are you go-ing to Lizzie's for lunch on Sunday?"

"Yes," I said.

"Well I'll see you then," she said. "And chin up."

I put my mobile phone away and took out my paper. Doing the crossword would calm me down. Bastard. *Bastard.* Fifteen across: *Fool about with high-flyer.* Seven letters, first letter, 'S." Couldn't do it. I stood up and rang the bell. As I made my way to the back of the bus an elderly man made a beckoning gesture.

"Why don't you join Dateline?" he said in a gravelly whisper. "Much safer. I think these personal ads are rather risky myself."

"Thanks," I said, "I'll think about it."

Fool about with high-flyer. I turned it over and over in my mind as I got off at my stop and walked down Ockendon Road. Oh God, there were cyclists on the bloody footpath again.

"It's the People's Pavement you know!" I called out as the boy whizzed past, practically clipping my left ear. God I was in a bad mood. A really bad mood. Damn Seriously Successful. *Damn* him. *Fool about with high-flyer,* I thought. High-flyer. And then it came to me—with a pang—*skylark.*

July Continued

By the next morning I was much, much calmer. "What a *bastard*," I raged to myself. I mean, what a copper-bottomed swine. Disgusting behavior. Part-time girlfriend indeed! Seriously Successful? Seriously Sleazy. Seriously Shabby. Seriously Scurrilous. But I have only myself to blame—serves me right for doing something so patently risky. Might have known there'd be a catch with this catch. I mean he's very attractive, at least I think so. And he's got very good manners, and he's very amusing and very good company and all that and yes, he's very successful, and very well-dressed and very sophisticated too and very charismatic. But he's also very *married*. Blast. Blast. I stabbed away at the antique roses—I've done two small petals actually—while I reflected on Seriously Successful's appalling behavior and my continuing bad luck with blokes. Then the phone rang. I went into the hall and picked up the receiver.

"Oh hello Tiffany, it's um—ha ha ha ha!—Peter here." Oh *God*. This was all I needed. "Tiffany, are you there?" I heard him squeak.

"Er, yes. Yes, I am," I said, "but . . ."

"Well, ha ha ha! It was so nice to meet you the other day, Tiffany, and I just thought we ought to arrange that game of tennis." Ought we? Oh God, no.

"I'm afraid I have to decline your invitation owing to a subsequent engagement," I said, recalling Oscar Wilde's solution to these dilemmas. Actually I didn't say that. I didn't say anything. I was thinking, fast.

"Can you go and get your diary?" I heard him say.

"Er, yes, hang on a second," I said, suddenly inspired. But I didn't go into my study. I went to the front door, opened it, and rang my bell hard. Twice. And then I rang it again.

"Oh Peter, I'm so sorry but there's someone at the door," I said breathlessly. "I'd better answer it . . ."

"Oh well, I'll hold on," he said cheerfully.

"No, don't do that, Peter, I'll ring you back. Bye."

"But you don't have my num—"

Phew. *Phew.* I went back into the sitting-room. And then the phone rang again. Bloody Peter Fitz-Harrod. Why couldn't he take a hint? This time I'd tell him. I'd just pluck up the courage to say, sorry, but that I'd prefer him not to call.

"Yesss!" I hissed into the receiver.

"Darling, what on *earth's* the matter?" said Mum. "You sound awful."

"Oh, hello, Mum. I *feel* awful," I said. "I'm pissed off. With men."

"Never mind," she said. "I'm sure there's someone nice just around the corner."

"I'm sure there *isn't*," I said.

"Haven't you met anyone new yet?" she inquired.

"Oh yes. One or two. But no one I'd bother telling you about," I said bitterly. "No one I'll be bringing home for tea, if that's what you mean. No one who's going to be any *use,* to use that old-fashioned phrase."

"Oh dear. It's just so difficult these days," she said. "It's not like it was when Daddy and I were young. I mean, when *we* were young—"

"I know," I interjected. "You just met someone you liked, and they became your boyfriend, and then before too long you got engaged, and then you got married, and you stayed married forever and ever. End of story," I said.

"Well, more or less," she replied. "I suppose forty years *is* forever and ever, isn't it?"

Forty years. My parents have been married for *forty* years. Four decades; four hundred and eighty months; two thousand and eighty weeks; fourteen thousand, five hundred and sixty days; three hundred and fifty thousand hours; twenty-one million minutes; one billion, two hundred and fifty-eight million seconds, give or take a few. They've been married all that time. Happily married, too. And no affairs. I know that. Because I asked them. And that's the kind of marriage I'd like myself. And I don't care what *bien-pensant* people say about the complexity of modern family life, the probability of divorce, the natural tendency toward serial monogamy and the changing social mores of our times. I know exactly what I want. I want to be married to the same man, for a minimum of four decades—possibly five, like the Queen—and no infidelity, thank you! I'm sorry to be so vehement on this point, I know that others may take a more relaxed view, but it's simply how *I* feel. I mean, the first time my mother met my father the only thing he offered her was a ticket to a piano recital at the Wigmore Hall. What did Seriously Successful offer *me* the first time we met? A position as his part-time girlfriend. Charming. Very flattering. Thanks a bunch. Well, you can bug off with your impertinent propositions, Seriously Sick—I decline. And then of course there's another reason why I wouldn't touch him with a barge pole, and that is that Seriously Successful is *ipso facto* an unfaithful fellow. Obviously he is, by the very nature of what he was proposing to me. Now, I *know* what it's like to be with an unfaithful man, and it's not nice at all. And I'm not doing that again. Not after Phil Anderer. No way. But then, well, that was my fault. Because it wasn't as though I wasn't warned about Phillip—I was. When I first met him everyone said, *"Don't Even Think About It!"*— because of his ghastly reputation. And what did I do? I not only thought about it. I did it. I got involved. And I got hurt.

"It meant *nothing,*" Phillip shouted at me, when I found out for certain what I had suspected for some time. "It meant *absolutely nothing.* Do you think I'd risk everything we've got for some pathetic little bimbo?" To be honest, I wasn't at all sure what we *had* got. Not sure at all, in fact. But he was very, very persuasive that I should stay.

"Do you think I'd do anything to jeopardize my relationship with you?" he said, in a softer tone of voice this time.

"You just *did,*" I pointed out tearfully. But later, I thought maybe I was being small-minded and unfair. Perhaps he just needed to do a bit more growing up—even though he was thirty-six. But quite frankly, when he came back from the "golf course" *again* with cheap, alien scent clinging to his House of Fraser diamond-patterned jumper, I was thrown into renewed despair. Another bloody "birdie," I realized bitterly. *Then you know exactly what they're up to*—his mother's words came back to haunt me. But then after three husbands I can understand her being, shall we say, a little circumspect. However, having persuaded me to stay, and let another year go by, Phillip had the nerve to dump *me.* It was horrible, and I'm never, ever, ever, *ever* going out with anyone dodgy ever again. So you can bugger off with your offensive offers, Seriously Slimy. Yes, just bugger *right off,* get lost, never darken my door again, let alone buy me dinner at the Ritz or flirt with me or pay me compliments or laugh at my jokes or make me giggle and . . .

Just then the doorbell rang. *Funny.* I wasn't expecting anyone. A man was standing there. With an enormous bouquet. Who the hell . . . ?

"Miss Trott?" he said.

"Yes," I said. Over his shoulder I could see a van marked Moyses Stevens.

"Flowers," he said. "For you."

I brought them into the kitchen, put them in the sink—they

wouldn't fit even my largest jug—and just sat and stared. It was like a floral fireworks display, a golden explosion of yellow gerbera, lemon-coloured carnations, saffron-shaded roses, banana-yellow berberis, white love-in-a-mist and buttery-colored stocks, all bound together with a curly, primrose ribbon and topped by delicately spiralling twigs. Heaven. And tucked inside the cellophane wrap was a letter.

My dear Tiffany,

I specifically asked the florist—Mr. Stevens does make *exceedingly* good bouquets—for something in yellow. Yellow for cowardice. *My* cowardice, at not being straightforward with you from the start. Can you forgive me? I must say I was rather taken aback by your anger—you were rather fierce you know—but I've tried to see things from your point of view. I can only apologize for having upset you with my facetious and offensive offer. I was, in fact, trying to be honest with you, but I appear to have insulted you instead and I can only say that I hope you'll forgive me enough to remain, at least, my friend.

SS

P.S. Graded Grains Make Finer Flowers.

Oh. Well. Gosh. *Gosh.* I mean, that's a nice letter. That's a *really* nice letter. And what an incredibly thoughtful thing to do. Perhaps I've been a bit over the top. Perhaps I've been too hard on him. How did he know my address? Oh yes, he had my card. But what a *lovely* thing to do. He *is* nice— Oh God oh God oh God, why does he have to be married? Just my luck. Maybe I should think about it. Maybe we could be friends. Why not? Everyone needs friends, and he's so funny, and so interesting, and he's got such good taste in ties, and we get on incredibly well. I'm sure we could at least be pals. I'm sure we could. I'm sure.

"You must be out of your *tiny* mind!" said Lizzie, as we strolled round Harrods Food Hall the following Saturday—or rather, as I traipsed after her while she filled her basket with an assortment of prodigiously expensive groceries in preparation for lunch in her garden the following day. "Don't have *anything* to do with him," she reiterated slowly.

"But I like him," I said, as we lined up at the charcuterie counter.

"That's got *nothing* to do with it," she said, as a jolly-looking man in a white coat planed slices off a Hungarian boar. "Seriously Successful is not available. He's married. And, what's more, he's told you that he's never going to get divorced—a pound of Parma ham, please—and you just *haven't* got time to waste. Oh, and I'll have six honey-glazed poussins as well. Basically Tiffany, you're nearly—"

"I know," I said wearily, "I'm nearly fifty."

"*Exactly*. So if you really want to get married stick to single men—God knows there must be enough of them out there. I mean, I really don't mind if you marry a divorcé, Tiffany," she added, as we surveyed the rows of French cheeses.

"That's a relief," I said absently.

"I mean, if you married a divorcé you could still get married in church, or at the very least have a blessing and wear a nice dress and everything. *And* have bridesmaids," she added. "But getting involved with a married man is not something that should be undertaken 'unadvisedly, lightly, or wantonly,' as they say. Half a pound of nettle-wrapped Cornish Yarg, please. In fact it should not be undertaken *at all*."

"But I'm not *going* to get involved with him—he only wants to be *friends*," I pointed out.

This was greeted with a derisive snort. "Friends? Don't you realize that that's a Trojan horse? If you become 'friends' with him, I guarantee it will be only a matter of weeks before you're sitting desperately by the phone dressed down to the nines in your La Perla, while his wife's private detective is parked outside your house with his video camera trained on your bedroom window. Is that really what you want? Because that, Tiffany, is exactly what happens to mistresses."

Mistresses? *Mistress*. What an awful word. God, no. No way. Lizzie may be brutal, but she's right.

"I'm only thinking of you, Tiffany," she said, as we wandered through the perfumery department on the ground floor. "You've been up enough dead ends with men to fill a cemetery. You can't afford another mistake. Just write to Seriously Successful, thank him for his flowers and tell him, firmly, but very politely, that you can't possibly remain in touch. Are you OK for moisturizer?" she added as she dotted "Fracas" behind her ears.

"Yes," I replied as I dismally sprayed "Happy" onto my left wrist.

"Have you tried the new Elizabeth Lauderstein ceramide complex containing alpha hydroxy serum derived from fruit acids?"

"Yes."

"Fantastic isn't it?"

"Incredible. Lizzie, do you think these expensive unguents really work?" I asked.

"I believe they do," she said simply. "OK, Tiff, let's head home."

THANK YOU FOR NOT SMOKING, said the sign in the taxi in which we headed up toward Lizzie's house in Hampstead. Lizzie pushed her Ray Bans further up her exquisitely sculpted nose and lit another Marlboro Light.

"You know, Tiffany, I've been thinking about it all and the fact is that you're going about this whole thing the *wrong way*."

"What do you mean, wrong way?" I asked, opening a window to let out the smoke.

"Well, you've been answering ads, and I think it would be far, far better to put one in *yourself*," she explained. "That way you'd be more in control. You could filter out the husbands and the head-bangers. I'll help you write it," she added. "I'm good at that kind of thing—we can do it *right now* in fact."

The taxi turned left off Rosslyn Hill and came to a stop halfway down Downshire Hill, outside Lizzie's house. A vast, white-washed early Victorian pile with a fifty-foot garden—and that's just at the front. Lizzie and Martin have lived here for eight years, and it's worth well over a million now. I struggled out of the taxi with her array of Harrods carriers, just like I used to help her carry her trunks up the stairs when we were at school. She went and tapped on the window and Mrs. Burton came and opened the door.

"Thanks, Mrs. B," she said. "We're loaded down with stuff for tomorrow. I've been a bit naughty in Harrods, but never mind," she added with a grin, "Martin can afford it, and he likes to feed all my girlfriends properly. Where *is* Martin, Mrs. B?" she inquired.

"Mowing the lawn," Mrs. Burton replied.

"Oh good. I told him it needed doing. OK, Tiffany, will you help me put this stuff away?"

Now, I'm not a jealous person—I'm really not. But, it's just that whenever I go round to Lizzie's house I always feel awfully, well, jealous. Even though she's my best and oldest friend, my envy levels rocket. I don't know what it is. Maybe it's the forty-foot Colefax and Fowlered drawing room and the expanses of spotless cream carpet. Maybe it's the artful arrangements of exotic flowers in tall, handblown glass vases. Maybe it's the beautifully rag-rolled walls or the serried ranks of antique silver frames on burnished mahogany. Perhaps it's the hundred-foot garden complete with rose-drenched pergola. Or perhaps it's the fact that she has two adorable children and a husband who loves her and who will never, ever be unfaithful or leave her for a younger model. Yes, I think that's what it is. She has the luxury of a kind and faithful husband, and she has pledged to help me secure same.

"Now, listen to me, Tiffany," she said, as we sat in her hand-distressed Smallbone of Devizes kitchen. Through the open window I could see Martin strenuously pushing a mower up and down.

"You are a *product,* Tiffany. A very *desirable* product. And you are about to sell yourself in the market place. Do not sell yourself short."

"OK," I said, sipping coffee from one of her Emma Bridgewater fig leaf and black olive spongeware mugs. "I won't."

"Your pitch has got to be right or you'll miss your target," she said, passing me a plate of chocolate olivers.

"It's OK, I know a thing or two about pitches," I said. "I mean I *am* a copywriter."

"No, Tiffany, sometimes I really don't think you understand the *first thing* about advertising," she said, glancing out into the garden.

"But my ads win awards! I got a bronze Lion at Cannes last year!"

"Martin!" she shouted. "You've missed the bit by the *cotoneasta!"* He stopped, wiped the beads of sweat off his tonsured head, and turned the mower round.

"Mind you, I don't know why you want a husband, Tiffany, they're all completely *useless*." Suddenly Amy and Alice appeared from the garden.

"What are you doing, Mummy?" said Amy, who is five.

"Finding Tiffany a husband."

"Oh good, does that mean we'll be bridesmaids?" said Alice.

"Yes," said Lizzie. "It does. Now go outside and play."

"I've *always* wanted to be your bridesmaid, Tiffany," said Alice, who is seven.

"I think I'm more likely to be your bridesmaid," I said, "when I'm about fifty."

"OK Tiff, this is what I suggest," said Lizzie, waving a piece of paper at me. "Gorgeous blonde, thirty-two, size forty bust, interminable legs, fantastic personality, hugely successful, own delightful house, seeks extremely eligible man, minimum six foot, for permanent relationship. No losers. No cross-dressers. No kids."

"I think it contravenes the Trades Description Act," I said.

"I know, but at least you'll get lots of replies."

"I am not thirty-two, I'm thirty-seven. I do not have a size forty bust, and I am definitely not gorgeous."

"I *know* you're not," she said. "But we've got to talk you *up* as they say in the City. It's all a question of perception. I mean Martin's always talking up his stocks and shares to his clients, and some of them go through the roof."

"Some of these men are going to go through the roof too," I said. "What's the point in lying? Lying will only get me into trouble."

"Men lie," she said, accurately; and into my mind flashed Tall Athletic Neville, a towering sex god, five foot eight.

"Well, I'm *not* going to lie," I said, scribbling furiously. "Now this," I said, "is nearer the mark: "Sparky, kindhearted girl, thirty-seven, not thin, likes tennis and hard work WLTM intelligent, amusing, single man, 36–45, for the purposes of matrimony. No facial hair. No golf players. Photo and letter please.' "

"You won't get *any* replies," Lizzie shouted down the path at me as I left to get ready for tennis. "Not a *single* one!"

Tennis always takes my mind off my troubles. Bashing balls about in my small North London club is so therapeutic. It gets the seratonin going, or is it endorphins? Maybe it's melatonin? God, I can't remember which. Anyway, whatever it is it releases stress, makes me feel happy. Or at least it would do if it wasn't for that wretched man, Alan—such a fly in the ointment. Whenever I'm playing, there he is: the solicitor with two heads. Bald; bearded; thin. The man of my nightmares. It's not at all flattering being fancied by an extremely unattractive man.

"Mind if I join you?"

"No. Not at all," I said airily as I sat in the sunshine on the terrace. We made our way onto one of the grass courts—at least he's not a bad player. We played a couple of sets—he won six-two, six-two, in fact he always beats me six-two, six-two— and then we went and had tea.

"Tiffany, would you like to see something at the cinema with me?" he said as he poured me a cup of Earl Grey.

No, not really. "Ummmmm," I began.

"The Everyman are doing a season of Truffaut."

"Well . . ."

"Or perhaps you'd like to go to the opera—the ENO are doing *The Magic Flute* again."

"Oh, er, seen that one actually."

"Right, then, how about something at that theater?"

"Well, you see, I'm really quite busy at the moment."

He looked stricken. "Tiffany, you're not seeing anyone are you?"

Sodding outrageous! "I really think that's my business, Alan," I said.

"Why don't you want to go out with me, Tiffany? I don't understand it. I've got everything a woman could want. I've got a huge house in Belsize Park; I'm very successful; I'm the faithful type, and I love children. I'd be a good father. What is the problem?"

"Well, Alan," I said, "the problem is that though you are un-doubtedly what they call a 'catch,' I for one find you—how can I put this politely? Physically repulsive." Actually I didn't say that at all. I simply said, "Alan, you're *terribly* eligible, but I'm afraid I just don't feel that the chemistry's right and that's all there is to it. So I'm not going to waste your time. I don't think it's nice to have one's time wasted. And if this means you don't want to play tennis with me anymore, then I'd quite understand."

"Oh no, no, no—I'm not saying that," he interjected swiftly.

"I'm not saying that at all. How abut Glyndebourne?" he called
after me, as I went downstairs to change. "In the stalls? With a
champagne picnic? Laurent Perrier, foie gras—the works?"

Oh *yes*. yes. Glyndebourne. Glyndebourne would be lovely.
I'd *love* to go to Glyndebourne—with *anyone* but you.

Why is it, I wondered later as I telephoned the classified ads
section of the newspaper to dictate my personal ad, that the
men I don't want —who I really, really don't want—are always the ones who want me? Why is it always the men I find
boring and unattractive who offer to spoil me and treat me well
and worship the ground I walk on? And *why* is it that the ones I
really, really like are the ones who treat me like dirt? Isn't that
odd? I just don't get it. But I'm not having it any longer—I'm
taking control. I'm going for what I want and I'm going to find
it, with my very own sales pitch in the "Ladies" section of a
lonely hearts column.

"I've put a lonely hearts ad in the Saturday Rendezvous section of *The Times,*" I announced slightly squiffily at lunch the
following day. Lizzie, Catherine, Emma, Frances, Sally and I
were sipping Pimms by the pergola. In the background, Martin
was painting the French windows, assisted by Alice and Amy,
while we all contemplated the first course of our annual al
fresco lunch—Ogen melon and Parma ham.

"My God that's so brave!" said Frances, stirring her Pimms
with a straw. "Very courageous of you, Tiffany. I admire that.
Well done you!"

"I didn't say I'm climbing backward up Mount Everest," I
explained. "Or crossing the Atlantic in a cardboard box. I
merely said that I've put a personal ad in *The Times*."

"It's still bloody brave of you, Tiffany," insisted Frances.
"What courage! I'd never have the nerve to do that."

"Nor would I!" chorused the others.

"Why ever not?" I asked. "Lots of people do."

"Well, it would be very artificial," said Sally, swatting away a wasp. "I prefer to leave my choice of mate to Fate."

"Me too," said Emma, adjusting the strap of her sundress. "I'd rather meet someone in a romantic way, you know, just, bump into them one day . . ."

"*Where*?" I asked. "By the photocopier? Or the fax machine?"

"Noooo," she said thoughtfully. "In the cinema queue for the films, or on the Northern Line, or on a plane, or . . ."

"How many people do you know who've met their partners like that?" I asked.

"Er. Er. Well, none actually. But I'm sure it does happen. I wouldn't do a lonely hearts ad because I wouldn't want to meet someone in such an obviously contrived way. It would spoil it. But I think you're really brave."

"Yes," chorused the others. "You're really, really brave, Tiffany."

"She isn't brave, she's stupid," said Lizzie forthrightly, "and I say that because her ad is completely truthful. I recommended the judicious use of lying, but she wouldn't have it. She's even put in her age. And 'One should never trust a woman who tells one her real age. A woman who would tell one that, would tell one anything.' " She smiled ingratiatingly. "Oscar Wilde," she explained. "*A Woman of No Importance*." Of course. From Lizzie's great days in Worthing.

"Did you ever hear again from that married chap you met at the Ritz?" asked Sally.

"Er, yes, yes I did actually," I said with a sudden and tremendous pang, which took me by surprise. "To be honest he's really not that bad, ha ha ha! Sent me some rather nice flowers actually. To say sorry. I wish . . . I mean I would like . . ." My voice trailed away.

"What Tiffany means is that she wishes she could see him again, but I have told her that this is *out of the question*," said Lizzie. "She's *got* to keep her eye on the ball. Martin! Don't forget to give it two coats!"

"What did you do?" said Emma.

"I wrote back to him and thanked him, but said that unfortunately circumstances would conspire to keep us apart."

"Maybe he'll get divorced," said Frances. "Everyone else does. Luckily for me!"

"He won't contemplate it," I said.

"Why not?"

"Because he's worried about the effect it would have on his daughter."

"So he'd rather have affairs instead," said Lizzie, rolling her eyes toward the cloudless sky. "Charming."

"Common," said Frances, fishing a strawberry out of her glass.

"Understandable," said Emma quietly. "If his marriage really *is* very unhappy." I looked at her. She had gone red. Then she suddenly stood up and helped Lizzie collect up the plates.

"Er, has anyone actually met anyone they like?" Sally asked.

We all looked blankly at each other. "Nope," said Frances. Emma shook her head, and said nothing, though I could see that she was still blushing.

"What about you, Sally?" I said.

"No luck," she said with a happy shrug. "Perhaps I'll meet someone on holiday next week. Some heavenly maharajah. Or maybe the Taj Mahal will work its magic for me."

"Like it did for Princess Diana, you mean," said Frances with a grim little laugh.

"*I'm* interested in someone," announced Catherine.

"*Yes?*" we all said.

"Well, I met him at Alison and Angus's dinner party in June. Tiffany was there. He's an acc—"

"Oh God, not that dreary accountant?" I said incredulously. "Not that boring-looking bloke in the bad suit who lives in Barnet and probably plays golf?"

Catherine gave me a withering look. I didn't know why.

"He's very nice, actually," she said coldly. "And he's interesting, too. And he's particularly interesting on the subject of art.
He's got quite a collection of—"

"Etchings?" I said.

"Augustus Johns, actually." Gosh. "I mean, Tiffany, why do
you assume he's boring just because he's an accountant?
You're quite wrong."

"Sorry," I said, aware of the familiar taste of shoe leather.

"And nor does it follow that men with interesting jobs are
interesting people," Catherine added. "I mean Phillip had an
interesting job, didn't he?" she continued. "And though I
would never have told you this at the time, because I wouldn't
have wanted to hurt your feelings," she added pointedly, "I
thought he was one of the most boring and conversationless
men I have *ever* met." This could not be denied. "And I don't
think Alex set the world on fire either," she added. This was
also true. "But my friend Hugh, who's an accountant, is actually rather interesting," she concluded sniffily. "So please
don't sneer, Tiffany."

"God I feel such a heel," I said. "I'm sorry. It's the Pimms.
Can I have some more?"

"Anyway, Augustus John was incredibly prolific and he
lived a long time, so there's a lot of his work out there. Loads of
it, in fact. And Hugh's been quietly collecting small paintings
and sketches for years. And after that dinner party he asked me
to clean a small portrait that John did of his wife, Dorelia, and
when he came to collect it yesterday he asked me if I'd like to
have dinner with him next week."

"That's wonderful!" I said, feeling guilty and also stupid.
"Try and find out if he has any nice colleagues. *Single* ones, of
course."

Suddenly Amy appeared, wearing a wide-brimmed straw hat,
party sandals, pink sun-glasses and clutching a small leather
vanity case. She looked as if she was about to set off on some

cheap Iberian package. "What are you all TALKING about?" she shouted. Amy has a very loud voice.

"We're talking about boyfriends," said Lizzie.

Amy opened her case and took out one of her eleven Barbie dolls. "BARBIE'S got a BOYFRIEND," she yelled. "He's called KEN. She's going to MARRY HIM. I've got her a BRIDE'S DRESS."

"Amy darling," said Lizzie. "I keep telling you, Barbie is never going to marry Ken." Bewilderment and disappointment spread across Amy's face. "Barbie has been going out with Ken for almost forty years without tying the knot," Lizzie explained patiently as she passed round the honey-glazed poussins. "I'm afraid Barbie is a commitophobe."

"What's a COMMITOPHOBE, Mummy?"

"Someone who doesn't want to get married, darling. And I don't want you to be one when you grow up."

"What are you all talking about?" said Alice, whose blonde pigtails were spattered with black paint.

"Boyfriends," said Frances.

"ALICE has got a BOYFRIEND," Amy yelled. "He's called TOM. He's in her CLASS. But I HAVEN'T got one."

"That's because you're too young," said Alice wisely. "You still watch the Teletubbies. You're a baby." Amy didn't appear to resent this slur.

"How old's your boyfriend, Alice?" Catherine inquired with a smile.

"He's eight and a quarter," she replied. "And Tom's mummy, Mrs. Hamilton, she's got a boyfriend too."

"Good God!" said Lizzie. "*Has* she?"

"Yes," said Alice. "Tom told me. He's called Peter. He works with her. In the bank. But Tom's daddy doesn't know. Should I tell him?" she added.

"*No,*" said Lizzie. "No. Don't. Social death, darling."

"Tiffany, have *you* got a boyfriend yet?" asked Alice.

"Er, no," I said. "I haven't." She went off and sat on the swing with a vaguely disappointed air.

"You know, it's horrible being single in the summer," I said vehemently. "All those happy couples necking in the park, or playing tennis or strolling hand in hand through the pounding surf . . ."

"Personally I think it's much worse in the winter," said Emma, "having no one to snuggle up to in front of an open fire on some romantic weekend break."

"No, I think it's worse being single in the spring," said Catherine. "When everything's growing and thrusting and the sun's shining, and it's all so horribly happy. April really is the cruelest month, in my view."

"Being single in autumn is the worst," said Sally ruefully, "because there's no one to kick through the leaves with in the park or hold hands with at fireworks displays."

"Well, I often envy you single girls," said Lizzie darkly. "I'd *love* to be single again."

"Well, we'd love to be you," said Catherine, "with such a nice husband."

Lizzie gave a hollow little laugh. I thought that was mean. I glanced at Martin, quietly painting away.

"Love is a gilded cage," said Emma drunkenly.

"No—'Love conquers all,' " said Catherine.

" 'Love means never having to say you're sorry,' " said Frances, with a smirk. "I'm glad that's true—otherwise I'd be unemployed!"

" 'Love's the noblest frailty of the mind,' " said Lizzie. "Dryden."

" 'Love's not Time's fool,' " said Sally. "Shakespeare."

" 'The course of true love never did run smooth,' " said Emma. "Ditto." And for some reason, that cheered me up—I didn't know why.

"Come on, Tiffany—your turn!" they all chorused.

"Er—'Better to have loved and lost than never loved at all,' " I said. "Tennyson."

"However," said Lizzie, "according to George Bernard Shaw 'there is no love sincerer than the love of food.' So eat up, everyone!"

August

On Saturday the first of August I opened *The Times*, turned to the Rendezvous section and found my ad, under "S" for "Sparky." I was quite pleased with it. It didn't look too bad, alongside all the "Immaculate Cheshire Ladies," "Divorced Mums, Thirty-nine," and "Romantic" and "Bubbly" forty-five-year-old females looking for "Fun Times." No, "Sparky" was OK, I reflected as I went up to the Ladies Pond in Hampstead to seek refuge from the blistering heat. "Sparky" might just do the trick, I thought to myself optimistically as I walked down Millfield Lane. NO MEN BEYOND THIS POINT announced the municipal sign sternly, and in the distance I could hear the familiar, soprano chatter of 150 women. I love the Ladies Pond. It's wonderful being able to swim in the open air, free from the prying eyes of men, totally calm and relaxed—though I must say my new high-leg Liza Bruce swimsuit with the cunning underwiring, subtly padded cups and eye-catching scallop trim is *extremely* flattering, and I do sometimes think it's completely wasted in an all-female environment. However, the main thing is not to pose, but to swim. To gently lap the large, reed-fringed pond, where feathery willows bend their boughs to the cool, dark water. To commune with the coots and moorhens which bob about in its reedy shallows; or to admire the grace and beauty of the terns as they swoop and dive for fish. But sometimes, when I'm sitting there on the lawn afterward, gently drying off in the warmth of the sun, I wonder about myself. I really do. I mean it's so Sapphic! Lesbians everywhere! Lesbians young and lesbians *d'un certain âge*; lesbians pretty, and lesbians physiognomically challenged. Lesbians thin and lesbians fat; lesbians swimming gently round the treelined lake, or disporting themselves in the late summer sunshine. And there I was, sitting on the grass, reading my "Sparky, kind-hearted girl" ad again and feeling pretty pleased with it actually, while discreetly surveying beneath lowered eyelids several hundred-weight of near-naked female flesh and wondering, just *wondering,* whether I found it even vaguely erotic, when this attractive, dark-haired girl came up to me, bold as brass, and put her towel down next to mine.

"Hello," she said with a warm smile.

"Hello." *Excuse me. Do we know each other?*

"Mind if I join you?" My God—a pick-up! My Sapphometer went wild.

"Er, yes, do," I said, pulling up the strap of my swimsuit and quickly adjusting my bosom. I discreetly surveyed her from behind my sunglasses as she removed a bottle of Ambre Solaire from her basket and began rubbing the sun lotion onto her legs. She was clearly a "lipstick" lesbian, I decided. The glamorous kind. Her nose and eyebrows were unpunctured by metal studs. She had no tattoos, no Doc Martens, and she did not sport the usual Velcro hairstyle. In fact she was very feminine with a slim figure, lightly made-up eyes and shining, mahogany-colored hair which fell in gentle layers down her back.

"My name's Kate," she said, with a smile. "Kate Spero."

"Tiffany," I said. "Tiffany Trott."

"Are you single?" she asked, nodding at my copy of *The Rules: Time-Tested Secrets for Capturing the Heart of Mr. Right.*

"Yes."

"So am I. Isn't it a bore? I'm looking for TSS."

"TSS?"

"That Special Someone."

"Oh. Well . . . good luck. Er—are you looking here?" I asked, casting my eyes around.

"Oh good God, no! I'm not gay," she explained, with a burst of surprised laughter. Oh. Got that wrong then. "No, I'm looking for a *man*," she added matter-of-factly. "But I just can't find one *anywhere*." And then she said, "Do you know, I never thought I'd get to thirty-seven and still be single." And that was really, really amazing because that's exactly what *I* say out loud to myself several times every day.

"I know," I said. "Isn't it a drag?" And then we immediately told each other all about our past unhappy relationships since about—ooh, 1978 or so—revealing them as children proudly display their scars, though I decided not to tell her about my ad. Anyway I'm happy to say that Kate is now my New Best Friend. I mean, we've go *so* much in common. We're the same age, both single and both desperate. Isn't that an *incredible* co-incidence? In fact, her birthday is a week after mine. Amazing!

"What did you do on your birthday this year?" she asked a few hours later as we strode across the Heath in the afternoon sunshine.

"I got dumped by my boyfriend," I said. "What did you do?"

"I cried all day," she replied happily. We walked on in silence for a while, stopping to watch a knot of children flying kites on Parliament Hill. And then Kate said, "You know, we should look for guys together. It's much easier hunting in a pack." This is probably true. I've often wished that Frances and Emma and Sally would consider it, but they're determined to leave their romantic happiness to the vagaries of Fate. Or God. But God really didn't seem to be doing that much at the moment. I preferred Kate's proactive approach.

"What we need is singles dos," she said firmly. "There are lots of them—Eat 'n' Greet, Dine 'n' Shine, Dateless in Docklands, that kind of thing. I'll do some research and let you know."

"What a brilliant idea," I said, as we parted. "You're on."

In the meantime I waited suspensefully—oh heavens, the torment!—for the replies to my small ad to arrive. Maybe Lizzie was right, I wondered as two and a half weeks went by. Maybe I wouldn't get a single response—no irony intended, ha ha! Perhaps there isn't much demand for sparky girls at the moment. Maybe dull girls are all the rage. But, just in case, I went in search of some more expensive unguents in order to look my best for any future blokes. I mean, at thirty-seven, one's got to take action because, as Lizzie says, my face is going over to the enemy. But I'm not having it—no sir! Crows' feet—eff off and die! Naso-labial lines—hold it right there!

"Yes, yes, tricky . . ." said the woman at the expensive unguents counter in Selfridges. She narrowed her eyes in concentration as she scrutinized my skin. "You've got a luminosity problem," she announced.

"Well, can anything be done about it?" I asked anxiously. "I'll pay."

"In that case the Helena Ardenique multiaction retinyl complex intensive lotion with added ceramides for active cell renewal should do the trick," she explained. "Firmness and elasticity are measurably improved, lines and wrinkles diminished by a guaranteed forty-one and half percent and luminosity and skin glow restored. What it does," she concluded, "is to make your skin 'act younger.' "

"That's *fantastic*," I said as I wrote out my check for seventy pounds.

Then I went home and there, there on the doormat, having arrived by the second post, was a plain, brown A5-sized envelope stamped, "Private and Confidential." And inside that plain, brown envelope, dear reader, were no fewer than thirty-two letters! And what an assortment of writing paper—Basildon Bond, Croxley Script, Conqueror, Airmail, Andrex—ha ha! Some even had hearts and flowers stuck to the envelope! Some were typed, some were word-processed, some were neatly handwritten, while others were almost illegible. Illegible, but possibly quite eligible none the less, I hoped as I ripped into them with lepidopterous stomach and pounding heart.

For crying out loud! A Norfolk pig farmer! And, at forty-nine well outside my stated age range! If I'd wanted a Norfolk pig farmer I'd have bloody well asked for one, wouldn't I? I'd have placed my personal ad in the *King's Lynn Gazette* or *Pig Farmer's Weekly*. Anyway, the other replies broke down as follows: five accountants, twelve computer software designers, one data collection manager, two probation officers, one natural catastrophe modeler, three chiropodists, one stockbroker, one master mariner and six solicitors including . . . including . . . well, actually, I'm furious. Because when I opened reply number nineteen—a nice, thick pale-blue watermarked envelope—I found a longish letter inside and then this photo fell out, and stone the crows, it was none other than two-headed Alan from my tennis club! What the hell does he think he's up to? He's supposed to be infatuated with me, offering to take me to Glyndebourne and everything, and here he is tarting around the lonely hearts columns. I was outraged. And what a flatteringly out-of-date photo—obviously taken in about 1980, he's much balder than that now! But I must say his letter was nice. It was very open, and said how much he'd like to get married and have children and what a good father he'd make, and how he wouldn't mind changing nappies or anything, and in fact would probably even enjoy it. He also said he plays tennis twice a week and likes going to the opera—especially Glyndebourne—and went on about how his heart's desire is a woman of good character complete with strong forehand. Well it's forty-love to me, Alan, because I'm not *bloody* well replying, because I don't think you should be two-timing me with sad women who advertise themselves in the personal columns of national newspapers. Actually, I feel a bit guilty about it, but I can't write back, can I? I suppose I could always lie and say that due to unexpected demand the vacancy has now been filled. But I think that in the circs it's better not to say anything.

Keep mum. Poor bloke, he'd be *mortified* if he knew it was me (must tell Lizzie—she'll *hoot*!). Then while I was reading letter number twenty-six—very witty actually—from the stockbroker, the phone rang. It was Kate.

"Eat 'n' Greet. This Saturday. Huge summer party in prestigious venue for Successful and Attractive Single People."

"Oooh goodee," I said. "Is that us?"

"Of course."

"Are we going, then?"

"Yes. We most certainly are."

The following day I was in my sunny sitting room going through my record collection; I've never had the heart to chuck out my vinyl, somehow CD's just aren't the same. I was sorting through the singles, and thinking as I did so that what I would really prefer is Long Play, when the phone rang.

"Tiffany!"

"Yes."

"It's me."

"Oh. Hello." He sounded rather cross.

"I got your letter this morning."

"Yes."

"And I just wanted to tell you how disappointed I am. Very disappointed. And hurt. Very hurt. *Very*."

"Well, I'm sorry," I said. "It's just that there really doesn't seem to be much point. In the circumstances."

"No point? No point in even being pals?"

"No," I said. "There's no point, because the point is that you're not free."

"But married people can have friendships, Tiffany. It is allowed, you know."

"Yes, but they have to choose them carefully. And I don't think our friendship would be wise."

"All I want to do is see you from time to time," he said plaintively.

"Well, that's not a good idea," I said.

"And I know you'd like to see me."

"Well . . ."

"You would, wouldn't you?" he persisted.

"Well, OK, yes, I admit it."

"Aha!"

"But circumstances . . ."

". . . will conspire to keep us apart," he said in an irritating sing song voice.

"Yes. Yes. That's right."

"But surely we could have dinner together sometimes," he persisted. "Or see a film? Now, there's a wonderful concert coming up at the Barbican," he went on animatedly. "Yo-Yo Ma is playing the Bach unaccompanied cello suites and I really want to go. Why don't you come with me?"

"Well . . . well it sounds lovely, but I just don't think I should."

"Why not?"

"Because I don't wish to be tempted. That's why."

"So you *are* tempted," he replied triumphantly.

"Well, well—"

"Say it!"

"Yes, I am. OK. Yes. I'm tempted. Happy?"

"You like me?"

"Yes. I like you a lot." *In fact I find you Seriously Sexy.*

"I like you too," he came back, more warmly now. "In fact, Tiffany, 'You're the Right One, the Bright One.' "

"Purleeze!"

"You're my One and Toblerony!"

"Now listen, Seriously Successful!" I said crossly. "This really won't do . . . anyway, what *is* your real name?"

"I'm not telling you," he said defensively.

"Why not?"

"I refuse to tell you, unless you agree to go to that concert with me."

"Well I'm not going to," I retorted.

"Oh, why not?" he said.

"Because I know that it would be wrong for me because I've got to keep my eye on the ball and frankly, you're way off-side."

"But Tiffany, we could have such fun . . ."

"I keep telling you, I don't *want* to have fun."

"We could do such nice things together."

"I can do nice things anyway."

"But Tiffany, we communicate so wel—"

I put the phone down. And then I said, "Sorry."

Who'd have thought that sorting out replies to a lonely hearts ad would be such a mammoth task? I mean, these bulging buff envelopes marked "Private and Confidential" just keep plopping onto the mat.

"OK, OK, I take it back," said Lizzie as we sat at my kitchen table going through the replies. "I didn't think you'd get any. No need to crow. But just think how many you *would* have got if you'd followed my advice."

"I think 114 is quite enough," I said as she lit another cigarette. "I'm not greedy."

We sorted them into three piles: Yes, Maybe, and You Have Got To Be Joking.

"Now here's a really nice one," said Lizzie, waving a blurred photo of Son-of-Quasimodo, fifty-seven, at me.

"You have got to be joking," I said crisply.

"Why? He's very suitable," she said.

"He isn't suitable. He's hideous," I replied.

"He's not hideous," she said indignantly, exuding two plumes of smoke from her elegant nostrils. "He's a senior partner in a City law firm. He's probably in 200k. I don't call 200k hideous. And make sure you phone that stockbroker."

"OK, I will," I said. "But only because he's OK-looking-bordering-on-the-almost-acceptable and because I liked his witty letter. It's not about money," I added. "I mean, Alan has a lot of money. But I don't care, because I'm not interested. All I'm looking for is a golf-hating commitophile with good character, reasonable backhand and complete absence of facial hair. Is that too much to ask?"

"Probably," she replied. "Now here's a *lovely* guy," she said with a smirk, handing me a piece of torn-off graph paper.

Dear Sparky Girl, I read. *Can I light your fire? My name is Stavros. I am art student. Are you blonde? I need pretty sexy blonde model. I do portraits. You could be chapter in history of art. You could be my model only. But maybe, if you really sexy, you could be more than model. But if you ring me, and if you sexy blonde, I buy you meal for sure.*

"Point taken," I said, wavering only slightly before consigning Stavros to the You Have Got To Be Joking pile. It was distressing to see how big that pile had grown; it was full of probation officers, undertakers, astrologists, men called Terry, and a bloke from Acacia Avenue, Billericay, who wrote, "If I am not in when you call, please leave a message with the security men, pool guy, my housekeeper, or one of my five full-time gardeners." One letter was all in German and contained a photo of a man with waist-length brown hair who said he worked in Düsseldorf airport. Another was from a computer consultant called John who wrote, "I am sexually insatiable and am looking for a gorgeous babe with class, intelligence, superb breasts and a big bum."

"Well, you've got the bum," said Lizzie.

"My God—look at this!" I said, holding up a red foiled-wrapped chocolate.

"Don't eat it!" Lizzie screamed, snatching it out of my hand and rushing to the bin. "It's probably *poisoned*!"

I glanced at the accompanying letter. "Oh Baby, the thought of you keeps me awake at night," the sender had written, "you're really playing havoc with my sleep patterns. Please, baby, don't be cruel to me. You know I really, really, really LOVE YOU."

"Eighty-five percent of these men appear to be deranged," I said. "And the ones that aren't deranged are largely boring." For the same tedious phrases kept popping up over and over again: "incurable romantic . . . all my own hair . . . red Porsche . . . all my own teeth . . . golf in the Algarve . . . almost divorced . . . tropical sunsets . . . no baggage . . . that special lady . . . two ex-wives . . . young at heart . . . five children . . . give me a call."

"I've got to stop," I said suddenly to Lizzie. "I can't take any more. It's making me feel *sick*."

"OK, we'll go through the rest another time, but *don't* forget to phone that stockbroker," she said as she left. "I mean a stockbroker would be fine—just look at me!"

Yes, just look at Lizzie, I thought, as she got into her Mercedes. She had gone from actorly impoverishment to a seven-bedroom house in Hampstead. But does she love successful-but-not-terribly-exciting Martin? I have never liked to ask. Anyway, I left a brief, friendly message on Ian the stockbroker's answer phone and then got ready for the Eat 'n' Greet Sensational Singles Party. Quick shower, then black cocktail dress, chunky pearls at wrist and neck, strappy sandals, hair piled up, mascara and lip-liner—*voilà*!

"You look lovely," said Kate generously, when she came to collect me at seven.

"No, you look *much* prettier than me," I said, "and much younger too, may I say."

"Oh, no you look *incredibly* young—only, ooh, twenty-five," she countered.

"But you look—*seventeen*!" I insisted. "Are you sure you're old enough to be in command of a motorized vehicle?" Having a New Best Friend who's exactly the same age as me and also single is marvelous—Kate and I compete to pay each other the most lavish, ego-lifting compliments which we would obviously be receiving regularly from blokes were it not for our tragic and frankly perplexing singledom. As we drove through south east London our confidence began to decline.

"It'll be full of desperate, desperate women and really sad men," I said as we cruised up the drive of the Dulwich Country Club, set in twelve acres of fabulous parkland. And was it my imagination, or were the regular members of the club sniggering at us as we walked up the steps? And I could swear that the girl from Eat 'n' Greet gave us a sweet but pitying smile as she ticked us off the list on her leatherette clipboard.

"Here we go," said Kate, as we were ushered into the champagne reception. She gave my hand an encouraging squeeze. "Just smile."

It's funny how human nature accentuates the negative. In the conservatory there were about 150 people aged between thirty and fifty-five, but somehow all I could see was men with gray hair and women *d'un certain âge* trussed up like Thanksgiving turkeys in shiny giftwrap frocks. My heart sank and my jaw was already aching from maintaining my rictus grin. This was hell. What was I doing here? it was dreadful, dreadful, *dreadful*. But then I began to notice a few men who were perfectly-OK-looking-bordering-on-the-almost-acceptable—in fact some of them looked quite handsome, especially in their DJs. And there were some rather gorgeous girls, too.

"Oh, *she's* pretty," I whispered to Kate as we circulated.

"You're here to meet men, Tiffany, don't look at the women. And just keep smiling."

It seemed to work. If you beam at a totally strange man, he will beam right back. In fact he will come up to you, politely introduce himself and ask you your name. Good heavens! We'd only been there ten minutes and we'd already met three chaps each! Then a gong sounded and we went in to dinner. I found myself chatting to a tall, blond, aristocratic-looking bloke called Piers. Bit of all right actually, and dead posh.

"I *say*," he said as he consulted the table plan. "You're sitting next to me, Tiffany, how lovely."

* * *

I think this singles scene is really marvelous. It's such fun. It really is. It's a gas. But there are drawbacks. I mean, there I was sitting next to aristocratic-looking Piers, and he was telling me *all* about his divorce and how his wife was unfaithful to him four times—oh how *could* she, I thought to myself as I stared into his cobalt eyes. And I was just about to start telling him all about *my* unhappy relationships, and really getting quite interested in him, and to be honest hardly saying a word to the man on my right, which was a bit rude really, except that he was quite happily chatting to a pretty redhead in personnel, when a gong suddenly sounded.

"We'd like the ladies to stay seated and all the gentlemen to move thu-ree tables to their left *purleeze,*" said the major-domo.

Piers looked stricken. "But I don't *want* to move," he said. "I'm really very happy *just* where I am." The blood rushed to my cheeks. I smiled shyly at him. "Well, I'll be back," he said. "After dessert. And we'll carry on from there."

"I'll . . . *wait* for you," I said encouragingly, as the white chocolate mousse with raspberry coulis arrived. Piers gave me a little wave as he headed off and then I saw him sit down at a distant table, next to a woman whose youth and attractiveness I could not accurately ascertain at seventy-five feet. Then two new men came to sit on either side of me, both of them OK-looking-bordering-on-the-almost-acceptable. From the other side of the table Kate gave me a little grin—she seemed to be having a jolly time too and was happily chatting away to a charming demolitions expert. Good, we were both getting our fair share of nice chaps.

"Hallo, erm . . . erm . . ."

"Tiffany," I said, helpfully holding up my name card. "Tiffany Trott." I shook hands with my new neighbor, who on closer inspection was rather handsome, though he seemed to have had a teensy weensy bit too much to drink.

"And who are you?" I inquired.

"My name's Terry," he said. *Terry!*

"That's interesting," I said, "because actually Terry is my *least* favorite male Christian name—ha ha ha! After Kevin and Duane, of course." Actually, I didn't say that at all. I simply said, "Hello and welcome." He laughed. I don't know why.

"Now Tiffany, what do you do?" he asked. Gosh! Getting right down to business here.

"Er, try and guess!" I challenged him teasingly.

"Well . . . er . . . I think you're a . . . um, secretary," he said as he poured us both some rather good Chablis. I must have looked a bit taken aback because he quickly added, "But you're clearly a very high-powered one. You probably work for a Senior Sales Manager." Now I must say this disappointed me. Why had he not assumed that I was employed in some more glamorous field, say as an actress, croupier, television presenter or international horsewoman?

"Wrong!" I said. "I'm a builder."

"Get away!" he replied. "Are you really?"

"No," I said. "I'm not. Actually, I'm in advertising. I'm a copywriter."

"What," he said, "writing ads? Go To Work On An Egg—that kind of malarky?"

"Yes," I said. "That sort of thing."

"Vorsprung Durch Technik?"

"Yup. That's it. What do you do?"

"I work on an oil rig. In the North Sea. Bloody dangerous. Never at home. Two divorces. Three kids. Loads of alimony. And how old are you, Tiffany?" he inquired, narrowing his hazel eyes.

"Guess!" I said boldly.

"Well, I think you're . . . twenty-nine," he said, passing me an Elizabeth Shaw after-dinner mint.

"I think I love you," I said.

"Do you? Tiffany, I think I may be a little bit thick for you, but will you marry me?"

   "Well, I don't know," I said. "You see, you've kept me hanging around. Normally I expect men to propose within five minutes but you've kept me waiting . . ." I glanced at my watch, ". . . twelve."

   "I think you're lovely."

   "I think you're a bit pissed."

   "Yes," he said as the band struck up for the dancing. "But in the morning I'll be sober, and you'll still be lovely." Ah. Obviously an educated fellow.

   "Well, that's very gallant of you," I said. Now, this banter was all very well, but dinner was well and truly over by now and I rather wished that Piers would come back and rescue me. Where was he? Not at his table. I glanced round the dance floor and suddenly my blood ran cold. *Piers!* Draped around an elegant brunette. How could he? The fickleness of men! I absently bit the burnt almond off a *petit-four* and poured myself another glass of wine. Terry was chatting animatedly to the woman on his left—no doubt proposing matrimony to her as well. Kat was deep in conversation with a tree surgeon. And I was completely alone. Here I was at a party with 149 other Sensational Singles and not one of them was talking to me. I know, I thought to myself, I'll go to the ladies' loo. That way I'll avoid looking as though no one's *remotely* interested in me. Three men and several dances later I found my way to the powder room on the floor below—very tastefully done up in pseudo Sanderson. As I went over to the basin I noticed two thirty-something women adjusting their makeup in the three-way mirrors.

   "God the men here are *ghastly,*" said one of them, whose voice I was sure I recognized.

   "Yes. Wish I was a lesbian," said her friend with a snort. "The girls are much better-looking than the guys!"

   "But then in my experience the men are always pretty useless at these kinds of things," said woman number one. "I really don't know *why* I bother." Suddenly she looked up at

he said this, and saw me squishing orchid-scented liquid soap
nto my hands. I tried to avoid her gaze, but damn! I'd been
potted.

"Tiffany Trott!" she said accusingly.

"Oh—ha ha! Hello, Pamela," I said. "Fancy meeting you
ere, ha ha ha!" I pulled down a paper towel from the dispenser.

"Long time no see," she said. Not long enough. "It's been
ears. How are you?"

"Fine. Fine," I said. "Fine."

"Still single, though?" she said, with just a hint of satisfaction.

"No, actually I'm married with five children," I said, "I just
ome to these sorts of occasions for kicks." Actually I didn't
eally say that at all. I said, "Yup. That's right. Single—ha ha!
'm freelance now, so I don't meet nearly as many people as I
sed to. This seemed like a sensible thing to do." I was aware
hat she was looking me up and down.

"You look very, *fit*," she said grudgingly. Fit. That was al-
vays the most generous thing she could ever manage to say.

"I *am* fit," I said brightly. "I play a lot of tennis these days."
ou should try it you hideous lardarse!

"Still in ad-biz?" she inquired, combing her short, wispy red
air. I nodded. "Doesn't the triviality of it ever get you down?"
he added. She always used to ask me that.

"Oh no, I find it rather stimulating, actually." *And in any
ase we can't all be English language teachers, can we?* God
his was awful—it was bad enough being abandoned by Piers
vithout running into ghastly Pamela Roach in the ladies' loo.

"Still in Stoke Newington?" she asked as she removed her
uge, pink preppy glasses and reapplied her trademark blue
yeshadow.

"No, I've moved to Islington actually."

"Oh. Doing very well for yourself then," she said resent-
ally. And suddenly I remembered exactly why I had never
ked her. This constant resentment, and the gatecrashing—not

to mention the time I had accidentally left my beloved cash
mere cardigan at her flat and it had come back two month
later, stuffed in a carrier bag, worn to bits, and stained wit
black ink from the topless felt tip she had been carrying abou
in one of the pockets. I never forgave her for that. But persis
tent and pachydermatous, it took her seven years to get th
message.

"Are you enjoying this evening?" she inquired carefully. B
which I knew she really meant, "Are you having a better tim
than me?"

"Oh yes—yes," I said. "It's quite good fun. I've met som
rather nice people actually. How about you?"

"Well, there are so few attractive men," she said.

"Oh, I don't know. I've met some very nice-looking ones,"
replied. *Though unfortunately the one I liked the most has ju*
deserted me for a gorgeous brunette.

"Well, *I* haven't spotted any," she insisted. "And I'm reall
not going to compromise. I don't see why I should."

I looked at her: spaghetti straps over Herculean shoulders;
strategically placed feather boa only half disguising the appar
ent lack of neck; the perpendicular line of her wide, squar
body uninterrupted by perceptible breasts or a waist; the larg
pudgy hands and platelike feet, and I thought, as I alway
thought when we were at college, just who are you trying t
kid? It's strange how it's always the least attractive wome
who express the most reluctance to compromise. And then
think of someone like Sally, and she says things like, "*Who o
earth* would want me?" But the fact is, Sally is beautiful. An
as for me, well my ambitions extend no further than Mr. OF
looking-bordering-on-the-almost-acceptable. God, I hope
find him.

"If you see any good-looking men, put them my way," Pame
instructed me as she applied another layer of black eyeliner.

"Er, sure," I said. "Anyway, it's nice to bump into you,"

carried on mendaciously, "but I'd better get back to my table—
I'm here with a friend."

"Have you got a card?" she asked as she replaced her
glasses. "I don't have your new address."

"Er—no, um—I'll pop one in the post," I lied.

"Keep in touch," she called after me.

"Yes. Yes." I *won't*.

Phew. Phew. Damn. That's the problem with these kinds of
events, I reflected as I found my way back to my table. It's such
a small world—and that's the pitfall—you could easily bump
into someone you knew and that would be so embarrassing,
so dispiriting, especially if you were feeling vulnerable anyway, being seen by someone you didn't even like and it was
ghastly . . .

"Tiffany?" *Aaaahhh!* What is this? What's going on? Oh my
God, I've been spotted again. Who the hell was this?

"It is Tiffany, isn't it?" said this tall, handsome chap with
gray hair and blue eyes whom I vaguely recognized.

"I've been trying to catch your eye all evening," he said.
"Jonathan de Beauvoir. Do you remember?" Of course.
Jonathan de Beauvoir. We'd met at that drinks party in Drayton
Gardens four years ago. He was terribly nice. He had a very
pretty girlfriend then—what on earth was he doing here?

"I remember you very well," I said. "We met at that party in
Kensington. You were with . . . er . . . Sarah then, weren't
you?"

"Yes. And you were going out with that architect who was
dead keen on golf."

"Yes, that's right."

"I assume that's over or you wouldn't be here. I must say I
didn't think you looked terribly happy."

"I wasn't. In fact," I said with sudden candor, encouraged by
his kind expression, "I was miserable. He was unfaithful. And
controlling. And chronically selfish, too. Luckily he dumped
me—ha ha ha ha! What about you?"

"Well," he sighed. "It's a long story. I won't bore you with it. But I'd just love to know how you are. Will you take a turn about the gardens with me?"

"Yes," I said, jumping up and hoping that Piers would see me leaving the dining room with this tall, drop-dead gorgeous bloke. "Yes, let's go for a little wander. That would be nice. It's terribly hot in here."

We picked up our drinks and headed off across the lawn. What a turn-up for the books, I thought to myself. Here I am with Jonathan de Beauvoir, the handsome auctioneer, and we're walking along arm-in-arm under a star-filled sky in the grounds of a prestigious venue at a singles event. I already had a soft spot for Jonathan the size of a Louisiana swamp. He was completely divine! As we skirted the tennis courts and headed off toward the rose garden I could feel my spirits lift. The evening was turning out well after all. In the distance I thought I could hear someone shouting "Tiffanneeee . . . Tiffanneeee," but perhaps it was only the wind in the trees.

"You see, I'm still incredibly fond of Sarah," said Jonathan. He had his head in his hands and he was sighing heavily. "But I'm not at all sure I want to marry her, and so I don't know what to do now. I just want to go on as we were."

"Well, you can't blame her for laying it on the line," I said brightly, trying to mask my disappointment that the only reason he had wanted to talk to me was to get womanly advice about his girlfriend. "I mean, eleven years is a long time. Sarah's thirty-five. So if you don't want to marry her, don't tie her up—it's not fair."

"Yes, but I don't want to marry someone because there's a gun to my head—it's so *unromantic*."

"But it's unromantic for women to feel they're with a man who won't commit. You've got to try and see it from her point of view."

"She gave me this ultimatum," he explained. "And then she

just—*went off*. Just like that. Didn't even say where she was going. And I didn't like it, so I decided to come to this singles party to see if I might perhaps fall for someone else. Of course I'm not going to," he added. "It's mad. I mean there's absolutely no one here I even *remotely* fancy. Anyway, thanks for listening, Tiffany. You're a *brick*. Now, what about you?" he added. "Did you go out with anyone nice after Phillip?"

"Yes, I did. He was an interior designer called Alex. He was very nice."

"So what was the problem?"

"Well, the main problem was that he was a commitophobic infantaphobe, though obviously I didn't know that at the time. And the other problem was that the only thing he wanted to do in bed was play Scrabble."

"Oh. Oh I *see*," he said delicately. "Didn't that make things rather, you know, *difficult*?"

"Not really. We used a travel set with magnetic letters. It was fine."

"Tiffanee—Tiffanee . . ." Suddenly the rose bushes parted and Kate appeared, a little *distrait* and slightly out of breath. "God, Tiffany, *there* you are. I've been looking for you everywhere. Are you . . . ?" She glanced suspiciously at Jonathan. *"All right?"*

"Yes, of course I am. Kate, this is Jonathan. Jonathan, meet Kate. Shall we go back inside? Golly it's one o'clock! No wonder I'm yawning."

"Tiffany, I was so worried about you," Kate whispered as we strolled back across the lawns. "You just disappeared—I thought you were being ravished in the bushes."

"Unfortunately not," I replied. "Shall we go now? It's terribly late." I waved at Piers, who was still wrapped around the elegant brunette on the dance floor, and then said goodbye to Jonathan.

"I will think about what you said, Tiffany," he said earnestly as we collected our coats. Then Kate and I drove back across London.

"It was rather fun, wasn't it?" she said.

"Yes, it was. I wonder whether any of them will want to see us again."

"Eat 'n' Greet will call us if they do."

At nine-thirty the next morning, I called Eat 'n' Greet. "Hello. This is Tiffany Trott. Have any of the eleven men I met last night asked for my telephone number?" I inquired.

"Er. No. No, they haven't," said an assistant. "But you're a bit quick off the mark. Don't worry. We'll let you know if they do."

In the meantime I had a date with the stockbroker who had answered my personal ad. Out of 114 replies, I had decided to meet only three men—and he was the first. He was thirty-eight, single, did not play golf, and had no perceptible facial hair. Brilliant. He might do nicely! I liked his amusing letter— three pages long. It was very funny, all about his passion for backgammon ("though, as a stockbroker, of course I don't believe in gambling") and his detestation of golf ("as Mark Twain said, a damn fine way to ruin a good walk"). I liked his sense of humor and his photo was reasonably attractive, so we arranged a seven o'clock rendezvous at a West End wine bar. I got there first and sat doing the crossword. At seven-fifteen a man came up to my table and said, "Tiffany?"

"Yes. Are you Ian?" He nodded. It's funny what your eye picks out when you meet a total stranger. He was wearing a rather cheap, baggy suit, which I disliked. And his tie was a garish shade of green. He just looked . . . undistinguished, I suppose. Medium height. Medium build. Medium brown hair. Medium brown eyes. Freckles and—horrors—a small nose, positively retroussé. The photo had been a very flattering one. What a dud, I thought. And he looked so young and inexperienced—like a little boy. Probably hadn't had that many girlfriends. But if I was disappointed with him, his body language suggested that he was not impressed with me. Bloody cheek, I thought. Oh well. Better sit it out. At least have a drink. Rude not to. He ordered some wine and we started to chat. I told him about my work, he told me about his—working for private clients on the stockbroking side of a small merchant bank. I had a few pre-prepared questions about the FTSE and the Hang-Seng, so the conversation wasn't entirely unsuccessful. But I was pretty bored and was just wondering how to exit in a diplomatic way when something really bizarre happened. I mentioned the name of my street and he suddenly said, "Oh, my nanny lives round the corner from you."

"Your *nanny*? Oh, I didn't know you had children," I said. "Your letter didn't say that."

"Yes. I've got two, both under five."

"Oh. You didn't say you were married."

"I'm not," he said. Curiouser and curiouser.

"Divorced?"

"No," he said matter-of-factly. "Widowed. My wife died." Ah. Sharp intake of breath.

"How *dreadful*. I'm very sorry," I said. "When did she . . . when did it happen?"

"Five weeks ago," he replied. Five weeks!

"Oh. How awful for you, but isn't it a bit . . . you know . . . soon to be . . . ?" My voice trailed away.

"Oh, no it's fine, because she took eighteen months to die— she had leukemia—so we had lots of time to say goodbye. We were at school together, she was my childhood sweetheart actually. We were married for fifteen years. We married young."

How could I just get up and leave after he'd told me that? I couldn't. So I sat there for another two hours while he talked about his wife and her illness and what it had been like discovering that she was ill, and knowing that she was going to die, and the whole process taking so long, and his struggle to look after the children. And then, at ten p.m., he said he thought he ought to go. And so we said goodbye, both knowing that we had no wish to meet each other ever again. And then I went home and I cried. It was *so* depressing. So dreadfully, dreadfully depressing. Other people's lives. *Poor* bloke, I thought. How terrible. What a tragedy. Poor, poor man. But then, as I dried my eyes, I thought, five weeks? What a *bastard*.

August Continued

"Five weeks!" I said to Lizzie. We were sitting in my kitchen the Saturday after my dismal date with the widowed stockbroker. "If I'd known he was so recently bereaved I would *never* have agreed to meet him. He should have said in his letter. Five weeks! How could he start looking for someone else so soon?"

" 'Thrift, thrift, Tiffany, the funeral baked meats etc. etc.,' " said Lizzie, drawing on another Marlboro Light. "Anyway, I don't know why you're so surprised. Men are heartless beasts when it comes to the Grim Reaper. Remember Jim Brown?" Oh *yes*. Jim Brown, our housemaster, who was publicly chasing wife number two while wife number one slowly shuffled off this mortal coil in a local hospice. Within a month of her death he had married again, his engagement announcement tastefully appearing in the same edition of the school magazine as his first wife's obituary.

"Men have an entirely different attitude to death," said Lizzie expansively. "As soon as wife number one has popped her clogs they pop down to the dating agency—that is if there was no one they fancied at her funeral. Whereas we women pine for *years*."

"Decades," I said. "Mind you, your mother married again quite soon, didn't she?" Lizzie shot me a poisonous look so I quickly changed the subject. There are various things I know I mustn't mention to Lizzie, and her mother's second marriage is one of them. I've met her stepfather a few times—he's rather nice, rather mild, rather, well, put-upon actually, a bit like . . .

"Martin's being such a *drag*," said Lizzie. "I've asked him to paint the shed and he just hasn't done it. Keeps saying he doesn't *feel* like it. That he's too *tired*. But I said, 'Well darling, I'm exhausted too, looking after two children and this house all day.' And then he said, 'But the girls are at school and Mrs. Burton comes every day. You can't be *that* tired.' And then he said, 'I mean it's not even as though you're working.' And I thought that was really below the belt, Tiffany, because of course I'm not working, I'm an actress, and he knows how devastated I was at not getting that part in *Casualty*."

"But it was nonspeaking," I said. "You told me you were going to be a *corpse*."

"Yes, but it's all work, you know. And I was going to be in shot and everything, and of course it might well have led to other things. *Anyway,* I said to him, 'Don't be so *bloody* unreasonable, Martin. You're *totally* unfair.' God, men are *beasts*, Tiffany—I really don't know why you're so keen to find one."

Now I've always liked Martin a lot. He's not that exciting or anything, but he's just, well, terribly calm, and nice, and kind. Lizzie's so lucky. He saw her in *A Woman of No Importance* when she was in rep at Worthing ten years ago, and he sent flowers to her backstage. I suppose he couldn't help acting on impulse. Just like Seriously Successful, just like . . . where was I? Oh yes. Lizzie, at Worthing. Anyway, she was thrilled, he was loaded, and of course he had a lot more hair then. But I really *hate* it when she goes on about him, which she does rather a lot these days. But of course I never say anything about it, I just try and change the subject.

"No one from Eat 'n' Greet has called me," I said. "It's been three days since the Sensational Singles party and not a peep. Big fat zero. I obviously went down like a lead balloon." Then, strangely enough, the phone rang.

"Hello Tiffany, this is Mary Ann from Eat 'n' Greet. One of

the guys has asked for your number." Hurrah! Social success. Who could it be? Perfect Piers? Doubtful, after his defection to the elegant brunette. Tipsy Terry? God I hoped not.

"Who is it?" I asked. "Tell me."

"It's Paul," she said.

"Who?"

"Paul, the property developer. He was on your table during the main course."

"He was?"

I had vivid memories of the poached salmon and puy lentils, but I couldn't remember anyone called Paul to save my life. I cast my mind back to the Dulwich Country Club. Nope. Paul in property rang absolutely no bells. But what the hell! A bloke's a bloke, so I told Mary Ann he could have my number anyway and, later that afternoon, he called.

"Now, tell me, Paul, did we actually talk?" I inquired.

"Yes," he said, a little stiffly, I thought. "We talked." And then he said, "We also danced."

"We did?"

"Three times." Oh.

"That's funny," I said, "because I have absolutely *no* recollection of you whatsoever. I hope you don't think that's rude," I added.

"Well, there were a lot of people there," he said diplomatically.

"Yes, I know, and I remember talking to lots of different blokes, but my mind's a *complete blank* when it comes to you," I insisted. "I must have early on-set Alzheimer's—what did you say your name was?!"

Much to my amazement, he asked me whether I'd like to have dinner with him later that week. I agreed.

"It'll be a bit like a blind date for me," I pointed out.

"Well, partially sighted," he replied. "But bring your white stick, just in case, and please write it down in your diary so that you don't forget to turn up." Touché.

He suggested meeting in Shepherd Market at Le Boudin Blanc—one of my favorite restaurants. This got things off to a good start. And when I was shown to his table, upstairs, he did look vaguely familiar—tall and well built, with hazel eyes and large, sinewy hands. Now to me, hands are very important. They're the first thing I notice after hair and eyes. They can make or break it for me. Seriously Successful had very nice hands—large, masculine and square. Phillip's were quite attractive, strong-looking hands, but Alex's were awful, very narrow, with exceptionally long palms, like a monkey's, and attenuated, feminine fingers which he had professionally manicured every week. I didn't like them. In fact they were a turn-off. But I did like Paul's, so that was a good sign. And now I remembered who he was—he was the chap on my right who had been chatting to the pretty redhead in personnel while I was talking to Piers. And later, when Piers had deserted me, and before I met Jonathan de Beauvoir, Paul had asked me to dance. But my mind had been elsewhere.

"It all comes flooding back now," I said. "You're in property, you live in Putney and you play the piano and Ping-Pong."

"Correct," he said, as the waiter took our order. "And you live in Islington, you're a copywriter, and you enjoy tennis and amateur neurosurgery."

I began to warm to him. He had a dry sense of humor, he was obviously doing rather well for himself, and he was passionate about the piano. He could play all the Chopin studies—wow! And he has a Steinway—fantastic!

"It's secondhand," he said modestly, his voice slightly muffled by a mouthful of smoked duck and dandelion salad with fresh caramelized figs and Parmesan.

"But they appreciate," I pointed out, tucking into my fresh market leaves garnished with walnuts, croûtons and foie gras.

He swallowed, and then said, "I appreciate you." Gosh!

"I'm really sorry about my memory lapse," I said. "It's either holes in the brain, or perhaps I really do have Alzheimer's."

"You shouldn't joke about Alzheimer's," said Paul with sudden severity. "My father died of it, actually."

"Oh God, I'm sorry," I said, spitting out a shoelace. "It's a really *awful* disease. How old was he when he got it?"

"Fifty-one."

"Fifty-one." Oh. Very young. Poor guy. And then I remembered that early-onset Alzheimer's can sometimes be hereditary. Oh *oh*. I looked at Paul. He was forty-three now. If I married him I'd probably be pushing him round in a bath chair by the year 2005 and wearing a large badge saying, "Hello! My Name's Tiffany—I'm Your Wife!" Maybe he already had it? I decided to give him a little memory test.

"How many Köchel numbers are there?" I asked casually, as the waiter served us.

"625."

"Wrong! There are 626." He was clearly in the early stages of dementia.

"And how many Nocturnes did Chopin write?"

"Nineteen. What is this, *Mastermind*?"

"And when was the battle of Culloden?"

"1746."

"And what's the seventh commandment?"

" 'Thou shalt not commit adultery.' "

So far so good. Very good, in fact.

"And who unraveled the mysteries of deoxyribonucleic acid?"

"Crick and Watson, of course. Do you want the year as well?"

"No. No need," I said. "And, um, what's the square root of 497?"

"I *don't know*," he said with sudden, and quite unnecessary, vehemence.

Why was he getting so ratty? I wondered. He really did seem to be somewhat irritated by me. I didn't know why, but then I was irritated by him, and no more so than when his tender rabbit with red pepper sauce arrived. I could not *possibly* fall in love with a man who eats bunny, I thought as I tucked into my sliced rump of veal. We chewed away in silence for a few minutes, and then, just as I was desperately trying to think of something—anything—to say, this funny thing happened. A bottle of Bollinger mysteriously arrived at our table.

"Gosh—how lovely, did you order that?" I asked.

"Er, no. No I didn't actually."

"Where did it come from then?" I asked.

"I really don't know," said Paul.

"Eet eez from ze *gentilhomme* in ze corner," said the waiter, in such cod French that I concluded that he could only have come from Penge.

"What man in what corner?" said Paul.

"Zat one. Zere."

I swiveled round in my chair. There, at a tiny table in the farthest corner of the low-ceilinged, wood-paneled room, was a familiar figure: beautifully dressed; absorbed in his crossword. A cloud of Amazonian swallowtails suddenly took flight in my stomach. Seriously Successful. Dining alone. In fact he looked decidedly sad and solitary. He'd probably been here the entire time that I had been here with Paul. Suddenly, he looked up, saw me staring, and gave me a funny, sad little smile. Then he resumed eating.

"Do you know that man?" asked Paul suspiciously, craning his neck for a clearer view.

"Not really," I said, removing the scribbled note from the ice bucket. "But I have met him. Once." I quickly read it, aware that my face was as flushed as my glass of red Burgundy.

TT

    I'm really sorry about the other day. I should have taken no for an answer. But this is just to show you that I don't bear a grudge about it, even if I do, in fact, resent it deeply. And also because I thought your partner's conversation looked as though it could do with a little fizz. I bet he doesn't drink Carling Black Label.

SS

"Does he normally do this kind of thing?" said Paul, clearly nettled by Seriously Successful's unexpected intervention.

"Probably," I said, as the waiter refilled our glasses. I scribbled a little note to him: *Thank you very much. That was Naughty but Nice,* and asked the waiter to deliver it.

"Do you mind?" I asked Paul.

"Yes, I do," he said, though he drank the champagne nonetheless. We ate the rest of our meal in relative silence—he was obviously fed up by the way the evening had turned out, and I was feeling, well, disturbed. The butterflies were still circulating, making it practically impossible to eat. And I could sense Seriously Successful's eyes bearing down on the back of my neck. Annoying man, hijacking my evening like that. He clearly likes to provoke. And yet, the fact was that I felt drawn to him as iron filings are drawn to a magnet. A few minutes later, I turned round again, to see that he was paying the bill. Then he folded his paper, and left. I wanted to follow him down the stairs. I wanted to run after him down the street like a dog. I wanted to hold his hand. I wanted to . . . Oh get a grip will you, Trott, I said to myself crossly, as I tried to concentrate on what Paul was saying. At least Seriously Successful hadn't ruined the start of a beautiful friendship. I wasn't enjoying myself much, and nor was Paul. I knew this for a fact because when the bill came he suddenly said, "Ok, let's go Dutch."

"Of *course,*" I said, though inwardly I was fuming as *he* had invited *me*—a fact he had clearly forgotten. Further proof of his deteriorating mental condition. I had been right to be circumspect. "I enjoyed meeting you again," I said. "Perhaps I'll see you at the next Eat 'n' Greet event?"

"Yes," he said. "Perhaps. Goodbye."

What a weird evening. Going home on the number 73 I drew up a questionnaire for future blokes entitled, "Do You or Any Member of Your Immediate Family Suffer From Any of the Following Possibly Inherited Medical Conditions?" Then I wrote down "Alzheimer's, diabetes, congenital heart disease, cleft palate, pigeon toes, BSE and any kind of cancer? Check as applicable." That would cover it. One couldn't be too careful. And then I daydreamed about Seriously Successful and what an incredibly irritating man he was and how sad it was that he was married. When I got home, the phone rang. Seriously Successful, with another tempting invitation! No such luck. Damn. It was Paul. What on earth did he want now?

"Tiffany?"

"Congratulations!" I replied. "You've managed to remember my name." Actually, I didn't say that. I simply said, "Yes?"

"The restaurant have just called me. They say you forgot your coat."

September

"You know what our problem is, don't you?" asked my New Best Friend Kate as we sat in Café Rouge on Saturday morning. It was clearly a rhetorical question. I could tell by the unusually vigorous way in which she was stirring her cappuccino. "Our problem," she continued thoughtfully, "is that we're in a sort of arrested adolescence."

"I don't know what you mean," I said, taking out my copy of *19* magazine.

"Instead of having conversations about grown-up things such as how to cope with a crying baby, or how to choose a good prep school, we have these incredibly teenage conversations about what to do if your boyfriend doesn't ring when he said he would—"

"Dump the bastard!" I interjected.

"Or whether or not it's OK to snog a guy on the second date."

"What's your view on that?" I asked.

"It's as though we're seventeen," she went on. "But we're not. We're *thirty-seven*. It's pathetic. Why can't we just grow up?"

"Yes," I agreed. "Why can't we just grow up and get married like, like, that Bianca on *EastEnders*."

"Yes," said Kate. "Like her. Then we could have proper, adult conversations about housekeeping and joint accounts and going to Tesco with our husbands."

"Mind you," I added. "She's just showing off. Just because she managed to get hitched. Getting it on the telly and everything."

"Yes," said Kate with uncharacteristic ferocity. "She's *showing off,* just because she got the rock, the frock, and the party."

"And the tiara."

"Yes."

"And the spread in *Radio Times.*"

Silence descended like a stone. Kate was thinking. I knew this because a small pleat had appeared on her brow. I picked up the *Mail* and looked at the Nigel Dempster gossip page. Such tedious tittle-tattle, I thought. I really don't know *why* people want to read that kind of stuff . . . ooh! That's interesting: *New Labour's Lawrence Bright, forty-five, is reportedly experiencing marital misery after his wife spotted him in the lingerie department of Harvey Nichols with a sultry thirty-something brunette.* Tsk tsk, I thought to myself. Another naughty MP. Don't they ever learn?

"Do you think we'll ever get hitched?" I heard Kate say.

"What? Oh. I don't know."

Kate was ready to talk again. "I mean, what are you looking for in a man, Tiffany?"

That was easy. "Common ground, a kind heart, reasonable looks, oh—and an *enormous* serve."

"And fidelity," she said.

"Oh yes," I said, glancing at the photo of Lawrence Bright in the *Mail.* "And fidelity." And then I thought of Seriously Successful again. "I'm not going out with anyone unfaithful ever again," I announced. And while we sat there, ruminating over our coffee, I rewound my mental video back to Phil Anderer. And I remembered how painful it was going out with him. And how embarrassing, too. Because men with bad track records, well everyone seems to know. Look at Bill Clinton.

"How do you *cope* with him?" people would say to me with

an awestruck smirk when Phillip and I went to parties together. And I'd shrug it off with a peal of laughter and rapidly change the subject, but inside . . . inside, I felt enraged. Well, how do *you* cope with being married to such an ugly woman? I'd inquire. Or, How do you cope with a husband who is, by common consent, a bore? Or, How do you cope with your alcoholic wife? Or your drug-dependent daughter? How do you cope with *that,* precisely? Though of course, I didn't say any of those things. I kept my outrage to myself. But privately, I felt ashamed of Phil Anderer because privately, I knew that they were right.

"Yes, fidelity is very important," said Kate with sudden feeling. "Very, *very* important."

I wondered what she meant by that, and why she was so emphatic. I didn't like to ask—there were lots of things I didn't know about her. I supposed she'd tell me if she wanted to. "Do you know," she said brightly, clearly trying to change the subject now, "I think it would be better to try younger blokes because if they're in say, their early thirties, they're less likely to be bitter, twisted divorcés, and they haven't quite got to the commitmentphobic stage yet."

"That's true," I said thoughtfully. "Just a few years younger would be fine. But how do we meet them?" How indeed? We chewed our baguettes thoughtfully.

"I know," she said. "Let's go to a rave."

"Yes," I said. "What a brilliant idea. *Let's.*"

When I got home I phoned the Ministry of Sound—dead upmarket so I've heard—and got the details for Friday night. We would have to queue, the woman told me, and we would have to dress appropriately.

"It's OK," I interjected. "I know *exactly* what to wear."

"Whistles will be worn," I told Kate over the phone a little later. "Carriages at six A.M. Dress—informal."

"Tropical," she said, "it'll be *hot.*"

In the meantime, a couple more replies had trickled in from

my lonely hearts ad. The most recent one, which was accompanied by two photos, one full face and one in profile, read as follows:

> Dear Advertiser,
>   I could not help noticing your very appealing personal advertisement two weeks ago. I must apologize for taking so long to reply but I am currently detained at Her Majesty's pleasure for the importation of illegal substances, and as inmates are only allowed to write letters once a week, this is my first epistolary opportunity. However, I am hoping to be released on parole shortly and I wondered whether you would care to meet up?

"You have got to be joking," I said to myself. I mean, what would they say at the tennis club if I turned up with an ex-con? More to the point, I didn't fancy him. And then there was an artist called Eric. I liked the sound of him and he was rather good-looking—tall with green eyes and blond hair. A few details jumped out of his letter—"Brighton art school"—"classic cars"—"tennis twice a week"—I really couldn't be bothered to take it all in. So I just wrote back my standard letter:

> Dear Eric,
>   Thank you for your recent letter in response to my personal advertisement. I had some pretty weird replies I can tell you, but yours was almost normal. Congratulations! If you would like to meet me, please give me a ring on the above number.
>   Yours sincerely,
>   Tiffany Trott (Miss).

Then I enclosed a rather good photo of myself taken at Glyndebourne with Alex last year (with a sticker over Alex's face obviously) and popped it in the post.

When Friday came Kate and I met in the queue outside the club at ten P.M. We blew our whistles and jigged up and down to keep warm, and actually we got some quite odd looks, which I attributed to sheer, naked envy—my stylish new Nike tennis shoes with the carbon rubber outersole, molded midsole, rear-foot trinomic cushioning and reflective trim for night visibility had cost £150! Finally we got to the head of the queue.

"You can't come in looking like that!" said the fierce-looking female bouncer. "This is a very *upmarket* nightclub, it's not a *rave*. No whistles, no running shoes. Smart club gear only."

Oh. Oh dear. Blast.

"But we've been queuing for forty-five minutes," I said.

"I don't care if you've been queuing for forty-five days," she replied. "You're not coming in looking like that. I suggest you go and change and come back later—the club stays open until six A.M." The thought of schlepping all the way back to Islington from the Elephant and Castle made me feel tired. Frankly, I couldn't be bothered. Nor could Kate.

"I know, we can come back tomorrow," she suggested.

"OK, we'll come back tomorrow," I said to the bouncer, "but could we just have a quick peek inside—now that we're here? Just to make sure we *do* want to come back tomorrow?"

"Yes. Just to make sure it's *our* kind of place," added Kate.

"Well . . . all right," the woman said reluctantly, "but make it snappy."

We went in and were hit by a wall of sound. Gosh it was loud. And what an amazing venue. And so dark. The walls were lined with tin foil; illuminated streamers hung from the ceiling and gnomic inscriptions were projected all over the walls: "Happiness exists," said one. "The world has a beautiful soul," said another. Well, quite. The floor was already heaving with bobbing bodies—two thousand people bouncing to the boom! boom! of the beat. There were some terribly handsome-looking young chaps—perfect! But then, just as we had satis-fied our curiosity and were preparing to leave, I caught sight of something odd—something wrong. Something, frankly, alien—and yet familiar at least to me. For in the far distance was an intriguing spectacle: a solitary, gleaming bald pate. The strobe light kept bouncing off it—frankly it stuck out a mile among the crowd of luxuriantly follicled youths. Wasn't that . . . no! It couldn't be—but it really *did* look like—gosh I *wish* he'd keep still, I thought to myself, and then I'd be able to see. Surely it couldn't be him, it was just someone who looked like him, but actually, I think it *was* him—Martin! At the Ministry of Sound! Martin, whose musical tastes run to nothing more adventurous than Gerry and the Pacemakers! Martin, who thinks Oasis is something you see in floral arrangements. In any case, surely Lizzie wouldn't let him come to a place like this? Was it him, or wasn't it? God, it was so hard to tell with all these people around and these blinding, flashing lights. Anyway, I was just making my way toward the dance floor, trying to get a better view, when suddenly I felt a hand on my shoulder.

"You two—out!" said the lady bouncer. "I said you'd have to be *quick.*"

"OK, OK," I said, as Kate and I followed her out of the double doors. "We'll come back tomorrow."

And we did. Suitably attired this time. Smart. Very smart. And no whistles. We were frisked on entry—it was just like being at the airport.

"What are you looking for?" I inquired, as another female bouncer went through my Prada handbag.

"Weapons," she said. "And drugs."

"I *never* take drugs," I said truthfully. And fortunately, I happened to have left my small but efficient axe in my other handbag.

Kate was dressed all in black; she looked particularly chic and I noticed several blokes looking in her direction as we eventually gained admittance. My Liberty silk floral two-piece with the large pearl buttons and the lace edging on the cuffs seemed to attract a lot of attention, too—but then it did go down *extremely* well at Ladies' Day last year. Anyway, Kate and I sat on a huge circular seat, shyly surveying the throngs of men standing by the bar. No sign of Martin—I must have got that wrong. Most of them were pretty young, and wore shirts of an hallucinogenic hue. They looked quite, well tough, I suppose. In fact, to be perfectly honest, they looked like Millwall supporters. Some of them had broken teeth. Still, the night was young, I thought to myself happily. I was sure some more eligible-looking chaps would turn up soon. But my God it was hot! And conversation was going to be tricky—this "home" music is so loud!

Suddenly a man came up to us. "Do you want some coke, girls?"

"Oh, er, yes please," I said. "A Diet Coke would be great."

"Yes. I'd like a Diet Coke too," said Kate. But the man just gave us a funny look and walked away. That wasn't very friendly, was it? Oh well. And then Kate disappeared to the loo because she was unhappy about her hair, and I was just sitting there listening to the bang! bang! of the beat and watching the strobe lights when another chap came up to me. He was very young, but rather good-looking in a brutish kind of way. What on earth could he want?

"   ," he said.

"What?" I replied.

"   ."

"I'm awfully sorry, I can't hear a word you're saying," I said. "I'm afraid your shirt's rather loud."

"   DANCE?" I just managed to make out this time.

"Oh, would I like to dance with you? Well, er, er . . ." But before I could make up my mind he had grabbed my hand and was leading me onto the dance floor, where I was soon lost in the heaving, bobbing, bouncing mass of bodies.

I can understand it now. I can quite see how it happens. I mean, you hear about kids going to raves and dancing nonstop for eight or ten or even twelve hours, and you think, How do they *do* that? But now I know—you just get drawn into the rhythm of the thump! thump! thump! and before you know where you are you have danced yourself into a trance. And so I wasn't at all surprised when I glanced at my watch at the Ministry of Sound to find that it was six A.M.

"That's it, everyone!" said the DJ suddenly. "Night night. *Gute Nacht.* Beddy byes. Bog off."

Suddenly the lights stopped strobing and the sonic boom! boom! ceased. I smiled at my male companion, the charming young Millwall supporter who had invited me onto the floor several hours earlier. At last! I would be able to talk to him. He was really rather good-looking despite the somewhat prognathous jaw.

"Thanks very much," I said. "That was fun. I'm Tiffany, by the way. What's your name?"

"Stephen," he said, with what I thought was a slightly odd, intense stare. "But my friends all call me Broadmoor."

"Er . . . what an amusing sobriquet," I replied.

"You can call me Broadmoor too," he continued, as we headed for the door. "Or," he continued, "you can call me Stephen. Whichever you like, really. Whichever you prefer. Stephen. Or Broadmoor. I leave it up to you."

"Gosh, um, thanks. That's er, very *flexible* of you. Well, see you again sometime. Broadmoor."

"*When* will you see me again, Tiffany?"

"When will I see you again? Er, to be honest, I really don't know."

"But I'd *like* to see you again, Tiffany. I really would."

"Well that would be nice, but . . ."

"What's your phone number, Tiffany?" He produced a small address book from his trouser pocket. "What's your phone number?" he asked again, with the same disconcerting stare.

"Er. Er. I don't know," I said.

"What do you mean, you don't know?"

"Well, it's probably because I'm so tired, but I really can't remember it. I know it's 2-2-6 something or other, but the rest of it . . ." I shrugged. "It's just gone."

"But I need your number, otherwise I can't ring you up." *Quite.*

"Well, the thing is . . ."

"What, Tiffany? *What*?" He was standing painfully close. I could have counted the beads of sweat on his face. Where *was* Kate? "You know, Tiffany," I heard him say, "you're just my type. You've got . . ." a loud, dirty sniff contorted his features, "class."

"Well, I think I'm a bit too old for you, Broadmoor. I really do. How old are you?"

"Twenny-free."

"Well, you see—I'm thirty-seven!"

"You're taking a piss!" He looked shocked. "I didn't realize you were *that* old. Fir-ee-seven? 'kinnell!"

"Yes, yes I am," I said crisply. "I'm practically middle-aged, ha ha ha ha ha!"

"Well," he said, replacing his address book and retreating, "it was very nice to mee chew. Fir-ee-seven? 'kinnell."

Then Kate emerged out of the milling crowd—she was talking to a rather attractive chap, actually—and we staggered outside, blinking into the sunlight like vampires. Our ears were ringing and the ground appeared to rock beneath our feet. I felt as though I had just arrived at Boulogne after a particularly choppy crossing.

"Wasn't that *great*?" said Kate, as we made for the station. Her complexion was as etiolated as a tin of Dulux "White With a Hint of Apple Green."

"Do I look as ill as you?" I asked her.

"No. You look worse."

"How do you feel?"

"Terrible, actually. But wasn't it great?"

"Er, yes," I said.

"That guy was really nice."

"What guy?"

"The one I was talking to. Mike. He's a doctor. He's twenty-eight. I gave him my card."

"That's good."

"But he works in Manchester."

"That's bad."

We got the tube, which is delightfully uncrowded at six-thirty on a Sunday morning. I whizzed up to the Angel and, at seven a.m., I walked through my front door to the deathly hush of an Islington dawn. Thank God. Peace and quiet, although there was still clamor in my ears. In fact there were bells ringing. Loudly and insistently—*ring ring. Ring ring. Ring ring. Ring ring.* And then I realized it wasn't just in my ears. It was the phone. It was the phone ringing. And this was very strange, because my phone does not normally ring at seven A.M. on Sunday mornings. Seriously Successful! No—of course not—don't be ridiculous, I said to myself as I picked up the receiver. Get a grip!

"Tiffany? Tiffany!" It was Lizzie. She sounded distraught. My God, what was going on?

"What's happened?" I said. "Where are you?"

"In bed," she said in a loud whisper. In the background I could hear strange gargling noises.

"Lizzie, what on earth's the matter?" She sounded close to tears. And what on earth were those peculiar sounds? "Lizzie, why are you calling at this time?"

"It's Martin," she said. "He's gone a bit . . . funny."

"Funny? What do you mean, funny? Martin's *never* funny."

"I know. But he did it again last night."

"Did what?"

"Disappeared." Suddenly I realized what the noises off were—it was the sound of strenuous regurgitation and it was emanating from Lizzie's en-suite bathroom.

"On Friday he disappeared without telling me where he was going," she continued with an audible sob. "He didn't reappear until *dawn*. I was frantic. And then last night he did the same thing again. Said he was 'going out' and that he didn't have to tell me where. Said he'd go anywhere he bloody well *liked*. Anyway, he came back half an hour ago *drunk* as a *monkey* and has now got his head down the loo."

"Well, that's very, um, uncharacteristic behavior, that's all I can say."

"And when I asked him where he'd been he just gave me this funny, lopsided little smile, and said nothing. *Nothing*." She sobbed. "You know what I think?"

"What?"

"I think—in fact, I'm sure—he's having an affair."

"Oh Lizzie, don't be silly. Martin's not the type."

"Well, that's what I've always thought, but maybe he *is* the type and I just didn't realize it. My God, men are such bastards!"

"Well, wait till he's sober . . ."

"I know he's got a new secretary—she's only twenty-four . . ."

". . . and then talk to him about it," I continued.

"It's probably her. Bet it is. Little tart."

"He probably *isn't* having an affair at all," I said.

". . . you know these women who work in the City are ruthless."

". . . you need to calm down a bit, and then very gently . . ."

". . . they're all the type who'd steal your husband. All of them. Except Sally of course. God, maybe it's Nicola Horlick! He met her once. In 1989."

". . . talk to him and ask him if there's anything wrong, or if he's unhappy about something."

"He'd be very stupid if he *did* have an affair," she suddenly announced. "Because I'd divorce him on the spot, and then I'd take him to the cleaners."

"Lizzie, you're jumping to conclusions."

"Specialist cleaners. *Very* expensive ones. In fact, the legal equivalent of Jeeves of Belgravia. I'd leave him without the shirt on his back. I'd . . . I'd . . . I can't talk anymore," she suddenly said. "I'llringyoulaterbye."

I simply couldn't believe that Martin was having an affair, I reflected as I got into bed. He just isn't the type. Now Phil Anderer's mother used to say in one of her many "advice-giving" sessions: "Tiffany—you can *never* tell. You've *always* got to be on your guard, because the *quietest*-looking men can go off and have an affair." But I don't believe Martin is capable of infidelity. I just don't think he would do that. Some men would and some men wouldn't. And Martin is in the latter category— unlike Phil Anderer. And unlike Seriously Successful, I thought bitterly. No, I don't think Martin's looking for a part-time girlfriend. And I say that with confidence, because into my mind flashed that bobbing, gleaming bald pate at the Ministry of Sound and the only thing I suspect Martin of is trying to have some fun.

September Continued

"I just don't know what to do," said Kit on Monday afternoon. He was sighing heavily as he stared into his cup of Algerian arabica. "God this coffee's a bit strong, Tiff—can't we just have Nescafé?"

"Yes, of course," I said, chucking both our coffees down the sink. He looked rough. Obviously hadn't slept. "Have a Jaffa Cake, Kit." I pushed the plate toward him. "And then we really ought to get on—we've got work to do."

"I'm too upset to work," he said, shuffling in his chair. "I've been up all night. Worrying."

"OK, let's talk about it," I said. "And then we must carry on with the pitch. We've got to win the Love Hearts campaign. I know we can do it."

"Yes," said Kit. "I think we can. Your copy ideas are really good. But"—he stared at the open packet of pastel-colored sweets—"it's totally depressing doing the artwork for it, when my own love life's going so badly." He read out the inscriptions on the sherbet discs. " 'Forever Yours,' " he said joylessly. " 'Love Me,' 'Be Mine,' 'Darling.' 'Yes Please,' " he added with a bitter little laugh. "Or rather, 'No Thanks.' 'Bog Off.' 'Get Lost.' " Then he rested his head in his hands. "Can't we just watch *Neighbors*?" he asked. "I really don't feel very creative today."

Now, Kit is a very cheerful kind of chap. He's always—how

can I put this?—*up*. That's what I'd say about him. He's usually animated and smiling and talkative and, well, *happy*. But Portia's giving him such a bad time at the moment—I haven't seen him smile for weeks.

"I just don't know what to do," he groaned. "She won't even return my calls." He turned the palms of his hands toward the ceiling in frustration—I could almost see the stigmata.

"Well, I've said it before, and I'll say it again," I said, "she's very lucky to have someone as devoted and considerate as you." *And I wish I'd married you myself when I had the chance.*

"Thanks," he said quietly. "And I think I'm very lucky to be with her."

"But why? She's a shallow, Styrofoam-brained creature who isn't fit to tie your shoelaces," I said. Actually I didn't say that at all. I didn't say anything, because one has to be very, very tactful when offering advice to lovelorn friends. I just looked at him. He was so nice, so good-looking, so creative and considerate and kind. Oh God, Mummy was right, I reflected. She was right. Dad was right. Lizzie was right. Everyone was right. I *should* have married Kit. If I had, then I would not now be a pregeriatric single, I would not now be going on blind dates with married men and losers, I would not now be a front runner for the Nobel Prize for Spinsterdom. No. If I had married Kit, as I should have done, I would be in my eighth or ninth year of domestic bliss, with at least four, or maybe even five, delightful children, allowing for the possibility of twins.

"I really try not to pressure Portia," Kit explained. "I know that's a big turn-off for women, if they're not quite sure about a guy. But then we've been together for eighteen months, and I want to get married, so I really feel that the crunch is coming. But she just won't talk about it. Maybe I shouldn't have bought the Discovery," he added.

"Well, it might have been better to wait," I said. "Until you were sure. Also, I really don't think you should keep dragging

her off to Hamleys—she knows you're fond of kids." He nodded in mute agreement.

"And I think taking her to Disneyland was probably a mistake. Does she ever explain why she's not ready to settle down
yet?" I added. "I mean, it's not as though she's that young—
she's thirty-two. You'd think that at thirty-two she'd quite like
to get married."

"Maybe she does want to get married—but just not to me,"
he said bitterly. *Oh, I do hope so, and then I can marry you
myself.*

"Well, I think if that really was the case, then she wouldn't
hang around at all," I said. "Women are very pragmatic. I
mean, she is fond of you, isn't she?"

"I suppose so," he said, popping a Love Heart into his mouth.
"I think so. She says she is, but then there are times when I simply don't believe her, because if she really was fond of me,
then she'd accept, wouldn't she?"

"Well, it's obviously more complicated than that," I said.

"Tiffany, I just don't know *what* to do," he said again, and
this time there were tears standing in his eyes. I was shocked. I
had never, ever seen him so distressed. It wrung my heart. I put
my self-interest aside.

"Don't be so nice to her," I said suddenly. He looked horrified. "Don't look after her and run around for her in the way
that you do."

"But she's very vulnerable," he said, eating another sweet.
"She needs me."

"You should withdraw a bit, and see what happens," I added.
"You let her take you for granted, because she knows that
you'll never give her a hard time. Perhaps you *should* give her
a hard time," I went on. He looked appalled. "Just for a little
while. I mean, perhaps you shouldn't always offer to pick her
up from work."

"Well, I don't like the idea of her getting the bus," he said,
eating another Love Heart.

"And maybe you shouldn't be quite so ready to rush round when her washing machine's on the blink . . ."

"But she's so impractical—I don't think she'd even know who to call."

"And if I were you I'd let her pay someone to do her garden— you don't have to do it."

"Yes, but it doesn't take long."

"Better still, let her do it herself." He looked shocked.

"And you're not a painter and decorator, so let her find a professional one next time her kitchen needs doing up. It's not as though she hasn't any cash."

"That's not the point," he said. "If you love someone you want to do lots of things for them, don't you?"

"Yes, but Kit—you do *too much*."

"So do *you*!" he said. "With men." This was true. That's why Kit and I are friends. We're the same. And we get walked on.

"We're both in the Love Gap," I said. "I read about it in *Options* . . ."

"Yes. I'm in the Love Gap all right," he interjected with a hollow laugh. "I'm in the Baby Gap, too."

"The French say that in every relationship there is one person who is offering kisses, and one who is receiving them," I said, as he stuffed a handful of Love Hearts into his mouth. "Well, you and I are kissers, Kit," I announced. "And kissers are losers, because we've got to get as well as to give. I mean, what do you get back from Portia?" There was what I can only describe as a pregnant pause.

"Not a lot, really," he said miserably.

"Exactly. You know, Kit, you're not a wimp," I added. "No, at all. You're a proper bloke. But when it comes to women you're hopelessly unassertive. Kit—please don't eat all the Love Hearts, we need them. You're too nice for your own good," I went on. "And you get exploited. You meet a woman and you become the human equivalent of a 'Welcome' mat."

"I am not a doormat!" he said, shocked.

"Yes, you are."

"Well so are *you*!" he retorted.

"No I'm *not*."

"You bloody well are," he said, eating another Love Heart. "May I remind you that when we were going out together you used to iron my shirts. I never asked you to."

"Well, you used to clean my shoes."

"You used to do my washing up!" he flung back at me. "Including, might I add, the nasty burnt bits on the bottom of the saucepans."

"You pruned my lilac tree for me," I replied venomously. "And my wisteria."

"Well, you used to take Fluffy to the vet for her flu jabs!"

"You repapered my bedroom!"

"You collected my prescriptions," he hissed.

"You . . . you . . . dropped off my dry cleaning, even though it wasn't on your route and wasn't at *all* convenient!"

"Well, you took my car in for repairs."

"You mended my bicycle. *Six times*!"

"You used to return my videos!" he retorted triumphantly. "Including the ones I hadn't even watched with you! And now you have the *nerve* to tell me you're not a doormat. You are, Tiffany! You're in denial. But you are!"

"Well, if I'm a doormat," I spat, "you're a bloody BOOT SCRAPER!"

Kit just looked at me. Then he went quiet. I had hurt him. Oh dear.

"Look, Kit, please let's not quarrel," I said, grabbing his hand. "I'm sorry. It's just that we're not talking about me. It's you we're discussing. Your problems. Not mine. And you've got to do something about this, Kit. I mean, you're going to have to be *very* assertive if you become a commercials director—you know what it's like on set."

"I can be very assertive professionally," he pointed out with a wounded air. "That's not a problem. In fact, I can be a complete bastard if necessary. But, yes, OK, OK—I admit it, I find assertiveness in relationships very hard. Otherwise I'd have *insisted* that you marry me all those years ago. Why didn't you marry me, Tiffany?" he asked. "Just out of interest."

"Oh, I don't know," I said, scribbling on my pad. "Or rather, yes I do," I added quietly. "It was precisely because we're too alike." But if I'd had a crystal ball to give me twenty-twenty foresight, and known then what I know now, perhaps I would have married him, I thought to myself. Was it too late? If Portia left him, then maybe . . . maybe . . .

"I wish you had you know, Tiff," he said. "We could have saved each other a lot of grief."

"Look, please would you stick to Portia," I said, to cover my confusion.

"I *am* sticking to Portia," he said. "The problem is that she won't stick to me."

"Well, why don't you do some personal development course of some kind?" I suggested. "Or go on one of those, you know, male bonding bonanzas?"

"What? Those weekends in the woods for wallys? You must be joking," he said vehemently. "Not my style at all. I'd never do that."

"Well, you need to do something radical if you want to keep Portia's interest, and my advice is to do something entirely contrary to your nature, and be a bit mean. Or rather, treat her as neglectfully as she treats you. Just show her what it's like to be on the receiving end of your partner's indifference."

"OK," he said, biting into a Jaffa Cake. "I'll think about it. But it's not going to be easy." He looked at his watch. "Enough about Portia—Love Hearts. Oh God, 'You're My Dream.' "

Three hours later, we finished. Or at least we had the bare bones of our pitch mapped out in Kit's scribbly pictures and my words. It was to be a TV campaign to be launched in the run-up to Valentine's Day next year.

"Are you having any luck with men?" Kit asked, as he left.

"Yes—bad luck mostly," I said. "but I've got one more bloke to meet from my personal ad. He sounds OK. In fact I'm fairly optimistic. I'm seeing him this Saturday. He's called Jake."

"What's he like?" said Kit.

"He's a film director, he's single, he went to Oxford—I mean, he sounds perfectly fine," I said. "On paper."

Now, "on paper" is an interesting concept and one to which I've been giving quite a bit of thought recently. You see, on paper, advertisements, especially TV advertisements, tend to look very, very silly. A cat that turns into a tiger inside a bottle of vodka. A panda shooting along on rollerskates. A man dressed only in an empty Vitalite tub diving into a forest pool. And then, when you see the ads on screen, they look really great. They work. They do the trick. But when it comes to romance I find that the opposite theory of "on paper" applies. You see, on paper, a lot of men look great. Take Jake, for instance. Now Jake was thirty-eight, five foot eleven, interesting job, well-educated, and with his own mews house in Camden. Fine, you'd think. And I'd thought that a film director would be rather interesting. I liked his letter, he was obviously very bright, with GSOH, and he was looking for a LTR. And he seemed to be reasonably attractive too, though the photo, just a headshot, was somewhat blurred. But, as far as I could tell, he appeared to be OK-looking-bordering-on-the-almost-acceptable. So on paper, Jake was a definite possible. Well-educated. Single. Never married. No alimony. No child support. No criminal record. No notifiable diseases. And all his own teeth. Anyway, he said that he would book a restaurant somewhere in Hampstead, and offered to "pick me up" at the tube. There were lots of great restaurants in Hampstead, I thought to myself happily as I came up in the lift at Hampstead station. I'd already been to most of them with Lizzie when she couldn't be bothered to cook. There was Byron's a few doors up from her on Downshire Hill—dead romantic; there was La Villa Bianca in Perrin's Court and that dinky little French one in Flask Walk. I glanced at my watch as I came through the barrier. I was about ten minutes late. Clearly he wasn't here yet—damn! There was just that scrofulous-looking fellow standing scrutinizing the local map. Dirty jeans, baggy gray jumper, tieless shirt, filthy, unkempt hair, and—horror of horrors—scruffy trainers. God! Some men have absolutely no idea. And I was just standing there wishing that Jake would turn up soon because I really *hate* standing around on my own in public places, when this putrid-looking bloke turned round, held out his hand, and said "*Hello.* You must be Tiffany. I'm Jake."

Disappointment. Disenchantment. Disillusionment. Dismay. That's what you let yourself in for when you set sail for Singles City. From a distance the view looks so attractive—hundreds of unattached, eligible blokes all jostling on the quay. But when you get up close—oh dear. I mean, as I say, on paper, Jake looked perfectly presentable. But in the flesh he resembled a genetic pile-up between Struwwelpeter and Uriah Heep. My heart sank so low it was practically underground.

"Good to meet you," he said. His hand felt like a wet haddock in mine. "Isn't this *fun*?"

"Yes," I said bleakly, "it's fun." We stood outside the Hampstead tube while he looked thoughtfully in both directions, his unbrushed, corkscrew curls flapping gently in the wind. How on earth could I get away? Perhaps I could plead a sudden migraine. Maybe I could remember a pressing deadline. Perhaps I could affect a fainting fit, though I didn't think I could manage it without fracturing my skull. Maybe I could simply run away.

"I'm awfully sorry, Jake, but I have an urgent appointment with my television," I said. "I'd forgotten—it's *Noel's House Party*." Actually, I didn't say that at all. I simply said, "Where have you parked?"

"Parked? Oh I don't have a car."

"Oh. Oh I see. But I thought you said you'd 'pick me up.' "

"Yes. I meant on foot. We can walk. It's not far."

"Oh, so you've booked somewhere, then?" I asked him as we made our way up Heath Street.

"No, no," he said. "I thought we could just play it by ear."

We passed the Calzone Pizza Bar—it looked rather inviting, with green tables and cane chairs—perfectly acceptable, and I was already feeling pretty hungry, having missed lunch.

"I *hate* pizza," he said. "Don't you?"

"No. No. I like it, actually. Pizza would be just fine," I said.

"Well, let's keep going, after all the night is still young," he said cheerfully. Oh *yes*, I thought miserably. The night was still young. And all the while we walked he talked, nonstop, about films, in this deep, curiously plummy, slightly over-elocuted voice. And, as he talked, his large Adam's apple lifted up and down in his scrawny throat like a bucket in a well. He was like a walking cinematic encyclopedia—"Truffaut . . . *Nouvelle Vague* . . . Eisenstein . . . Fassbinder . . . *Three Colors Blue* . . ." I heard him say.

"My friend Kit wants to be a director," I said.

"What sort?"

"Commercials."

"Oh," he replied, with evident disdain.

"What sort of films do *you* make?" I asked.

"Well, I've got a couple of things in development," he said. "But I haven't got funding yet. You see my style is fairly, well, experimental. My heroes are Cocteau and Buñuel, and of course Peter Greenaway and Derek Jarman." He turned to me with an expression of exaggerated concern. "Don't you think it's really *worrying* that we have so few avant garde film directors in this country?" Worrying? *No*. The only thing that was worrying me was the fact that I was hungry, in Hampstead, with this hideous-looking man. What's more my new shoes were beginning to rub—I couldn't even make a run for it. We paused outside La Sorpresa—a pretty little Italian place with flickering candles, potted palms and pink tablecloths, but he thought it looked too crowded.

"Too many smokers," he declared briskly. "I wear contact lenses and my eyes are particularly sensitive. Thank God all the cinemas are smoke-free these days," he said, as we wandered off again. "Have you been to the National Film Theatre recently?"

"Er, no. But I have been to the Odeon Leicester Square, ha ha!"

He looked shocked. "The NFT are doing a *fantastic* season of early German cinema at the moment. There are new prints of *The Blue Angel, Pandora's Box* and Fritz Lang's *M*—one of the great classics of German Expressionist cinema. It's an incredible movie. And they're showing some great Senegalese films too, including *four* by Ousmene Sembene. Isn't that interesting?"

"Er, very," I replied, though the only thing I found interesting was the prospect of something to eat. We passed La Villa Bianca—*so* pretty, with a wrought-iron balcony and red and pink geraniums tumbling down the whitewashed walls. I just managed to catch a glimpse of the menu in the window— venison at £12.50 and grilled fillet of beef at £14.50, before Jake had walked straight past it, muttering disapprovingly about the price.

"I wouldn't go there on principle," he said. They probably wouldn't let him *in* on principle, I thought, surveying his dishevelled appearance. In Hampstead High Street I spotted Café Rouge.

"Café Rouge," I said. "That'll be fine. Let's go there."

"Well, OK, I'll ask, but it looks pretty full to me." He shot across the road and reappeared a moment later. "As I thought. Full up. Packed."

"But I'm sure I can see a couple of free tables at the back . . ." I said, but Jake was already heading down Rosslyn Hill. A wonderful Tandoori tang emanated from the Taj Mahal and I drew to a halt outside. "I really don't like curry," he said.

"But I *do*," I said. "In fact I *love* it. And if there are so many things you don't like why didn't you book somewhere you *do* like—especially as it's a Saturday?"

"I think we'll find something more suitable nearer the Heath," he said, ignoring me and turning down Pond Street. And then, semidelirious with hunger, something began to obsess me. I was trying to remember the name of that French film in which there's this group of people who *never get to eat*. Either they meet on the wrong day, or they turn up at the restaurant only to discover the owner's corpse, or they finally sit down to a fantastic dinner only for the army to burst in. What was it? Jake would know.

"What's that French film where they never get to eat?" I asked as the Royal Free hospital came into view.

"Oh, *The Discreet Charm of the Bourgeoisie*. One of Buñuel's greatest. Made in 1972 with Stéphane Audran, Fernando Rey and Michel Piccoli. It's a brilliantly sophisticated satire on the French establishment. It got the Oscar for Best Foreign Language Film. Wonderful *ensemble* playing." Suddenly he stopped, and I found myself staring in amazement at this vast, painted sombrero. "Viva Zapata, Mexican Bar and Restaurant" said the sign. "Eat All You Want for £5 a head!" Jake appeared to breathe a sigh of relief.

"Now *this*," he said, "should be fine."

"You have got to be joking!" I said. I surveyed the tin foil trays of chicken legs and guacamole marinating in the window, the plastic chairs and tables, the hanging ponchos and synthetic cacti, and suddenly my hunger vanished. "I don't want to eat here," I reiterated.

"Why not?" he said. "It has charm and character."

"I'm afraid I simply don't want to eat anywhere that says 'Eat All You Want for £5 a head.' What do you take me for?"

"I take you for an incredibly bad-tempered woman," he suddenly said.

"I am *not* bad-tempered," I hissed, outraged.

"Yes you *are*," he countered. "All you've done, *all* evening, is complain. I find you very irritable. And rude." Rude?

"I am NOT rude," I spat. "I have been extremely PATIENT and POLITE!"

"No you *haven't*."

"Oh yes I *have*." I could feel my eyes begin to fill, while blood from my blister trickled down my right heel into my shoe. "You invited me out," I shouted, "you didn't bother to book anywhere, you've made me walk a mile and a half, and you've raised objections to every single restaurant we've stopped at. And now I know the reason why—you wanted to come here because it's so *cheap*."

"Who are you calling cheap?" he shouted back.

"*You*. And you can bloody well stay here on your own because I'm off." I saw a yellow light coming down the hill toward us and stepped off the curb to flag it down. "AND," I flung at him as I got into the cab, "you look a total MESS!" Now that *was* rude. But I didn't care. It made me feel better. Gradually my tears subsided and my heartrate slowed. What a nightmare. What a nightmare.

"What a nightmare!" I said to Lizzie the following morning. She had just dropped the girls off for their weekly tennis lesson.

"How ghastly," she said. "What a creep. I'm amazed you stayed more than five minutes. Did you cry?"

"Only when I got into the cab."

"And were you rude to him?"

"A bit," I conceded, "not rude enough, actually."

"Never abuse men, Tiffany—however gruesome, simply walk away. Maintain your dignity and composure at all times."

"But Lizzie, if it had been you, you would probably have *punched* him," I pointed out accurately. She ignored this, or perhaps she was too busy lighting another cigarette to hear what I said.

"Just keep your head," she said, exhaling audibly, "and remember, that old cliché about kissing frogs is true."

"I have absolutely no objection to frogs," I pointed out. "A frog would be fine. It's the toads that get me down."

"Well, this morning, *my* toad announced that he's going to his mother's next Friday," she said, narrowing her slate-blue eyes as she inhaled. "He says he wants to go on his own. So I said, '*Fine.*' But I think it's *very* suspicious, Tiff. However, I'm no longer convinced that he's having an affair with Nicola Horlick," she added.

"That's a relief," I said.

"No. I'm pretty sure it's Jade Jewel."

"Jade Jewel? The daytime TV presenter?"

"Yes. He's been videoing *Pet Passions* and *Tip Top!* a lot recently. And every time she's on he sits there, sighing, and saying to me, in this very pointed way, how 'nice' he thinks she looks. It's very peculiar."

"She probably *is* nice, Lizzie."

"Look, if she's having an affair with my husband, she is *not* nice, QED. What's this chart?" she asked, peering at the kitchen wall.

"Oh, it's something I did last night to cheer myself up. A reward system for ghastly dates."

Lizzie read it out loud. "For not instantly running away when faced with hideous man on blind date—one gold star. For staying more than five minutes with same hideous man—two gold stars. For staying more than one hour—three gold stars. For not crying in public during course of bad blind date—one silver star. For managing not to be unspeakably rude to hideous man during course of bad blind date—one red star. For losing grip and insulting hideous man on bad blind date—one black mark.

"What's the prize?" she asked.

"Well, I've already got three gold stars from my horrible date with Jake," I explained. "When I've notched up twenty I'll be the lucky winner of a ticket in the stalls for *Aspects of Love* followed by dinner for one in a top London restaurant."

"You're going mad," said Lizzie, with gratuitous brutality. "It's all getting too much for you. You're really becoming quite eccentric. You keep making these endless, obsessive lists, and I caught you talking to the vacuum cleaner the other day. You didn't think I'd heard you, but I did. You said, 'You silly thing, look, you've missed a bit'! You see, you've been living on your own too long, Tiffany. You're becoming very *singular*. In fact, you're clearly losing your marbles."

"If Prince Charles can talk to his plants, I can talk to my Hoover," I said.

"That doesn't follow," she replied. "Because Prince Charles is, at least, addressing another life form. Whereas you're not even doing that. And do you also sometimes say to it, 'Shake and Vac, Put the Freshness Back!' like that idiotic woman on the telly?"

"Yes," I said. "If I want to. Why not? I'm not *hurting* anyone, am I?"

"Tiffany," said Lizzie, stubbing out her cigarette, "may I suggest a holiday?"

"Well, I'm not sure," I said, "I'll have to discuss it with my dishwasher."

Though, actually, I *had* been thinking of taking a holiday. The Kiddimint job was over and the agency were happy with it, and Kit and I didn't have to submit our Love Hearts pitch for another month. Why *not* go away? I had enough money, and I hadn't had a holiday for two years. Not since I went to Marbella with Phil Anderer. That was a golfing holiday, of course, though obviously I didn't play—I just watched. For five hours a day, every day, for two weeks. I wanted to go on a drive to Granada to see the Moorish architecture, and the Palace of the Alhambra. It looked so wonderful in the travel guide. But

Phillip said it would be much too hot sitting in the car for two hours each way, so we didn't go. But while he played golf, I read. In fact, I read an awful lot that holiday. I read all twelve volumes of *A Dance to the Music of Time*. So I got something out of it. But that was ages ago. And Alex never had time for a holiday. Lizzie was right. I really *did* need a break—but who would I go with now? Maybe Kate would be up for it.

"Fantastic idea," she said, when I phoned her. "I'm pretty exhausted myself. I know, we could go on a singles holiday— meet lots of chaps."

"What, like Club 18–50, you mean?"

"Club Med," she said.

"Club Mediterrané?"

"Yes. Let's go to the one in the Bahamas."

"But Kate, the Bahamas aren't *in* the Mediterranean," I pointed out.

She appeared to ignore this. "Paradise Island, on the Bahamas," she persisted. "I've seen it in the Club Med brochure. It looks fantastic, and apparently it's stuffed with eligible single men."

"OK," I said. "Book it. Let's go tomorrow."

"Er, a bit soon. How about next week?"

"Next week it is then."

October

OK—bikinis (two)—tick; swimsuits (two)—tick; Philips Lady-shave (one)—tick; Vidal Sassoon professional travel turbo hairdryer (one)—tick; adaptor plug for Vidal Sassoon travel turbo hairdryer (one)—tick; Braun Style 'n' Go cordless tong and brush (one)—tick; Carmen classic hot airbrush styler (one)—tick; sundresses (fourteen)—tick; sarongs (five)—tick; beach towel (one)—tick; waterproof mascara (three)—tick; sunglasses (five pairs, four of which I will lose)—tick; high-factor sunblock—er, still got to get that; cardigans for cool evenings (two)—tick; tennis racket (one)—tick; tennis dresses (four)—tick; tennis shoes (two pairs)—tick; Swiss army knife (one)—tick; antique roses tapestry kit (one)—tick; small knapsack for excursions (one)—tick; mosquito spray (two bottles)—tick; medical kit (one)—tick, including Arret—just in case, though I'm told the food at Club Med is v good—tick; shampoo (three bottles)—tick; conditioner (ditto)—tick; assorted toiletries (one lge bag)—tick; smart dresses for evening cocktail parties and disco (twenty-three)—tick; inflatable neck pillow for greater in-flight comfort (one)—tick; improving books (seven)—tick; portable CD player (one)—tick; notepad in case I get brilliant idea for slogans (one)—tick; travel alarm clock (one)—tick; concealer (two)—tick . . .

"Tiffany, why are you always making lists?" said Kit, with evident exasperation.

"Because I need to," I said. "For my holiday. So I don't forget anything. I'm just being sensible, that's all. How many thermos flasks do you think I should take?"

"But Tiffany"—he picked up my pad of A4—"this list runs to seventeen pages. You can't possibly need all this stuff. It's a beach holiday, not a round-the-world trip. You're not Michael Palin."

"Yes, but I might meet some nice chap and I've got to look my best. Kate says its going to be a bloke-filled Bahamian Rhapsody. She says Paradise Island is—and I quote—'Stuffed with eligible single chaps.' Isn't that marvelous?"

"Yes," he said. "It's wonderful. You really need a break. I don't think you realize how stressed you are. The constant list-making, and the obsessive counting. And I've noticed you talking to the microwave recently."

"Have you? But the microwave's cracked."

"And I heard you muttering something to the fridge the other day."

"No, that's not true—I find the fridge a little cold."

"Tiffany, when are you off to Club Mad?"

"The day after tomorrow."

"Good. The sooner the better. In fact, I think you should bring it forward. I'm going on a bloke-filled holiday too," he added.

"You *are*?"

"Yes. I've been thinking about what you said, and I've signed up for it."

"What?"

" 'Menswork—Discover Your Inner Warrior Weekend Workshop.' " My *Gaard*! "I'm going down to Winchester this Friday."

"Have you told Portia?"

"No. I simply said—and God I hated not telling her what I was doing—but I simply said that I 'wouldn't be around' at the weekend. That's what I said, just like this: 'Portia, I'm afraid I

won't be around this weekend.' I don't think she liked it
much."

"Well—good," I said.

"Yes," he said. "I'm going to celebrate my manhood. Do a
bit of bonding, with eighty other blokes."

"I don't think you should drive down in the Discovery,"
I said.

"No, I've thought about that," he said. "I'm going to do
something really macho—I'm going to hitch."

"Why don't you just get the train?" I suggested.

"Well, because . . . I've been looking at the brochure and
I've got to start as I mean to go on," he replied. "I've got to take
risks—push out boundaries, do things I wouldn't normally
do—and basically, men who are in touch with their 'inner warrior' don't get the eight forty-five from Waterloo."

The thought of Kit's forthcoming weekend had lifted his
spirits, and I felt similarly uplifted by the thought of my holiday on Paradise Island. Sun, sea and sand swam in my imagination; Kate and I would have a fortnight of fun. But there
were hidden dangers. I popped down to Oxford Street to get
some sunblock to keep the Caribbean rays at bay.

"I need factor ninety-five," I said to the young girl on the
sun protection counter in the department store. "I'm going to
the Bahamas, and I'm concerned about my collagen."

"Why don't you just wear a balaclava," she suggested as she
took the money for five large bottles of Factor Thirty Extra-
Waterproof Total Bloc—otherwise known as cement. "Or better still," she added, "go to Iceland."

"Why don't you get lost?" I said. Actually, I didn't say that at
all. I simply said, "What an *excellent* idea. I'll go round to the
travel agent right now and ask them to change my ticket. I've
heard October's a *particularly* good month for Reykjavik."

"I've heard October's a *particularly* good month for the
Bahamas," said Kate when I met her at the British Airways

check-in at Gatwick two days later. "It's the beginning of high season—the weather should be *brilliant*."

"I mean, it's going to be *really* hot," she reiterated five hours later as we sat in the departures lounge, still waiting to board our delayed flight. "I mean it's going to be *boiling*. We'll really have to be careful. Especially you."

By this time I had finished reading *How to Make Anyone Fall in Love with You* and was halfway through *A Suitable Boy*.

"There'll be *lots* of suitable boys at Club Med," quipped Kate happily as she returned from her seventh visit to the Alders Duty Free shop.

"I think I'd prefer a suitable man."

Finally, our flight was called. We boarded the plane, fastened our seatbelts and took off for Paradise Island. But isn't twelve hours a long time to sit on a plane? Especially when the in-flight entertainment is appalling, every windowseat is taken, there's a two-hour stop in the Caymans, and your next-door-neighbor is a crying baby?

"God, I feel dreadful," said Kate as we shunted our luggage through Nassau airport at three A.M. the following morning. "Still, at least we're guaranteed to have good weather. It'll be sweltering. I wonder how we're meant to get to the resort?"

We found the answer outside the airport in the form of a handsome young man. In one hand he was grasping a sign saying CLUB MED. In the other, he was holding aloft a large, black, dripping umbrella.

This *Melrose Place* is brilliant. I've been watching it every day. In my room at Club Med. But I find myself wondering two things: a) Why does Heather Locklear still look twenty-five? Is she bathing in ass's milk, or drinking the blood of young virgins? And b) When is it going to stop raining?

"Sorry folks, it's the tail end of a hurricane," said one of the *Gentil Organisateurs* or GOs, as we Club Medders say. "The sun will shine again," he said; and then he quickly added, "*Le

*soleil brillera encore; die Sonne wird scheinen; el sol volvera
a brillar; sola skinner nok igjen; mata haremasuyo.*" Because,
you see, all these GOs, they're multilingual. Apparently they
can say, "OK everybody, let's party!" in twenty-three different
languages. That's what's so nice about Club Dead, I mean,
Club Med—it's dead international. I mean, we've met—well
actually, we haven't met anyone yet because of the rain, but
when it stops, I'm sure we will. We'll meet *lots* of people then.
It's only a matter of time. Millions of single chaps. From all
over the world. Thank God we booked for two weeks, because
it's been raining nonstop for four days now. And how clever of
me to bring my Clarins self-tanning cream. Anyway, fortunately there are seventy-two channels on the TV. So when I'm
not watching *Melrose Place* I watch reruns of *Peyton Place* on
the nostalgia channel, and there's the CNN twenty-four-hour
weather channel and of course I'm taking a close interest in the
ads. Some of them are really gross. Ads for herpes treatments,
hernia trusses, and toenail fungus creams are, unfortunately,
common. Thank God it's not like that in the UK. Thank God
we have such rigorous advertising standards. Thank God we
only show ads for Tampax, sanitary towels, dandruff sham-
poos and anti-thrush treatments. Oh yes. And another thing
I've been doing is writing postcards. It helps to pass the time.
I've already sent fifty-six including three each to Frances,
Sally, Catherine, Emma, Kit, Lizzie and Martin. But of course
I'm not sending one to Seriously Successful. That would be
stupid. Anyway, this morning, very, very early, I was suddenly
awoken by a loud knocking on my door. Clearly someone
wanted to speak to me. It was Kate.

"I'm just off to the beginners' step-aerobics exercise class,"
she said. "I thought I'd let you know. It's only six-thirty. You
can go back to sleep now."

"Thanks."

When I got up three hours later—still feeling the effects of
jet lag actually—I couldn't help noticing that it had stopped

raining. Fantastic! I dashed over to the restaurant for breakfast and there was Kate, chatting to this rather charming chap.

"Tiffany, this is Jurgen," she said. "He was in my step-aerobics class this morning."

"Hello," I said. "Tiffany. Tiffany Trott."

He smiled, and then he said, "Are you students?" *Students!* He had *got* to be joking!

"Er, no," we said. "We're both working. We've both been working for quite a long time, actually—years and years. In fact we're practically *retired*!"

"Ach so." He looked rather surprised. "Well, you look so young, I thought you must be students." I was beginning to enjoy this holiday.

"Are *you* a student?" I asked him pleasantly.

"No," he replied, "I'm thirty-five—I left university last year. I'm a tax lawyer now."

After breakfast we all went down to the beach. The sea was so warm, and the sun was incredibly hot. This was more like it.

"Do you like that German chap?" I asked Kate as we spread out our towels.

"Well, he's very nice," she said. "I think I do. But do you like him?"

"Well, yes, he's OK, but, I mean, *you* saw him first," I said.

"Well, I wouldn't want to stand in your way, Tiffany, you know, if you really felt that you'd like to get to know him."

"Oh no, no, no, no—don't think about me. In any case, I'm sure he likes *you*."

"No—I think he likes *you*, Tiffany. I get the impression he likes blondes."

"No, I think he's keener on brunettes. He's definitely keen on you—his body language was notably positive. I think you should make an effort to talk to him again."

"Well, OK, then," she said reluctantly, "I will. As long as you're sure."

"I'm sure," I said, giving her a reassuring smile. Just then we saw Jurgen walking toward us—hand in hand with a rather attractive blonde. Blast.

"Hullooo," he said. "Zis is my fiancée, Gudrun. She has been having golf coaching all zis morning and now ve are going to sit on ze beach until lunch."

"Well, just make sure you don't put your towels down on the best sun-loungers!" I said. Actually, I didn't say that at all. I simply said, "Hello, Gudrun."

Got that one wrong, then. Oh well. And in fact, to be perfectly honest, there did seem to be rather a lot of couples. Fun-loving couples, I suppose you'd call them, all frolicking in the sea, cuddling under the palm trees, rubbing suntan lotion into each other's backs, or strolling hand in hand through the pounding surf. Bloody sickening.

"I thought you said that Paradise Island was full of single blokes," I said to Kate as we built a small, but impressive sand castle.

"Well, I thought it was," she said.

"In fact, do correct me if I'm wrong," I continued, "I distinctly remember you saying that it was 'absolutely stuffed with eligible single men.' "

"Well, that's what I was told. Maybe it's one of the other Bahamian Club Meds, maybe I got them mixed up . . ."

There were, we also couldn't help noticing, quite a few same-sex, fun-loving couples. Particularly women. At lunch later that day we met a couple of rather fierce-looking worshippers at the shrine of Sappho—Jane and Sandra from Solihull.

"What does your girlfriend do?" Jane asked me as Kate went up to the buffet to get some more seafood salad.

"My girlfriend? Oh. Oh, Kate's not my *girlfriend*. Well, not in *that* sense, ha ha ha!" I said. "We're just having a holiday together. That's all."

"Oh I see—you're just good friends, are you?" said Sandra with a rasping laugh. "Heard that one before!"

"No, no, no, no, really," I added, adjusting my sarong. "I mean, I wouldn't like you to think . . ."

"It's all right, Tiffany. Don't get your bikini bottoms in a twist about it," said Jane as they got up to leave. She gave me a wink. "See ya later."

"Kate," I said, when she sat down again. "I think I've identified a problem here. There seems to be an assumption that we're gay. I don't think this is going to assist us in our search for Mr. Right. I think we should do something to counteract this ridiculous presumption as soon as practicable."

"OK," she said simperingly, "I won't hold your hand in public anymore, darling. Promise."

"No, but seriously, Kate . . ."

"Ooh, go on, give us a kiss."

"For goodness' sake, Kate, this could be a *real* problem."

"I really *love* it when you're angry."

"I know—let's talk about our exes in a loud voice," I suggested. "To indicate our unambiguous heterosexuality. So tell me what your ex-boyfriend did to *you,* Kate?" I inquired as I ate my apricot ice cream.

"Well, he was really *horrible,*" she said. "He never used to ring when he said he was going to."

"What a *bastard,*" I replied.

"Yes. And he used to make me go Dutch on dates. And," she added, "he used to drink far too much at parties and embarrass me. What about you?"

"Well, my ex-but-one, Phillip, was a golf-bore. He used to play the whole time, it was *awful*. But he'd never, ever do anything *I* wanted to do."

"What a *selfish creep!*"

"Yes. And he was very controlling. He used to tell me what to wear all the time, and even made me change my clothes!"

"How *outrageous*! I once had a boyfriend who was *just* like that. He used to scream at me if I wore something he didn't like."

"How *appalling*," I replied. "How *pathetic*. Also," I added, "this man, Phil, was unfaithful. I went through *hell*!"

"How *horrible*!" said Kate. "Well, my ex was unfaithful too—and he got someone else *pregnant*!" Suddenly we were aware that everyone had stopped talking and was listening avidly.

"My God," I said quietly. "How terrible." Kate hadn't told me this before. "What happened?"

"She had it!"

"What?"

"The baby."

"Oh no. What did you do?"

"I stood by him," she said simply, "and helped him. Even though I felt dreadful. I'm an expert on the Child Support Agency," she added with a sardonic little smile. "Ask me anything you like." Poor Kate.

"Then what happened?" I asked.

"Well, when it was all over, but not until then, he dumped me."

"No!" said a woman at the next table.

"Yes," said Kate. "Then I got post-natal depression."

"How *horrible*," I announced, outraged, as people shook their heads and tut-tutted sympathetically. "You *poor* thing. Well you're *well* shot of a *cad* like *him*! Well, get this," I continued. "My last boyfriend, Alex, was a *cross-dresser*!"

"Get away!"

"Yes. I kept finding him in my bedroom wearing my sexy underwear."

"Oh God!"

"*And* my summer dresses. But the worst thing was finding him in my Bellville Sassoon *ballgown*—he'd torn it very badly round the bust."

"*Bastard!* Did he get it repaired?"

"No, he *didn't*! And then the last man to take an interest in me was this guy I'd met through a lonely hearts ad, and do you know *what* . . . ?"

"*What?*" she said obligingly.

"He was already *married*! He just wanted me to be his part-time girlfriend!"

"How bloody *insulting*! MEN!"

"Yes. MEN!"

We glanced around the restaurant; those few single men that there were—and I had identified one or two—were scraping back their chairs. All except that nice-looking chap of about forty-five who looked a bit like Hunnicut in *M*A*S*H*. He was having lunch alone, outside on the veranda. Now he quite interested me, because when I was about twelve, I was in love with Hunnicut. And he was a tennis player—I knew this for a fact because I'd spotted him carrying a racket about. Now normally, I'm not at all pushy with men, but maybe, just for once, I'd be pro-active.

"Excuse me," I said, going up to him. "My name's Tiffany. Tiffany Trott."

"Er, Todd," he said. "Todd Schellenberg." American! Or, possibly, Canadian.

"I hope you're not Canadian," I said. "I mean, *are* you Canadian?"

"No. I'm from L.A."

"Oh good. Well, you see, I couldn't help noticing that you're a tennis player, and I wondered if you could direct me to the courts."

"Oh well, er," he gulped his coffee down, "sure. Here, let me draw you a little map. It's at the south end of the resort—about a five-minute walk. Near the main gates. The best thing is if you just turn up there and ask to join in the coaching," he said. "It's every morning at eight-thirty. Of course it's been too wet to play over the last three days, but the forecast's fine for tomorrow. See you there," he said with a smile as he stood up to leave.

"Kate," I said as we left the restaurant, "what you just said, just now, about your ex. Is that true?"

"Yes," she said quietly.

"God, how awful for you. Er, do you want to talk about it?"

"No, I don't," she said wearily. And then she added, with sudden, studied brightness, "I want to go back to the beach!"

The next morning I got up early, did my stretching exercises, put on my best Fred Perry tennis dress, full makeup—God, I hoped it wasn't going to get too hot otherwise it would all come sliming off—and headed for the tennis center. Twenty courts—what bliss. I spoke to a coach called Sebastian, who looked just like Tom Cruise—only two feet taller—and he said that I should be in the top group.

"Is the top group Todd's group?" I asked.

"Yes," he said. "It is." And I went and joined the group which consisted of five chaps—including Todd—and me. Anyway, Todd asked me to be his partner in the backhand exercise class and it was going really, *really* well, except that he stopped halfway through and came round to my side of the net and said, "Tiffany, please would you stop saying 'Sorry' every time you hit the ball out of the court."

"OK," I said, "sorry."

And then when the lesson ended he said, "I'm staying here on my own, actually. Would you like to have dinner with me tonight?"

"That would be lovely," I said, explaining that I was here with my friend Kate and she was currently doing the step-aerobics class followed by beginners' golf followed by beach volleyball followed by intensive Ping-Pong, and he said he'd see us both in the beachside restaurant at eight. Pity I forgot to put on my sunblock, I thought to myself later as I looked in the mirror. I'd already gone rather pink. Damn.

October Continued

After lunch, Kate and I went down to the beach again, and there we were bobbing about in the sea in our bikinis and I was telling her all about Todd's really exciting work as a cameraman for NBC when one of the GOs shouted, "OK everybody, it's the Ladies' Coconut-Throwing Competition! *OK folkens, na kommer Kokosnottkonkurransen! Fate attenzione, è arrivato il momento del tiro delle noci di coco! Achtung! Der Kokosnusswettbewerb geht los!* The winner gets a free piña colada!"

Being rather competitive, I naturally decided to enter. Quite a lot of women went for it, some of them could hardly lob at all, it was pathetic. I went last—shot-put fashion—and I threw it the farthest! Everyone clapped—I felt quite overcome—and I was just about to claim my free cocktail when, out of the blue, this really slim, tall, frankly rather attractive Belgian girl called Stella turned up and she said *she'd* like to have a go. I thought to myself, huh! She won't chuck it very far. But she did. In fact she threw it farther than me. By about three feet actually, which not only irritated me, it surprised me too as she only weighs about eight stone. And afterward she put her sunlounger next to Kate while she sipped her piña colada, and she and Kate got chatting, and before I knew what had happened Kate had invited Stella to join us for dinner, too.

"What a *good* idea, Kate," I said.

"She's *terribly* nice," Kate replied. "Very impressive. She's a stockbroker. She's got a boyfriend, he's a banker—Débit Suisse, I think. But he's in the middle of this really, really big deal worth *billions,* and too busy to take a holiday, and so she decided to come here on her own. She's very pretty, isn't she? I think she's loaded, too."

"I should say so," I said, "judging by her coordinating cruisewear."

Anyway, at eight o'clock we went to meet Todd in the harborside bar and I introduced him to Kate and Stella, and then we all went into the restaurant which was delightfully situated, overlooking the sea—and Todd was being *so* charming, *so* amusing, *so* attentive—to Stella! It was bloody sickening. "OK Todd, I know she's beautiful, rich, slim, successful and clever as well as being a marvelous coconut-thrower, but that's no reason for talking to her all the time and ignoring me," I said. Actually I didn't say that at all. I just kept rather quiet. She was talking about skiing.

"Did you just say you were an *Olympic skier*?" Todd asked her with an expression of fanatical admiration.

"Yes. Yes, I am," she said with a giggle. "I mean, I was. In 1984, at the Sarajevo Winter Olympics."

"But I thought Belgium was flat?" I said. "And not particularly snowy."

"Oh yes that's true," she said. "But I was educated in Switzerland and I learnt to ski there." Of course. Switzerland. Where else?

"Did you get the gold?" Todd asked.

"Oh no, of *course not,*" she said with a descending arpeggio of tinkling laughter. "Only the silver. I keep it in the bathroom to impress my friends! Have you ever skied, Todd?" she asked, as I maliciously wondered how good she was at avoiding trees.

"Just once," he replied. "It was fun, but we Californians prefer surfing. Mind you, I've heard the skiing in Vermont's beautiful."

"Yes, it is," she said. "I go to Vermont every February. It's really wonderful, and I also love heli-skiing in Canada—now that really is *very* exciting."

"Very *dangerous,* too," said Todd. Dangerous? *Good.*

"Yes, very," she said. "Though of course you have a guide. But right now I'm really into sub-aqua—I've done a lot of scuba diving in the Mediterranean. I've just qualified as an instructor, actually."

"Wow!" said Todd. His jaw was visibly slack; his tongue had practically hit the floor. "You Belgians are *so* adventurous," he added. Frankly, that was the stupidest thing I've ever heard. But then I've noticed that Americans do have this tendency to generalize about other nationalities. *"So* adventurous." He was now shaking his head in open disbelief.

I, for one, was bored by this conversation, though, depressingly, Kate seemed to find Stella's many accomplishments as mesmerizingly interesting as Todd. But I was fed up with the unbashful Belgian with the baby-blue eyes and the strawberry-blond hair and the big bank balance. I wish Seriously Successful were here, I thought to myself bitterly. He wouldn't ignore me, he'd talk to me and tell me jokes and flirt and make me laugh. Maybe I *would* send him a postcard after all. But what on earth would it say?

"Wow! What a woman!" I heard Todd say. "All that and coconut throwing too!" I thought I was going to throw up.

"Did you say your boyfriend is the chairman of Débit Suisse?" I suddenly asked Stella. "Or the president? I can't quite remember."

"Oh he's only the *vice*-president," she replied with a girlish giggle, fingering the fashionable "commitment ring" on her perfectly manicured right hand. Todd shifted uneasily in his chair.

"But vice-president, that's *fantastic,*" I said. "He must be *really* clever. Is he going to join you here?"

"Oh, no, he hasn't got time. He's in the middle of this deal which is worth, well, *billions,*" she said with an amused shrug of her slender shoulders. Todd was now looking distinctly crestfallen. And then suddenly, for the first time that evening, he looked at me properly. In fact, he was positively peering at me.

"You know, Tiffany, you've gone rather pink," he said. "You'd better be careful in the sun." Nice of you to care, I thought to myself bitterly. And then he added, in this quiet voice, "I've learnt that lesson the hard way because, well, actually, I've had skin cancer." Oh *no*.

"Well that's *very* easy to cure," I said quickly. "As long as it's caught early, which yours obviously was."

"Actually my surgeon keeps on having to chop bits off me," he said with a grim little laugh. "I think I've put his kids through high school on the proceeds."

"But skin cancer's *nothing* these days," said Kate, looking vaguely distraught. "It's terribly common. *Everyone* in Australia's got it. It's really *not* a big deal. I wouldn't worry."

But then Stella said, "Oh no, that's not true. It can be *extremely* difficult to cure. In fact I had a very dear friend and she got it, and she died of it."

"Have you been throwing coconuts long?" I asked her.

"She got a tiny mole on her big toe," she continued, "and, within six months—that was it. *Curtains*. It went through like wildfire."

"Oh, look, there's the sea!" said Kate.

"She suffered horribly," said Stella. "It was really frightful. I was *terribly* upset."

"Do you like the Bahamas?" I asked her, passing her a *petit four* whilst stealing a surreptitious glance at Todd, who had an expression of polite interest Superglued to his face.

"Yes, skin cancer's the most *terrible* thing," Stella concluded, shaking her head sadly. Then, what can only be called a deathly hush descended. "Well, I think I'll go for a little late walk on the beach," she said. "Do any of you want to join me?"

"Er, no thanks," said Todd quickly, politely standing up as

she pushed back her chair. "I'm all in," he said. "Tiffany really took it out of me on the tennis court this morning." Fortunately, my blush was concealed beneath the roseate glow of my incipient sunburn. Then, as we sat drinking our coffee, we heard, in the distance, the strains of "Dancing Queen."

"Oh gosh, the disco's just starting," said Kate. "Are we going to go?"

"I'm going to hit the sack, actually," said Todd. And then, as we left the restaurant he said, "Tiffany, would you give me a game of tennis tomorrow morning before the lesson? At about eight? I could really do with some practice."

Now eight's a little on the early side for me. In fact as far as I'm concerned eight A.M. is still the middle of the night. But, as Kate and I headed off toward the nightclub under a starlit sky, I said, "Yes, Todd. Eight a.m. would be just fine."

By now it was ten-thirty, and the nightclub was already crowded—knots of Japanese honeymooners and infatuated Italians bobbed in a desultory way to the beat. It all looked a bit lackluster to be honest, and I'd made a mental decision not to stay, when suddenly Sebastian the tennis coach leapt onstage to the accompaniment of a fanfare and flashing lights.

"OK everyone," he announced. "It's Party Time! We're going to do some proper dancing now—starting with the 'YMCA'!!!!"

Young Man! . . .

"OK, you put your hands over your head like this—*attenzione tutti quanti, mettete le mani in alto così; alors, haussez les mains dessus la tête; poned las manos sobre la cabeza; Händer über den Kopf, so; Opp med hendene slik; Konoyoni ryote wo ue ni agete kudasai.*"

There's no need to feel down, I said. . .

"Now drop your hands like this—*ahora dejad caer las manos, de este modo; abaissez les mains, ainsi; adesso lasciate andare le mani verso il basso; jetzt lassen Sie ihre Hände*

fallen so; Ned med hendene slik; kondo wa konoyoni ryote wo
oroshite kudasai."

Young Man, get yourself off the ground, I said...

"Oh, God, Kate, I'm not doing this," I said, "it's silly."

"Turn around everyone, in a circle, like this," yelled Sebastian.

"Come on, Tiffany," said Kate. "Do it."

"No—I feel embarrassed."

So many ways—to—have—a good time!

"Come on, you're on holiday!"

"No way."

YMCA!

"That's it," shouted Sebastian. "Make the letters with your
hands everybody—*faîtes les lettres avec les mains; fate le let-
tere con le mani in questo modo; formad las letras con vues-
tras manos; zeichnen Sie die Buchstaben mit den Händern so;
Lag bokstavene med hendene slik; konoyoni ryote de moji wo
tsukutte kudasai*—YMCA!"

It's fun to stay at the YMCA. It's fun to stay at the YMCA-AY.
They have ev-ery-thing for young men to enjoy. You can hang
out with all the boys.

"Look, Kate, I just don't want to do this kind of thing—it's
really not *me*."

You can get yourself clean! You can have a good meal...

"Can't we go now?"

You can do whatev-er you feel!

"Oh, God, I've had enough," I reiterated under my breath.
And then suddenly, the music changed to "La Bamba" and this
divine-looking bloke grabbed me by the hand and started dancing with me.

"Hola!" he said, as he wiggled his snakelike hips to the
Latin beat. "You wanna dance with me, baby?"

"Um—OK. Yes," I said, and luckily I happened to have done
a bit of salsa. Just three lessons actually, but enough to get the
gist. One, two, three, *step*. One, two, three, *step*. What fun!
This was more my thing, and he was so good-looking. A mop

of dark, shiny hair, smoldering brown eyes, and that wonderful
V-shaped torso which drives women wild.

"What your name you?" he breathed hoarsely into my left ear.

"Tiffany, Tiffany Trott."

"Teeffanee. Very nice. You do salsa good, Teeffanee."

"Gosh, thanks."

"Me—José."

"How do you do," I said, "Spanish?"

"Brazeelian. I from São Paulo. Very beeeg ceeteee." Very big.

By now I was really beginning to enjoy myself as we spun
and shimmed around the floor but then—well, it was rather
embarrassing really, because José suddenly leapt up onstage,
pulled me up behind him, and began a Conga line—with me at
the front! This was ridiculous—I mean this was seriously *silly,*
though I can't say I didn't enjoy the feel of his manly hands
around my waist.

Der da da da da da DAH!

I mean I don't mind dancing as long as I know what I'm
doing . . .

Der da da da da da DAH!

. . . but all this Conga business wasn't my kind of thing at all.

. . . *di di dee deee!*

Whatever next—the hokey cokey?

. . . *di dum dee da!*

"Right, everybody form a large circle!" shouted Sebastian.
"OK? Now—you put your *left* foot in . . ."

That was the point at which I decided to leave. Call me a
spoilsport, but I went. I really felt I'd done my bit. Anyway, I
was exhausted after my exertions on the beach, and I had an
early rendezvous with Todd. But then the Brazilian . . . he was
rather nice. *Very* nice, in fact. José. I wouldn't mind seeing him
again.

Ooooooooohhh—the hokey cokey! I heard in the distance as I
made my way slowly back to my room through the coconut
grove.

Oooooooohhh—the hokey cokey . . . I mean, nothing wrong with Brazilians, I thought as I passed the beginners' golf course. Brazilians are very attractive.

Ooooooohhhhhh—the hokey cokey . . . They're very family-minded too, of course—they're known for their love of kids.

That's what it's all ABOUT!

"OK everybody," said our tennis coach, François, at nine-thirty the next morning. "You made some very good progress today. Tomorrow, we'll work on your volleying. *Demain, le smash. Morgen, werden wir an Eurem Volley arbeiten; I morgen trener vi på volley 'en. Domani rivediamo il gioco aereo* . . . "

"Excuse me, sir," Todd interjected politely, "but we're all English speakers, actually. I just thought I'd save you a little time here."

"Oh. Oh. Well, sank you," said François politely.

Then Todd and I made our way to the restaurant for breakfast in the already blistering heat. We spotted Stella at a distant table, but Todd didn't seem interested in joining her. In fact he was being quite attentive toward me.

"Tiffany, you seem quite distracted this morning," he said as we went up to the breakfast buffet. "Are you sure you're OK?" he inquired as we sat down with our croissants and yogurt. "I sure hope you didn't overdo it last night."

"Oh, thanks, no, I'm fine," I said, waving at Kate and hoping that José would turn up. José was a laugh. José was a bit of all right. And then right on cue—José arrived. He rushed up to our table, and gave me a kiss! My God. These Latin types. Delightfully spontaneous.

"Hi Teeffanee!" he said. "You tired? I give you hard time last night, no?" Todd suddenly looked uncomfortable.

"Er, no, it was um *fun*," I said truthfully.

"But I make you go on too long, I think."

"Oh, no, the length was just fine," I said. "I could take it. Really."

"No, I theeenk I make you do theeengs you deedn't reeely wanna do. No?"

"Excuse me, I think I need another croissant," said Todd, scraping back his chair.

"Er no, José. It was great fun. Are you going to be there again tonight?"

"Tonight? No. Not tonight. Tonight I on plane."

"Plane? Oh. Oh, that's a pity. You're leaving. On a jet plane, ha ha ha!"

He didn't laugh. He just said, "Yes. I leeving tonight. I bin here one week. I very sad."

"Well *we're* very sad," I said sadly.

"Get his *address*," Kate hissed.

"Well, I hope I'll—we'll—see you again, José. Here . . ." I scribbled on a paper napkin. "This is my address in London, and this is Kate's. Do come and stay."

"Oh *grasias*—yes I weel come and veesit you." I waited for him to give me his address, but he just poured himself a cup of coffee.

"Can I have *your* address, José?" I said.

"Your dress? Yes, your dress is very nice," he said. *"Very nice."*

"No. I'd like your *address*. Where you live."

"Yes, I leave. I leave today."

"No. Your *ad*dress. So *I* can visit *you*," I said. "I've never been to Brazil. Can I come and visit you?"

"Yes, I *weel* visit you. I veesit you very soon. Very soon. I have to go now. I have to go to Nassau, to the bank. So I say goodbye, Teeffanee. You keep dancin'. We do salsa—in London!" He grabbed my hand, kissed it, and was gone.

Kate looked at me. "Oh well," she said. "There's always Directory Inquiries."

"Yes," I said, "São Paulo's not that big."

"No. That's right. Only ten million people," she pointed out

as she buttered her toast. "Pity you don't even know his sur-
name, though."

"Yes. That could be a bit of a drawback . . ."

"But I'm sure it's worth pursuing," she added. "I mean you
both communicated so well."

After breakfast I wandered over to the Club Med shop,
where, like everything else in the Bahamas, the prices are
thrillingly high. A T-shirt—forty quid. A swimsuit—one hundred and twenty. I decided to buy a postcard. I found a tasteful,
artistic scene of a solitary palm tree leaning over a vast
cerulean sea. And then I sat down and wrote on it, "I'd really
like to shake your coconuts!" Actually I didn't write that at all.
Even though Seriously Successful would have laughed like a
drain. I just didn't have the nerve. I'd save it until later, when
felt braver—maybe this evening after the dolphin excursion.
Because, you see, Kate and I have booked to go on this amazing Dolphin Encounter on the Blue Lagoon, a short boatride
away. And it should be *really* brilliant because not only can you
see real dolphins—you get to swim with them. It would be an
amazing experience because swimming with dolphins is
proven to benefit people with all kinds of serious conditions—
autism, epilepsy, depression—and it can have miraculous
healing effects. I found myself wondering whether it could do
anything for terminal singleness. Anyway, we walked down to
the quay where we joined a large group of people from another
hotel. Then we stepped on board a cruiser and headed out
toward the lagoon. And it was quite ironic really, because
nearly everyone else going on the Dolphin Encounter trip was
either Japanese or Norwegian.

"I suppose the last encounter you had with a dolphin was
between two halves of a sesame-seeded bun," I said to a couple
of Japanese honeymooners sitting next to me. Actually
didn't say that at all. I just smiled at them politely. And as for
the Norwegians—God, they were a noisy bunch, it was the en-

tire sales force of the Oslo branch of Black and Decker on an incentive travel freebie.

"We met our targets," said one of them proudly. "This trip is the reward. I sold twelve thousand cordless multidrills in the first six months of this year."

"Congratulations!" I said. "That's marvelous. How many did *you* sell?" I asked this other bloke, who was tall and blond and built like a Viking.

"None," he said. Oh.

"So what are you doing on this trip, then?" I said accusingly.

"I'm not Norwegian," he said. "And I don't work for Black and Decker. I'm an artist, I'm English and I'm staying at Club Med." Oh. I hadn't spotted him there. "I arrived yesterday," he explained. "My name's Eric."

To be quite honest, Eric looked a little bit familiar, though I couldn't put my finger on the reason why. Anyway, he joined our group as we all jumped into the water with life-vests while "our" dolphin, McIvor, swam around us, chirruping like a bird, splashing the water with his leathery fins or leaping over our heads in high, elegant parabolas. Being so close to a dolphin, gazing into his clever, watchful eyes like that—well, it's the kind of thing that makes me believe in God.

"Wasn't that wonderful," said Kate, as we made our way back to Club Med.

"Fantastic. Did you see the way that dolphin looked at me?"

"You're really a sad case," she replied. "Let's ask Eric to join us for dinner," she said, as we disembarked in the late afternoon heat. A couple of hours later the three of us were sitting on high-stools at the harborside bar, sipping banana daiquiris beneath a slowly revolving fan.

"Tell us about your paintings," I said, as a bead of sweat rolled down my neck into the small of my back.

"Well, they're not really paintings," he said. "I mostly do conceptual work."

"Rotting cows' heads? Bisected sheep?" Kate inquired politely.

"There's more to conceptual art than bits of dead animal," he said slightly resentfully. "I'm not Damien Hirst. I use photography a lot."

"Can you actually, you know, paint and draw?" Kate asked innocently.

"Of course—but art's about more than pigment and paper."

"Where did you train?" I asked him.

"Brighton art school."

"And where do you live?"

"Hackney. I've got a house on London Fields." That sounded familiar too.

"And do you also own a vintage Jaguar?" I asked him. Actually I didn't ask him that at all, because I didn't want to embarrass him in front of Kate. Because by now I knew who Eric was—which explained the strong case of *déjà vu* I'd had all afternoon—he was the bloke who had answered my lonely hearts ad. He was Eric the artist with a restored racing Jag who'd been to Brighton art school. What an amazing coincidence, I thought. Of all the Club Meds in all the towns in all the world, he had to walk into mine. And had he twigged who I was? He'd seen that photo of me at Glyndebourne, but by now my face was so disfigured by my failure to use sufficient sun block that he probably hadn't recognized me at all.

"I know who you are, by the way," said Eric, after supper, as we sat by the pool, drinking brandy and listening to the distant trill of the cicadas. Kate had gone to get some more mosquito spray. "You're the 'sparky tennis player' in *The Times*, aren't you?"

"Yes," I said, as a coconut tumbled off an adjacent palm tree with a muted thud into the grass. "What an amazing coincidence," I added. "If I were a writer and I put this in a book it would be dismissed as an improbable fiction."

"I know."

"Do you know how many Club Meds there are?" I asked him.
"No."

"A hundred and twenty. And you chose this one. Actually I'm amazed you recognized me," I added, rubbing my flaking nose. "I'm not normally this color. I've been a bit silly with the sun. I look like Michael Gambon in *The Singing Detective*."

"You look fine," he said. "I knew it was you when I saw you on the boat this afternoon, but I decided not to say anything in case you were embarrassed. Did you meet anyone nice through your ad?"

"Er, no. I met a guy whose wife, it transpired, had *expired* just five weeks earlier. And then I had a Saturday nightmare with a budding film director who wanted to take me to a Mexican restaurant in Hampstead where they charged five quid a head."

"Oh dear," he said. "Bad luck. The funny thing is that I was just about to ring you last week, and then I decided to have a week's holiday. And here you are—in the very same place. Weird," he said. "There's obviously a karmic connection here."

"Yes. There is." But was there any other kind of connection between us? Well, to be honest, not really. I liked him. He was extremely interesting. And he was nice. But not as nice as Seriously Successful, I couldn't help thinking. Not as funny. Not as sophisticated. Not as attractive, either—at least not to me. And certainly not as well-dressed. When I got back to my room I stared at the blank postcard, and then picked up my pen and wrote: *Anytime. Anyplace. Anywhere. Tiffany. x,* briefly wondering, as I did so, what the precise difference *is,* exactly, between "anyplace" and "anywhere"—surely they're the same thing aren't hey? Any*place*? Any*where*? Any*way,* I then filled in the address, which to be honest I didn't know, but I knew that if I just put *Albany, Piccadilly, London, W1,* it would probably get there. However, it was not lost on me that the name Seriously Successful might not mean much to the porters. So in brackets underneath I wrote, *Tall, really quite good-looking and* very *amusing publisher who plays the cello and wears Hermès ties.* That should do it, I thought happily, and then, because I was slightly tipsy—although normally I'm very careful about my alcohol intake and never drink more than twelve glasses—I ran straight over to the letter box and dropped it in! Oh God. Oh God.

"Oh *God,*" I said to Kate at breakfast the following morning.

"What's the matter?" she said as she sipped her paw-paw juice.

"Well, you know that thing you're not meant to do. That thing about writing to someone when you're drunk and then posting it before you can change your mind?"

"Yes," she said. "I know."

"Well *I did it.* I wrote an affectionate postcard to Seriously Successful at two o'clock in the morning. And then I posted it straightaway. And I got up too late this morning to retrieve it. It is winging its way to Piccadilly as we speak."

"Tiffany," she said, very slowly. "Can I give you some advice?"

"Of course."

"You should never, ever, *ever,* write to anyone when you're pissed. Also, you should never, ever, *ever,* rush out and post something without giving yourself proper time to pause and reflect. Because you might well regret it."

"Thanks, Kate," I said. "I'll remember that. Oh God oh God oh God," I continued. "What have I done? What a disaster!"

"Is it?" she said with a shrug. "It's only a postcard."

"Yes, but my message was *extremely* provocative."

"What did it say?"

I told her.

"Oh, I see," she said seriously. "That *is* extremely provocative."

"I know," I said. "It sends all the wrong signals, and he's

disastrous—a married man looking for a mistress. I ask you! Seriously Unscrupulous. And now he'll think I'm very keen on him."

"You *are* very keen on him," Kate said. "Oh, look—there's Todd."

Todd was having breakfast with the attractive Croatian hairdresser who had won the Paper Plane Throwing Competition on the beach the previous day. "No, really, I thought your design was brilliant—you fully deserved that piña colada," I heard him tell her. "The aerodynamics were truly outstanding."

Todd, we knew, was due to leave later that evening, and Kate and I were going the following day because suddenly, our two weeks were up. Bye bye Bahamas. Pip! Pip! Paradise Island.

"Come and visit me in L.A.," said Todd, giving us both a hug.

"Yes, please. And do come and stay if you're ever in London on one of your assignments."

"I'm having a private showing at my gallery in late November," said Eric when we went to say goodbye to him. "I'd love you both to come."

"We'd love *to* come!" said Kate happily.

"I'll send you an invite," he said as we handed him our cards. "It's on November twenty-eighth. See you then."

And that was it—back to reality; back to work; back to an empty house, and no boyfriend. Back to the vacuum cleaner. Back to the dishwasher. Back to the microwave. And the fridge.

November

"I haven't phoned her for twelve days," said Kit triumphantly on Tuesday morning. His normally smart, curly black hair was a wild, uncombed mess, he had four days' growth on his usually close-shaven chin, his shirt was open at the neck and there were traces of mud on his jeans. "It's driving her completely mad," he added with a wild grin. "She's left twenty messages on my answer phone ranging from the casual 'just wondered if you're back yet' to the hysterical 'why aren't you phoning me back you bastard, why why why? Are you seeing someone else? I bet you are you bastard I'll never speak to you again.' In her last one she threatened unspeakable violence if I didn't phone her back *immediately*. She said she'd never been treated so disgustingly in her entire life and she was going to tell her parents. It's *brilliant*. Gosh you look brown, Tiffany."

"*Did* you phone her back?"

"No," he said. "I'm going to leave it until Thursday. And then I'll tell her, very, very calmly, that the reason I didn't call was that I was busy and didn't have time."

"Well don't overdo it, Kit, I think you've made your point."

"I can't help it. I feel *different* now, Tiffany, after the bonding weekend. I feel liberated. Oh Tiffany—you're *still* making lists!" He snatched my shopping list out of my hand, which I had been scribbling on while he talked, ripped up all five pages, and then dropped them into the bin.

"Why did you do that?"

"To help you, Tiffany," he said purposefully. "To release you from the tyranny of compulsive enumeration."

"Look, could you please just give me the top ten points about the Inner Warrior Weekend," I said. "I'd like to write them down so that I get it straight."

"It's changed me fundamentally," he said forthrightly. "That whole thing I was taught as a child about being considerate and respectful to women, well that's fine—as long as they're considerate and respectful to *me*. And Portia hasn't been. I'm making up for the all the times *she* never phoned me, all the times she made *me* feel insecure, all the sleepless nights *I* had. And I'm making up for all the times she pushed me around as though I were her amanuensis, not her boyfriend, and what did I get out of it—what? What? What? *What?*"

"Er, well, I agree with you, Kit, but please don't go *too* far."

"By the way, Tiffany," he said. "I've been thinking about your Love Hearts copy. Some of it's crap, you know."

"Oh. Is it?"

"Yes. It just doesn't convey the benefits of the product at all. I think you'll have to come up with something better than that, otherwise we'll lose the pitch. I'm selling the Discovery," he added. "I'm buying a Ferrari. Turbo twin-engined." Good God.

"And I've cancelled *Parenting* magazine and I'm getting *GQ* and *Loaded* instead."

The Inner Warrior had certainly been released in Kit. Along, I feared, with the Inner Brute, the Inner Beast and the Inner Bastard. This was not what I'd had in mind.

"Kit, I wasn't recommending a complete personality change—just a minor modification. Don't you think you're going a bit far? Don't forget—you're *fond* of Portia. You don't want to drive her away." *Although it would be nice if you did, because then I could go out with you again instead.*

"Yes, I *am* fond of her," he said quietly. "I don't want to lose her." *Oh. Fair enough.* "But I don't want to lose myself either. I'm remolding myself," he added. "I need to. It's an inevitable 'blokelash' against years of oppression. I mean I did a lot of sharing with these guys—we showed each other our 'wounds.' "

"What do you mean, 'wounds'? You haven't got any wounds."

"Our pain. The pent-up pain of years. The pain of wounds received in childhood, in adolescence; wounds inflicted by our parents, our siblings, our children . . ."

"You haven't *got* any children."

"I *know*. I'm just speaking metaphorically . . . where was I? Oh yes, wounds from our uncles, our aunts, our grandparents, our cousins, our teachers, our friends, our next-door-neighbors, our delivery men and, especially wounds from our wives and girlfriends. I mean, there was this one guy there who worked in the City and he'd had a *terrible* time—much worse than me— I'll tell you about him in a minute. Anyway"—he paused for breath—"we showed each other our wounds and we *cried*. And crying helped us to rediscover our maleness, because real men *do* cry, you know. That's what the bloke running the course said. He said, 'Male tears are beautiful.' And they are. And that's what we did, we released our tears and rediscovered, and celebrated, our manhood, our maleness—our nonoppresive, positive maleness." Kit had a faraway, messianic look in his eyes as he gulped down his Nescafé.

"Do you know what else we did, Tiffany?" he said, biting into an éclair. "We chopped wood. Heaps of it. Like lumber-jacks. And we beat drums. Big drums, deep in the woods, and the sound of eighty men all beating out this rhythm was in-credible, it was infectious, you just got totally sucked into it— and now, now, I feel really, really *strong*."

"Er, oh good. That's lovely," I said.

"Yes, and we all hugged each other—no-holds-barred. And it's perfectly OK to hug another man. It's not poofy, or wimpy. It's OK. There were eighty of us, all hugging at the same time. I *like* hugging men, Tiffany," he added enthusiastically.

"Well, don't do it too often, Kit. I mean, you know—just do it . . . now and again."

"Anyway," said Kit, "there was this one guy, the one I mentioned just now, and his wife had walked all over him. I mean we *really* bonded—he gave me a lift down there actually, he stopped for me on the M3 and it turned out that he was going to the Inner Warrior Weekend too."

"How did he manage to get away for this bonding jamboree if his wife's so domineering?" I asked.

"He told her he was staying with his mother. And his mother had to lie for him, because his wife kept ringing up and demanding to speak to him; and apparently it was really touch and go. Anyway, this bloke, he's forty-seven now, and we got on really well, and I knew that I would end up like him if I didn't change—if I didn't start to make demands in any relationship instead of just giving, giving, giving all the time."

"Who was that, then?"

"Well this poor bloke, he'd been slaving away in the City for years so that they could have this big house and accounts at Harrods and Harvey Nichols, and private education for their kids and designer clobber for her; and his wife didn't even appreciate it at all and she didn't even work, right, because she was this not-very-successful actress, and wouldn't even consider doing a part-time job or anything when she was out of work. She seemed to give him nothing, but it was obvious from what he said that she expected him not only to bring home the bacon, but to cook it, dish it up, and wash everything up afterwards as well."

"Oh. Poor chap. How unfair."

"I know. But, I mean, this guy didn't just sit there and bitch about his wife, we all had to draw it out of him, bit by bit— what a cow—she's got really expensive tastes, and he's just a walking wallet as far as she's concerned. He doesn't even feel that she loves him or appreciates him or has any respect for him—actually, that was when he cried, when he told us that. And she's obviously a mad cow because she accuses him of having affairs with other women, which he said he's *never* done, and she keeps saying he's having it away with Nicola Horlick . . ."

"But that sounds . . ."

". . . which is totally ridiculous because everyone knows that Nicola Horlick's got five children and is far too busy for affairs . . ."

". . . just like . . ."

"And he said if he was going to have an affair with anyone in the public eye he'd choose Jade Jewel, because she looks so nice . . ."

"But this sounds like . . ."

"Please don't keep interrupting me, Tiff. I'm trying to tell you something. Anyway, this bloke, they've got a huge house in Hampstead, and he pays for his wife to have help in the house but *he* still has to mow the lawn and paint the garage, because she says they can't afford a gardener and a handyman, even though they obviously *can*. And I kept thinking, that's what it would be like with Portia and me unless I change. That poor, broken man is me in ten years' time."

"That poor broken man sounds just like Martin," I said.

"What? Yes. Martin. How did you know his name?"

"Is he rather thin on top?"

"Yes—it's probably caused by all the grief *she's* given him."

"Does he work for Jack Carpel?"

"Yes. How did you know?"

"Because Martin is Lizzie's husband—that's how."

"My God! I didn't get it. But then his name isn't Bohannon, it's Keane."

"Bohannon's her maiden name. She's never taken his."

"Then it's just about the only thing of his she *hasn't* taken, from what he said. So why haven't I ever met Martin before?" Kit asked, clearly puzzled. "I've met Lizzie often enough."

"The reason why you haven't met Martin is because he never comes to my parties—he's too exhausted to socialize because he gets up at five-thirty to be in the office by seven A.M. And then he stays at his desk for twelve hours. And so when he gets home at eight all he wants to do is collapse, or read a book, or watch TV, because he has to be in bed by ten. So Lizzie always comes on her own. That's why."

"Poor bloke. Poor sod. And he seemed to be so successful—he really seemed to have it all. But he just looked at me when we said goodbye on Sunday evening, and he said, very slowly and very sadly, *"Just don't end up like me."*

Two days later, on November the fifth, I went to Martin and Lizzie's annual Guy Fawkes party. Every year they invite thirty or so of their friends to stand in their back garden and watch the fireworks explode over Hampstead Heath—they have a wonderful view from their house. At seven-thirty on Wednesday we stood by the pergola, stamping our feet in the bracing cold. Then BANG! POP! KER-ACK! The night sky began to fill with huge, fiery blooms—gigantic dahlias and chrysanthemums in metallic mauve and yellow and red. The children shrieked and gasped. The adults ooohed and aaaahed. The sharp aroma of cordite hung on the freezing air. On and on it went, then BOOM! WHEEEEEEEEEEEEEE! CRACK! went the final rockets. FFFFZZZZZZ! Aaaaaahhhh! A curtain of silvery sparks descended and at *that* point, Martin arrived.

"Daddy, Daddy you missed it!" shrieked Alice.

"Sorry, darling," I heard him say as we all trooped inside. "I couldn't leave the office any earlier." He followed us into the drawing room and started refilling our glasses with mulled wine while the children ran into the TV room to watch a promised video.

"What are you going to watch?" I asked Alice.

"Nightmare on Elm Street Four."

"Oh dear, sounds horrible," I said.

"Yes," she said happily. "I hope so. Have you seen our new sofa?" she asked. "In *there*."

"It's lovely," I said, glancing at the pale-gold damask three-seater sofa positioned in the drawing room bay window.

"It was *very* expensive," Alice confided. "Mummy chose it."

"Martin—thank *God* you're here at last!" Lizzie shouted as she came in from the garden. "Could you get the olives from the kitchen? Black ones. No, not *those* ones, you idiot," she hissed at him as he came into the drawing room. "We don't want *green* cocktail olives, I said the *black* ones. Black, Martin. Not green. *Black*. They're in the fridge—and make sure they're the Italian ones, not the Greek." He obediently took the offending olives back into the kitchen while we all pretended we hadn't heard.

"Husbands," said Lizzie, rolling her eyes heavenward. "Hopeless! You just *can't* rely on them."

Martin came back in with the "right" olives and started circulating. He looked so tired. But then he always looks tired.

"Hello, Tiffany," he said, giving me a kiss on the cheek. "How lovely to see you—what exciting campaign are you working on at the moment? I'm sure whatever it is your ad will make me want to buy it."

"Well, just some brochure copy actually, for Thames Water," I said with a smile. "And I've just won a pitch to do a TV ad for Love Hearts."

"Love Hearts? Well, you *do* have an interesting job, Tiffany."

"Well, yes. Sometimes it is."

"I wish I could do something really creative like that," he said with a sigh. "All I do all day is stare at figures on a screen and calculate two-way spreads and price-to-earnings ratios."

"Well, what would you do if you *could* do something else?"

"I don't know," he said, "I love archaeology and anthropology—that's what I read at Cambridge. But until the girls are older I've got to keep on chasing those rats." Just like me, I thought bitterly.

"Tiffany," said Alice, who had suddenly appeared. "Are you getting married yet?"

"No—no I'm not," I said. "Didn't you like the film?"

"No. It's boring."

"Is Amy still watching it?" I asked her.

"Yes. She *likes* it. But Tiffany, *when* are you getting married?" she asked again.

"I really don't know," I said, sipping my wine.

"But you said I could be your bridesmaid."

"You can," I said, "but I'm afraid I just can't tell you when."

"Well, will it be *soon*?"

"No, it won't," I said.

"But I've never been a bridesmaid. Can I be *your* bridesmaid?" she asked Sally. Sally almost choked into her orange juice. Why *was* Sally only drinking only orange juice? I wondered—she wasn't normally averse to a bit of booze.

"Sorry, Alice," said Sally. "I'm afraid there are absolutely *no* husbands on *my* horizon. Try Frances."

"Can I be *your* bridesmaid, Frances?"

"No darling, I'm afraid you can't," Frances replied, biting into a mince pie. "I've got no intention of tying the knot, ever. Ask Emma!"

"Oh Alice, I'm afraid I've got awful problems in that department," said Emma cryptically. What on earth did *that* mean? Then Alice went up to Catherine, who was standing next to Hugh—it was their first appearance in public together. Catherine looked nervous, but happy.

"Catherine, are you getting married?" Alice inquired.

"Er, er, ha ha ha! What a silly question Alice," said Catherine, fiddling with the fourth finger of her left hand.

"Great kid!" said Hugh, with a nervous sip of his mulled wine. "Great kid."

"My mummy says all men are *useless*," said Alice, giving him a penetrating stare.

"They *are*!" Frances exclaimed.

"Well, *some* are," said Catherine judiciously. "But a lot aren't. For example, Hugh isn't useless. Are you?"

"Er, ha ha! No," he said. "No."

"Well, Mummy tells my daddy *he's* useless," Alice persisted. "Doesn't she, Daddy? She says you're useless."

"She's only joking," I lied, while we all studied the carpet.

"Martin, can you see what the children are up to!" Lizzie shouted across the room. Martin obediently disappeared with Alice into the TV room. Fifteen minutes later he reappeared, clutching his first glass of mulled wine.

"They're watching this really gruesome film," he exclaimed. "There's this fellow called Freddy Krueger, who appears to need a manicure. Gosh, I'm knackered," he added, sitting down on the new sofa with an exhausted smile. But then this awful thing happened. He was *so* tired he sat down too hard, and the mulled wine sloshed all over the pale-yellow damask fabric. A huge, red stain spread across one corn-colored arm, like blood.

"Oops!" he said. "Oh dear. Now I'm going to cop it." He was right.

"Martin, you are an *idiot*!" said Lizzie. She dashed into the kitchen, a blue light flashing on the top of her head; then she reappeared with a cloth and bowl of soapy water.

"Look, don't just sit there," she said as she rubbed away at the crimson splash. "At least get some *salt* or something. Oh God, it's not coming out. Oh really, that was so *careless* of you, Martin. You just weren't *concentrating*. But then you've obviously got *other* things on your mind at the moment," she spat. "Which is why you're hardly ever here!"

We all fiddled with the stems of our wineglasses. My face felt as hot as my mulled wine and was probably a similar shade.

"The FTSE's doing awfully well, isn't it?" I said to the man standing next to me—a colleague of Martin's.

"God you're *so* clumsy!" I heard Lizzie say.

"Yes," said the man, "though of course the instability in the Far East is bad news for us in London."

"Of course."

"And unfortunately I think interest rates are bound to go up again."

"I mean it's really *chronic*," Lizzie hissed. "You're so uncoordinated."

"What do *you* do?"

"I'm a copywriter."

"I mean, I leave you alone for one minute, and there's a complete *disaster*."

"Oh—Go To Work On An Egg, that kind of thing?"

"Yes, that's right," I said. "Vorsprung Durch Technik, and all that."

"Oh God, Martin, do you *know* how much this sofa cost?"

"Yes," he said wearily, "I do."

"It cost two and a half thousand pounds."

"Yes," he repeated. "I know that. And I know that because I *paid* for it."

"What?"

"I said, I paid for it. *You mad cow*."

"Martin!"

"Just as I paid for everything *else* in this wretched, unhappy house you call a home, because *you've* never lifted a finger . . ."

"*Don't* make a scene, Martin . . ."

"And do you know what? I don't *care* if there's a wine stain on it . . . in fact . . ." He picked up a bowl of chilli sauce and dripped its contents all over the sofa, ". . . I don't think it's stained enough. Let's see . . ." Then he picked up the taramasalata and slopped that onto it too.

"Martin—have you gone *mad*?"

Then he sprinkled honey-glazed sausages over it, holding them daintily between thumb and forefinger and distributing them with meticulous care.

"What the *hell* do you think you're doing?" screamed Lizzie. "Martin, put that down at once." He had picked up a tray of cheese and spinach mini-roulades and had tipped them all over the seat. Then he began to work the mess into the fabric with the tips of his fingers. Then he said, "Hang on a moment . . ." wiped his hands on a nearby napkin, and disappeared into the kitchen.

"Martin! Martin—*put that down*!" He had reappeared and was clutching, in both hands, the tureen of lukewarm mulled wine. Lizzie's mouth opened, but no sound came out, just an asthmatic gasp. Then she said, very quietly, "Martin, please Martin—Martin *don't*."

But it was too late. He emptied the viscous red liquid all over the sofa, spattering and spilling with as much care and precision as if he were Jackson Pollock. Then he got his coat and walked out of the house, closing the door quietly behind him.

"Well, it's been a lovely evening . . ." I heard someone say. "Must be off—I'll just get the kids."

"Yes, well I think I'd better make a move," said Frances.

"Thanks a lot, Lizzie . . . er . . . I'll give you a ring," said another voice. "Come on, Tom. Polly? Home now. Say bye bye to Alice and Amy." Then there was silence, all except for the loud sobbing emanating from the hand-distressed kitchen.

"What a *bastard*," howled Lizzie. "What a copper-bottomed *bastard* . . ." Her breath came in great shuddering gasps. Her face was puce and wet.

"Here," I said, handing her a paper towel.

". . . humiliating me like that. Ruining the evening. My God, people will talk about this for *years*. It's all because he's having that *affair*," she wept. "It's making him behave oddly. Totally out of character."

"Lizzie, he *isn't* having an affair," I said.

"Yes he bloody well *is*," she sobbed. "With Jade Jewel."

"No he isn't."

"He *is*." Her cheeks were streaked with molten mascara. The whites of her eyes were bright pink. "I didn't tell you this, Tiffany," she said, clutching the tear-sodden tissue, "but last weekend he went away, and he said he was going to his mother's. But when I phoned him there, his mother kept saying that he was chopping wood for her. But she has a *gas* fire! She was just covering up for him. Because he's having an affair." Then she started crying again, her slender shoulders shaking with every sob.

"That sofa cost *two and a half grand,*" she wailed. "It was custom-made—it took me ages to choose the fabric. I went back *three* times. And he's ruined it. Useless, *useless* man. God, I'll divorce him," she muttered as she lit a cigarette. "I'll take him to Jeeves of Belgravia. I'll leave him without the shirt on his back, I'll . . . Tiffany, why are you looking at me like that?"

"You're *so* unfair," I said quietly. "Martin's so *nice* and you treat him like dirt." I was trembling, I thought I was going to cry.

"He's *not* nice," she hissed. "He just *ruined* my new sofa and humiliated me in front of *all* my friends. I don't call that nice at all." Two plumes of smoke streamed from her elegant nostrils. It wouldn't have surprised me if she had actually breathed fire. "There's no excuse for what he's just done," she added ferociously. "None."

"He's reaching," I said. "Can't you see it? He's breaking out. You've crushed him for years and years and years and now he's breaking out."

"He's breaking *down,* you mean," she said derisively. "Losing his marbles."

"Well yes. Yes, he probably *is* having a nervous breakdown," I said. "And it's not surprising, because he's exhausted all the time because he works so hard, and he doesn't even *like* his job, but he does it so that you can have this house and all the fancy *stuff* you've got—and you aren't even *nice* to him! Poor man. Poor, downtrodden man. In fact," I said as I began to stack the dishwasher, "you're *horrible* to him. I don't know *why* you're horrible to him. But you are. You walk all over him.

Ever since you had the girls, you've treated him like another child. I've noticed it," I said as I scraped guacamole off a spongeware plate. "It's been impossible *not* to notice it." I turned and looked her in the eye. "You know, you were quite ghastly. But it was bearable. Almost endearing. Bossy old Lizzie Bohannon—bit of a battleaxe, but terribly kindhearted. But since you've had Alice and Amy you've exhibited distinctly dictatorial tendencies and I can't see your kind heart anymore. Maybe there was a mix-up at the IVF clinic and they gave you testosterone instead of estrogen—I don't know. All I know is that these days you're so far over the top you're almost out of sight."

"Tiffany, I really don't think you should be talking to me like this," she said with quiet menace. "You're supposed to be my *friend*."

"I *am* your friend," I spat.

"Then you should take *my* side when I tell you that my husband is a useless, bloody man."

"He's *not* useless," I groaned. "He's a wonderful husband. He's a kind and devoted father. You don't know how *lucky* you are to have someone as nice and decent as Martin as your husband. You don't realize . . ." My voice trailed away. I felt the familiar aching in my throat.

"What do *you* know about husbands?" said Lizzie with a contemptuous snort. "You haven't even *got* one!"

That was it. I burst into tears. "I *know* I haven't," I retorted, stuffing my knuckles into my eyes. "And yes, I wish I *did* have one, I'd *love* to have a husband and I'd especially love to have a husband as nice and kind as *yours*!"

"Well, why don't you have him?" she said. "Feel free. Or perhaps . . . perhaps it's not Jade Jewel I should be worried about. Perhaps it's *you*," she added.

"What?" I said. "Oh Lizzie, you are out of your mind."

"That's *rich*," she shouted, "I mean, that's *really, really*

RICH, coming from a woman who talks to her DOMESTIC APPLIANCES!"

At that point Alice and Amy appeared. "Why are you and Tiffany SHOUTING, Mummy," shouted Amy.

"We're NOT shouting," Lizzie shouted. "We're just having a discussion."

"Mummy, have you seen the sofa?" Alice exclaimed. "It's a *mess*!"

"Mummy, where's Daddy?" said Amy with a bewildered air.

"He's gone out."

"Is he going to read us a story?" she asked.

"I don't know," said Lizzie. She wiped her eyes with a casual air while I surreptitiously mopped at my own.

"Why are you both crying, Mummy?" said Alice.

"We're not crying," she sobbed.

"Aren't you and Tiffany friends anymore?"

"Of *course* we are," I heard her say as I wearily retrieved my coat from the hall. "Don't be so silly, Alice. We are friends, aren't we, Tiffany?" Lizzie shouted after me as I made my way down the path.

"Tiffany?" I heard her call, as I shut the gate behind me. "Tiffany? *Tiff-a-neeeee?*"

November Continued

The next morning I awoke with dread in my heart and the terrible events of the previous night still swimming before my eyes. I trudged downstairs in my dressing gown. It was only eight o'clock, but a stack of mail bound with a rubber band was already lying on the mat, and, floating free, a white envelope, written in Lizzie's large, sloping hand. She must have stuffed it through the letter box overnight. I opened it first, of course: *Hampstead. Six A.M. Please don't be beastly to me, Tiff. You've no idea how miserable I am about Martin and Nicola. Or Jade. Or whoever. Do you know where he went last night? Madame Jo-Jo's! I'm feeling desperate. Haven't been to bed. Can I come round soon? Please. L. xxx.*

Poor Lizzie, I thought. And I rang her straightaway. Then I went into the kitchen and looked at the mail.

In the first envelope was an invitation, stiff as a plate and edged in gold: *Miss Tiffany Trott*, it said in the top left hand corner. Then, beneath, in black italic lettering so pronounced I could have read it with my fingertips like braille: *Jonathan de Beauvoir and Sarah Rush invite you to celebrate their engagement at a reception at the East India Club, 16 St. James's Square, London SW1, on Thursday 20th November. 6:30 to 8:30. RSVP.* And on the back, Jonathan had scrawled, *Thanks so much for your sensible advice at the Eat 'n' Greet party, Tiffany. You're a brick.* Good old Sarah, I thought—she had managed to pin him down. Eventually. It took a while, but it paid off. In the end. That old "flouncing off" tactic clearly works, I thought. And then, in another envelope, was an invitation to Eric the artist's private showing at the Oscar Reeds gallery. So what with all the film premières, charity balls, book launches, cocktail parties, gala concerts, fashion shows, award ceremonies, business receptions and, of course, 237 Christmas bashes, my diary's pretty full right now—ha ha! Just joking. Anyway, it's really nice of Jonathan to invite me to the party. I'm looking forward to it. Should be fun. Might even meet TSS there—That Special Someone. Though I rather doubt it—to be perfectly honest, my prediction is that it will be full of suffocatingly posh people.

Anyway, when the twentieth came I put on my LBD—little black dress—Jean Muir, secondhand, actually, from one of these agencies that flog the castoffs and fashion mistakes of fabulously wealthy women, and then I headed off toward Piccadilly on the number 38. I really like the 38—there's something satisfying about getting on a bus which matches one's bra size. The 36b's quite good too, though I don't get the 41— that really is going a little far.

"May I see your pass please, young lady?" said the conductor. *Young lady!* Get that!

"Oh yes, yes, of course," I said happily, holding up my annual season ticket. This was an auspicious start to the evening. I was obviously going to have a very good time. I stared happily out of the window—oh God! Christmas decorations in the shop windows *already*—that really gets me down . . . then I jumped off outside the Ritz. The Ritz. Now, I can't help it, but every time I go past the Ritz I automatically think of Seriously Successful—or rather, Seriously Unsuitable. Damn and blast, blast and damn—why did I always have to fall for someone who was either totally unmarriageable or hopelessly unavailable?

Lizzie has a new theory about this. "You know what you are,

don't you," she said when she came round for our reconcilia-
tory tête-à-tête. She had brought me a rose to plant in the garden. She said it was a late birthday present, but when I looked
at the label, it said, *Peace,* and then she gave me this awkward
hug and she looked really upset—well, she was crying actually, and I couldn't help crying too. After all, we've been
friends for so long. Anyway, after she'd helped me plant it we
sat at my kitchen table and she said, "Tiffany. In the twenty
years we've known each other we've never really quarrelled
before, have we?"

"No," I said quietly. "We haven't."

"Apart from that incident at college when you stole one of
my eggs from the communal fridge."

"Oh yes," I said. "I vaguely remember."

"I had written LB on it quite clearly," she continued, "and
you ate it."

"Sorry," I said.

"And then there was that time in 1986 when I lent you my
Valentino leather jacket, and you kept it for a week longer than
you said you would." This was true. I sighed regretfully. "But
until last week," she added, "we had never ever had a *serious*
falling out, had we?"

"No."

"And I think you may have hit a few nails on the head,
Tiffany. You really gave me food for thought. About my attitude to Martin. And why he may have gone off his rocker a bit
recently. And because of that, I know you won't mind, both
of us having spoken our minds so freely, if I point out an
important home truth to *you*."

"Please do," I said apprehensively. "Go ahead."

"OK," she said. "Here goes. Tiffany, you're a closet commitophobe." This was news to me. I couldn't have been more
surprised if she'd said, "Tiffany, you torture small animals," or
"Tiffany, you take hard drugs."

"I'm *not* a commitophobe," I said. "I'm the opposite—I'm a spouseomane."

"But you're not having much *luck*, are you?" she pointed out. This could not be denied.

"I mean, you're about as likely to find a husband in the next six months as I am to split the atom.

"Why do you think that is, Tiffany?" she continued, cocking her head to one side in a slightly smug and irritating fashion which I had never observed before.

"I think it's because . . . well, because I'm just—incredibly unlucky, that's why. Unlucky. That's all there is to it. In fact I've decided to become a professional card player."

"No," she said, with a sad and yet knowing smile. "It's got *nothing* to do with luck. The reason why you're not married is because you're a closet commitophobe. You can't see it yourself," she added, "but I can because, you see, I've been reading this book about relationships after our little, um, *contretemps*."

"Oh God, not *Women Are From Pluto, Men Are From Uranus,*" I said, "I *hate* all that pop psychology."

"No. Not that one. Another one. What's it called, er, *Women Who Don't Love Enough,* or something like that—can't remember. Anyway, the point *is* that I've been trying to work a few things out. And so I've taken a long hard look at everything and I've been turning everything over in my mind and really doing some serious, serious soul-searching, and trying to be more analytical about what's been going wrong and the mistakes that have been made—and I've worked out *why* you're still single. And you're still single because, secretly, you don't *want* to get married," she explained triumphantly. "That's why you keep going for such useless or unavailable men."

"Lizzie, I think it would be better if you psychoanalyzed yourself rather than me—after all, you're the one with the shaky marriage."

"Well, I am looking at myself, of course," she said. "But the fact is, I'm looking at you too. Because I'd really like to help you, Tiff."

"Er, thanks," I said.

"And so I began thinking about you and what's gone so horribly wrong with your love life."

"Oh."

"Yes, I began to reflect on this succession of disasters that you've had and this constant, *constant* rejection. Because, let's face it Tiffany—you're a complete failure with men. But having known you for so long, I've now been able to work out *why* you've experienced nothing but abject and humiliating *failure* and spectacular unsuccess."

"OK, OK, you've made your point."

"You see, Tiffany, I've spotted the pattern," she went on. "You always go for men who can't or won't commit. Like that rugger player at school—John Harvey-Bell—the captain of the Fifteen. It all started with him—now he wouldn't make a commitment to you."

"Lizzie, he was seventeen."

"And then all those useless chaps at college, like that boring actor whatsisname, Crispin Wilde—God I saw him on the box the other day, he was hopeless. God knows how he gets the work. Anyway, he wasn't interested in marrying you either, was he?"

"We were only twenty."

"And ever since you graduated it's been just one romantic disappointment after another for you. Unremitting failure. Chronic. You spent a long time with Phil Anderer, and of course *that* didn't work out—because we all warned you about him, didn't we?"

"Yes," I said dismally.

"And what did you do? You went right ahead and laid yourself down on his sacrificial altar and handed him the knife. And then Alex turned out to be useless too, didn't he?"

"Yes. OK, OK." Oh God I wished she'd stop.

"And *yet* . . ." Lizzie continued, theatrically holding up a forefinger and cocking her head on one side again in that irritating way, ". . . there have been *plenty* of men you could have married—if you'd wanted to. Take, for example, Alan from the tennis club. Mad about you, from what you said."

"Yes. But there was that small matter of the second head."

"And that actuary from Acton."

"Oh, him. The human anaesthetic."

"And that accountant—Mick—he liked you. What was wrong with him?"

"I didn't fancy him. End of point."

"And Peter Fitz-Harrod was keen."

"I told you what I thought of him."

"Not to mention *Kit*," she concluded. "Why *didn't* you marry Kit, Tiffany?"

"Because . . . because . . . he was . . ."

"Decent and kind and interesting and good-looking and *extremely* considerate and very suitable!" she said triumphantly.

"No. Because if I'd really wanted to marry Kit then I could have done because he wanted to marry me but I *didn't* want to marry him because although I really liked him and think he's wonderful and yes I happily admit that we have an awful lot in common it just didn't *feel* right, because we were simply too alike and would have driven each other mad although yes I do sometimes have regrets about it now and wonder what would have happened if we *had* got hitched and what it would be like with our five children and what we would have called them and yes if Portia does dump him and I don't find anyone else and he's still interested in me in that way which frankly I very much doubt after all this time then I might *very* well be tempted to marry him, does that make it clear?"

"Oh it's all very clear, Tiffany. You see, there are men who might have done, but you didn't want them. And the reason why you didn't want them is because they were available, perfectly acceptable men, who might have ruined everything by marrying you! So what you do is reject them and go for useless commitophobes. And Seriously Successful fits this pattern, too. Because the point is, Tiffany, that Seriously Successful has a wife."

"I know that, actually,"

"And so he's not likely to marry you."

"I know that too."

"And yet you still like him."

"No I don't. Not really. Not much."

"And you still think about him."

"No I don't—hardly ever in fact."

"Yes you do, Tiffany. You think about him all the time. Why?"

"Why?"

"Yes—why do you think about him?"

"Why do I think about Seriously Successful?"

"Because he's got a wife, that's why! So here is yet another *utterly* useless, unavailable man who isn't going to marry you in a month of Sundays—*perfect*! And moreover," she continued, "I bet that if his wife were to meet with some unfortunate accident—"

"Lizzie, please don't say things like that. I wouldn't wish that on him or anyone."

"Yes, but if, purely for argument's sake, she was, shall we say, off the scene, and he was suddenly available, I guarantee that you'd instantly lose interest in him," she concluded. "Because that would ruin your little game. Do you know, psychiatry's the most *fascinating* subject," she added. "I'm thinking of doing a course in it actually. In fact, I'm thinking of giving up acting altogether and becoming a counselor."

"Oh God. I mean—oh good."

"Yes, I really think I've got quite a gift for this kind of thing you know, Tiff," she said, lighting a post-counseling cigarette. "I've got emotional insight. I mean I've got you figured out, haven't I? If Seriously Successful was suddenly Seriously Single, then you'd run a mile!"

Would I? *Would I?* That was just the question I was asking myself as I passed the doors of the Ritz on my way to Jonathan's party. The Ritz! His local! Local. God, perhaps he was in there, right now. He probably was, no doubt interviewing some other hapless woman for the position of part-time sweetie. Absolutely outrageous. Seriously Swineish. I bet that's where he was. Bastard. Wonder if he got my postcard? As I walked past the hotel, well, I just couldn't resist—I decided to have a little teensy weensy look.

I went through the swinging doors in Arlington Street with a pounding heart. No sign. I could hear the blood pumping in my ears, like a fetus hears the beat of its mother's heart. My cheeks felt hot and flushed. My mouth was Sahara-dry. I felt the familiar fluttering of Amazonian swallowtails against the lining of my stomach. I must be mad, I thought as I penetrated the pink and green Rococo interior. I must be off my rocker. Still, I reflected, if I *did* bump into him—God forbid—but if I *was* unlucky enough to see him, at least I knew I was looking OK in my Jean Muir and my luxurious-looking fake leopardskin coat which I bought in New York last year for a song and which everyone says really suits me. Elegant outerwear is *so* important . . .

"Tiffany!" I turned round. Oh God. Oh *no*.

"Hallo," I said. "Er, how nice to see you. How are you?"

"*Splendid!* Ha ha ha ha ha! *Splendid*. How are you?"

"Fine."

"Did you get my messages?"

"Er. No. No. I didn't."

"I left a couple of messages for you in the summer. On your answer phone."

"Oh I've had *such* problems with that machine," I said, rolling my eyes in mock exasperation. "Sorry not to have got back to you, but it obviously didn't record them."

"Anyway, what are you doing here?" he said. Bloody cheek!

"Well actually, Peter, I didn't like to tell you this before in case you were a bit of a gold digger, but the fact is I live here. Yes. That's right. In one of the deluxe suites on the top floor. They're only six hundred and ninety-five pounds a night plus VAT." Actually, I didn't really say that at all. I just said, "I'm on my way to a party in St. James's Square and I've just popped in to see a friend, in fact . . ." I looked at my watch. "Ooh! I'm running late—must dash, but *so* nice to see you again."

"Yes," he said. "We must have that game of tennis!" Must we?

"Oh yes, we must," I said. "We must. Yes."

"Yes. Ha ha ha ha ha! I'll give you a ring."

And then—as if in a dream—I saw him. I thought I must be hallucinating. But I wasn't—it was him. I mean I hadn't *seriously* expected to see Seriously Successful. But now, here he was. This was Seriously Surprising. And he had seen me too. But he didn't stop—he walked straight past me; and the reason *why* he did that is because he could see that I was talking to another man and he was filled with jealous rage. And he thought that if he *did* stop, he'd probably *kill* Peter Fitz-Harrod. Fell him with one mighty blow. Or hurl his puny body across the crowded bar. Who the hell am I kidding? The only reason why Seriously Successful didn't stop to speak to me is that he was with *another woman*! A beautiful woman with a lovely figure and long, curly chestnut hair. And she looked very close to Seriously Successful indeed. She was leaning toward him slightly, and they were both talking in low voices and smiling. And I wanted the ground to swallow me up. And the lingering aroma of his Givenchy made me almost faint with desire.

"I'm going now," I said to Peter weakly. "Bye."

"Oh—ha ha ha!—er goodbye, Tiffany! I'll ring you!"

"Yes. Don't," I said as I pushed on the revolving door with my head.

What a bloody fool you are, I said to myself as I stomped down Piccadilly. What a bloody fool. Because the fact is, that if I hadn't gone into the Ritz, I wouldn't have seen Seriously

Successful with that gorgeous brunette. Damn. Damn. Damn. And *damn* Peter Fitz-Harrod for being there and speaking to me and holding me up, because otherwise I might just have walked straight out of the hotel again, in which case I would *not* have seen Seriously Special with that other woman and had my life completely ruined. And now I was going to have to go to a party when I was no longer in the mood for it, because all I wanted to do was go home and lie down on my bed and howl.

As I marched down Jermyn Street my high heels pinged on the pavement, the noise ricocheting like gunfire around the surrounding buildings. By the time I turned into Duke Street my heartrate had slowed to about 185 and I felt slightly calmer. Though depressed. Terribly depressed. But he's *married*; I repeated it over and over, like a mini-mantra. So he's no *use*. He's just looking for a bit on the side. Nothing to get very excited about. Really, Tiffany, get a grip. You've got a party to go to here. Wonder if he got my postcard? Wonder what he thought of it? Wonder how long he's known that attractive woman. Wonder if he loves her? Hope he didn't show her my card. I was then tortured by thoughts of Seriously Successful and Gorgeous Girlfriend lying in bed, naked, in his exquisitely appointed apartment in the Albany, having a postcoital laugh at my provocative postcard before consigning it to the elegant leather bin which they'd bought on a romantic weekend in Florence.

I stamped up the steps of the East India Club, a grand, white stuccoed building in the corner of St. James's Square. I found the cloakroom, splashed cold water on my burning face, reapplied my lip gloss and concealer, then found the Clive Room on the ground floor. Inside, about two hundred people were chatting away as though they'd known each other all their lives. Probably had, I reflected. I really wasn't in the mood to make tiny talk over the canapés with a crowd of total strangers. Then, luckily, I saw Jonathan.

"Tiffany, how *lovely* to see you!" he exclaimed. "So glad

you could come. Now this is Sarah—but you've met before, haven't you?"

"Yes, briefly," I said, raising my voice above the cocktail cacophony.

"That's right. We met at that party in Drayton Gardens," she said animatedly. "You were with . . ." Oh God, please don't say it—please don't remind me about Phil Anderer.

". . . that architect. He was very keen on golf, wasn't he? Talked about nothing else. I can't remember his name."

"Nor can I—ha ha ha!" I said. "I'm afraid that's all blood under the bridge now." Oh God, what a complete drag this evening was turning out to be. I'd started out feeling happy and hopeful and it had all gone horribly wrong. "So tell me," I said, with neon brightness, "when's the big day then?"

"In March," she said. "March the ninth, actually. You'll get an invitation."

"Oh my, I didn't mean—I mean I don't expect you to *invite* me. I was only asking, ha ha ha!" In fact, I was only making conversation. Trying to change the subject. God, now she'll think I'm one of these awful people who drops hints.

"Oh no, Tiffany, we really *want* you to come," she said earnestly. "Jonathan told me how helpful you were to him at the Eat 'n' Greet Sensational Singles party. He said you helped him 'see the light.' " She giggled. "You've no *idea* how grateful to you I am! Of course we'd like you to be there."

"Oh well, thanks . . . I love weddings. Especially other people's." I grabbed a glass of champagne from a passing tray; two sips and my stress levels began to drop down to stratospheric. Now, who else was here? I began to circulate. I was right about the posh factor.

"—we stayed with the Hurds last weekend . . ."

"—Rebecca's still at Benenden . . ."

"—well, in our corner of Kensington . . ."

"—no, we go down to Somerset . . ."

"—and then our younger son's at Eton . . ."

"—super little place near Bordeaux . . ."

"—no, no, not the Norfolk Higham-Hamiltons, the Suffolk ones, yes . . ."

"—her husband's an equerry you know . . ."

Oh my God—Pamela Roach! What was she doing here?

"What are *you* doing here?" she said with impertinent surprise.

"I gatecrashed," I replied, taking in her Full English Make-Up and tentlike dress. "Just like you." Actually I didn't say that, I said, "I was invited. I know Jonathan. How about you?"

"I was at school with Sarah. A couple of years ahead. I hadn't seen her for years but when I saw the engagement announcement in *The Times* I thought I'd ring her up to congratulate her . . ." Oh, that old tactic. ". . . and when I asked if they were having a party she very kindly said, 'Oh do come along.' It was nice of her."

"Yes," I said, "it was." God, how could I get away? I discreetly glanced round the room seeking an exit, and my eye just caught a rather handsome-looking chap. Standing alone. Tall and good-looking, in dark gray serge. Pamela followed my gaze.

"He's rather a dish, isn't he?"

"Who? Oh, him, Er, yes. I suppose so." *I couldn't care less if it was Pierce Brosnan, I'm in love with Seriously Successful.*

"He's got a very pretty girlfriend," she added maliciously, giving me one of her fishy smiles. "She's just gone to powder her nose. Have you got your business card on you?" she added. "You never sent it to me."

"No I haven't," I said. "I've forgotten to bring it again. Well, must circulate."

"Keep in touch," she said.

"Yes," I said. *I won't.*

Phew. I wish I could have brought Kate with me, I thought. But I remembered her advice at Eat 'n' Greet. "Just smile," she had said. So I gently made my way through the crowd, smiling in a general, all-purpose kind of way. And it does really, really work. Or at least, it does for some people, but it didn't for me. No one seemed to want to talk to me at all. And so I decided to study the paintings—the walls were lined with portraits of mustachioed Bengali lancers and Victorian viceroys. I wandered around, taking in their faces—"Sir Arthur Phayre, First British Commissioner for Burma, purchased Singapore for Britain . . . Major General Stringer Lawrence, 'Father of the Indian Army' . . . Sir George Pollock, took part in march to Kabul after the massacre by the Afghans . . ."

"Trotters!" What? I spun round. A handsome chap in a pinstripe suit was smiling enthusiastically at me.

"I'm sorry?" I said. "I mean have we . . ."

"Trotters! I've been trying to speak to you for the past quarter of an hour."

"I really don't think we know each other . . ."

"You're Tiffany Trott. Trotters."

"Yes, but you see I haven't been called that since I was at—"

"Look here, Trotters, this just won't do!" he said, whoever he was. "You don't remember me, do you? Can't say I'm entirely surprised. I mean I've changed a bit since I was thirteen." And then, suddenly, I got it.

"Nick," I said faintly.

"That's me," he said happily

"Nick Walker. School House."

"Yes. I used to deliver Harvey-Bells's *billet-doux* to you."

"Yes, of course—my God, how funny."

"And I used to offer to carry your books."

"You've grown a bit."

"And you had this incredibly sweet tooth, and I used to get stuff for you from the pastry shop. Chocolate éclairs—that's what you liked. And Jaffa Cakes."

"You were a little boy last time I saw you."

"And you were a real woman of sixteen. I worshipped you!"

"It's so nice to see you again, Nick."

"And do you know what, Trotters—you look just the same as you did then. Only, um, a bit slimmer."

"Oh *thank you,*" I said, "I think I love you." Actually I didn't say that at all, I simply said, "But I didn't have crows' feet then!"

"You were my one and only," he said.

"Well, there wasn't much choice—there were only ten girls," I said.

"Yes, but you were the one for me. I remember you standing on the touchline at rugger matches, Tiffany."

"Yes, and you used to lend me your scarf!" By now I was drowning in a sea of sentiment. I was sixteen again. I was at Downingham, surrounded by boys all offering to carry my books. Or asking me to help them with their prep. Or teasing me about my weight.

"Who do you know here?" I asked

"Jonathan. I work with him at Christie's. He heads my department—English furniture. I could get you a very good deal on some Chippendales," he said with a laugh.

"Oh, yes please!"

"And I'm very hot on Hepplewhite!"

"Oh good! Do you still see anyone from school?" I asked as we sipped our champagne.

"Oh yes!" he exclaimed enthusiastically. "Lots. How about you?"

"Well, not many, just Lizzie really."

"What, Battleaxe Bohannon? God she was bossy!"

"She still is."

"She was always telling me to cut my hair, and she wasn't even a prefect. Are you both coming to the OD dinner next week?"

"I don't know, hadn't thought about it."

"Well look, I'm going. Why don't you come too?"

"Oh, I don't know. I've never been to one of those school reunion things."

"I wish you would," he said, "I'll be able to talk to you properly then, you see I've got to go now. But look, it's next Wednesday, please do."

"Oh, I don't know . . ." My voice trailed away.

"Go on," he said enticingly.

"Well . . . maybe . . . I don't . . ."

"Good, you're coming then, Trotters—that's settled. And it'll be *great* fun!"

November Continued

"It'll be *great* fun," I said to Lizzie the following day. "Please come."

"Well, I'd love to. In theory. But I'll just have to check it with Martin."

"Sorry?"

"I'm going to check it with Martin," she repeated very slowly. "You know, Martin, my husband."

"Well, quite."

"Just to make sure he's happy for me to go."

"Oh, well . . . good idea," I said. "Er, ask him." I could hear the phone clatter onto their George the Third sideboard, and the sound of Lizzie's footsteps echoing down the hall. "Darling," I heard her say. "Tiffany wants to know if I'd like to go to the OD reunion dinner at the Law Society next Wednesday. But I said I'd ask you first. So I am. Asking you. Is that OK, darling? If I go? You sure? Sure you don't *need* me? Oh you *are* an angel. And you don't mind putting the girls to bed on your own? Sure? Oh all right then. I'll tell her yes, shall I? If you're really sure you don't mind. Thank you, darling." Then I heard her approaching footsteps. "It's firm," she announced. "He says he doesn't mind if I go. So sweet of him—so yes, I'll come with you. We'll see all those boys again. What a scream! And there's another reason, of course, for us going, Tiffany."

"What's that then?" I asked.

"You might *meet* someone you *really* like!" This was true.

And indeed that possibility had not been lost on me. It had already occurred to me that there might be boys who, like Nick, had metamorphosed from grubby caterpillars into handsome butterflies in the intervening years.

So the following Wednesday I met Lizzie at Chancery Lane. She looked very elegant in a black Donna Karan trouser suit with a silver velvet devoré scarf, her short, white-blonde hair tucked back behind her dainty ears. She was calm and smiling, and somehow she'd lost that—how can I put this nicely?—*violent* look.

"How's Martin?" I asked casually, as the banistered steps of the Law Society came into view.

"Martin's *fine,*" she said with a beatific smile. "He's *fine.*"

"So he's not having it off with Jade Jewel, then?" I said. Actually, I didn't say that. I just said, "Good."

"You know, that weekend with his mother really *did* something for him," she added. "He came back with a much more— I don't know, positive, *purposeful* air. Perhaps it was all that wood-chopping he did."

"Perhaps."

"Chopping wood's such a wholesome, *manly* activity, isn't it?"

"Oh yes."

"I like men to behave like *men,*" she said. "Don't you?"

"Er, yes," I said, as a vision of a surprised-looking Alex clad in satin and black lace hove into mental view.

"We've ordered the new sofa," said Lizzie. "I wasn't mad on that other one anyway."

"Same color?"

"Oh *no,*" she said, "not that *awful,* wishy-washy yellow. *Totally* impractical. I realize that now. No, it's going to be a deep red. 'Claret,' I suppose you'd call it, or possibly 'Bordeaux.' Or maybe 'Mulled Wine.' We'll christen it at Christmas," she added.

"Good idea," I said. *You could get Martin to grind some*

mince pies and brandy butter into it and then set it on fire.
"Here we are." We went up the steps of the Law Society and
then downstairs to the cloakroom.

"Do you know, I feel quite nervous," I said as I carefully
reapplied my lip gloss. "These guys haven't seen us for twenty
years—what if they don't recognize us?" Fear gripped my
heart. "What if they have to ask us *who we are*?"

"Don't be so negative, Tiffany," Lizzie admonished me as
she carefully combed her hair. "I'm sure they'll all tell us how
incredibly *young* we look." She took a step back and appraised
her reflection in the full-length mirror. "You know, we really
look perfectly OK . . ."

". . . considering that we're practically fifty."

"Quite. But isn't it amazing, Tiffany?" she said as she
dabbed "Opium" behind her ears.

"What?"

"The fact that you went to school with seven hundred boys,
and yet here you are, two decades on, *still* single!"

We went upstairs to the library for predinner drinks. The
walls were lined with tooled, leather-bound legal books as thick
as telephone directories. Two hundred men in dinner jackets stood in small groups, drinking, smoking, and gossiping
noisily.

"—no no no, I was in Dewar House. With young, whatsisname—Downer."

"—I was in Gordon's. I was the only one who wasn't gay—
hur hur."

"—oh God, women—always thought it was a damn shame
the way they let gels in like that. Glad it didn't happen in *my*
day."

"—did you hear about Cockayne? Damn shame. He was a
good man. Good man. Got five years."

At the far end of the room was a seating plan, with year of
entry next to each name. Lizzie peered at it.

"There are quite a few chaps from our generation," she said, raising her voice above the stentorian din. "But none of the other girls seem to be coming. I would have thought Isla Moray might have turned up. Anyway Hennessy, Jamieson and Bass are all coming. And—ooh good—Johnny Rothman's going to be here too. I always liked him. He was in my history set. I heard he's in TV drama now—maybe he could get me some work, just to tide me over of course till I start doing my counseling . . ."

"Bohannon, you old battleaxe!" Lizzie's face had frozen in horror. A middle-aged, red-faced man with beads of perspiration on his brow was bearing down on us. Roger Six-Pack! Mad Irishman. God he'd aged. It was frightful. He looked forty-eight but could only be thirty-nine at most.

"I used to fine you for smoking, didn't I, Bohannon! I see you haven't kicked the filthy habit. Hello, Trotters! Well, I must say . . ." He took a step back to scrutinize us. "You two look . . ."

"Older?" I volunteered happily. *Like you!*

"Yes!" he said, with a roar of laughter. "And even lovelier. I used to fancy you rotten, Bohannon, despite the fact that you always smelt like an old ashtray. Yer married?"

"Yes," she said, giving him a permafrost smile. "*Happily* married."

"And what do yer do with yerself?"

"I'm an actress," she said, clearly miffed that this was a fact of which he was patently unaware. Had he not spotted her name in the listings in *Radio Times* in 1991, or seen her in that bit part she had in *The Bill*? Evidently not.

"An actress, eh? And what about you, Trotters?"

"I'm in advertising—I write copy."

"Oh—Go To Work On An Egg and all that? Now, did you know that was written by an OD—Salman Rushdie! Poor blighter."

"No," I said. "It was Fay Weldon, actually. Salman Rushdie

did . . . oh look! There's Tim Flowers. He used to tease me about my weight."

"Trotters!" said Tim Flowers with a smile. "I'd hardly recognize you."

"Thanks," I said.

"You look—different. You used to be a bit on the plump side, didn't you, but that's obviously all behind you now! Ha ha ha!" Very funny, I thought, as I felt my face redden. And then I suddenly remembered what the boys used to say. It was never, "Where do you come from?" They always said, "So tell us, Trotters, where were you *reared*?" and then run off down the street in hysterics. Oh yes, I thought that was marvelously witty. They really should have charged me for that one.

"Hallo, Trotters!" boomed Jamie Worthington. "Got any tuck? That's what you used to say, 'Got any tuck?' I remember you stuffing your face with chocolate éclairs."

"Yes," said Lizzie, "while all the other girls had anorexia. You never could spot a trend, Tiffany."

"Your old flame John Harvey-Bell is coming," said Tim. "We remember what you used to get up to with *him*."

"I didn't get up to anything with him," I said frostily.

"Yes you did—come on."

"I did not."

"You did, he said you did."

"Then he was lying."

"Come on, Trotters, admit it!"

God, these blokes hardly seemed to have *evolved*. They were still the barely pubescent public schoolboys of the late 1970s. In fact they could have offered themselves up to science for embryo research. Still, I thought to myself, I shouldn't complain—I'd enjoyed my two years at Downingham a lot. OK, I'd been teased quite a bit. Well, all the time, actually. But there were some very nice blokes and quite a few foreign boys which lent the place an international air—for example, there was Hans Heineken, George Budweiser, Philippe Gauloise and

Jean-Marc Courvoisier. No Krugs—they went to Eton, of course. But no, it was a very *mixed* school—those Schweppes twins were charming.

Then as we all trooped into the dining room for dinner, Nick came running up the stairs. "Hallo, Tiffany—I'm a bit late— oh gosh, you look nice. Can I carry your handbag for you? And can I get you some éclairs?"

"Stop it, Nick! Do you remember Lizzie?"

"Nick Walker—your hair needs cutting," she said. "And how dare you be so good-looking when I'm a married woman!"

He laughed. "You're not married are you, Tiffany?" he said, peering at my left hand.

"No," I said.

"Oh good," he said, and blushed. I glanced at him beneath lowered eyelids as a hush descended for grace. He really was *very* good looking. I couldn't connect this six-foot Adonis with the angelic little boy with curly blond hair who used to turn up at the girls' house with little notes for me. How old was he? Probably thirty-three.

"Benedicat benedicatur," intoned the Chairman of the Board of Governors, Sir Andrew Bass. And then dinner began.

"—Tripp House have done awfully well this year, won the rugger and the cricket."

"—I hear Whipper Wilson got the sack—he was a bit of a brute."

"—yes, he taught me in the LSD block."

"—these mushrooms are bloody good."

I looked at Lizzie. She was locked into conversation with Johnny Rothman. "—Tiffany and I both went to Bristol, and after that I went to drama school. No, not RADA. Why not? Well, I didn't *get in*, actually. No, not Bristol Old Vic—yes, I agree it's an excellent drama school. Well, it's very competitive, you know. No, not Central either. Yes, yes, I had a go. No no, *not* LAMDA, either. Where? Well, it was the Prudence Rutherford Academy of Dramatic Art, actually. Yes, in Thames

Ditton. That's right, PRADA. Well . . . you know . . . bits and pieces, I did have an audition for the RSC once. In 1984. Yes, it went *awfully* well. I did, 'Out, out damned spot . . .' No, I *didn't* get in. So tell me, have you cast *War and Peace* yet? I can do a *very* authentic Russian accent . . . Whadaya mean—*too old*?"

"Tiffany?"

The waiters were clearing away the first course.

"Tiffany?" My God—my old flame, John Harvey-Bell. The captain of the Fifteen and school Colossus. Except that his heroic luster was subsequently somewhat bedimmed by his unfortunate failure to get into Cambridge. But gosh, he was good-looking, though much of the muscle had turned to fat. I'd forgotten how blue his eyes were. Like Wedgwood, though his once-blond hair was now visibly tinged with gray. How typical of him to arrive during the main course. He was always late for everything—except a rugger match.

"How are you, Tiffany?"

"I'm fine. How are you?"

"I'm OK. Married. Four kids. Did medicine at Edinburgh. I'm in Harley Street now. The About Face Clinic for Cosmetic Surgery. What do you do?"

"Advertising."

"Oh, I know—Only the Crumbliest Flakiest Chocolate etc., etc." Funny that he should remember that one.

"And are you married?" he asked as the sherry trifle arrived.

"No. No. Too young."

"Ha! Quite. Well, here's Walker—he's single, aren't you?"

"Oh yes," said Nick, giving me what looked suspiciously like an adoring smile. "I'm single," he repeated as he poured me a glass of port.

"Now look, Harvey-Bell," Tim Flowers shouted across the table. "Worthington and I want to know *exactly* what you got up to with Trotters in your study in Michaelmas term 1978."

"Oh for God's sake," I said, passing the bottle to my left.

"Did you or did you not—"

"Bloody cheek!"

"With Tiffany . . ."

"Pur-leeze!"

"And if you did, what was she—"

"I'm sorry, I've got to go and talk to Glen Fiddich," I said. "Haven't spoken to him all evening. Excuse me."

"Anyway," said Worthington maliciously, "you're all barking up the wrong tree, everyone knows that Trotters was in love with the *Badger*!" This stopped me dead in my tracks.

"I was *not in* love with the headmaster," I said. "Even though he was, admittedly, an extremely attractive, charismatic, cultivated, liberal and sensitive man."

"I remember the way you used to look at him in chapel," said Worthington accusingly. "The rapture on your face when he strode up to the lectern in his gown. You were *mad* about him."

"I was not," I said crisply. "I just admired him, that's all." This produced an explosion of mirth.

"Well I admired the way he sacked me," said Flowers, "just for a couple of kilos of hash—I ask you. It wasn't even my fault. I was looking after it for my parents. I think it's very good of me to come along to these dinners in the circumstances."

"Look, I really don't want to discuss your substance abuse," said Worthington drunkenly. "I want to know *exactly* what Harvey-Bell and Trotters got up to in his study in 1978."

This was pathetic. I was bored. No potential husbands here. And Lizzie was rolling her eyes and pointedly tapping the face of her watch. Time to go.

"Oh don't go yet," said Nick. "Come to Annabel's with us. Worthington's a member."

"Well, maybe another time," I said. "I want to get home—I've got some slogans to write. Bye, everybody." I waved. "It was fun. Bye bye, John."

"Bye, Tiffany, nice to come across you again," he said with

an indolent smile. "And please don't hesitate to give me a ring."

"A ring?"

"Well, you know. I'd be delighted to give you a discount . . ."

"Discount?"

"Well, I could give you a very good rate on liposuction or a chin tuck."

"Oh, well that's very generous of you."

"That offer goes for you too, Lizzie," he said. "My boob lifts are pretty impressive."

"Thanks," she said acidly.

"Oh it's nothing," he added as he lit a Havana cigar. "Old school tie and all that."

"Well, we'll certainly bear it in mind," she said as she swept out of the dining room with a flourish of her devoré scarf.

"Tiffany!" It was Nick. Running down the wide staircase after us.

"Yes, Nick."

"Harvey-Bell didn't mean to hurt your feelings. He's a bit dim really—always was."

"It's all right," I said. "I know he meant it nicely." But Lizzie was in no mood to be mollified. She stamped downstairs toward the cloakroom, leaving me with Nick.

"I just wanted to say that *I* think you still look very young."

"Thanks, Nick."

"No, really, just like you did at school. Only slimmer of course. Much."

"Thank you."

"I mean, to me, you'll always be sixteen."

"Well, that's very sweet of you to say so."

"In fact, Tiffany—it's been so nice running into you again. I wondered, I mean I know you're very busy with your slogans and everything, but would you have dinner with me next week?"

"What? Um. Well. Yes," I stammered, "that would be *lovely*. Here's my card. Er, give me a ring."

Two days later I came back from a walk on Highbury Fields to find the answer phone flashing at me frantically. My finger sprang onto the "Play" button. *Beep. Beep. Beep*

"Hello, Tiffany—ha ha ha ha! It's um, Peter here." Oh God, not him *again*. "It was so nice to bump into you the other day ha ha ha—how are you? I just wondered whether you'd like to have that game of ten—" I hit the fast forward button. *Beep*.

"Hi, Tiffany." It was Sally. Phoning from *work*. That was un-usual. She never normally had time to make social calls from the office. "Tiffany," she said calmly, above the babble of busy options traders. "Don't you think life is just *amazing*? Don't you think it's *wonderful*? I know I do!" What on earth was she talking about? "I mean, I'd always thought that when it came to life's journey I was a hopeless map reader," she went on calmly. Oh God, she must be drunk! And it was only eleven-thirty. "But," she added mysteriously, "I think I've just found the way." Found the way? Oh! So that was it—she'd had a re-ligious conversion. That would explain it. She'd been indoc-trinated by some sect, though I didn't think the Jehovah's Witnesses could get up to the fifteenth floor of Chelsea Har-bor. "I'm sure you'll find the way too, Tiffany," she concluded happily. "Bye for now!"

Bizarre, I thought, as the tape wound forward for the next message. Her brain's gone AWOL. All that slaving away in the City had finally taken its toll. *Beep*.

"Tiffany!" It was Emma. Sounding distressed. Close to tears in fact. "Tiffany, don't you think life is a complete bitch," she said crossly. "Don't you think that it's all just *horrible* and messy. And aren't men horrible too! With their beastly . . . *complications*!" she spat. "And never ringing when they say they will. Just thought I'd share that with you. Oh God I'm pissed off!" she added splenetically. "Sorry about this—just letting off steam here. And I can't get hold of Frances—she's in court all day. Anyway, can't really talk now, I'm in the staff room. But give me a ring, will you?" *Beep.* What on earth was going on there? *Beep.* But the next call put Emma's problems—whatever they were—right out of my mind.

"Tiffany! Hi! It's Nick." Hooray! I'd really hoped he was going to ring. "Tiffany, how about that dinner—are you free on Thursday? Will you meet me at Orso's? Only ring me back if you can't make it, otherwise I'll see you there."

On Thursday I put on my new Phase Eight silk dress which I'd bought specially for the occasion, and a modest amount of makeup, then found my way to Wellington Street. When I went downstairs to the restaurant the manager told me that Nick had already arrived. He stood up as I approached the table, smiled and then kissed me on the cheek.

"Oh Tiffany, it's so lovely to see you again," he said happily as the waiter spread a large napkin over my lap. His evident warmth was terribly touching. And he looked gorgeous. He was wearing a dark gray, pure wool suit with a pale yellow tie and interesting-looking cufflinks. And he smelt nice, too. I smiled at him and felt myself transported back twenty years.

"You were always so nice to me at school," he said, pouring me a glass of Pouilly-Fumé. "Even though I was a little squit, then. But you used to make me toast and coffee when I came round with those notes from Harvey-Bell. Well, they weren't really from Harvey-Bell," he added quickly, and he blushed. "They were from me, actually. He was useless at English. In fact he hadn't a clue. He didn't even know that *Hamlet* was by Shakespeare! So I used to write them for him like Cyrano de Bergerac. You know, he didn't deserve you, Tiffany," he added seriously. I gazed at him. He was incredibly handsome. And he was thirty-three. Not such a big age gap really. I began to go through a list of famous men with older partners—Alfred Molina and Jill Gascoigne, Greg Wise and Emma Thompson, um . . . there must be others. Anyway, it's not unusual, I thought to myself as I sipped my wine. What does it matter if a bloke's a few years younger?

"Did you enjoy the OD dinner?" Nick asked as our starter arrived—cured ham in aspic for him, tomato and mozzarella salad for me.

"Yes, sort of," I conceded. "It was just like being at school again!"

"I go to those dinners every year," he said.

"Gosh, do you?"

"Oh yes," he said enthusiastically. "I mean, Downingham was such a wonderful place, wasn't it?" he added with passionate sincerity.

"Well, yes. I really enjoyed it. I mean—it was fun."

"The sight of the chapel on frosty mornings could bring tears to my eyes," he went on sentimentally. "Even the memory of those awful dormitories can bring a lump to my throat. They were the best days of our lives, weren't they?"

"Um, well, I don't know . . ." To be honest, I think my happiest time was at Bristol, so I decided to turn the conversation to other things. I found out about his family; he was an only child, like me, and his mother had died when he was at prep school.

"My father lives in the States now," he said. "I don't see him very often."

"And tell me about Christie's," I said as our main course arrived. Smoked trout for him, pan-fried Dover sole for me.

"Oh, it's fine. The sales are fun. I've been there so long, Tiffany—fifteen years—you see I didn't go to university. I went straight onto the Christie's trainee course after school. Now," he said with sudden animation, "do you remember when Courage House did *The Government Inspector*?"

"Um, vaguely," I began, racking my memory.

"Oranjeboom had the main part," Nick went on enthusiastically. "He was brilliant."

"Mmmm," I began. "You must have a better memory than me, Nick, to be honest I can't say I really remember it."

"And *you* were *fantastic* in that Chekhov," he added. "God, I'll never forget it. *The Seagull.*" His eyes appeared to mist over. I glanced at his cufflinks, they were two teardrop-shaped pieces of amber set in eighteen-carat gold.

"And what sort of things do you do in your spare time?" I inquired.

"Well, I do enjoy the odd game of tennis," he said. Tennis? Ooh good.

"Oh I love it too," I said happily. "I like to play at least once a week."

He leant forward. "Do you remember when Watney won the public schools tournament?" *No.*

"Um . . ."

"God, he played like a demon. Slaughtered this chap from Harrow six-love, six-love." Suddenly, a doubtful expression passed across his face. "Or was it six-love, six-two . . ."

"And what else do you like to do when you're not working?" I persisted as our desserts arrived. Chocolate ice cream for me, compote of preserved fruits for him.

"Well, I'm very keen on cricket," he said. "Oh Tiffany, wasn't it funny when Tom Player bought a bull from the local cattle market and released it onto the Close during the house cricket final? Bloody funny," he added, shaking his head with a gentle laugh.

"Oh yes. Ha ha! Yes, it was," I said.

"Bloody funny," he said again, with a grin. "We did get up to some jolly japes, didn't we?" he went on happily. "I'll never forget Roger Speed getting expelled for defecating out of a top window in Crack House while Sandeman stood in the quad below and caught it in a saucepan."

"Oh yes, I do remember that," I said weakly, looking down at my ice cream.

"Mind you, it was bloody dangerous," Nick added seriously.

"It was a very high window. I mean Sandeman could have been *killed*."

I glanced around the restaurant and realized what had been troubling me. There were no windows. It was below ground, so you couldn't see out. There were just these white-tiled walls, and absolutely no view onto the street. I was glad the meal was coming to an end, I suddenly felt overcome by claustrophobia, in fact I was almost gasping for air.

"Oh Tiffany, it's been such fun seeing you again and talking about old times," said Nick as he got the bill. "I'll be away for most of December, I've got to spend two weeks in New York for work, and then I'm going to go up to New England to spend Christmas with my dad. So I won't be able to see you again before January, but can I ring you early in the New Year?"

"Yes," I said. "That would be lovely."

"There are so many more things for us to talk about, Tiffany," he said as he gallantly handed me into a cab. I pulled down the window. "So many things. Do you remember when . . ." he began.

But the cab had already started to pull away.

November Continued

"I've made a conquest," I said to Kate over the phone the following morning. "Nick Walker. He's adorable."

"Adorable? Oh—that means you're not really interested," she said.

"Well, I don't know," I said. "Maybe I am. He's terribly nice. And very good looking. But he's rather young. He's only thirty-three."

"But Tiffany, that's nothing. My mother is seven years older than my father and Mike's nine years younger than me." Oh yes, of course, her new chap, Mike, the Man from the Ministry. He's working in London now, and Kate's very keen.

"Age gaps really don't matter," she went on. "Personally I *like* younger men, I keep telling you that. And they're much better for—"

"Kate," I interjected. "I like Nick a lot. He's very nice. But I'm just not sure. We've only had one date."

"Well, are you going to see him again?"

"Yes," I said. "But not until the New Year. So I'm not going to think about him until then. Now where shall I meet you tonight?"

"Let's meet at the gallery," she said. "It's just off Piccadilly. I'll see you there at a quarter to seven."

I knew nothing about the Oscar Reeds gallery except that it specialized in conceptual art. And although I'm really not keen on that kind of thing—in fact I hate it—it would at least be, well, interesting, and Kate and I were both looking forward to seeing Eric again. He was nice. He was good looking. He was obviously set for artistic success. Perhaps I ought to try and fall for Eric, I thought to myself as I passed Hatchards. Maybe I could be his muse, and in a few years' time, when he's famous, art critics would acknowledge my influence on his work, just as they acknowledge the influence of Françoise Gilot on Picasso, or of Camille Claudel on Rodin. And in newspaper interviews Eric would say things like, 'Of course, I owe it *all* to Tiffany. Without her I'd be lost. I'd be *nothing*. She's my inspiration. She's the source of all my creativity, just as the mountain stream is the source of the sea.' Ye-es. Perhaps I should pay a little attention to Eric, I thought. Anyway, now that Seriously Successful has found himself a gorgeous brunette to be his bit on the side, I can go out with anyone I like. Anyone. At. All. How could Seriously Successful *do* that? I thought to myself bitterly as I passed Fortnum and Mason. Oh no—more beastly Christmas decorations. And it's only November. And I *hate* November—it's such an incredibly *long* month, it goes on for ever. I mean how could Seriously Successful be so fickle—just because I turned him down? That didn't give him the right to look at other women. Bastard. What a pity I have to come to Piccadilly so often, I reflected. Where Seriously Successful lives. With his glamorous neighbors, such as Alan Clark. Maybe Alan Clark's to blame, I thought bitterly. Leading Seriously Successful astray. Teaching him a few tricks in the infidelity department. Wonder what Seriously Successful's flat's like, I thought. Wonder what he's doing right now. Wonder whether he still thinks about me. God I wish he lived in Pinner rather than Piccadilly, then I could forget him more easily.

Kate was already waiting outside the Oscar Reeds gallery, and we went in together. It was thronging. What a crowd! Very . . . male. Very . . . urban. Ooh! Lots of pierced noses and studs in eyebrows and shaven heads and Doc Martens.

"Hello you two!" said Eric, giving us both a kiss. "Really glad you could come. Go and get yourselves a drink and then come and talk to me."

"We'll be right back," I replied, moving into flirt mode. "Now, don't you go away!"

A forty-something man with floppy blond hair, horn-rimmed glasses and a very fat behind was standing by a table on which there were some bottles and glasses. He ignored me completely.

"A pint of white wine, please," I quipped happily, "and a packet of pork scratchings."

He gave me a filthy look. He was clearly immune to my charm. "I'm not a bloody barman," he said testily. "I own this gallery."

"Well I'm sure that's very nice for you," I replied, "but my friend and I would like a drink." My hackles, needless to say, were vertical.

"Get it yourself," he said, nodding at the bottles of table wine.

"Thanks very much," I said curtly. "Kate, would you like bad red, or bad white?"

"Red," she said, reddening. "Tiffany, let's go and look at the pictures."

"What a *rude* man," I said in a deliberately loud voice as she led me away by the sleeve.

"Shhh. Don't react. It's not worth it."

"He *owns* this gallery and he treats guests like that! How does he sell any pictures?"

This was actually rather a good question. How indeed? Eric's work consisted of body parts, photographed from odd angles and blown up to huge proportions. A woman's foot, so enlarged as to give the dainty bones the scale of gothic fan vaulting; a clenched fist photographed in such a way that it looked like a range of jagged hills; an ear lying, like a huge conch shell, on a deserted beach; an enormous blue eye, like a lake; a pair of cavernous nostrils, three feet across.

"Snot very good," I said to Kate. "It's *really interesting,*" I lied to Eric two minutes later. "*Terribly* original and thought-provoking. I *love* conceptual art."

"My work is about the topography of the body," he explained seriously. "We each have a physical landscape with ridges, and furrows and crests . . ."

". . . and plains."

". . . yes, and plains."

". . . and crags."

". . . yes, and crags."

". . . and grassy knolls."

". . . yes, yes, quite."

". . . and peaks," I said.

". . . yes. And peaks."

"Mine are size thirty-eight, ha ha ha!"

He didn't seem to find that funny. "Please don't trivialize my work, Tiffany."

"Sorry," I said, "but really, I do think your work is awfully interesting." *Why don't you try watercolors of Norfolk instead?* I looked around. The crowd certainly was interesting—very modern, very chic. Lots of men, giggling.

"—ooh Kevin, you are a one!"

"—Saatchi was here earlier, you know."

"—Tracey Emin—fabulous."

"—give me Marcel Duchamp any day."

"—did you hear Damien on *Kaleidoscope*?"

"—uses his own blood."

"—I hear Oscar Reeds is in big trouble."

"—Brit Art is really *great*."

"—gallery's been threatened with closure."

"—waxwork ding-dong."

"—*no* money."

"—I prefer American minimalism myself."

And as we circulated it was the detail that jumped out. A man with a heart-shaped birthmark on his right cheek; a late sixty-something woman with a suspiciously taut lower face; a young chap in his twenties, with hair as white as Warhol's. And people weren't really looking at the pictures at all—they were looking at each other. Women discreetly eyeing men. Men eyeing men. Men eyeing women.

"What the hell's that man staring at?" I suddenly said to Kate. She followed my gaze.

"*You,* you idiot," she said. "Look, I've got a really bad headache. You stay a bit longer, but I'd quite like to go home. Do you mind?"

"Er no," I said.

"And also, I'd like to see Mike," she admitted, blushing visibly.

"That's all right, Kate. You don't have to explain," I said. That's the last I'll see of her for a bit, I thought ruefully as she left. I decided to stay a little longer. Perhaps have another chat with Eric. But that bloke was still staring at me. Did he know me? He certainly looked vaguely familiar. And then he began moving in on me. He was about five foot ten with dark curly hair and a long, Paxmanesque nose. About forty-five. Where had I seen him before?

"Hell*ooo,*" he said, extending his hand. "Mungo Brown." Mungo Brown. Now that was quite familiar. But whence?

"I *know* that name," I said. "But I don't know why. Have we ever met?"

He chuckled. "No, we haven't. Because if we had, I would certainly have remembered your name." Oh, what a *nice* thing to say, I thought happily.

"My name's Tiffany," I said. "Tiffany Trott. Now, *why* do I think I know you?"

"Well, ha ha ha!" He coughed delicately. "I think it's because, well, you've probably seen me . . ."

"On the number 731!" I said.

"No. On the television, actually." Television? *Television?* Oh *yes.* Of course.

"Got it," I said happily. "You're a reporter."

"Correspondent, actually," he said slightly huffily. "*Special* Correspondent. Social Affairs. ITN." *Oh yes.*

"I'm sorry I didn't remember you straightaway," I said, "but to be quite honest the only reporters who stick in my mind are those incredibly brave foreign reporters, like George Alagiah, John Simpson, James Mates . . ."

"Yes, yes," he said distractedly.

". . . Mike Nicholson, Lindsey Hilsum, Bridget Kendall . . ."

"OK, OK."

". . . and of course Kate Adie." He rolled his eyes. "But I'm afraid when it comes to domestic news the names don't really register at *all*. What have you done recently?"

"A very interesting piece for *News at Ten* on problems in the Welsh clam industry."

"Oh, is there much to say about that?" I asked.

"Yes," he said, "clams have a lot to tell us . . . look, I'm really rather bored of this show. Would you like to come and have a drink with me?" Gosh—very forward. Ummmmm.

"OK," I said. "Why not?" I said goodbye to Eric, gave Oscar Reeds a valedictory glare, then exited with my new acquaintance.

"Where shall we go?" he said

"The Ritz!" I said. "It's not far." *And we might see Seriously Successful, whom I love.*

"Er, I don't think I want to go there," he said. "My tie's not quite smart enough for that."

"Oh, I think your tie's fine," I said.

"Let's go to the Red Lion," he said. "It's just behind St. James's church."

So we did. And he bought me a half of lager, and he sat there and told me *all* about himself.

"I'm just getting divorced," he explained. "I was married for fifteen years. My wife didn't understand me. I said she should go to a shrink. She said she didn't need one. Bloody ridiculous." He was really rather an attractive man, I thought to myself as he talked away. And he's getting divorced. Ah *ha*. And he had a good job. A very good job. And that would go down well at the tennis club, wouldn't it? "Oh hallo, Mrs. Chumleigh, this is my husband. Mungo Brown. Yes that's right. *The* Mungo Brown. Yes you have seen him. On the television. That's why he looks so familiar. Yes, that's right. On ITN. After the break." Mmmmmm. Wonder how encumbered he is.

"Do you have any children?" I inquired with a casual air.

"Yes," he said. "Five." *Five!* For crying out loud. Still, perhaps they were all grown up and off his hands.

"They're eleven, seven, five, three and eighteen months," he explained.

"Oh. Lovely ages. Lovely ages," I said, while mentally deleting him from my list of potential life partners. Damn and blast. He really was rather good-looking. But then, on the other hand, I do *like* kids—I could be like Maria with the von Trapp children. All singing songs and escaping dangerous situations and doing amusing things in harmony. I could hear them now. "Oh Tiffany, we're so lucky to have *you* as our stepmother."

"Can I get you another drink?" I said to Mungo.

He gave me a grateful smile. "Yes please," he said. "I'll have a triple Grouse."

December

Canned carols. Hateful holly. Crass cards. Grotty grottoes. Miserable mistletoe. Tedious, tawdry tinsel. Effing fairy on top of the evergreen, plastic tree. Santa and Rufus and sleighbells going *ring ting ling a ling, ring ting ling a ling ling*! Gosh I love Christmas! The Salvation Army band. Piping choristers with apple-cheeks and crisp, pleated ruffs. Sitting by a blazing log fire with the man of your dreams, joking and laughing and . . . oh God oh God oh God—it's *that* time of year again. The Bleak Midwinter. Jingle Bells. Such a wonderful time for us Single Belles. Deck the Halls with Boughs of Holly, tra la la la—tra la la la! 'Tis the Season to be Jolly Pissed off, actually. And, of course, Christmas in all about babies, isn't it? Being "in the sixth month" and all that, swaddling clothes and cribs and all the rest of it, and then giving birth in some sub-NHS middle-eastern manger with a steady stream of concerned visitors.

Siii-lent Night. Ho-ooly Night, droned Bing Crosby in Selfridges today. And the annoying thing was—I mean talk about the potency of cheap music—but the annoying thing was that it really *got* to me. I tried not to let it, but it did. In fact, it was extremely embarrassing.

"Why are you crying, Tiffany?" Alice demanded as we stood in the queue for Father Christmas on the fourth floor.

"DON'T ask her THAT," shouted Amy. "Tiffany's CRYING because SHE'S NOT MARRIED. She HASN'T got a HUS-

BAND. She hasn't EVEN got a BOYFRIEND. THAT'S her PROBLEM."

"I am *not* crying because of that," I said indignantly, while wondering what on earth Lizzie said about me to the girls when I wasn't there. "I'm simply crying because I've got some dust trapped under my contact lenses, that's all."

"Of *course* you have, Tiffany," said Lizzie handing me a tissue. "OK Alice and Amy—don't forget, one request only."

"Oh *Mummy*," they wailed.

"Last year they asked for sixty-three things each," she said. "It was hideously embarrassing. They'd brought a list and refused to leave until they'd got to the end of it. I had to drag them out. Hope it's not the same man this year. And if he attempts to sit *either* of them on his knee," she added fiercely, "I'm *suing*."

"Look, I'll wait outside," I said. "There's no need for me to come in too." I wandered down to Menswear to get a tie for Dad. I looked through all the different makes. Dunhill, that might do. Lanvin—lovely, but a bit flash for him. Yves St. Laurent—not quite his thing. Ralph Lauren . . . Ralph Lauren . . . that reminded me. It reminded me of the time I bought Phillip a silk tie from Thomas Pink. It was rather nice, silvery-gray with a scattering of tiny scarlet motifs. It wasn't for his birthday or for Christmas. It was just a present. And I felt quite shy about giving it to him because I hadn't been going out with him that long—just a couple of months—and I really, really hoped he'd like it and I knew that it would go with his favorite gray suit. But when he opened it, he looked at the label and his face fell, and he said that he wouldn't accept it because he only wore ties from Ralph Lauren. I bet Seriously Successful wouldn't have done that, I thought to myself. If I'd given *him* a tie, he wouldn't have said to me, "Look, I'm sorry, but I only wear Hermès ties." He'd have said, "How lovely, Tiffany. Thanks very much. I really like it." And I think he'd have said that even if he *hated* it. Even if he thought it was the most hideous tie ever produced in the history of neckwear. Because Seriously Successful may have a wife, and quite possibly a girlfriend too, but he's also got good manners. I bought Dad a nice tweedy, speckly sort of tie in olive green, and then met Lizzie and the girls in the mezzanine café.

"God it was embarrassing," said Lizzie as Alice and Amy went up to get some more cake.

"Why?" I said. "Did they ask for too many things?"

"No. It wasn't that. It was the fact that I knew Santa! I recognized him from drama school. He was the star of my year—he played Romeo. And after that I saw him on TV once or twice and then he seemed to disappear. And here he is—in the Selfridges Christmas grotto."

"Did you say anything to him?"

"Of course not!"

"Why not—did you think he'd be embarrassed?"

"No. It's just that the girls *believe* in Father Christmas. How could I say, 'Hallo, Jeffrey, I remember you from drama school.' The game would really be up then."

I caught the number 73 home, while they took a cab back to Hampstead. And I sat staring out of the window, at the tinsel-dressed windows, and the frosted glass, and the bright lights swinging overhead in the stiff breeze, and the souped-up synthesized carols kept circulating in my head. *No crib for a bed. . . lays down his sweet head . . . infant lowly, infant holy . . . he smiles within his cra-adle . . . a babe with face so bright.* And I thought about babies, as I often do these days, and wondered whether I would ever have my own special delivery. A sweet little cherub, with downy head and huge blue eyes and bendy little arms and legs and . . . oh God, what a *din*! I wish that baby would *shut up*! I turned round and glared. Some people just let their babies scream their heads off on public transport, don't they? *Waah! Waah! Waah!* Totally sickening for everyone else. Where was I? . . . oh yes. Babies. The infant Jesus. Christmas. And, to make things worse, the forecast is for snow.

That nice man John Kettley was right. Six inches came. Overnight. This morning I walked down to Highbury Fields, my feet crunching into the thick layer of glistening, pristine white. The air was clear and clean. The sky a refulgent blue. Snowflakes drifted down from the trees, and were whipped up by the thin, sharp wind into meringue-like peaks and folds. And the roar of the traffic was dulled by this dense, blue-white blanket. All you could hear was the shrieking and laughter of a hundred children at play. There they were, all bobble-hatted and cherry-cheeked, being pulled along on toboggans, pelting each other with snowballs or building portly, serious-looking snowmen.

"Mummy! Mummy! Faster! Faster!" a little boy yelled as his mother pulled him along behind her on a plastic sled. They were both giggling, almost hysterical. I thrust my hands deeper into my pockets and turned up the collar of my old loden coat. The snow crunched and groaned underfoot, the sharp sunlight stung my eyes. And as I stood watching them I wondered whether I could ever go it alone. On my own. With a baby. Whether I could be a single mother. A lone parent. Like Sally. *Sally!* Of *all* people. I mean, I just couldn't *believe* it. Of all the women I know, Sally was always the least likely to go down that road. Sally, who just a few months ago said that she would never ever have a baby without a bloke, is intending to do just that.

"I've known for sure since mid-October," she said last night as we sat at my kitchen table, "although I didn't want to say anything in case it didn't, you know, happen. But now I know it's definitely on its way."

"When?" I asked.

"May."

"Wow! Well, um, congratulations!" Is that what one said on

these occasions? Were congratulations necessarily in order when one's single girlfriends announced that they were pregnant? I wasn't at all sure. I looked at her—she certainly looked very happy. And she looked different. Her face seemed to shine as if something was radiating her from within. Her eyes were animated and lucent, not red-rimmed from lack of sleep. And she hadn't got out her laptop all evening. She had sat with me in my kitchen, talking and laughing—though I had wondered why she'd refused to drink, just as she had at the firework party—and then, as we sat down to eat a looping mound of spaghetti carbonara, she had quietly dropped her bombshell.

"I've found the way," she concluded happily as she replaced her fork on her plate. So *that's* what her bizarre answer phone message was about. "I've found the way," she repeated. "And this is it. At least, for me. Aren't you going to ask me who the father is?" she added mysteriously.

"No," I said, "I'm not. Because it's absolutely *none* of my business. Er . . . is it anyone I know?"

"No," she replied with an odd little laugh. "It's no one *I* really know either." Curiouser and curiouser.

"He was my guide," she explained. "On holiday, in Rajasthan in August. A well-heeled young English guy working for the company, doing lecture tours of the Mogul palaces. We were all staying in the Lake Palace at Udaipur and, one night . . . well, it's a very romantic spot."

"I know," I said. "That's where William Hague went on honeymoon. Are you going to tell him? I don't mean William Hague," I added quickly. "I mean, your um, your um, father. Not *your* father, though you probably *are* telling your father— I mean the chap. The father of your child."

"No," she said. "I'm not."

"Why not?"

"Because he's only twenty-two." *Gosh.* "And he's about to start a Ph.D. at Oxford in Indian architecture. How could I impose a responsibility like that on him just as he's starting out?"

"But he might *want* to know," I pointed out.

"I very much doubt it," she said. "And it's better if he doesn't. What good would it do? We're not in a relationship, and we're never going to be in one. It was just, you know, a moment really. And anyway, it's my choice to have the baby. Not his. I mean, no one *has* to have a baby, do they?"

"Did you do it on purpose?" I asked.

"No," she said thoughtfully. "But nor did I take any particular measures to avoid an 'accident.' "

"Nor did he, it seems."

"I know. But he's very young. And a bit silly. And he believed me when I said he didn't have to worry."

"Oh. Oh. I see."

"In any case his parents are very pukka, rather uptight people from what he said. I'm sure they'd be absolutely horrified. Just like mine are."

"*Are* they?"

"Yes. Completely. Can't accept it at all, though I guess they probably will when they see the baby."

"But you said your parents would *love* you to have a baby. You said they were always going on about how much they'd like to have grandchildren."

"Oh yes," she said, "but not like *this*. I'm afraid it's gone down like a cup of cold sick at home."

"But you're thirty-eight."

"I know. But I'm still their little girl," she explained. "And I'm their only daughter. So naturally they're disappointed that I'm not going to have the white wedding of their dreams to their fantasy son-in-law. Anyway," she continued, "they're pretty unhappy about it, and for the time being they don't want to know. And that's why I'm telling you, Tiffany."

"Well, it's nice of you to confide in me," I said as I got out the double-chocolate ice cream. "I promise I won't breathe a word."

"No, no, it's more than that. I didn't just want to tell you to get it off my chest. I wanted to ask you something."

"Yes?"

"A favor."

"Yes. If I can."

"It's a big favor."

"Ask away," I said as I shut the freezer door.

"It's a *very big* favor."

"Sally, I really don't mind. You know I'd do *anything* to help."

"OK then. Will you be my birth partner?"

"WHAT?"

"I'd like you to be there with me when I have the baby."

"Er. Well. I'm terribly squeamish, you know."

". . . and I was wondering if you could come to some of the ante-natal classes with me."

"I'm not sure I'd be much use, really."

"You see, I need someone to give me moral support . . ."

". . . just doesn't sound like my kind of scene at all, Sally."

". . . as I don't have a man."

"Oh God, oh God."

". . . and you're the only person I know well enough to ask. I can hardly ask my younger brother," she continued, "my mother's absolutely anti, and I don't have any other women friends to whom I feel sufficiently close."

Gosh. Well. Flattery does work wonders, doesn't it? But to be honest, I was a bit surprised, because although I like Sally a lot, I really do, I would never have said we were best friends. But it's *me* she wants. Me! How amazing. "Well, *of course* I will," I said.

"Thanks, Tiffany. You're a *brick*."

And so this morning, it really got me thinking about the whole subject. Babies. I suppose if Fate handed me a card like that I'd probably play it too. But some women—they set out to be single mothers. Deliberately. They have a one-night stand, or they ask a friend to oblige, or they pop down to the sperm bank. But that's always struck me as highly risky because you don't know what you're getting, do you? I mean, it would be OK if you could go down there and say, "I'd like some Pierce Brosnan please, or if you're out of him, I'll have some Kevin Costner or possibly a little Bill Gates." But it isn't like that, is it? It could be any ugly, scrofulous student with criminal tendencies and a genetic predisposition to athlete's foot. No. No way. I'm not doing that. At least Sally knows what she's got. And by May she'll be a mum. Gosh.

Anyway, I arrived back home after my walk in the fields to find the answer phone flashing at me in a cheerful fashion. Ooh goody. A message. Not from Seriously Successful, who appears to have given up on me completely, but from Mungo Brown.

"*Hello,* Tiffany," he said in his slightly affected drawl. Or maybe he was drunk. "It's *Mungo* here. I hope you're *well.* I really enjoyed meeting you at the Oscar *Reeds* gallery last week and, um . . . I wondered *whether* you'd like to come to a little *dinner party* I'm having at my house *in Shepherd's Bush* on Friday. Just a small do. Just *six* of us. Hope you can make it. Around eight? Give me a ring will you, to let me *know.*"

On Friday I put on my long Nicole Farhi sweater which conveniently covers my bum, and a woollen miniskirt which really flatters my legs, popped on my leopard-skin coat and a fur-trimmed hat, and set off for Shepherd's Bush. Bit of a schlepp frankly, and the Central Line's so slow! *Please Mind the Gap,* said that annoying woman over the Tannoy again. Well yes, I *will* mind the gap, I thought to myself. I really *do* mind the gap. That fifteen-minute gap between trains. God, it was eight o'clock already and I was still stuck at Oxford Circus. I hate being late for dinner parties. And I hate it when people are late for mine—turning up at half past nine by which time the first course is curdling and the main course is practically carobonized. So I always try to arrive on time for other people's. But this time I knew I was going to be late. Damn. And I'd forgotten to bring my mobile phone. Well, I hoped they'd all have started without me. Much better.

"Oh I'm so sorry I'm late," I said to Mungo when he opened the door to me in Stanlake Road. "I do hope you've all started . . ." I stopped. All? What all? Where were the other people? He had said it was a dinner party for six.

"Oh, are the others all later than I am?" I asked, handing him a bottle of rather good Sauvignon. "It's eight forty-five already."

"Well . . ." He gave a little laugh. "I'm afraid there aren't any other people, actually I . . ."

"What, you mean they all canceled? Oh *bad* luck!" I said. "It's terribly annoying when that happens. That happened to me on my last birthday. I had forty-four cancellations. Perhaps you should have rescheduled for another day. I wouldn't have minded."

Mungo didn't say anything, he just took my coat with a rather lingering look which swept up from ankles to throat. "What a fabulous fur," he said. "I love leopard-skin."

"Oh it's not real of course," I said swiftly. "Budget won't stretch to it, ha ha ha ha! Just joking. I wouldn't wear real fur. Of course not. But that doesn't mean I'm vegetarian. I'm not." And then I noticed something. Or rather an absence of something. Cooking smells. No aroma of roasting lamb, or grilling fish, or baking quiche. Nothing. Just a dusty, fusty smell. And what a bare, tiny place. Like a studio flat. Just a sofa and a telly in the living room, and a few badly upholstered chairs. He'd said "house." His "house" in Shepherd's Bush. That was funny.

"Nasty little place you've got here," I said. Actually, I didn't really say that. I said. "Well, the December air has made me quite peckish!"

"I'm a hopeless cook," he said, "so I thought I'd order in take-away." A take-away? Astonishing. "Do you like Indian?" he inquired.

"Er. Yes," I said, "I do."

"Or perhaps you prefer Chinese?"

"No. No. Indian would be fine," I said. "Fine."

"Would you like a drink?" he said.

"Yes please."

"Sauvignon OK?" he said with a laugh. My Sauvignon, evidently.

"Yup. Sauvignon would be just fine. How long have you lived here?" I asked as he poured me a glass of wine and then opened a tiny packet of peanuts, like the sort you get given on planes.

"About six months. Of course it's a bit cramped. But my wife got the house in Hammersmith, the law being the ass that it is."

"Well, I suppose she needs it with five kids."

"Yes, maybe, although I would have preferred it to be sold. But there you go," he added with a sardonic little smile. "Divorced men get a bum deal."

"Why *are* you getting divorced?" I asked boldly.

"I don't know. She just kicked me out. She became a religious nut actually, started going to this weird church in Notting Hill . . ."

"Gosh—I'm surprised she had the time to go to church with five kids."

"—and they indoctrinated her. They convinced her that I was this mean, uptight, drunk, lascivious, domestically useless chap who she should never have married in the first place," he said. "That's bloody sects for you."

"Oh dear. Is your wife very impressionable, then?"

"No I wouldn't say so. Anyway, it's all a drag," he said. "Let's order some food. They usually take about forty-five minutes to deliver." He handed me a leaflet from the Tip Top Tandoori House in the Uxbridge Road.

"I'm going to have a number seven, a number forty-three and a number fifty-six," he said.

"Oh, I'd like the prawn garam masala and the chicken tikka, and some pilau rice, please—that's number six, number twenty-nine and number forty-one." Gosh—it was just like doing the lottery! Mungo phoned the restaurant while I stared at the walls. The Anaglypta wallpaper was lifting off at the sides, like a scab.

"Could I just use your bathroom?" I asked. He showed me where it was, and I went in. It was disgusting. Unwashed bath. Scabrous toilet. Taps that were encrusted with lime. An old toothbrush holder and some tiny soap, clearly from a hotel or airline. I had a quick peek in his cabinet—always fascinating, isn't it, the contents of other people's bathroom cabinets? My God! Women's makeup, and deodorant. A small bottle of Oil of Olay, and a can of hairspray. Whose was that? I was happy to see that it was Head Start—the one that Kit had worked on. Then I sat on the sofa again while Mungo fiddled with a rather ancient, portable cassette player. He put on some Ella Fitzgerald. This was undoubtedly the worst dinner party I'd been to since college. How long would it be before I could get away? Still, he was, at least, attractive. Extremely attractive, in fact. And I was starving. That's the trouble with drinking—one glass of good white wine and I'm ravenous. I'd eat and then plead an early night.

The bell rang. He went to the door and took delivery of the food, in four paper carrier bags. Then I heard him say, "Tiffany, I'm a bit short. Have you got any cash?"

"Er, yes, hang on a minute," I said, mentally renaming him Mungo *Mc*Brown whilst I reached for my bag.

"I need another fifteen pounds." Fifteen pounds! "Thanks."

He went into the tiny kitchen with the food, and reappeared with plates and plastic forks, and little sachets of salt and pepper which bore the legend, "Dan Air." At least the food was good, I thought to myself as he poured me another glass of wine. And then, I don't know what it was, perhaps it was just the fact that I felt replete and comfortable and slightly tipsy, I just sat back into the sofa. Which is why I didn't really care as he sat there and talked about his wife and his divorce.

"—outrageous really, she got an ouster order . . . kicked out of my own home . . . and most of the money that went into that house was mine you know . . . she didn't really work . . . just a bit of teaching . . . her parents never liked me . . . big problems with her father . . . he's a lawyer, so of course they're going to shaft me . . . should never have married her . . . mind you the kids are great . . . though she's trying to turn them against me . . . those people at her church should be strung up."

"Why don't you ask me something about myself?" I said indignantly. Actually, I didn't say that at all. Because the fact is that I couldn't have cared less. I knew I was never going to see him again, even though he was, really, very, very attractive. I just nodded and made polite noises as his monologue reached fever pitch.

". . . and no sex, you know. She wouldn't."

"Well, she did five times at least," I said.

"Yes," he said morosely, "if they're all mine."

"Oh dear."

"Do you like my suit?" he said suddenly, fingering his viscose jacket.

"Yes," I said. "It's very nice." *Nice and shiny.*

"It was only thirty-five pounds," he said happily. "In a warehouse sale."

"That's good," I said with a discreet glance at my watch. Ten past ten. Good, I could leave soon.

And then something odd happened. Mungo stood up, went to the light switch, and dimmed the overhead light to an amber glow. Then he went to the TV and put in a video. And then he came and sat next to me—right next to me, so that our thighs were touching—on the sofa. What, I wondered, was going on? The TV flickered into life. Then he turned and gave me a lecherous smile. Oh God, not a dirty video, I hoped. Pur-leeze. I

found myself staring at his collar, the ends of which were curling up as if in disgust. And the collar was getting closer and
closer and then I realized he was going to snog me. Definitely.
Yup. This was about to become a snogging situation. His face
approached mine, his lips pulled back from this wall of even
white teeth. Oh well. A snog's a snog.

"Dawn over Aberystwyth . . ." said the voice on the video,
which I instantly recognized as his. I looked over at the television. There was Mungo, standing on a Welsh beach, the collar
of his trenchcoat turned up against the wind. "This is home to
the Welsh clam," he said as he walked along the sand. "A cot-
tage industry which provides employment for hundreds of
local people. And now . . ." he said, turning and looking dra-
matically out to sea, ". . . the clams are drying up."

I glanced at Mungo, sitting next to me on the sofa. He was no
longer looking at me. He was gazing with an expression of intense but happy concentration at his own projected image.
"This bit's really good," he whispered confidentially, as the
picture cut to an interior scene in a local restaurant. And there
was Mungo again, napkin tucked into shirt, spoon poised over
a bowl of soup. He dipped it in, took a sip, and gave the camera
a thoughtful sort of smile. "The clam chowder you can eat in
Aberystwyth is as good as any you'll find in New England," he
said. Suddenly, Mungo stopped the video, and rewound it.

*The clam chowder you can eat in Aberystwyth is as good as
any you'll find in New England . . .*

"You see, what's so good about *that,*" he explained, "is that
I had never before attempted to record a link with my mouth
full."

"Well, it was marvelous," I said in a bored kind of way.

"Yes, I really was pleased with that. The camera crew were
very impressed." He started the tape again, and I sat through
the feature to the end, complete with interviews with Welsh
clam workers, indignant local people and poignant shots of
young children whose future as packers in the local clam fac-

tory hung perilously in the balance. Then Trevor McDonald came into view. "That was Mungo Bwown weporting from W-Wales," he said. The item had taken over ten minutes.

I turned to Mungo to ask for another glass of wine, but he was fiddling with the remote control. The screen scrambled, then cleared, and suddenly there was Mungo Brown again, sitting on a rock, in a windswept field, the collar of his trenchcoat turned up. "Here in the Outer Hebrides," he began, shouting over the gusting wind, "life has continued in much the same way for decades. Centuries even. But now the late twentieth century is impinging on the peaceful life of these crofters, and a new threat . . ." Suddenly a farmer in a Range Rover drove by shaking his fist at the camera. "Oops, we had to cut that bit out—we were on his land," Mungo explained. "Hang on." He wound it forward. ". . . a new threat is looming to the traditional way of life here in the form of a virus on the island's computers . . ."

Half an hour later, after I had sat through Mungo Brown in Nottinghamshire talking to ex-miners, Mungo Brown in Staffordshire with pottery workers, Mungo Brown in Lincolnshire with bulb planters, I had had enough of Mungo Brown.

"Look, this is fascinating," I said, standing up. "But I've really got to make a move."

"No—I'm the one who's got to make a move," he said with a drunken giggle as he grabbed me by the waist and attempted to wrestle me to the ground.

"For God's sake—get off! I don't even know you," I hissed as he started to loosen his tie.

"Oh come on, Tiffany, I know you want to."

"Bloody outrageous. How dare you! Who do you think I am?"

"You came here on your own," he said indignantly.

"I did not. I came here expecting to be one of six people," I retorted. "I had no idea it was going to be tête-à-tête."

"Well." He stood up, reddening. He straightened his polyester tie. "I seem to have made a mistake."

"Yes," I said. "You have."

"But I thought you might just want to—you know—"

"What?"

"Go with the flow."

"I do want to go with the flow," I said. "With the flow of traffic. I'm leaving now. Could you get me my coat? Thanks. Goodbye and . . ."—what should I say? A thank you was hardly in order—". . . good luck with your divorce."

December Continued

Being single isn't so bad really. In fact, there are lots of good things to be said for it, and every time I have a bad date I cheer myself up by enumerating the many advantages of living on one's own. On my way back from Shepherd's Bush I passed a pleasant half hour listing them in the little notebook I keep in my bag for this purpose.

TEN GOOD THINGS ABOUT BEING SINGLE:

1. You can spend a lot of quality time with yourself.
2. You can eat potato chips in bed.
3. Your Janet Reger is secure.
4. You are not married to a bastard, or even to Mr. Not-Quite-Right.
5. You do not have to be totally meticulous about cleaning the bath after use.
6. You do not have to look and smell alluring twenty-four hours a day.
7. You can put on weight if you wish.
8. You can watch *Xena: Warrior Princess* without being sneered at for you plebeian taste.
9. You can watch *Blind Date,* ditto.
10. You can put that buttery knife in the marmalade jar.
11. You can, in a no-panties situation, retrieve yesterday's pair from the linen basket.

12. You can converse uninhibitedly with your domestic appliances.
13. You can sleep diagonally.
14. You can fall in love.
15. Being single is an important fashion statement.

"You're right—being single and female is very chic," said Frances on the phone the following morning. "It's cool. I'm glad you've come round to my way of thinking, Tiffany. Marriage is passé—we're Lone Rangers. We're hip."

"I thought we were SINKs," I said, "Single Income No Kids. Or what's the other one? SINMOSSs: Single Income Never Married Owner-Occupiers. Or aren't we SINBADs? Still No Boyfriend, Absolutely Desperates?"

"No. We're Lone Rangers," she reiterated. "There's nothing desperate about us. We don't even need Tonto, because we're bright, independent, happy career women, who are having it *all*."

"All, that is, except for the husband and children."

"Yes. But we don't *need* a husband and children, Tiffany. We're the generation of women who can take or leave all that. Who can be perfectly fulfilled without it. And better a self-reliant single than a sad divorcée."

"Yes, that's right," I said. "We're single-minded."

"Quite."

"I mean, better sadly solo than miserably married."

"Er . . . yes," she replied uncertainly.

"Better suicidally solitary, than dismally divorced."

"Er . . . sure," she said hesitantly. There was a sudden lull in the conversation. Quite a long lull, actually. And then Frances said, "Anyway, men are so boring."

"I know," I said.

"Complete and utter *bores*. All of them."

"Oh yes, Frances."

"I mean, what is marriage, Tiffany, but the triumph of hype over experience?"

"Absolutely. Frances, did you know Sharon Stone didn't get married until she was thirty-nine?"

"Didn't she?"

"And Jenny Agutter was thirty-eight."

"*Really?* Oh well, I must say that's rather encouraging," she replied. "Anyway, I'll see you here for Christmas drinks next Monday, from seven P.M. OK?"

"I'll be there," I said.

Frances's parties are always jolly, even though a lot of her lawyer friends are frankly rather dull. All they ever talk about's the law. You try and get them onto some neutral subject such as the price of tomatoes, and before you know where you are you're knee-deep in European Directives and Common Agricultural Policy legislation and test cases before the European Court of Human Rights on conditions for workers in the Italian tomato industry. Frankly, it's a bit of a bore. Still, at least Kit's going to be there, I thought to myself, and Lizzie, and amazingly Martin's going to come too. I don't think he's ever been to one of Frances's parties before. He and Kit can carry on bonding. Maybe bang a few drums together. Or chop up the furniture. Or perhaps offer each other some voluntary body contact. But, before then, I've got to gen up on babies. It's Sally's first ante-natal class on Saturday morning. In Highbury. I told her I didn't mind coming over to her local group in Chelsea, but she felt it was unfair on me to have to travel that far.

"But it's not just that, Tiffany," she told me over the phone. I really don't *want* to go to a group in Chelsea."

"Why not?"

"Because the other day I went to an introductory evening at a house in Royal Avenue, off the King's Road, just to check it all out, and some of them weren't very nice to me."

"What do you mean, they weren't nice to you?" I said. "How could anybody not be very nice to you?"

"Hang on, Tiffany—can I put you on hold a sec, Washington's on my other line—sorry about that, where was I? Oh yes, well, one or two of the husbands—and some of the wives—but especially the husbands were rather, well, disapproving. They kept staring at my left hand and saying things like, 'I suppose your husband's too busy to come this evening—away on business, is he? Tied up in the City?' And when I told them that I didn't have a husband, they looked absolutely appalled. And then when I said I didn't even have a partner, they looked at me as though I were Myra Hindley. And then this fat bloke who works for Morgan Grenfell said that he thought it was a 'damn shame.' So I said, 'What do you mean, "damn shame"?' And he said, 'For the brat, of course.' "

"Outrageous," I said, outraged.

"I know," she said. "So that was it. I left. And all the other local groups are fully booked. But I've found one I like the sound of in N5 and that'll be easier for you." To be honest, this was true.

"I've had an EDD confirmed," she added excitedly.

"EDD? What's that?"

"Expected Date of Delivery," she said. "It's the first of May."

"Labor Day," I said.

On Saturday morning I met Sally at a house in Ronalds Road, just off Highbury Corner, not far from where she used to live before she moved to Chelsea. Sally's really keen on this whole pregnancy thing—really, really enthusiastic. But the funny thing is, although she's eighteen weeks, she doesn't look pregnant at all.

"Are you *sure* you're pregnant?" I asked her as we stood outside the tall, Victorian house at ten A.M.

"Absolutely sure," she said happily, tapping her tummy

which was as flat as a Dutch bulb field inside her size ten jeans. "I had another scan last week," she added. "And guess what?"

"What?"

"It's a girl!"

"Well, that's wonderful. If that's what you want."

"Yes I do, actually, I was really hoping for a girl. They say boys are a lot more work, so a little girl would be easier for me to manage as a single parent."

"What are you going to call her?"

"I don't know. Laetitia, possibly. Or perhaps Lydia. Or maybe Laura."

"Something beginning with 'L' then," I said. "How about Lois? Or Lycra?"

Just then the door opened. A large, gray-haired woman dressed in a loose-knitted tunic of an indeterminate shade of buff smiled at us beatifically. I found myself staring at her feet. She was wearing open-toed Birkenstock sandals, with no tights. In December.

"Hallooooo," she said. "I'm Jessie. Please do come in out of this bitter cold."

"Sally Peters," said Sally, extending her hand. "And this is my birthing partner, Tiffany Trott." Inside, about ten pregnant women had already gathered, with their partners, and were sitting around on beanbags in the large, double drawing room. "Desarts of vast maternity," I said to myself as I surveyed their mountainous forms. They sat there, sipping herbal tea and babbling about babies and bumps.

"—when are you due?"

"—morning sickness was awful."

"—chorionic villus sampling."

"—nuchal translucence, actually."

"—yellow nursery."

"—no, Johnsons' are supposed to be better."

"—pre-eclampsia is a nightmare."

"—very good offer this week at Mothercare."

Jessie clapped her hands, as though to attract the attention of small children at a dancing class, and the session began. The point of these classes, she said, was to prepare mother and partner for the baby's birth. The main activity would be yoga, in order to improve breathing to facilitate an easy delivery.

"The first thing I want you to do, is all introduce yourselves," she said.

"I'm Sally Peters, and I'm eighteen weeks!" said Sally happily, after everyone else had spoken up.

"You don't look *one* week!" said a rather vast woman to her right impertinently.

"Well, it's very hard to tell whether you're pregnant yourself," I said, "perhaps it's all blubber under that attractive marquee you've got on." Actually I didn't say that at all, I just glared at her.

"Oh I *am* pregnant," said Sally with a good-natured laugh. "It just doesn't show much yet, that's all."

What a mixture of people — most of the women were in shapeless khaki tunics and ubiquitous black or gray leggings. Sally, by contrast, was in a pink silk shirt and fitted stonewash jeans. And I couldn't help noticing that some of the men were looking at her. In fact, they couldn't take their eyes off her. And then they looked at me, out of narrowed eyes, with a somewhat prurient air.

"Er, I'm Tiffany. Tiffany Trott," I said when my turn came to speak. "I'm a copywriter and —"

"Go To Work On An Egg!" shouted one of the men, with a guffaw.

"Well, you obviously have!" I quipped back. "Anyway, *as* I was saying, I'm a copywriter and I'm Sally's birthing partner. But I'm not her *partner* partner, if you see what I mean, ha ha ha ha! Certainly not. No. Not that she isn't, of course, *extremely* attractive." And then I felt really annoyed because why should I feel I had to explain my relationship to Sally? It was none of anyone else's business. After all, we might be lesbians, and that's perfectly fine, because that other same-sex couple, Pat and Lesley, they certainly were. Lesley was having the baby, and Pat was, well, her other half. I knew that because when it came to the first yoga exercise, and we all had to get into the appropriate positions with our partner, I saw Pat give Lesley a discreet but tender kiss. Well that was entirely their own concern. *Nothing* to do with anyone else. Nothing at all. Though I did find myself wondering whether they'd got a friend to donate, or if Lesley had had a one-night stand, or maybe they'd gone down to the sperm bank, and if they had, who they had asked for? Peter Mandelson? John Prescott? Or maybe The Leader himself. Or possibly Seriously Successful . . . ? His offspring would be *very* high quality, I was quite sure about that. And then I thought, perhaps, if Seriously Successful's sperm *was* available for the purposes of self-insemination, I might go it alone after all . . .

"Tiffany, wake up!" hissed Sally.

"Sorry," I said. All the mothers-to-be were removing their shoes for the foot massage and the air was suddenly filled with the warm tang of unshod, sweaty feet. At least Sally's feet were nice, I thought, as I massaged them for her while she went, "Ooooooooooohhh! Hummmmmmmm . . . ooooooooooooooh! Hummmmmmmmmm . . ." like a mantra in a Buddhist temple. I glanced around the class. There were some really ghastly feet —thick, cheesy heels, dirty nails, cracked and calused soles, and toes, undulating with corns. But then I suppose your feet— are rather difficult to get at when you've got an enormous pro-tuberance in front. I made a mental note to get Sally to have a pedicure when she got too big to attend to her feet properly. She could afford it. After the foot massage it was time for the break.

"Now, all you chaps, and you ladies who are partners, I want you to make the herbal tea for your other halves," said Jessie.

"And your task is to make it while simultaneously holding, under your left arm, one of these soft toys. Do you think you can manage that?"

Well, it was going to be touch and go. We all snatched a toy from the pile—I just managed to get Peter Rabbit—and went into the kitchen. To be honest, making a herbal infusion one-handed isn't easy. And Peter Rabbit was absolutely no help. When I took the mug of fennel tea back into the drawing room the expectant mothers were all busily bonding, although the air crackled with catty competitiveness and a kind of bitchy solicitude.

"—oh you *do* look *tired*."

"—do you have a *problem* with water retention then?"

"—well of course we'll be getting *everything* from Osh Kosh."

"—we prefer Jacadi in *Harrods,* actually."

"—I wonder whether your breasts will *stay* like that — "

"—varicose veins are *so* unsightly, aren't they?"

"—I've heard they can go like empty bags afterward."

"—you must be, what, *eight* months?"

"—four and a half, actually."

"—what are *you* having, Sally?"

"A girl."

"Oh, *bad* luck!"

"Oooh . . . hummmm . . . oooohh . . . hummmmmmmm," Sally intoned as we walked down Ronalds Road in the crisp mid-morning air. "That was brilliant," she said. "I think I'm going to go for the natural approach, Tiffany. No drugs. Nothing. I want it to be a *real* experience, an epic, unforgettable event."

"Er, well, I wouldn't do that actually . . ."

"No really, I've decided. I'm going to give birth at home, in a warm pool."

"But I've heard hospitals are really wonderful places,

Sally, with lots of nice drugs and epidurals and lovely gas and everything . . ."

"I don't mind how long it takes."

"Not too long, I hope."

"I want to bring Lauren into the world in a memorable way," she said as she climbed into her soft-top BMW.

"But I'm sure Lucy would prefer a nice, neat Caesarian," I said, although I don't think she heard me. Natural childbirth? Twenty-five hours of crawling around on her hands and knees bellowing like a bull? You have got to be joking! I thought. Especially if I've got to be there.

"Yes, I'm going to have Lottie naturally," I overheard Sally say to someone at Frances's party the following Monday. "I really think it's the best approach. I don't want to be some anonymous body on a production line in a hospital."

"Which *is* your local hospital?"

"The Chelsea and Westminster."

"Oh, I've heard that's wonderful."

"Yes. Yes it is. It's fabulous. Like a five-star hotel. But that's not the point, is it?" she continued.

"Isn't it?"

"No. I want to give birth at home, in a pool, with soft music playing."

"Well, my specialty is medical negligence and let me tell you that I have to handle a lot of cases where home deliveries have gone horribly, horribly wrong." Sally shifted uncomfortably from one foot to another. She didn't want to hear this. "Now, let me just give you the background to one *particularly* fascinating case I handled in 1989," the man carried on. "It really was gruesome—in fact the baby died. Now the midwife in question . . ."

"I'd love to hear about it, but could I just get a refill first," I heard Sally say. "Back in a sec," she fibbed as she escaped toward the kitchen. Sally's always so tactful. It's one of her nicest qualities. That's what I noticed most when I first met her ten years ago. I'd been commissioned to write a brochure about her bank, Catch Manhattan, and she was chosen to brief me about the options and futures market. We've been friends ever since then. And I've never, ever seen her lose her rag, or swear, or show even the slightest irritation with anyone. Ever. She's got fantastic self-control.

Suddenly, the doorbell rang and there was Kit, with Portia. Oh *why* didn't I marry Kit? I thought, yet again, with a pang.

"Tiffany!" He gave me a lovely, enfolding hug. *Why didn't I?*

"Hallo, Kit," I said. "Hallo, Portia." Portia smiled at me. Very warmly. And this was unusual. And she looked . . . different. On the few occasions she'd agreed to come to my parties with Kit, she had stood around with a patently bored air, rudely tugging at his sleeve, or rolling her eyes at him in a conspicuous fashion to indicate that she'd had enough. This evening she looked more—animated. And she was holding Kit's hand. Quite possessively. I'd never seen that before.

"Sorry we're late," said Kit. "We just popped in to the Blow Coward Spank party for half an hour." That's why Portia was smiling, I thought—she'd obviously had a couple of drinks already.

"What a wonderful Christmas tree, Frances," Kit exclaimed. And it was. It barely cleared the ceiling, and it was beautifully dressed—no vulgar swags and bows in carefully coordinated colors, but a polychromatic confusion of pretty glass baubles and spangly beads, covered by a cobweb of white, twinkling lights. On the top was a porcelain angel with huge, gold chiffon wings.

"Kit, will you give me a hand in the kitchen?" said Frances. "I need someone to help me mix the cocktails."

I was left standing with Portia by the Christmas tree. She was so tall. She and Kit always looked a bit comical together, because he's five foot nine and she's almost six foot. Six foot three in her heels. But today she had flat shoes on. That was unusual. While she leant her elbow on the mantelpiece to steady herself, I subtly scrutinized her face: cheekbones you could stand a tray on, luminous skin, and large, gray-blue eyes which looked almost turquoise in the flickering half-light of the fire. It's not hard to see why Kit loves her. She's beautiful.

"I'm bleeding pissed off, Tiffany," she said in her native Streatham. "I've just done this *awful* shoot for *Harpers & Queen*. At Longleat."

"But it sounds fun."

"Well, it wasn't."

"Why not?"

"It was for swimwear, that's why. I'll be lucky if I don't get pneumonia. And that bloke who owns it, Christopher Thynne, he was hovering around."

"Perhaps he's looking for another 'wifelet,' " I suggested.

"Oh darlin', thank you," said Portia, as Kit brought us a couple of *enormous* Martinis and then slipped away into the crowd.

"In fact, Tiffany," she continued, knocking back half her cocktail, "I'm pretty fed up with being a model." Gosh. I mean, Portia had never really bothered to *talk* to me at any length before, let alone confide in me. "I'm thirty-two," she said, "I'm burning out. I'm much too old for it—the other girls all call me 'Grandma'—and the shoots are boring as hell."

"What about the catwalk?" I asked. "Isn't that fun?"

"I *'ate* the bleeding catwalk," she said vehemently, taking another mouthful of Martini. Gosh, she was really loosening up. "All that getting up at five-thirty to be at some airport. All that hanging around backstage with the other girls, bitching about the designers. I've made enough money," she added. "I want to do something more *meaningful*. I want to use my brain."

"Won't that be rather *academic* in your case?" I said. Actually I didn't say that at all. I just said, "What would you like to do?"

"Maybe work for the Samaritans," she said with another

large swig. "I'd like to help other people. I'd *reely* enjoy that. Sorting out their troubles. I've listened to enough problems from other girls over the last fifteen years to last a lifetime— drugs, drink, anorexia, bulimia, boyfriend problems, divorce, domestic violence, custody battles . . . the things I've heard. You'd hardly believe it. I'll ave to do a course, of course."

"Of course," I said, astonished. Gosh, this Martini was really, really strong.

"But the most important thing of all," said Portia, "is that I want to spend more time with Kit."

"That's a good idea," I said.

And then she looked at me and said, "Tiffany, why didn't *you* marry Kit?"

"Oh really, Portia, what a funny question . . . ha ha!"

"No, reely, Tiffany . . . why didn't you?" I pretended not to hear.

Standing just behind us were Lizzie and Martin, and they were talking to Catherine. "No we're not going skiing—we're going somewhere rather special, actually," I heard Lizzie say. "In January. Chile and Easter Island. Martin's *always* wanted to go to Easter Island, haven't you, darling?"

"Yes," he said happily. "I have."

"He's always had a bee in his bonnet about those massive stone statues."

"Yes," he responded, "ever since I was a little boy."

"They're really interesting," said Catherine excitedly. "No one knows how on earth they got there! I did them for A Level geography. You *lucky* things."

"Well I thought it was about time Martin got to do something *he* really wanted to do," said Lizzie, giving his arm an affectionate squeeze. "He works so hard. So my mother's going to come and look after the girls."

Then I saw Kit and Martin engaged in animated conversation—and wondered whether they'd ever told Portia and Lizzie where it was they'd gone that weekend.

"I know you think I've been a bitch to Kit," I heard Portia say. What?

"Good heavens no!" I lied, with a nervous sip of my Martini. "Why ever should I think that?"

She threw back her head and swallowed the rest of her drink. "Because I ave been a bitch to him, that's why. But he was so suffocating," she continued, waving her spiked olive at me and swaying slightly. "All that pressure. I couldn't stand it. All that pressure to have babies—as though that was all he needed me for. I wasn't even sure I *wanted* kids. I'm still not sure."

"Well . . ."

"And all those Teletubbies videos," she went on. "And the trips to Ikea. And I felt such an idiot in that bleedin' Discovery. It really got me down. He never understood, Tiffany. Until recently, he never understood that I wanted to choose, in my own time."

"Well, that's very understandable," I said.

"Yes. And at last he seemed to realize that," she said tipsily. "I don't know what it was, but he stopped being so claustrophobic. He changed. In fact he . . . but Tiffany, I just wanted," she leant forward. "I just wanted . . . to tell you something else." Oh my God, I didn't think I could take any more confessions from her. She put her hand on my arm. "I just wanted to tell you . . . how important you are to Kit," she said. Oh God, oh God, I couldn't take this. "And I'd never, ever stop you being close to him, because I know how much you mean to him. You always will." I could feel my contact lenses slip and slide as my eyes began to fill.

"Thanks," I said. "I feel just the . . . really don't know what I'd do without . . . er, sorry. Won't be a sec."

I sat in the downstairs loo, crying quietly. I can't take it when people get emotionally upfront with me. Can't deal with it at all. Especially in my present, pre-Christmas, pissed-off frame of mind. And she'd hit the nail on the head. Why *hadn't* I married Kit? It was too late now. But if I *had* married him then I wouldn't have had such an awful time with Phillip, or such a frustrating relationship with Alex, and I wouldn't now be going to hideous "dinner parties" in Shepherd's Bush or pining after married men with girlfriends. I could have avoided all that, if I'd simply said "Yes" to Kit eight years ago. But I didn't. I said "No." So it's all my own fault and I've been taking the consequences ever since. I splashed water on my face and went back into the sitting room, where the party was now in full swing.

"We're going to Easter Island together."

"Well, we'll be in Verbier."

"We're going to the South of France, actually."

"We'll all be up in Norfolk."

"We always go to John's parents."

We, we, we. All the way home. That's what Christmas was about. We. Us. Our. But I wasn't we. I was me. Myself. I. One. Singular. Single. Not double. A Lone Ranger. That was it. Lone. *Alone.* I probably always would be, I reflected miserably. With my crossword puzzles and my cross-stitch and my increasing cross*ness*. I'd never ever, ever find my spiritual twin now. It was too late. And if I did he'd be married, just like Seriously Successful. Gosh, how much had I drunk? What a mistake, it always made me maudlin. I decided to leave. I could feel myself coming perilously close to emotional meltdown. Portia had simply triggered what had been welling up for weeks.

"Oh Tiffany, do stay!" Frances boomed.

"Well, it's nine forty-five and I'm quite tired," I said. "But thanks for a lovely evening. I think I'll just slip away."

"Can't I call you a cab?"

"No, I'll get one on the high street, really."

The pathetic fallacy was clearly not fallacious at all, I reflected bitterly as I left Frances's house in the rain. The York flagstones were blurred beneath my feet as I tramped down Leverton Street and turned right onto Kentish Town Road.

What a dismal scene. Litter, heavy with water and streaked with dirt, lifted up and down in the gutter. A Coke tin rattled out into the road and was crushed like paper under a passing car. The shop windows were rimmed with white glitter and winked and blinked with cheap lights. No sign of any taxis, and I'd forgotten my mobile phone. I'd have to wait for a bus. Damn. But as I stood at the nearest stop a man suddenly emerged out of a dark doorway and staggered toward me, a can of Fosters clutched to his concave chest. He was probably only forty-five but looked sixty, with his gray-white hair and beard, his gnarled, arthritic hands and painful, shuffling gait. Oh God, winos at Christmas. Run away, Tiffany. Run away.

"HAPPY CHRISTMAS, YONG LADY!" he bellowed and then, oh God, oh God, he began to sing. In this cracked, but curiously lusty voice. " 'way in a-a MANGER, no crib . . . A BED . . . the little Lord JAYSUS . . . oh JAYSUS lady, have you a little somting for the homeless?" he said.

I dug in my pockets and felt a couple of pound coins. I handed them to him. But not kindly. Not in the spirit of good-will, but simply to get rid of him. I wanted him to go away. Just leave me alone. I couldn't take it. And there was no sign of a bus, and no taxis, but still the man stood there, belting out Christmas carols. And then he reached inside his coat and took out a postcard, and on it was a photo of Princess Diana in a pink satin gown and a diamond tiara, and her picture was seamed where it had been folded, and it was creased and cracked from wear. He showed it to me, and then he held it up with both hands and kissed it reverently, as orthodox Christians kiss icons. Then he slipped it back inside his fraying coat.

"She was a ministhering ANGEL," he said. "An ANGEL, that's what she was . . ."

"Yes. Yes," I said dismally, and then the carols began again.

"HARK THE HERALD ANGELS SI-ING . . ." That was it. I couldn't stand it. He wasn't going to move, so I'd have to. I'd have to wait at the next stop. And, as I walked away, my feet splashing into the puddles in the cracked paving stones, Seriously Successful hove into mental view again. I wondered whether things like this ever happened to him, and how much money he'd have given the man, and where he'd be spending Christmas. Not at home, with his parents, partnerless, like me. Probably with that beautiful girl I'd seen him with in the Ritz. The girl who'd had a good laugh at my silly postcard from Club Med. He'd probably take her skiing. Or perhaps whisk her away for some winter sun in, say, Tunisia, or Spain. Or perhaps she'd prefer Barbados. I was just torturing myself in this way and cursing myself again for not bringing my mobile phone with me when I found myself standing outside Radio Rentals. A thick bank of television screens flickered and danced in the window—all tuned to different channels. There was Jade Jewel, on location, somewhere exotic—where was it? It looked like the Cape. Next to her was David Dimbleby, waving his script at the *Question Time* studio audience, and peering over his pince-nez. And there was Barbra Streisand in *Hello, Dolly!* on Channel Five. And on the TV next to that, Trevor McDonald on *News at Ten,* introducing some report . . . and suddenly—oh God, wouldn't you know it?—there was Mungo Brown reporting from—where was he reporting from today? London. Kingsway. The word "Live" suddenly flashed up on the screen. He was standing with a group of homeless people, who were queuing for soup from a customized ice cream van. And Mungo was interviewing them, holding a large microphone under their bearded chins as they shivered in the damp, cold air. And then the camera followed him as he walked up to the van, and the shot closed in on the man in the thick donkey jacket who was dishing out the soup and . . . I caught my breath. What? What on earth . . . ? *Why* didn't I know that? Why didn't I know he did that kind of thing. My heart was banging in my chest. Why didn't I know that Seriously Successful helped the homeless? I pressed my face to the window, but of course I couldn't hear a word. What *was* he saying? I

desperately wanted to hear. I wiped the rain off the glass and
tried to lip read. I couldn't make it out at all. But I could see
that he looked vaguely irritated with Mungo, because Mungo
then suddenly turned back to the camera, looking slightly dis-
comfited, and I could see that he was signing off. I watched his
lips: "This is Mungo Brown. For ITN. In Central London."
And then there was Trevor McDonald again.

I was practically catatonic with shock. Seriously Successful,
helping out with a soup van. Seriously Saintly. Oh God, oh
God, and I'd thought so many bad things about him. I wished I
hadn't turned him down, I thought as I stepped onto the number 24.

I wish I hadn't said no to his part-time offer, because if I had
said yes, then at least I'd have been able to spend time with him.
We could have breathed the same air. Breathed the same . . .
Ooooohhh! Hummmmmmmm! Oooooooooohhh! Hummmmm-
mmmm! Ooooooohhh! Hummmmmmmm! These breathing exercises are terribly good for calming yourself down.

"Are you all right?" said the woman sitting next to me.

"No," I said. "I'm not. I mean, yes, I am."

"You don't *look* very well," she said solicitously.

"I'm fine," I said. "Really—thanks. Hummmmmmmm . . ."

"You're not pregnant, are you?" she asked.

"Well, not exactly," I said.

December Continued

"Hallo, Mungo," I said, the following day. "It's Tiffany here."

"Oh, hallo," he said, somewhat unenthusiastically.

"I'm just ringing to say that I saw you on the news last night."

"Well, you know, that's not unusual."

"Oh I know, Mungo. I mean, you're never off the small screen. But I just wanted to say that I thought your report about the homeless was really fantastic. *Very* hard hitting."

"Yes," he said, "it was."

"It had me really staring at the television set."

"Thanks."

"With my hands reaching into my pockets."

"Oh, good."

"And that chap you interviewed, whatsisname . . . oh I don't know, the bloke dishing out the soup . . ." I waited for Mungo to tell me his name. *Please tell me his name, will you, Mungo? Please.* "Er, I can't quite remember what his name is from the report . . ."

"Oh, that bloke in the van, you mean."

"Yes. Very interesting-looking chap." *Tell. Me. His. Name.* "I just wondered . . ."

"Interesting? Bloody unhelpful, actually. Didn't even know who I was and didn't seem to want to be interviewed at all." *Just tell me his bloody name, will you!* "Despite the fact that I was giving him a chance to appear live on national TV. He blew it, in my view."

"Who is he, Mungo?"

"Oh, I don't know. There are lots of them. Well-heeled volunteers who make soup every week for the homeless and dish it up from an old ice-cream van. He's loaded you see, they all are—that's how they salve their consciences, by dispensing oxtail to the poor."

"Yes, but, his name. I need his name."

"God, I can't remember. Never found out. He pissed me off, to be honest. Anyway, why do you want to know?" he added suspiciously. Ah. I'd already thought of that.

"Well, I'd quite like to get involved with a charity like that myself, and I thought he might be able to give me some advice."

"You'd be better off speaking to his girlfriend."

"Oh." A shard of glass pierced my right aorta.

"At least I assume that's who she was. I spoke to her before we began filming. She was hovering in the back of the van, out of camera shot."

"Oh." Of course.

"Rather attractive, actually," he added. "Long curly hair. She's called Grace. I managed to get her work number. Anyway, she'd know."

"Yes. I see. Well, not to worry."

"Don't you want her number, then?"

"Oh. No. No. It's OK, thanks. Anyway, er, Happy Christmas!"

All this had me thinking about Phil Anderer again. He used to go on and on and on about the homeless, about how disgraceful it was, and how pathetic the Tories were and how shameful that our streets should be filling up with unemployed people with no roof over their heads. He'd get quite hysterical about it, actually—well, he got hysterical about lots of things. And getting steamed up about the homeless was fine. In a way I liked it, but for the fact that I never, ever, in three years, saw him give money to a person on the street. Nor did he ever, ever, not even once, buy a copy of the *Big Issue*. In fact he'd walk straight past the vendors whilst I stopped, and I'd have to run after him to catch up. But he'd rant about it nonetheless. He saw no paradox in this, none at all—but his unconscious hypocrisy shrieked at me. And now here's Seriously Successful quietly, anonymously, trying to do his bit. Oh dear. I think I love Seriously Successful. Even if he has got a wife. And a girlfriend.

"Welcome to you all," said Father Ambrose, "whether you're regular parishioners or what I like to call my 'hardy Christmas annuals.' " Mum and I giggled—we fall into exactly that category. She's not the great churchgoer, and nor am I. We're lapsed Catholics. Incidentally, why is it that Catholics seem to have the monopoly on lapsing? Why do we not hear about lapsed Protestants, lapsed Methodists or lapsed Muslims? Or lapsed Seventh Day Adventists? Or lapsed Mormons? Or lapsed Jehovah's Witnesses, or lapsed Quakers or even, for that matter, lapsed Buddhists? Funny, isn't it? Anyway, lapsed or not, we'd hate to miss Midnight Mass. It's a ritual—no irony intended—a vital part of the year's end. And our local Catholic church in Shropshire is so beautiful: Victorian Gothic revival, with an elegant, dizzying spire, and an altar designed by Pugin. Anyway, at twelve-thirty on Christmas morning, the final chords of the last carol died away . . . *Oh come let us adore hi-im, Chri-ist, the Lord!,* and then everyone filed up to see the huge nativity scene in the side chapel. There was Jesus lying in the hay-filled crib, his blue eyes and his tiny palms turned heavenward; next to him, Mary, looking distinctly un-postnatal considering what she'd just been through. And there was Joseph with a shy and mildly surprised expression on his plaster face; then two kneeling shepherds, a donkey and a lamb, and, in the distance, the approaching Magi, led by a shining star.

Mum and I put some money in the offertory box and then

knelt down to pray. Now, I'm not very good at praying. I usually find it rather embarrassing—well it *is* awkward isn't it—like trying to make small talk at a drinks party with an irritatingly reticent stranger. *What do you do then? What, the entire universe? Oh, that must keep you busy.* Oh no, I really don't find it easy talking to Him. But this time, I don't know why, the words just seemed to flow.

"Dear God," I said. "Now, I really don't want to sound negative or anything, but I don't feel you've lived up to expectations over this past year. In fact, to be perfectly blunt, I think I've had quite a bum deal. Was it really necessary for me to be dumped on my birthday like that? Was that a crucial part of your divine plan? Well, to be quite frank, I'm not impressed, and I really think it's time you pulled your finger out. I mean I *now* you're *extremely* busy, what with the Middle East, Northern Ireland, the Russian Mafia, and world hunger et cetera, et cetera. And of course I realize that in the greater scheme of things I'm less than the size of a pimple on the face of a sub-atomic particle. But on the other hand you are omnipotent, and I'm sure you could deliver the goods for me if you really wanted to. So—no pressure or anything—just sort it out will you, say, within the next six months? Oh, and please bless everyone I love, including Seriously Successful, and if you could make him, miraculously, available, that would be greatly appreciated. Thanking you. Yours sincerely, Tiffany Trott, brackets Miss, close brackets."

"What about that nice accountant?" said Mum as we sat in the sitting room, after the Queen's Speech. I looked out onto the garden—behind the yew hedge were open, rain-soaked fields, and an almost uninterrupted view across six miles of Shropshire countryside.

"Er, I didn't fancy him," I replied as she cut the Christmas cake. "I've told you that."

"Well, what about that boy you were at school with—the rugger player?"

"Married. Four children." I looked at Dad. He was doing the crossword. He usually does it in twenty-five minutes, which is the average length of time it takes me to do one clue.

"And what about Roger whatsisname from Bristol?" Mum continued.

"Haven't seen him since he stood me up at the National Theatre in 1988."

"Oh. Do you want a bit with a robin on, or a snowman?"

"Er, snowman, please."

"And what about Peter Blake?"

"Immigrated to Australia."

"Oh dear." We chewed away in silence.

"Well, what happened to Conrad Taylor, from the advertising agency."

"Engaged. I saw it in the paper last week. Lovely cake, Mum."

"And what about that radio producer you used to know?"

I shuddered. "Oh him—he was so *camp*. It was embarrassing. Everyone thought he was gay."

"Oh yes," she said. "I remember that now. But then Alex was a bit . . . limp, too."

"Yes, he was." Oh yes.

"Darling. Why do you keep going out with pathetic men like that? I really don't understand it."

"It's a pattern," I said, putting down my plate. "I go out with a bastard who behaves like a complete bastard. And then I react to that by going out with a wimp who behaves like a total wimp."

"Well, I should try and break that cycle," she said sensibly.

"I agree. Kristin Scott Thomas had the same problem," I added as I unhooked a cracked bauble from the Christmas tree. "She said in an interview that she used to go for men who were 'either cads or bastards, or ones who weren't interested i girls.' So I'm not alone. Well I *am* alone actually," I added as I rearranged the tinsel. "But you know what I mean."

"Now, what about that nice little boy who used to partner you at dancing classes?"

"That was thirty years ago, Mum."

"And Brian Docherty?"

"Dead."

"Oh yes. Oh dear. Well, are you sure you're not overlooking anyone from your past, Tiffany? You did have such a lot of friends, I'm sure there must be someone you once knew who might want to get in touch with you again."

"Don't think so, Mum. Sorry."

"Oh darling, *why* didn't you want to marry Kit?"

"Yes. Why didn't you, Tiffany?" said Dad.

On New Year's Eve I was shuffling down Oxford Street, shoulder to shoulder with thousands of other shoppers and trying not to succumb to pavement rage. But people kept treading on my toes, and walking right into me, or inadvertently bashing me with their shiny carrier bags. And it was impossible to do more than one mile an hour—you simply had to go with the slow, human flow. And all I wanted was just one thing, and it didn't even have to be in the sale—a simple cocktail dress in which to welcome in the New Year. But where would I find it? "Red Sale" signs were plastered on every window, like wounds. "Forty percent off!" announced the signs in Selfridges. "Universal Savings!" said D.H. Evans. I decided to try Monsoon, and I was just inching my way toward it amidst the barrage of bargain-hunters, when a man attempted to thrust a leaflet into my hand.

"I'm sorry," I said, "but I can speak English already."

"It's not for a language school," he said with an enigmatic little smile, "it's for something *much* more interesting." What could he mean? I took one, and glanced at it as I walked along. *ingle?* it said in bold type at the top. It was for something

called Captivate. *Do you have someone special in your life?* it
asked.

"No," I said.

Do you feel that you will always be alone? it inquired.

"Yes," I said. "I do."

*Do you find it difficult to meet lots of stimulating new single
people?*

"Yes again," I said.

*Do you want to remain on the bottom rung of life's Romantic
Ladder?*

"No," I thought. "I don't."

*Well then, don't leave it to chance—choose! With Captivate
Join us and you'll meet your match.*

Inside was a questionnaire, and a postage-free address to
which it should be returned. *Don't leave it to chance—choose.
Don't leave it to chance—choose!* But then you hear such awful things about introduction agencies, don't you? They take
your money and then go into liquidation; they promise you
hundreds of eligible people, most of whom turn out to have
two heads. They sell their mailing list on to commercial com-
panies, leaving you with a lifetime's supply of junk mail. Introduction agency? You have got to be joking! I thought, as I
fought my way into John Lewis. That really is scraping the bottom of the barrel. I mean, answering a lonely hearts ad is one
thing, I said to myself as I stepped onto the escalator. Going to
a singles event—well that's OK, too. Perfectly acceptable. I'm
not normal. Gosh, seventy-five percent off evening wear. But
joining an introduction agency is for the Seriously Sad. Not the
Seriously Successful. Because the Seriously Successful—
well, they don't need it, do they? Nope. Agencies are for sad,
sad people, I thought as I went up to the fourth-floor café.
They're for pathetic inadequates and hopeless losers. They're
for people who are so unattractive, so desperately dreary and
unappealing, that they bloody well *deserve* to be single, I decided as I queued for a cup of tea. They've brought it upon

themselves by being boring and ugly, I reflected as I sat down at a vacant table. Yes. It's awfully sad for them, but they've only got themselves to blame. And then I opened my bag, took out my pen and carefully filled in the form.

"New Year resolutions!" yelled Sally as we stood on her balcony, watching the fireworks up-river at Tower Bridge explode into the velvety sky.

"I'm going to do something reckless!" said Emma drunkenly, as we heard the first chimes of Big Ben. *Bong!* "And I'm going to land myself in trouble!"

"I'm going to dumb down," said Frances. *Bong!*

"I'm going to drink too much!" said Catherine.

"And I'm going to take drugs," said Hugh. *Bong!*

"I'm going to be a counselor," said Lizzie, as she filled our glasses with Taittinger. *Bong!* "So I'll be able to sort you *all* out."

"And I'm going to have a *baby*!" said Sally, whose stomach was by now decidedly swollen. *Bong!*

"That's cheating!" shouted Emma. "That's a life event, not a resolution. Try again!"

"Er. OK. Um . . ." *Bong!* ". . . I'm going to give more money to charity." *Bong!*

"I'm going to exercise more," said Frances. *Bong!*

"I'm going to recycle my bottles!" said Emma. *Bong!*

"I'm going to stop thinking about Seriously Successful," I said. *Bong!*

"I'm going to start thinking about my husband," said Lizzie giving Martin a kiss. *Bong!*

"I'm going to paint the shed," he replied.

"And I'm going to join an introduction agency," I added. *Bong!*

"Happy New Year everyone!" we said simultaneously, as we kissed and hugged and chinked glasses. "Happy New Year. Happy New Year!"

The others shivered and retreated inside. But I stayed on the balcony for a few minutes, watching the Thames flowing strong and dark below; and I thought, well, maybe it *will* be a happy New Year—after all, a year's a long time.

January

Why oh why oh *why* do I keep dreaming about Canary Wharf?
And the Lloyds Tower? And sometimes, but less frequently,
Centre Point? I just don't understand. Maybe it's because I've
been thinking about Phil Anderer again, and so tall buildings
are on my mind. Not that his were very tall, you understand.
Quite low, actually. Conversions and extensions, rather than
anything which scaled the heights. I mean I wouldn't exactly
have put him in the Norman Foster or Terry Farrell league. And
what would he have built for me? A broken home. Mind you, to
be fair, his knowledge of building regulations was *extremely*
comprehensive. But I have found myself thinking about Phil
Anderer lately, because, of course, it's all his fault. Because if
he hadn't wasted my time, and then dumped me, I would not
be in this situation now. I would not now be on the verge of
having to join an introduction agency where I will be forced to
meet, and quite possibly marry, some very, very sad, unattractive and abysmally unsuccessful people. Yes. It's all Phillip's
fault.

Mum doesn't agree. "It isn't his fault," she said over the
phone this morning. "He was just being—himself. It's your
fault for going out with him in the first place. You had a choice."

"Well, it's Alex's fault then," I said. "He wasted my time,
too."

"Darling, you wasted your own time—that's what you don't
realize. Because you didn't have to stay with either of them,

and if you'd left them earlier, as you should have done, then you might by now have found someone far more suitable. But you didn't, you chose to stay. Sometimes I suspect you don't really want to get married at all, Tiffany."

"Oh no, no that's not true!"

"Well, please would you stop going on about Phillip and Alex—it's very boring for me, and it's bad for you. They're old news now. Anyway, would you seriously want to have married either of them?"

"No," I said, "but that's *not* the *point*."

"What *is* the point then?"

"The point is that *they* should have wanted to marry *me*!"

"Thank goodness they didn't, Tiffany," she said quietly. "Now, will you please pull yourself together. You're feeling nervous, that's what this is about."

Mum was right. I was. *Extremely* nervous. Because I was about to take the plunge. Join Captivate. They would have had my form by now. They would be contacting me to come in and see them for an interview. My stomach was tied up in knots. The butterflies were as big as birds. I mean, the artifice of it— being match-made. Having to acknowledge failure. Defeat. The lack of a bloke. Relying on some outside agency to do the trick for me when Fate, and God, had failed. How totally abject. How humiliating. What a bloody climbdown. And my God—if anyone knew—it would be mortifying. Terrible. Deeply, deeply embarrassing. But then, on the *other* hand, introduction agencies aren't such a big deal. After all, every religious culture had its matchmaker—they were a vital part of the community. And did not Dr. Johnson himself say that he believed all marriages should be arranged, on the orders of the Lord Chancellor, without either party having any say in the matter? And these days, it's *so* common. I mean, *everyone's* doing it. Everyone. I can think of at least . . . um . . . well, nobody actually, because people don't really talk about it, do they? They keep it quiet. Can't say I blame them. Who'd *want* to admit to it? I know I certainly wouldn't. Absolutely not. No way. Not that it's a *big deal* or anything, and in fact there's something rather romantic about being set up with someone by a concerned third party. A fairy godmother. Or father. A wave of whose magic wand might bring untold happiness into one's utterly sad, pathetic and desolate life. I mean, if I was buying a house I'd go to an estate agent, wouldn't I? I'd get professional help. If I was buying a car—not that I *would* of course, with their horrible, poisonous fumes, and anyway what's wrong with the number 38? —but if I *was*, then I'd ask an expert to help me choose it. And if I was looking for a bloke—well, I can get professional help for that too. Because I'm not going to leave something as important as my choice of life partner to the vagaries of Fate or the whim of God.

Anyway, I read the other day that Mel Gibson met his wife through an introduction agency. And he's been happily married ever since. At least, I think he has. I don't think he's been divorced. That's Harrison Ford isn't it? Is Mel Gibson still on his first marriage? Don't know. Must check. But if an introduction agency is good enough for Mel, it's certainly good enough for me. Wonder if Prince Edward met Sophie Rhys-Jones through an introduction agency? He probably did. Perhaps it was the very same one. And I bet that's how Jerry Hall met Mick. Anyway, I'm really looking forward to getting started at Captivate, and, well, *cracking* on with it.

"I think it's a brilliant idea," said Kate. "I really do." I was at her flat in Maida Vale while she demonstrated to me the benefits of the Mediwave "Take Five" nonsurgical face-lift machine. She's just bought one: £250. Frankly I find it all a bit alarming.

"It only takes five minutes," she said as she attached four pairs of electrodes to her face. "That's why it's called 'Take Five.' Isn't that a good name?"

"Brilliant," I said. "But take care."

"Now, what you do is to connect these pads here to the main facial muscle groups. Like this." She looked like Frankenstein's monster as she sat on the sofa, trailing wires. Then she threw the switch on the unit, and suddenly her face began to twitch.

"I'm passing a current through the . . . zygomaticus muscles now," she said, as her cheeks began to jump. "They're the upper cheek muscles. I'm also going to concentrate on my . . . naso-labials because I'm a bit . . . worried about those. No, I think joining a . . . dating agency is a wonderful idea," she continued in the two-second gaps between spasm-inducing bursts of electricity. "I may do it myself one . . . day if it doesn't work out with . . . Mike. Basically, this is a workout for the face," she continued. "I mean we . . . exercise the muscles in our arms and legs . . . don't we?" she said. "And this . . . works on the same principle." She tweaked the dial. "I'm just going to . . . increase the contractions by upping the . . . ampage a bit," she added. This time her cheeks and upper lips didn't just twitch, they convulsed, the muscles above her eyes contracting with a force to rival that of Herbert Lom in *The Pink Panther* or John Tusa in his *Newsnight* days.

"I think I've got the idea," I said, "but I find it quite hard to talk to you."

"Not much longer . . . Tiffany . . . hang on." Suddenly the machine emitted a high-pitched whine to indicate the end of the session. Kate removed the pads, leaving hectic red spots where the current had stimulated the skin. "My face," she said with an air of triumph, "has just done the equivalent of a half marathon followed by a couple of sets of tennis. Do you think I look younger?"

"Yes," I said truthfully, "I do."

"Do you think I look twenty-eight?" she said. "Like Mike?"

"Well. Yes. Probably. But Kate, why are you doing it? You don't need it."

"Because now that I've got a man it's more important than ever to preserve my looks."

"Yes, but Mike knows your age, doesn't he?" Silence. "Doesn't he?"

"Not *yet*," she said judiciously. "He thinks I'm thirty. If it gets serious, and I think it might, then obviously I'll tell him, but I'm just, you know, trying to keep the flesh all nice and firm. And of course it's far too early for a facelift," she said. "I mean, knife begins at forty."

"If he really likes you, then he won't mind the fact that you're a few years older," I pointed out.

"Yes," she said, "I know. Anyway," she added, "if it doesn't work out with Mike then I'll do what you're going to do. When do you join?"

"Quite soon. They're going to give me a call."

The call came the following morning.

"Miss Trott?"

"Yes. Hallo. That's me," I said.

"Well, *hallooo,* Miss Trott. My name is Stuuaaart," said a male voice. Who on earth was this? "I'm from Capteevate Personal Introductions."

"Oh. Yes. Hallo," I said again.

"Thank you for your appleecation," he droned, "and I am deelighted to be able to tell yew that yew qualify for an introductoree interview."

"Oh. Good . . ."

"So, we would like yew to come and see us at our London office," he continued. "May I suggest this Monday?"

"Oh, Well. I'd like to know a little bit more about it over the phone first," I said.

"Oh, I do not fink that will be necessary becorse it's much more better for you to meet with one of our executeeve consultants."

"But there are things I need to ask . . ."

"Becorse, Miss Trott, you are obviously looking for a quali-tee eligibew gentewman," he added. "End we have many such male members on our register."

"OK, but for example how—"

"You are obviously a very busy and successful lay-dee," he added.

"Er, yes, I suppose I am," I said.

"And you have reached an age where all your friends are married."

"Well, no. Not all of them, actually."

"They are *all* marreed," he continued happily, "and you find it hard to meet quality single people like yourself."

"Er. Well, yes."

"And so you have decided to come to us. You are a casualty of the serciety what we live in."

"How much does it cost?" I got in quickly.

"Ooh! We cannot divulge that information over the phone," he said.

"Why not?" There was a momentary hesitation at the other end.

"Becorse there are many levews of membership," he replied.

"Oh. I see. But, you know, roughly—just a ballpark figure would do." I persisted breezily, as my hackles continued to rise.

"But that is impossible," he insisted. "Becorse there are sev-eral levews of membership."

"Yes, yes I know. You just said that."

"And we would have to choose one that would be appropri-ate for you."

"Why couldn't *I* choose it?" I asked.

"Becorse it would not be appropriate," he replied. "I reely do suggest that you make an appointment with us today to come in at your earliest convenience."

"Look," I said. "I'm not going to make any such appointment unless you can give me some clear idea over the phone, now, as to what it's likely to cost."

"I'm afraid it would not be appropriate for me to tell yew that."

"I really don't see why," I said.

"Becorse we never deescuss fees over the phone."

"But I still don't understand why you can't say, within certain parameters, how much your company charges," I insisted.

"Well, becorse it depends on *so* many things," he said. "We never deescuss fees before meeting our clients."

"Well, I think you should," I said.

"I beg your pardon?"

"I said, I think you should," I reiterated crisply.

"Why should we?" he said defensively.

"Because it's extremely helpful for potential clients to know beforehand how much money they're going to be in for," I said firmly. "I mean, one hears some awful stories about cowboy agencies who take thousands of pounds from innocent people and then—"

"Miss Trott—are yew normally as bad-tempered as this?" he suddenly said.

"I am *never* bad-tempered," I hissed.

"Becorse if you are I can understand a few things . . . I can understand why you're not marr—" I put the phone down. Breathing heavily. Ooooooohh. Hummmmmmmmmm. Ooooooooohhhh. Hummmmmmmm. Dammmmmmmmn.

"Captivate sound like a bunch of wankers," said Sally succinctly, when I met her for the post-Christmas yoga class on the fourth of January. "You'll have to do some research if you're going to do this thing properly," she added. "You mustn't fall into the kind of trap that you fell into with Seriously Successful. You're got to know what's what."

"I know."

"You hear dreadful stories about dating agencies."

"I know that, too."

"You ought to ring the professional body and get them to recommend a couple. I'm sure there must be an association of some kind."

"*Brilliant* idea," I said. "Oh, hello, Jessie."

"Hallooooo," she crooned. We stepped inside the house, for the weekly heavy breathing session. This time it was, *"Oooh oooh oooh—aaah aaah aaah—oooh oooh oooh—aah aah aaah,"*—I thought I was going to faint from hyperventilation. And then we went back to humming.

"These breathing exercises will teach you all how to be calm and accepting during childbirth," said Jessica as the entire class hummed away—unfortunately not in harmony. "Purposeful humming noises will help to channel the pain of labor and bring your baby closer to you." Some women closed their eyes beatifically while they hummed and breathed. Sally kept hers open. Then it was time for the cat position —on all fours.

"How are you feeling?" said Lesley to Sally during the herbal tea break.

"Oh I'm fine," she said. "Sailing through it, so far at least. How are you?" This triggered a ten-minute monologue about morning sickness, wind, appalling indigestion, varicose veins, bloated feelings, pains in the wrist, insomnia, and constipation.

"You *poor* thing," said Sally sympathetically. I glanced at Lesley's partner, Pat. She was big, rather than big with child, and she seemed, for some inexplicable reason, to latch on to me.

"I don't let Lesley carry the shopping," she boomed at me manfully, as we made our way down Ronalds Road after the class. "I'm not having it. I keep telling her that she's *got* to take it easy. I bring her breakfast in bed every morning," she went on, "and I make her put her feet up on the sofa for at least two hours a day. Now, she thinks I fuss over her too much," she told me confidentially, "but I'm not having her straining herself. She's carrying our precious baby. Are you the same with Sally?"

"Sorry? Oh no. I mean, we're just friends. I'm just helping, really," I said. "Lending moral support. That's all."

"Of *course* you are!" she said with a loud laugh. "No need to be embarrassed, Tiffany," she added, slapping a brawny arm around my left shoulder. "Did you see that excellent program on car maintenance last night?"

That afternoon I looked in the phone book, found the British Association of Introduction Agencies and gave them a ring. A friendly woman gave me a list of the association's members, with telephone numbers, and I decided to try three. The first one was the Ruby Penhaligon Personal Introductions Agency. Established since 1940. That sounded quite good—it had been going a long time, and the emphasis, said an assistant, was on marriage.

"Although it's *not* a marriage bureau as such, our clients are almost all looking for marriage," said a pleasant-sounding woman over the phone. "Shall I book you in for an appointment with Miss Penhaligon?"

"Miss?" I said.

"Yes. Miss," she said, with a little laugh.

The following Wednesday I went over to Primrose Hill for the interview. The agency was in a narrow, flat-fronted house in a square just off Regent's Park Road. I waited in the hall downstairs, and was then shown up a winding wooden staircase to a large sitting room, furnished in forties chintz, with lots of pretty *objects* on occasional tables. It looked rather inviting, with a reassuringly old-fashioned air, though Ruby Penhaligon herself looked a little forbidding. Tall and slim, she had a distinctly teacherly air. I felt as though I was being called in to see the headmistress after a particularly disappointing report.

"You may wonder, Miss Trott, why I'm not married myself," she said with a soft laugh.

"Oh no, no, no," I lied.

"Well, you see, my fiancé died . . ."

"Oh, I am sorry."

". . . in a car crash in 1955, and I was therefore prevented from entering into holy matrimony myself. But I am *exceedingly* gifted at helping others into that happy estate." Oh good. Perhaps she could help me, then. I glanced round the room. It was very low-tech. No computer screens. No telephone switchboards. Just this pleasant-looking sexagenarian with a ring binder.

"Now, Miss Trott, please do tell me about your obviously *very* unhappy past," she said, with an expression of sympathetic concern. Oh gosh. Well, I wouldn't exactly put it like that.

"I wasted a lot of time on a couple of complete tossers," I said. Actually I didn't say that at all. I said, "Commitophobes. Two of them. That was the problem. Not *simultaneously,* of course," I added hastily.

"Oh dear me, dear me, a *common* problem," she said, shaking her head so vigorously that I thought the hairpins were going to fly out of her auburn-tinted hair. "A very common problem. But Miss Trott, you will be pleased to know that the gentlemen who come to me are not commitophobes. They are, in fact, commito*philes*.'

"Oh, good," I said.

"They actively *wish* to marry," she said, fingering the lace collar of her pin-tucked cotton blouse. "And they know that they can trust me to match them up appropriately." Well that sounded all right. In fact it sounded jolly good. Visions of hundreds of men, all proffering Posh Spice-sized engagement rings, swam before my eyes.

"How *do* you match people up?" I enquired as I sipped my Earl Grey.

"Intuition," she replied, tapping her temple with her left fore-finger. "And, of course, forty years' experience as a professional matchmaker. Some of these newer, you know—dating agencies—" she enunciated with delicate disdain, "—are *extremely* unreliable and frankly *dangerous* organizations. With their computers and their databases and I don't know what! Now, I don't use photographs," she added, "because in my experience looks are, well, very, *very* subjective." Are they? I wasn't quite sure about that. Pierce Brosnan is, for example, an *objectively* fantastic-looking bloke, and Winona Ryder is, objectively, one of the prettiest actresses in the world. Subjective? No. Alarm bells began to ring. No photos? If I was to become one of their clients I think I'd much prefer to see who she might be setting me up with. And surely they would, too.

"You would look on me as a friend," Miss Penhaligon was saying, "a wise intermediary with only your *best* interests at heart."

"And how much do you charge?" I inquired.

"A thousand pounds." A *thousand*!

"And, um, how many suitable chaps might you, um, have, on your, um books?" I asked.

"Register, Miss Trott. Please call it a register."

"Oh. Sorry." She opened the ring binder. It contained a thin sheaf of typed notes.

"Well—for someone like you, intelligent and successful, there would be just a *few* introductions," she said.

"Oh," I said, placing my teacup on a small mahogany side table. "Only a few?"

"Yes," she said. "Just a few. Because of course, Miss Trott, your age—it is a problem."

"A problem? Oh."

"Yes, you see, most men, in fact I would say, the *majority* of men, want a woman of thirty-five or under. So I think we may have a difficulty here."

"But my friends tell me I'm attractive."

"Oh yes, Miss Trott. Indeed you are. But that's not the point, is it, Miss Trott? The point is not that you are intelligent, successful and attractive. The point is that you are over thirty-five and men don't wish to meet—"

"But not *all* men are so narrow-minded," I interjected, feeling a combination of disappointment and growing irritation. "Can I just ask you how many men you have on your books, I mean, register?"

"Oh, Miss Trott, I'm afraid I could not *possibly* divulge that," she said, fiddling with her teaspoon.

"Oh. In that case, could you tell me, just for argument's sake, who you might match me up with, you know, in theory."

"Well," she said, rustling the bits of paper. "I do have one charming chap. Very nice. Very successful. He's a chartered accountant aged forty-one. But . . ."

"But what?" I said.

"Well, he is, very . . ." I leaned forward in my chintz-covered chair.

"Very what?" I said.

"Very, *fat,*" she whispered. Then she said, "Do you *mind* fat men, Miss Trott?"

"Er. I've never given it much thought, to be honest," I said. "How fat is he exactly?" *I mean, are we talking Robbie Coltrane here?*

She shifted uneasily. "Well, very fat, actually," she said quietly. "*Very* fat." Oh.

"Well, to be frank I think that might be a problem," I said. "You see I'm rather keen on tennis."

"But Pavarotti plays tennis, Miss Trott."

"Oh yes. So he does. But to be perfectly honest I think I'll give fatso a miss," I said. Actually I didn't say that at all. I said, "Do you have anyone else?"

"Yes. Yes, I do," she said animatedly. "Another *charming* man. He's a financial journalist. Now, he's a *very* interesting fellow and he has excellent genes—for example his ninety-three-year-old father still goes hill-walking."

"That's *wonderful,*" I said. And then I thought, ninety-three? "Er, how *old* is this chap that you've just mentioned?"

She gave me what I thought was a nervous sort of smile. "Fifty-two." *Fifty-two.*

"Oh," I said. "Well, I think that's rather a large age gap, actually. Fifteen years. I really don't think I'd want to marry someone of fifty-two. Unless he was very good-looking, of course, but even then it wouldn't be ideal. *Is* he good-looking?" I inquired.

"Looks are *so* subjective," she said again, with an ingratiating but slightly anxious smile.

"Well, I don't really think they are. Could you possibly describe him?"

She brushed an imaginary crumb off her dirndl skirt and then nervously sipped her tea. "Well . . . he's medium height, and he doesn't have a *lot* of hair, and he is rather thin I suppose, well . . . *very* thin, actually. But I'm sure he'd *love* to meet *you,*" she added.

"But to be honest, I'm *not* sure I'd want to meet him," I said.

"Yes, but he's *very* keen to marry again," she said.

"Yes, but I'd have to find him appealing," I replied, "and from what you say I don't believe I would."

"And he wants to have more children, Miss Trott. He's only got one."

"Well, I'm sorry," I said firmly, "but I just don't think he sounds right for me."

"Yes, but Miss Trott, at *your age* . . ." she said with an expression of excessive sympathy.

"Look," I said, "I might as well go down the sperm bank if this is the best you can do." Actually I didn't say that at all. I simply said, "Well, it's been interesting meeting you, but I think I'm going to have to give this some very careful thought. Thank you for the tea," I added, and then turned to find my way out. But as my fingers clasped the worn, brass doorknob, Ruby gave a delicate little cough.

"Miss Trott? Aren't you forgetting something?" she said.

"I'm sorry?"

"I think you've forgotten," she whispered coyly.

"Forgotten what?"

"The fee, Miss Trott. The *fee*."

Oh. Of course, the twenty-five quid upfront just for the privilege of meeting her. It had completely slipped my mind. I quickly wrote out a check and left. Then I crossed over Regent's Park Road, walked to the top of Primrose Hill and took in the view. I sat on one of the Victorian benches with the stiff breeze blowing my hair, and surveyed the scene below. The whole of London was spread beneath my feet—from Battersea Power Station in the west, to Canary Wharf in the east, and the lights were beginning to glint and shine and blink in the gathering dusk. And out there, I knew for a fact, were slightly more single men than single women. Hundreds of thousands of them. Several football stadia-full in fact, and all I wanted, all I needed—was one. Surely I deserved better than an obese forty-something and a thin, bald man of fifty-two? Yes, I said to myself, I *do*.

January Continued

Poor Phil Anderer. I almost feel sorry for him. It must have been such a shock. That supermarket, collapsing like that. Killing 500 unsuspecting consumers. And he was so proud of that building. It was a two-year project, and he was the chief architect on it. It was his biggest professional break. Literally. The worst damage was in the root vegetable section, which was particularly crowded that day due to a special offer on Spanish parsnips. He's been charged, of course. With professional negligence. And I doubt that even his detailed knowledge of building regulations is going to be of much help to him now. Anyway, there he was, sitting in jail, having been refused bail, and feeling pretty low when, to make matters worse, he picked up an old copy of *OK!* from mid-December. And he was just flicking through it, trying to distract himself from his appalling problems by reading about "Princess Stephanie and the New Man in Her Life" when he suddenly caught his breath. In "Caroline's Society Diary" on page sixty-five he saw a photograph headlined, "Celebs Turn Out in Force at Oscar Reeds Gallery in W1." And underneath the picture of Richard Branson and Charles Saatchi there was a photo captioned, "Celebrated ITN reporter Mungo Brown with award-winning copywriter Miss Tiffany Trott." And Mungo had his arm round me, in a gently proprietorial fashion, and luckily, it was a very good photo of us both. Poor Phillip. That must have been very tough for him—seeing that, at such a time. I really felt sorry for him. So much so that I was just planning to take him a pile of old *Hello!* magazines to help him pass the time when I suddenly woke up. Damn. But it was a great way to start the day. It really cheered me up, in fact. Because of course, it's all Phil Anderer's fault. I don't care what Mum says. I blame him.

"Yes Phillip, it's all your fault," I said to myself as I made my way to the Destiny Dating Agency in Wandsworth a couple of days after my meeting with Ruby Penhaligon. "You, Phillip, are entirely to blame." I had dressed neatly, in a sharp little navy suit and my best winter coat, which barely kept out the biting cold. The weather has turned Siberian. It makes it quite hard to work, actually, as my heating isn't very reliable. I sit upstairs in my study, wrapped up to the nines—granny pants, thermal vest and long johns, three cardigans, scarf, hat, mittens—the works—writing brochure copy for Cox and King's Namibian Odyssey and trying to imagine what thirty-five degrees of desert heat feels like. I mean it was *so* cold this morning that my lip gloss had frozen over—I had to break the ice on it with a flossing stick. Anyway, there I was, making my way down Wandsworth High Street and looking for Destiny and not doing very well, because of course these places don't exactly have their names up in large flashing neon letters. But, eventually, I found it, and got myself buzzed in. At the top of the stairs a friendly-looking blonde woman of about forty-five was waiting to greet me.

"Hello Tiffany—I'm Gabriella," she said. "I run the agency. Do come in. Would you like a cup of coffee?"

She was terribly nice. She put me at my ease, Some of my anxiety evaporated, because naturally it's quite nerve-racking doing this kind of thing: putting yourself on the line; rendering an account of yourself and your romantic failures to a complete stranger who may, or may not, be able to help. Anyway, I really liked her. The vibes were good. And the initial consultation was free.

"I'm sure we can help you, Tiffany," she said after about fifteen minutes of general chat.

"What about my age?" I said.

"What do you mean?"

"I've been told elsewhere that I'm too old."

She gave a derisive snort. "That's absolutely ridiculous," she said. "You're just the right age, and you're very attractive. You're absolutely fine."

"I think I love you," I said. Actually, I didn't say that at all. I just said, "Well, that's an enormous relief."

"Now, I do need to know a bit about your history, Tiffany." Three and a half hours later, I'd finished telling her all about my past unhappy relationships. She was *such* a good listener.

"But it was the Bellville Sassoon ball gown that really got me down," I concluded. "Though Alex was, at least, quite a nice person," I added, so that she would think me fair-minded.

"Well from what you've told me he sounds like a closet gay," she said. I rather liked the forthright way in which she said this, though to be honest it wasn't something I had ever really given much thought, although there were times when Alex and I went out together, when I had felt like attaching a label to my back saying, "My Other Boyfriend's a Man!"

"Now, what I'm going to do," said Gabriella, "is to let you go through the files, to see for yourself the kind of men this agency attracts. They're all well-educated, professional men, who are looking for a committed relationship. We don't have an emphasis on marriage here," she continued, "but it's safe to say that everyone is looking for a permanent relationship, and that very often does mean marriage." Then she got down four *enormous* ring binder files which were bulging with men's profiles in plastic sleeves. Gosh—there were *hundreds* of them—this was a far cry from Miss Penhaligon and her unhappy few.

"I'll leave you alone with these for at least, well, thirty minutes," said Gabriella, glancing at her watch. "Do give me a shout if you need any further information."

Gosh, she was *so* nice. So charming. I felt quite at ease as I happily flicked through all the forms. This was so encouraging. Really, really encouraging. And there were photos. Now, that's absolutely critical, I thought to myself. You've got to see what the person looks like. Anyway, there I was, happily going through the A–F file, when this funny thing happened. I saw someone I knew. Sam Clarke. He'd been at primary school with me. I'd never liked him much. He was rather aggressive. He used to pinch me in the playground. And now, here he was, at Destiny. His profile said he was an electronics engineer, divorced with three children, and that he liked motorbikes and hard rock. His face hadn't changed that much, but his hair was almost entirely gray. Gosh. Oh well. Small world, isn't it? And then I flicked through the G–M section and this time I spotted someone *else* I recognized—Sandy Ritts, a former colleague of Phillip's and, frankly, a bit of a wimp. In fact he'd rung me a few times after Phillip dropped me, but I'd managed to wriggle out of it. I'd never found him attractive, and his photo was at least ten years out of date, I noticed indignantly. Then I turned over a few more pages, and there were some quite nice-looking chaps who were accountants, solicitors and teachers, that kind of thing. And then I went through the N–R file and saw someone *else* I knew. Mike Shaw. An account executive at Gurgle Gargle Peggoty, who I'd worked with seven years before. He was all right, but A Bit of a One, as they say. And then I turned to the last file, S–Z, and I'd hardly got a third of the way through when I found myself staring at a very familiar photo. And the reason why it was so familiar was because I possessed a copy of it too. In fact it was the one I had sent to Eric the artist, with a sticker over Alex's face. It was of us both at Glyndebourne, standing on the lawn, by the ha-ha. And I remembered how much Alex had liked it, and it was indeed a nice one of him. And here it was, with me cut out of it, of course, though you could just make out a tiny bit of my blue satin skirt. I was gobsmacked. Alex! Who had said he never wanted to marry anyone, ever. Alex—who had said he didn't want a woman "messing up his things." Alex—who had said he couldn't stand the thought of babies. Alex, who had dumped me on my birthday. Alex, who had totally wasted nine whole months of my entire life! A tsunami of surprise mingled with nausea swept over me, leaving me gasping for air. Good God! Of all the dating agencies in all the towns in all the world . . . why was he *doing* this? Parental pressure, almost certainly—his two younger brothers are married and I knew his mother was always dropping hints about him "settling down." I peered at his profile. "What sort of partner would you like to meet?" it said. Now, for most people this seemed to be the key question. So they tended to answer it quite fully, and specifically. They'd say, for example: "I'd like to meet someone bright, confident, socially skilled, kindhearted, affectionate and yet independent too." That kind of thing. Or, they might put, "I'd like to meet someone aged up to thirty-eight, a nonsmoker, who will share my enthusiasm for ten-pin bowling and ceroc." Or they might say, "I'd like to meet someone, preferably without children, who is prepared to travel with me on business from time to time and help me entertain clients." That way, you get a very strong idea of what that other person is looking for. But Alex just wrote, "Surprise me!" Surprise me! What was *that* supposed to mean? I felt like annotating that section of his profile. In fact I felt like crossing out "Surprise me!" and writing down "A man!" I stared at his photo—he was in his dinner jacket which had the advantage, from his point of view, of disguising the weediness of his tall, light frame. By now I was so cross I felt like scribbling all over his form. He declared himself to be a nonsmoker. "You *do* smoke!" I nearly wrote next to that. He described himself as "romantic"—"but useless in the sack and not at all w/e!" I almost added. And he wrote that he was a "stylish" person. Stylish. "You do *not* look stylish dressed in late eighties Laura Ashley," I was tempted to scribble. Oh God. Oh God. This was going horribly wrong. Because, if I did join

Destiny I really wouldn't want Alex to know—let alone the other three men I'd recognized. Because they would of course see me in there. And if I was to go in the Confidential File, that would cost quite a bit more—£800, rather than £600. What a drag! Oh God, oh God. I couldn't join this one. I just couldn't. But what would I say to Gabriella?

"What do you think, Tiffany?" she asked when she came back into the room. "Do you feel positive about what you've seen?"

"Well . . . well . . . erm . . ." I couldn't tell her about Alex. I really couldn't. He was a client of hers. If I'd known that before, obviously I wouldn't have said a thing about him. In fact I probably wouldn't have gone there at all. Better to keep quiet, and go elsewhere. "Well, they all look very nice," I said. "But I would just like a few days to think about it."

"Of course," she said with a smile. "I quite understand."

Damn and blast, I thought to myself as I got the number 77a back to the center of town. Damn and *blast*. Destiny would have been perfect had it not been for the fact that I had recognized several of its clients. Too many for comfort. That's the trouble with the London singles scene—it's a very small world, obviously it is, because we're all looking in the same places. So there's nothing surprising about going, say, to Eat 'n' Greet or a dating agency and seeing people that you know there, because there are only so many places for the unattached to try. But of course, that can be a problem. A big problem, as I was now finding out.

My last shot was the Caroline Clarke Introduction Agency in Hertford. And perhaps, being close to North London, that might be a better bet for me in any case. And Caroline had sounded very nice over the phone. By now, I was familiar with the form. I knew just what to do. So when she welcomed me into the office above an interior design shop in Hertford High

Street I felt quite relaxed. I knew what she would want to know about me, and I found it very easy to tell her.

"What about my age?" I said, discreetly surveying the wall-ful of wedding photographs behind her.

"You're just the *right* age," she said. "I know that lots of chaps will want to meet you, if you do decide to join." Once again, I was left alone with the files. And she had so many blokes. It was amazing—there were loads of them—and there were at least three photos of each one, so you could really see what they looked like. There were men climbing up mountains, men sitting in canoes, men leaning casually against their cars, or standing in fields wearing Barbour jackets. There were men on the beach in swimming trunks, men with dogs and horses. And, best of all, I didn't recognize a single one. Not one. And their profiles were so nice. They all seemed to be looking for women aged "up to forty," if they were, say, in their mid to late thirties, and the word "independent" and "intelligent" featured a good deal in the "ideal partner" section. What's more, they were attractive. Very attractive. I felt my confidence lift. This was the one for me.

"What do you think?" Caroline asked.

"I think it looks wonderful," I said truthfully. And I signed up on the spot.

"It's such a sensible thing to do," I said when I went swimming with Sally the following evening. She belongs to the Chelsea Harbor Club, because her flat's close by, and recently I've been going swimming there with her, to help her do her aquatic relaxation exercises. She lay on her back, in the shallow end, her watermelon-sized middle thrusting upward into the air, while I supported her underneath. She was like an iceberg in reverse, I thought, seven-eighths of her were *above* the surface.

"You're big enough to sink the *Titanic*," I said tastelessly.

"Please don't talk to me, Tiffany," she said, keeping her eyes firmly closed. "The book says that while floating I have to find the stillness and peace inside, and focus on the natural rhythm of my breathing."

"Sorry. I mean, how much does this place cost? You don't exactly get much pool for your money."

"Tiffany!"

"Let's face it, they built this club from scratch, so why on earth did they put in such a small swimming pool?"

"Oh Tiffany, I don't know. I'm trying to surround the baby with white radiant light and loving, welcoming thoughts—oooooooohhh. Hummmmmmmm. Ooooooooh. Hummmmmmmm."

"Still, at least it doesn't reek of chlorine." My arms were beginning to ache by now and I was just wondering whether to ask this Sloaney-looking girl in a velvet headband and green, waxed-down swimsuit if she'd stand in for me for a while, when Sally decided she'd had enough. She went over to the wall and did a few side lifts and leg circles, like a ballerina practicing at the barre, and then we went to get changed.

"No, I think introduction agencies are a brilliant idea, Tiffany," she said as we retrieved our clothes from the lockers and sat down to change on the slatted wooden benches. "I'm really glad you're doing it. I'll probably do it myself one day, when Lorelei's about two years old."

"It helps take my mind off Seriously Successful," I added as we dried ourselves and dressed. "Because ever since I found out that he's kind to homeless people, naturally I like him even more, which is why it's so important for me to meet someone else."

"Er, yes, I see," said Sally as she pulled the waistband of her maternity leggings over her expanding midriff. "Why exactly *are* you in love with him?" she asked looking at me in a somewhat puzzled way.

"Because he's OK-looking-bordering-on-the-almost-divine," I began as I combed through my wet hair. "Well, at least *I* think so. And he's very funny, and he has a comprehensive knowledge of advertising slogans combined with a highly developed social conscience. But unfortunately he's also got a wife," I added sadly. "And a girlfriend. Which, let's face it, *is* a bit of a drawback."

"Er, yes," she said. "It certainly is."

"Anyway, that's why I've joined the—" I looked around, then lowered my voice to a whisper—"Caroline Clarke Introduction Agency. So that I can fall in love with someone else."

"What about that chap you were at school with—hasn't he phoned you again?"

"Yes he did. The week after Christmas. Then he went skiing. But he said he'd ring me when he got back."

"Well, what about him?" she said as we blow-dried our hair in front of the mirrors. "He sounds rather nice. Wouldn't he do?"

"Well. Yes. Maybe. Possibly," I said airily. "Perhaps. Potentially. I do like him," I added truthfully. "And he's incredibly attractive. It's just that I've only had one proper date with him—so I'd like to see him again. Anyway, how are you feeling?" I asked her.

"Oh fine," she said happily. "No more morning sickness—and look, my hair's gone thicker. I've ordered a wonderful jogging buggy," she added excitedly. "Just like Madonna had. For Lourdes."

"What about Lourdes?" I suggested. "Or maybe Lyons."

"Wait till you see what I got in Paris!" she said happily. We walked down Lots Road toward Chelsea Harbor. Sally's flat's in the Belvedere, a huge pagoda-like building which dwarfs the rest of the development. We shot up to the fifteenth floor in the lift and she opened the door to her apartment. It's huge—open plan, and nearly all white, with white leather furniture, and white marble flooring and white rugs and a white open-plan kitchen with shining steel worktops and gleaming white cupboards. Through the French windows we could hear boats quietly chugging up the river and the clattering of trains over Chelsea rail bridge. On the other, northern side of the flat was a view of the marina, where Khashoggi-style yachts gently rocked back and forth on their moorings, their rigging lines rattling against their aluminum masts.

Sally put an Enigma CD on her Bang and Olufsen music center, popped a frozen pizza into the oven, and then produced a number of expensive-looking carrier bags from which she took out eight or nine tiny dresses. They were adorable, and all in pink, with pink ruffles, and pink velvet edging, and pink sprigged flowers with pink satin sashes and pink-and-white broderie anglaise collars.

"They're lovely," I said. "They're like doll's dresses."

"I love French clothes for kids," she said, fingering the fabric. "These are from Tartine au Chocolat and Galeries Lafayette. Loretta will look adorable in them."

"But I thought you said you'd wait until Lola was born before buying any gear for her."

"Oh no, Tiffany. I'm really getting myself thoroughly organized. Come with me." She took me through to the back of her apartment. There, a spare bedroom which I had remembered as white, like everything else, was now pastel pink, with a border of coral roses at wainscot and ceiling, a light shade which danced with pink elephants, and a deep rose wall-to-wall woollen carpet. In one corner was a large cot with alternating pink and white rails, like a pack of marshmallows. On it was a satin coverlet, the color of early cherry blossom, and above it eight fluffy pink rabbits circulated gently in the sudden breeze from the open door. Against the far wall was a child's wardrobe, painted in pale salmon and stenciled with large pink peonies. Sally opened the door, revealing about twenty tiny outfits, all in varying shades of pink, and ranging in size from newborn to about two years.

"Gosh," I said. "How lovely. Lucky Lily."

"Well, I think it's really good to be prepared," she said.

"Same time this Saturday for the yoga class?" I asked her as I left.

"Yes," she said enthusiastically. "And Rosie's coming back

to the group to tell us all about her birth," she added happily. "I can't *wait* to hear about it."

I picked up the phone.

"Hallo Trotters!"

"Hello, Nick! How are you? Happy New Year!"

"Happy New Year to you."

"How was the skiing?"

"Oh, it was fun. But I'd love to see you. Now, will you have lunch with me on Thursday? At Green's Oyster Bar?"

"That would be lovely," I said. And so on Thursday I made my way to Duke Street and met Nick there. I was close to Piccadilly again—Seriously Successful territory, though no sign of him today, thank God. And in any case, I was thinking about Nick. I was looking forward to seeing him again. I really was. He was nice. And he was charming. And terribly attractive. And today he looked even more attractive with his Verbier tan. He kissed me on the cheek, and smiled.

"Oh it's *so* nice to see you again, Tiffany," he said. "I've been thinking about you a lot, you know." I blushed. I suddenly felt ridiculously happy. He was really a *very* nice chap. And he seemed keen. Maybe he was the answer to my prayers, I thought. Maybe he was. Maybe. We ordered a large bowl of mussels to share.

"Tom Player was in my chalet," said Nick as we sat scooping out the soft salty insides. "Do you remember him?"

"Er vaguely," I said, dipping my fingers in the silver water bowl.

"And Peter Croft came out for a few days, too."

"Oh great."

"They both remember you really well."

"Do they?"

"Oh yes. I told them you'd lost weight."

"Thanks."

Nick rinsed his fingertips and then took another sip of

Chardonnay. Suddenly he laughed. "Do you remember when Peter stuck that car on top of the chapel?" he said.

"Oh yes," I said. "I do. How could anyone forget?"

"Bloody funny, wasn't it?"

"Yes," I agreed. "Rather dangerous, though."

"Oh yes," he replied. "That driver could have been killed."

"How did he get it up there?" I asked.

"He hired a crane of course."

"And do you remember when Jack Daniels dyed the water in the swimming pool bright red?"

"Oh yes," I said wearily. "I do."

"Hell of a shock on a Monday morning."

"Er, yes." I was a bit sick of school stories to be honest, so I tried to change the subject. "So tell me about the States," I said. "What did you do?"

"Well, I spent a fortnight in New York—we had three big furniture sales. And then I stayed with my father for a week over Christmas. He was at Downingham too, you know, Tiffany."

"Oh. Look, why don't you ever talk about anything but school, Nick?" I said. Actually I didn't say that. I said, "How's your salmon teriyaki?"

"Delicious."

We finished our meal in silence, and then looked at the dessert menu.

"Trotters," said Nick. Suddenly he reached for my hand and looked me in the eye. "I mean, Tiffany," he said again.

"Yes?" I said, slightly disconcerted.

"Tiffany—would you . . . I don't know how to ask you this. It's a difficult thing for a chap to ask. But Tiffany . . . would you . . . would you . . . please would you . . . choose the choco-late éclairs?"

"Of, of course I will," I said with a peal of laughter, which was underpinned with relief.

But he was still holding onto my hand. "And would you go

out with me?" he added casually. "I mean, be my girlfriend?"
Oh God. "You know how much I like you."

"I like you too," I said.

"You see, you remind me of what it was like to be thirteen."

"Ah."

"You remind me, Tiffany, of some very happy times."

"I see."

"You take me right back to another *epoch* almost," he added
with a contented sigh.

"Oh. Thanks." I felt vaguely depressed.

"What do you think, Tiffany?" *What should I say?*

"Well Nick, I think you're a lovely person. But . . . but I just . . .
don't . . ."

"It's OK," he said quietly, letting go of my hand. "You really
don't have to say."

"I just don't think I'm the right person for you Nick, that's
all."

"I'm only four years younger than you are, Tiffany," he said.
'It hardly figures, you know." This was true. But that wasn't
the reason.

"It's not really the difference in our ages," I said. "It's just
that I can't help seeing you as I saw you at school." *Because
you don't seem to talk about anything else, you twit.* "Can't we
just be friends?" I asked.

"Of course we can," he said with a sigh. "Let's change the
subject," he added with sudden studied brightness. "Let's talk
about your slogans. I think they're marvelous," he continued
enthusiastically. "That one for *Which?* magazine was brilliant—
how did it go, now? Oh yes, that's it, Don't Get Done Get
Which? That was a classic."

"That was years ago," I said.

"But I still remember it," he said, "which proves it must
have worked. And that one for Dulux paint. Your Most Brilliant Liquid Asset, wasn't that it? Fantastic. What are you
working on now?"

"Love Hearts," I said, "for Valentine's Day. A TV campaign—the manufacturers are spending a fortune on it. It's a big risk for them."

"How are you going to do it?"

"Well, you know the inscriptions on the sweets," I said.

"Yes. 'Love Me,' 'Be Mine,' that kind of thing."

"Yes, exactly. Well, I've made up these poems out of them, and they'll be recited by actors—with club music and special effects and fast editing. It sounds silly," I added apologetically, "ads always do sound silly when you describe them cold, but I think it'll look quite good."

"That is *so* brilliant," he said admiringly. "It sounds marvelous."

"Oh it's only advertising, Nick," I said. "It's not exactly world-changing stuff. It doesn't prevent wars, or feed the hungry." Or house the homeless, I thought ruefully. "How's Jonathan?" I added. "Is he getting nervous about the wedding?"

"Oh yes—he worries about it the whole time. It's only two months away. You are going, aren't you?"

"Yes I am."

"Well, Yorkshire's a bit of a trek," he said. "Why don't we go up together?"

"Yes," I said happily. "That would be fun."

"Hummmmmm . . . Oooooohhhhh . . . Aaahhhhhhh . . . Hummmmmmmm . . . Oooooohhhhh . . . Aaaaaaaah!"

"OK—it's time for our break," said Jessie. "Let's take ten minutes, and then Rosie's going to tell us all about the birth of little Emily. Aren't you, Rosie?"

"Yes I am," said Rosie, with a shy smile.

Pat and I made a dash for the soft toy pile—I got Rupert Bear—and then we went into the kitchen. "I can't wait to hear Rosie spill the beans," boomed Pat as she tucked Paddington more firmly under her left arm.

"Nor can I," I lied as I put a camomile teabag into a gaily painted ceramic mug.

"I suspect she'll make it sound easier than it really was," Pat continued, as we one-handedly stirred the infusions and then carried them back to the drawing room. "Did you see the game last night?" she added.

"Game?"

"Arsenal blasted Chelsea four–one—*phenomenal* score. Or is rugger more your kind of thing?"

"Er, no," I said. "Tennis, actually."

"Tennis, eh? Now, Martina Navratilova's one of my heroines."

"Really?"

"And Billie-Jean King, of course—what a star. So, tennis is your scene, is it Tiffany?"

"Uh, well . . ."

"Suppose you'll be going to Eastbourne?"

"Er, no . . . don't think so."

"So you follow the women's game," she said with a loud, dirty laugh.

"I wouldn't put it like that," I said. "I mean I *do* like tennis. But actually, what I really prefer is synchronized swimming."

"Ladies' tennis! Ha! Bet you've got a good forehand, Tiffany!"

I handed Sally the mug of herbal tea, trying not to slop it all over the stripped wooden floor. She was wearing a smocked denim top and loose-fitting trousers.

"I can't *wait* to hear what Rosie has to say," she said. Suddenly, Jessie clapped her hands to bring the break to an end.

"OK Rosie—all yours," she said, giving her a beatific smile. Rosie, a pretty girl in her late twenties, stood up. Her baby slept peacefully in a moses basket at her feet.

"Well," said Rosie. "I had Emily two weeks ago. At University College hospital. It was quite an experience."

All eleven expectant mothers craned their necks forward eagerly.

"In fact it was—unbelievable," Rosie went on. "It was incredible. It was completely unforgettable and I'm *never bloody well doing it again*—at least, not without five epidurals. It was *horrible*," she added roundly. "And if you think I'm going to stand here and tell you how brilliant it was, and what a wonderful, life-affirming experience, well you're in for a disappointment."

"Oh Rosie, please don't say that," said Jessie, looking distinctly uncomfortable. But Rosie was just getting into her stride.

"I'd been having contractions for twenty-four hours—I thought I was going to burst open like John Hurt in *Alien*. And when people say that giving birth is like trying to shit a melon—they're wrong. It's more like producing a sack of coal. The pain's disgusting," she said. "I was bellowing like an animal, I had bodily fluids pouring out of every orifice . . ."

"Oh Rosie—please!" said Jessie.

"No Jessie—I'm going to tell the truth," said Rosie. "There's this conspiracy that we all have to pretend that childbirth is wonderful—when it isn't, it's horrible, horrible, and so stressful. And I felt totally degraded. Not human at all—I've seen a cat give birth with more grace than I did. But I couldn't help it. I howled, I screamed, I bellowed. I cried out for my mother. 'Mummy, Mummy, Mummy!' I yelled. My husband couldn't take it—he left the room, I don't blame him. In fact I told him to get lost. Because I didn't want him to see me in that state. Thrashing about like a stuck pig. Screaming and crying. And I hated the baby for doing this to me—it practically tore me in two, and I had to have forty-five stitches and I couldn't walk for a week afterward. And all the humming and all the deep breathing in the world didn't make the slightest difference—the only thing that would have helped me was a nice, neat Caesarian." Silence descended like a stone.

"Well—thank you, Rosie," said Jessie. "I'm sure everyone will find that very encouraging."

We all sat there, stunned. I made a mental decision to adopt. Then I looked at the girl sitting next to me—her baby was due the following week. She was staring at the floor, swallowing visibly. And then I looked at Lesley, who had less than two months to go. She was blinking back a tear, and Pat's arm was around her. Poor Sally, I thought. Poor, poor Sally. I looked at her. She was—oh for God's sake—she was smiling!

"What an absolutely *amazing* experience that must have been," she whispered to me excitedly. "What a vital, searing, *epic* thing to go through."

"Didn't it put you off, then?" I asked, amazed.

"Oh—of course not," she said with a giggle. "Don't be silly, Tiff. And in fact it only makes me more determined than ever to have the baby at home."

February

Now, according to the February edition of *Brides and Setting up Home* magazine, *the* fabric of choice for this summer's wedding belles is shot satin. Personally I much prefer good old silk dupion, but apparently that's frightfully old hat. What can I be thinking of—walking up the aisle with all these nice men from the Caroline Clarke Introduction Agency in a hopelessly unfashionable frock! I can almost hear the titters in the back pews now. "Silk supion? I ask you! Well, she never did have much of a clue. Still, could be worse, at least it's not polyester moiré. But poor old Tiffany. Yes, she never was terribly, you know, *stylish*." Stylish. That's what Phil Anderer used to say to me—I'm sorry darling, but it's just not very, stylish. Look, would you go and change?" And, like an obedient dog, I would. Isn't that appalling? Who'd have guessed that I had a brain, and a spirit, free will and self-respect? But, you see, I knew that if I said to him, as I should have done, "No I won't *bloody* well go and change and, by the way, who the *hell* do you think you are?" he'd have got hysterical, as he so often did, and I really hate unpleasant scenes. Can't cope with them at all. Now, professional disputes I can hack. I'm quite prepared to stick to my guns. For example, when I was at Gurgle Gargle Peggoty I once got very *very* worked up about Tiny Tears at a board meeting. But when it comes to heated confrontations with boyfriends, it's a different story. So I've always given in.

Gone along. Chickened out. Backed off. Shied away. It's not that I'm a coward, you understand—it's just that I'm afraid. Oh no, I'm really not one for rows.

Thus did my mind wander back and forth as I picked snow-drops in the front garden this morning. And I reflected, with a considerable degree of satisfaction, combined with cautious optimism, that I had, at least, made a very positive start to the New Year. I mean I've kept one of my resolutions—I've joined a dating agency. However, I must confess that I have broken my other one, in that I have not yet quite stopped thinking about Seriously Successful. In fact I think about him rather a lot, even when I'm asleep because, you see, he tends to come back to me in my dreams. But obviously, once I start to meet blokes from Caroline Clarke, then obviously I will stop think-ing about him, because, obviously, I'll fall in love with one of them instead, obviously. Anyway, I completed my form and sent in three very good snaps of myself taken last year; they're flattering without being, I believe, in any way misleading, and—imagine my agitation, dear reader! —I should start to re-ceive some profiles soon. OK, this is how it works. If, say, A likes the look of B, then B is sent A's profile. And if B likes A's profile, he/she tells the agency, and the phone numbers are ex-changed. Simple. It's going to be quite an adventure. I'm bound to fall in love. And that will solve all my problems. I must say it would be nice if I would fall in love before Valen-tine's Day next week. I'm dreading it. And OK, I know it's only a commercial thing—and God, I mean, *who cares* really, such a load of bull, isn't it? But the fact is that if you're single, and all you get on February the fourteenth is an overdue notice on your council tax, or a reminder to have your three-yearly smear, well, frankly, you feel like killing yourself. And the shops have been selling those wretched cards with their sickly, syrupy, saccharine sentiments since Boxing Day, so it's im-possible to avoid. Anyway, I decided to distract myself from the anxieties of being excluded from the nation's annual love-fest by boning up on childbirth. I still wouldn't know an episi-otomy from a pineapple and, as Sally's determined to be so laborious about the whole business, I suppose I'll have to know what's what.

This morning I went down to Waterston's and came back with an armful of baby books—*Having a Baby, Your Pregnancy—Questions and Answers, Planning for a Healthy Baby, Having Babies, Natural Pregnancy* and *The Baby Bible.* Some of the photos—my *God*—I had to find a chair before I could bear to look at them, and I thought to myself as I sat there with my legs crossed, Childbirth? You have got to be joking. I now definitely plan to adopt. Two children. Aged eighteen. When I've got myself a nice bloke, that is, which shouldn't take too long. Because, actually, the profiles have now started to arrive. This morning. In the post. An envelope stamped "Personal" plopped onto the mat containing profiles of men who want to meet me. Quite a lot of them, actually. There's Derek from Datchett who's in computers and likes "evening barbecues and moonlit walks with a warm scented breeze." Well how about a moonlit walk with a warm, scented Tiffany Trott, Derek? And there's Kevin from Hounslow who believes "a sense of humanity is essential"—hear hear, Kevin! And Toby from Barnes who is looking for someone "environmentally aware." Well that's me, Toby! I always put my bottles in the recycle bin, and I am a *passionate* devotee of public transport over the nasty, noxious motor car! Then there's John who's into black-and-white photography and ooh—is that a Ferrari he's leaning against in the photo? Then I quite like the look of George, for whom "traditional values are important, particularly trust." Well I'm right with you on that one, George! Trust me. Then there's Jeff, who is divorced and lives in Clapham with his three young sons, oh *"and their nanny."* And I must say Leo, a data collection manager from Thames Ditton, sounds rather nice. He's not that atractive, but he says he's looking for someone with a "sense of fun." Well that's me, Leo! Fun's my middle name. Actually, it isn't—it's Nicola—which was a bit of a silly choice, really; I mean, when I was at Downingham the sight of my initialed trunk used to cause guffaws—and occasionally panic. Where was I? Oh yes, looking at Leo and, um, Roger who's a librarian and describes himself as "a bit of a character" who enjoys "lively socializing" and "sun worshipping." And then, and then, there's Patrick. Now Patrick is forty-one, divorced, and a management consultant. He plays tennis and is also a qualified pilot. He has no children—oh *oh,* hope he's not infertile, I'd better ask him—and he claims to be "easy-going, loyal, honest, open and trustworthy." That sounds really good. He's also, may I say, *rather* tasty-looking, with black hair and blue eyes, about six foot. And in his photo he's standing on a hotel balcony with what looks like the Eiffel Tower in the background, so he's obviously terribly widely traveled too—*and* he's got a lovely smile. And nowhere on his form does the word "golf" appear at all! Now, Patrick purports to be looking for "someone with a sense of humor who doesn't take themselves too seriously. Someone who is intelligent, independent, successful, supportive and kind." Well Patrick, look no further!

"He does look rather a dish," said Lizzie when she came round on Monday. She had just got back from Easter Island and looked very tanned—because of course it's hot in Chile at this time of year. And she seemed happy. Very happy. Glowing. She flicked through my pile of profiles with a thoughtful, judicious air.

"What you want," she said with her customary emphasis, "is someone who is your *equal* in every way—someone who you won't want to dominate, and who won't dominate *you.* That's the secret of success you know, Tiffany—a balanced relationship where *neither* partner has the upper hand *too* much. I think that's why Martin and I have been *so* happy all these years."

I stared at her. I didn't say a thing. As I say, I try to avoid rows, so I simply said, "You're absolutely right."

"But," she added sensibly. "You *musn't* put all your eggs in one basket. Patrick looks nice, but you should see some of the *other* chaps, too. You may find that you *really* like them, and then you'll have a *choice*."

"Only if they like me," I said.

"Of course they'll like you, Tiffany," she said. "Don't be stupid." And that made me feel good. So I phoned the agency, right there and then, and said yes to four of the ten blokes including, well, *especially*, Patrick.

"You know about Emma, don't you?" said Lizzie as she showed me her holiday snaps.

"No. Haven't seen her for ages," I said. "She's gone rather quiet. Have another Jaffa Cake. Gosh, these statues look amazing."

"They're incredible. Basalt. The tallest are thirty feet high. No one knows how they put them up. Anyway," she added, "about Emma. I suppose you've *heard*?"

I looked at her blankly. "Heard what?" I replied. Gosh I do hate it when people gossip about other people who they know. "Tell me *all* about it," I said. "What's happened?"

"Well," said Lizzie, lighting another cigarette. "She's met someone."

"That's brilliant news," I said. "Oh, that's a lovely one of you Lizzie. That explains why I haven't heard from her for weeks. Apart from one or two rather odd messages on my machine. But I don't blame her—in the early stages you just don't want to talk about it, do you? Easter Island's quite bleak, isn't it?"

"Oh yes, it's not tropical," said Lizzie. "Nothing much in the way of palm trees or piña coladas. But there's another reason why Emma's not talking about her chap."

"Oh. What's that?"

"He's married!"

"Gosh," I said. Well that was entirely her own affair, as

it were. Of absolutely no concern to anyone else. "Who is he?"
I said.

"It's one of the parents. She'd been giving his daughter
some extra tuition after school, and he used to come and pick
her up, and apparently he picked Emma up at the same time."

"Oh." And then I had an awful, awful thought. "It isn't Seriously Successful, is it?" I certainly hoped Emma wouldn't stoop
so low as to steal other single women's married boyfriends from
right under their noses, even if they weren't actually going out
with them and in fact had only ever met them twice. And then I
remembered, his daughter's at Benenden. Phew.

"Tiffany—you're obsessed with that man."

"No I *am*," I said indignantly. We sipped our coffee in
silence. "That surprises me about Emma," I said as I bit into
my seventh Jaffa Cake. "I wouldn't have thought she'd have,
you know, *done* that."

"Well, she has," said Lizzie, "and the ordure is about to hit
the ventilator. Her headmaster's found out about it and her
job's on the line." But this was terrible. Her job had nothing to
do with her private life.

"They're hoping to keep it out of the papers," Lizzie added.

"Why on earth would it be *in* the papers?" I said.

"Because the man in question is a Labour MP."

That's the drawback about having such a big majority, isn't it?
Too many MP's, not enough work to go round, with the net re-
sult that some backbenchers, frustrated by their lack of promo-
tion and left with too little to do, are tempted to, well, put it
about a bit. Yes, I blame the government. But poor Emma.
What a ghastly situation. Imagine going to the newsagent one
morning, on what seems like a perfectly normal day, to find
your face splashed across the front page of the *Mirror,* the *Mail*
and the *Sun* above headlines such as these: TOTTENHAM
TROLLOP TEMPTS LABOUR'S LARRY! PLEASE MISS!
A BLACK MARK FOR LABOUR'S LAWRENCE BRIGHT!

I was horrified. It was disgusting. I bought them all. Still, at least they were nice pictures—she looked very pretty, even if she was staring mournfully out of an upstairs window as though she were a hostage which, in a way, she was. Poor Emma, I thought. Trapped by the tabloids. So *she* was Lawrence Bright's "sultry thirty-something brunette." But what a mess. And it made me realize how very foolish it is to get involved with married men. It always leads to disaster and sordidness and frustration and tabloid exposure and, well, thank God *I* hadn't gone down that road myself. I decided to send her an anonymous Valentine card to cheer her up in her darkest hour. I also thought I'd give her some advice about deep breathing— after all, this was a crisis.

"Emma, it's Tiffany. Can we talk?" The drama of the situation lent things a certain *frisson*.

"Of course we can talk," she said.

"I'd like to give you some advice about breathing."

"Why?"

"To help you feel calm."

"I do feel calm, Tiffany."

"Why do you fell calm, Emma?"

"Why not?" she said with a laugh.

"Because you're being trashed by the tabloids, that's why. I mean I don't want to rub it in, but they're successfully given fifteen million people the impression that you're a cross between Bienvenida Buck and Mae West."

"But that story's rubbish," she said with a sigh. Oh. I felt rather disappointed.

"Do you mean to say you're *not* involved with Lawrence Bright?"

"No. I mean, yes. I am." Oh good.

"Since when?"

"Oh I don't know—not that long. A few months," she added vaguely.

"Isn't he married?"

"Yes, he is. But they've conveniently overlooked the fact that his wife moved out after Christmas. He lives on his own now." Oh. I felt vaguely cheated.

"Why are the papers interested then?"

"Because they think she moved out because of me."

"Did she?"

"No. Well, not really. Don't ask me that, Tiffany. Basically she left because . . . because . . . oh I don't know. I mean, *she* thought they were happily married. But the fact is that he didn't feel the same way."

"Why did you meet him?"

"At a parents' evening last June. I liked him, but I knew he was married. Sometimes he'd come and talk to me when he collected his daughter from school, and then he started asking me out."

"Did you go?"

"Yes."

"Even though he was *married*?" *Oh Emma, Emma, how could you?*

"Well, yes," she replied. "But only because I knew he was unhappy—he told me that he was miserable, and that the marriage was coming apart . . ."

"But he might have been lying."

"Well he wasn't. He definitely told me the truth. I mean, look, his marriage *has* come apart, hasn't it? And so, yes, I did start seeing him, but obviously I couldn't talk about it to anyone. Not even Frances. And, to be honest, Tiffany, I didn't tell you because I thought you might disapprove."

"Oh no, no, no, no. I wouldn't have disapproved," I said.

"Well, I think you *would*, Tiffany. It was a complicated situation, but I certainly wouldn't say I broke up his marriage, though the papers are saying I did. And yes, his wife is saying that too. But it's not the same as what my stepmother did," she added, slightly too quickly, I thought, "just stealing my father away from my mum when they were perfectly happily married. And Lawrence Bright isn't Robin Cook." This was true. "I'm going to sue, of course," she added calmly. "Frances says she'll do it for me, *gratis*. She says a bit of libel will make a nice change for her, and the publicity will undoubtedly help Larry's career. I mean, look what happened to Paddy Pantsdown—his popularity rating soared."

"Gosh. Well . . . who tipped off the press?"

"I don't know. It might have been one of the parents. There's one mother who hates me because I told her that her precious little thug was as likely to get his GCSEs as I am to win a Nobel Prize. Or it might have been Larry's wife. She loathes me of course. But I'll probably never know for sure."

"What a ghastly situation. You're being very brave."

"Oh well, this is my fifteen minutes of fame, I suppose. Tiffany, I've got to go now, I want to watch Larry denying any impropriety on the six o'clock news."

"I'm afraid you got the wrong end of the stick there," I told Lizzie over the phone, later. "Emma says that his marriage was falling apart, and now they're separated. It's not a big deal."

"I still don't see *how* she could *do* it," she replied.

"What do you mean, 'do it'?"

"How could she *bring* herself to."

"What do you mean, Lizzie? She says she didn't steal someone else's husband."

"We don't know that, Tiffany. And anyway, I couldn't care less if she did. That's none of my business. What I find so shocking is this . . ."

"*What?*"

"A *Labour* MP, for God's sake!"

Anyway, I thought that I would still send Emma a Valentine card—just in case she did feel a bit depressed by the whole beastly business which rumbled on for several days. It was quite surreal seeing her in the *News of the World* the following Sunday, and Catherine was phoned up by the *People* and was

offered *huge* amounts of money to dish the dirt. Anyway, I
went to W.H. Smith and looked at the vast array of cards. Now,
which one would *I* most like to get, I thought, were I embroiled
in an unpleasant and highly public sex scandal with a Labour
MP? I surveyed the display of crimson hearts and pink flowers
and teddy bears and standard issue red envelopes. *Valentine, I
love you,* shouted one. *You're lip-smackin' gorgeous,* said
another. *Hug Me Darling!* said a third. Some were sordid—
others were simply sickly. I'd love to get one, I thought, as I
paid. Just one. It doesn't have to be expensive. It doesn't even
have to be in good taste. In fact it can be utterly nauseating—
I'm really not fussy. Perhaps Nick would send me one, I
thought to myself. Then I thought, why on earth should he,
when I had told him I only wanted to be friends? Maybe Seriously Successful would send me one, or Mum. Or Lizzie. Or
Kit. Or Terry from Eat 'n' Greet. Or Pierce Brosnan. Or Kevin
Costner. Or Elvis.

On February the fourteenth I stared, in disbelief, at the front
doormat. I couldn't believe my eyes. It was absolutely extraordinary. Exceptional. Phenomenal. Unbelievable. And incredible.
Nothing. Not even a Reader's Digest Prize Draw notification
form. Not even a gas bill. Not even a Kaleidoscope catalog or a
"special offer" flyer from the National Center for Cosmetic
Surgery. Not even a postcard from José in São Paulo. Not even
five more profiles from Caroline Clarke. Not even a minicab
card. In my head I could hear Karen Carpenter's cello-like
voice . . . *a card or a let-ter, the sooner the bet-ter* . . . Well,
there were no letters and certainly no cards. There was nothing. Zilch.

Hang on a mo! Maybe there was a rational explanation.
Maybe the post hadn't actually arrived yet, some mishap having befallen John the postman, thereby preventing a normal
delivery. I opened the front door and peeped over the hedge at
number twenty-four. A wadge of brown envelopes—and a red

one—were jammed in the brass letterbox. Damn and blast.
Blast and damn. Gloom descended like a cloud and I could feel
my shoulders hunched more than normal as I sat at my desk,
writing copy for Cox and King. I threw myself into the job, and
at least, once I'm really engaged on a project, time does tend to
fly. In due course I became aware of a vaguely hungry feeling,
which told me it was lunchtime. I went downstairs and peeped
at the front door with pounding heart, just in case my six or
seven Valentines had arrived by second post—but no. *Nuls
points* for Tiffany Trott in the Eurovalentine card contest. Just
the newspaper. That's all there was. Of course—*the paper*! I
turned to the special Valentine's Day pull-out—3000 small ads
swam before my eyes, surely one of them was for me! I spent
a couple of hours anxiously skimming through the snuggle-
bunnies and the pumpkin-pies, the fluffy bottoms and snookum-
wookums, but there was no mention of a single Tiffany, or
Trotters, or indeed any other ludicrously infantile sobriquet to
which I could have possibly laid claim. I cooked myself an in-
dividual Marks and Spencer steak and kidney pie with a tiny
bag of peas, and then returned to my study. I stared at my computer screen again, and then, within what seemed like mere
minutes, I was hungry again, and the room was virtually dark,
except for the soft, whiteish glow from my Apple Mac, and it
was very, very cold. I put on yet another cardigan—all this
knitwear makes me look vast—and went and switched on
Channel Four news. Jon Snow looked very chirpy—but then
he'd probably had a sackload of Valentine cards from admir-
ing viewers. Unlike Tiffany Nicola Trott, spinster in the parish
of Islington. Now I don't do this very often, but I was so pissed
off that I opened a bottle of red wine. Well why not? I said to
myself. I need it. I've been working for ten hours, and anyway,
everyone knows that a couple of bottles of red wine are very
good for you. Very good for the heart, I believe. And particularly good for raising morale when a Valentine's Day dinner à
deux with scrummy man in upmarket eaterie has inexplicably

failed to materialize. I tried to cheer myself up by re-reading *Brides and Setting up Home*—"Fashion for Modern Brides!", ran the headline. "The Experts Sort Out Your Bouquet"; "Where to Find that Dream Dress!" I wished the experts could tell me where to find that Dream Man, I thought bitterly as I poured myself some more Macedonian Merlot. And—oh God—why had I drunk so much?—two third of a bottle already. Why, why, why, why, *why*? On the other hand, why not? I poured myself another glass and looked at all the baby books again, spread out on my coffee table. Oh God, when did the third trimester—or was it semester—begin? Was it at eighteen weeks, or twenty? I'd have to look it up in the Dorling Kindersley *Pop-Out Book of Parturition,* and now the bloody phone was ringing and I'd have to bloody well answer it.

"Yess?" I said. "Hisit?"

"Hello Tiffany."

"Hello!" I said, as I leaned against the wall to steady myself against the romantoholic collapse, inexplicable happiness and the intestinal tickling of tortoiseshells.

"How are you, Tiffany?"

"Bit—ha ha ha ha!—um . . . oh dear . . ."

"Tiffany, are you drunk?"

"Only a lot."

"Why are you drunk?"

"Because, A Million Housewives Every Day Pick Up a Bottle of Booze and Say . . ."

"Tiffany, I just rang to say Happy Valentine's Day."

"Happy . . . tine's Day to you too."

"Did you get any cards?"

"Nope." Ooh—mistake. "I mean yeah," I said quickly. "LOTS. Hundreds, and 'dreds, in fact I'm still opening them— 'staken' me all day. Did you?"

"No." God, what a crackly line. I couldn't hear him properly.

"Speak up, will you?" I said. "This line's awful."

"Sorry. I'm on my car phone."

"Where are you?"

"Well, I'm in Islington, actually."

"Thassa coincidence 'cause . . . can't remember whether or not you know thish but, I, you know, um—live in Isl-ton . . . sh'ly."

"Do you? Good heavens! Well I'm in Oriel Road."

"Thass *'credible,*" I said. "Because . . . donno whether or not I tol' you thish, 'cause we've only met, twice, sh'ly—but thass my road."

"In fact I'm parked outside number twenty-two."

"Well, thersh 'nother 'credible coincidence because . . . oh . . ." I could hear a car door open and then shut. Then I heard the deep, throaty click of its central locking. And now I could hear sharp footsteps pinging on the pavement and the familiar squeak of my garden gate and then . . . my bell rang.

"Sorry, look, just gotta get that—hang on, won't be a min . . ." I went to the door, which is half-glazed, with red and blue stained-glass panels. A vast, wide shape looped eerily through the glass, half lit by the amber glow of an adjacent street lamp. I opened the door a crack. I saw something red. And green. And it was wrapped in cellophane. And it was very bulky, and it was bound at the bottom by an enormous red ribbon which lifted up and down in the thin wind. And then the red thing disappeared and there was Seriously Successful, standing behind it, smiling.

"Are you from Moyses Stevens?" I asked.

"No," he said. "Extraflora."

I laughed, though to be honest, what I really wanted to do was cry. He still had his mobile phone clamped, awkwardly, to his left ear. I looked at it inquiringly.

"I thought I'd like to have a One-2-One with you," he explained as he snapped it shut, "though I wish you weren't tipsy Tiffany, it does make communication rather difficult. Now, is this chronic dipsomania?" he inquired. "Or just a little sorrow-drowning? And Tiffany?"

"Yes?"

"Can I come in?"

I pulled back the door and he came into the house. I was filled with shame. My Ring of Confidence had collapsed. Because here was the love of my life and here I was half-cut and looking a total dog. Not even a pedigree dog, for example an elegant Saluki or beautiful Borzoi. Not even an English Trend-Setter. No, I looked pure Scrufts—six layers of ancient Aran and Shetland wool over thick gray leggings, which were visibly laddered behind one knee. Unbrushed hair. Unpolished, broken nails. No makeup—not even lip gloss—and no aroma of expensive scent. And the house—well, it was a tip.

"Sorry about the mess . . . like a drink?"

"Of course not Tiffany—I'm driving."

"Oh yes, sorry. Sorry. Wasn't thinking. Been drinking."

"I know. Why?"

"I drink therefore I am."

"Very funny," he said unsmilingly. "Look, could I make you some coffee?"

"Yes . . . kitchen's at the back . . . somewhere. Lovely roses. Lovely, lovely, lovely roses. Lovely . . . you're lovely . . . you're so nice to homeless people and sad spinsters and everything," I said, sinking into the sofa. "Even when they're clearly pissed." I flopped face down into the cushions and moaned softly into the chrysanthemum-yellow velvet devoré while Seriously Successful clattered about in the kitchen. God, I hoped he wasn't going to ask me where the Gold Blend was. Instead I heard him say, "Have you got any really strong coffee, Tiffany?"

"Yes," I said, suddenly remembering Alex's espresso. "I've got some thermonuclear Algerian . . . cupboard over the word processor. *Food* processor." Oh God, oh God. I looked around the sitting room—magazines and newspapers strewn everywhere, a chaotic pile of books on the coffee table, several small vases of half-dead snowdrops, and a depleted bottle of cheap red wine. Waynetta Slob, eat your heart out, I said to myself. Blanche Dubois, c'est moi! And that awful thought shocked me and made me want to sober up. I scooped things off the floor, then covered the mess on the table with a copy of the *Mail*—the one with Emma on the front page. Then I opened the window and inhaled deeply. Hummmmm . . . oooooh! Hummmmm . . . ooooooh!

"Tiffany, what *are* you doing?" Seriously Successful inquired as he brought in a tray with two cups.

"Breathing 'cises," I said.

"Oh." We sat, drinking the atomic coffee in silence, looking at each other. I began to feel a little better. Though, if I shut my eyes, I got the whirlies. I decided to keep them open.

"Thank you for the roses," I said. "They look lovely in that bucket."

"Well, I would have sent them to you, but I was away on business and didn't have time, and I thought it would be nice to, well, bring them over in person."

"It was nice. I mean it *is* nice. Very nice. You *are* nice. They're wonderful." I'd forgotten how powerful the coffee was—I felt the caffeine flood my veins like cocaine. I began to feel better. Much better.

"I'm sorry about my lack of personal grooming," I said. "And the charity shop couture. If I'd known you were coming I'd have washed my hair . . ."

"Your hair looks fine."

". . . and quite possibly restyled it too with the hot brush. And I'd have put on a pretty dress and elegant hosiery and a discreet amount of makeup. And I'd have taken 'ticular care over my 'cessories. Oh, and I'd have shaved my legs."

"You look very nice as you are."

"Thass not true, but thank you." I put my hand to my brow.

"Tense Nervous Headache?" he inquired solicitously.

"No. Shame and mortification. The headache's scheduled for tomorrow morning. After the raging thirst and before the postalcoholic panic." I looked at him. He wasn't in a suit today. He was wearing jeans and a thick, gray jumper, and his dark, curly hair was slightly damp.

"I saw you on the news," I said.

"Oh. That reporter was a bloody nuisance. We told him we didn't want him there. He hadn't asked beforehand. It was rude, and very intrusive."

"You looked so nice in your Savile Row donkey jacket."

"Thank you."

"What flavor was it?"

"What?"

"The soup," I explained. "Was it minestrone? Or mulligatawny? I don't suppose it was clam chowder, was it?"

"I can't remember. I didn't make it," he said. "I just help dish it out for two weeks of the year before and after Christmas. That's all. How are your campaigns?"

"They're fine. Have you seen my Love Hearts ad on the box?"

"Is that yours?"

"Yes."

"Those romantic poems?"

"Yes."

"It's really good," he said. "I didn't get a Valentine card this year," he added. "Would you recite one of your poems to me?"

"Oh. OK." I cleared my throat. " 'Be Mine/Blue Eyes/Trust Me/Nice Boy/Don't Be Coy/UROK/My Ideal . . . My Joy.' Of course, it's better with the club music," I added, "and the attractive actors and the eyeball-busting camerawork. You get the full effect, then. Do you want another one?"

"Oh yes."

" 'Forget Me Not/Dream Guy/My Love/My Buddy/My All/Be True/Why Not/Say Yes . . . Just Nod.' "

Seriously Successful was looking at me with a wistful intensity. "One more, please."

"Oh. Oh, OK, um . . . 'Cheer Up/Funny Face/My Sugar/My Pal/No Tears/I Love You/So Relax/Smile Dishy . . . You Win.'

They sound really stupid like that," I said quickly. "But on the TV they do look quite good, and the manufacturers are happy—they say it's been good for sales. And that's the bottom line. Sales. There's always a bottom line, isn't there?" I added thoughtfully as I replaced my cup in its saucer.

"Yes, there is," he said. "What's yours?"

"My bottom line is that I don't get involved with married men in any circumstances, even if I really like them. *Especially* if I really like them. And *your* bottom line is the fact that you're married." The wine had made me bold. That and the fact that I was on home ground.

"Yes," he said wearily, "I suppose that is my bottom line."

"And the penultimate line is the fact that you've got a girlfriend."

"No I haven't," he said with sudden indignation.

"Yes you have."

"No I *haven't.*"

This was outrageous. He was lying. Can't stand it when people lie to me. "Yes you bloody well have, because I saw you with her in the Ritz."

"That's not my girlfriend," he said with quiet exasperation. "That's my sister, Grace. Her boyfriend runs the small charity that organizes the soup run every year. She just wanted my help."

"If she was only your sister, why didn't you speak to me then? You just walked straight past, as though you were avoiding me. As though you had something to hide."

"I *was* avoiding you. Because you were with another man."

"Oh." Got that completely wrong then. How odd. "So you didn't go to Barbados then?"

"Sorry?"

"With your girlfriend."

"I've just told you I haven't got a girlfriend," he said.

"But surely you must have one," I persisted.

"Why must I?"

"Because you were looking for one."

"Doesn't mean to say that I found one," he said.

"But you must have done," I insisted, yet again.

"Look Tiffany—would you please stop telling me that I have a girlfriend when I don't have one," he said. Gosh, he was getting quite annoyed.

"But let's face it, you were going to considerable trouble to find one, advertising in the newspaper and everything, so I would have thought you'd have got one by now."

"Well, I haven't, OK."

"Because you said you were looking for someone to spoil a little or even a lot, and I'm sure there are any number of women out there who'd be only too happy to let you spoil them. Whereas I didn't want to be spoiled because I didn't know that you can only be spoiled by someone who's got a wife, like you."

"Tiffany, you're not making much sense . . ."

"And I'm only interested in single blokes who wouldn't dream of spoiling me. Ever."

"Tiffany, I won't spoil you," he said.

"Good," I said, looking at the three dozen long-stemmed red roses.

"But I don't want to spoil anyone else, either."

"Why not?"

"Because they were so boring," he said vehemently. "I did meet other women—about ten others from that ad, but they weren't . . ."

"Attractive?"

"Well, some of them were, but they weren't, I don't know . . ."

"Well dressed?"

"No, not even that, they were, but they weren't very . . ."

"Successful?"

"Oh no, some of them had very good jobs," he said, running his left hand through his curly brown hair. "It's just that they weren't . . ."

"What?"

"They weren't memorable. That's it. They were ordinary. Forgettable."

"I see."

"But I haven't forgotten you." He came and sat next to me on the sofa, and then he took hold of my left hand.

"I haven't forgotten you, either," I said quietly, and I could feel myself coming close to tears.

"And so I didn't bother with anyone else," I heard him say. "I wanted to see you, but you wouldn't see me. You wouldn't even be friends. That's what I couldn't understand."

"What's the point in being friends?" I said. "I'm not looking for friends—I've got lots of friends, I've got Lizzie, and Kate and Sally and Frances and Catherine and Kit and . . . and . . . and . . ." I grabbed the copy of the *Mail* which was lying on the top of the mess on the coffee table. "And I've got Emma," I said, pointing to her face. "She's a very good friend of mine."

"Oh God, that woman having an affair with Lawrence Bright?"

"Yes, but it's not her fault," I said emphatically. "He's unhappily married."

Seriously Successful gave me a penetrating look. "So it's OK for her, but not OK for you."

"What do you mean?"

"Well, I'm unhappily married, too. You know that."

"Yes, I do."

"But you won't see me." He looked upset.

"No, I won't."

"Why not?"

"Because I don't want to go out with someone who's not only married—they're *unfaithful,* too," I said.

"But I haven't been unfaithful!"

"Yes, you have," I said.

"No I haven't," he retorted.

"Well, why haven't you been?" I asked indignantly.

"Because the only person I wanted to be unfaithful with was you, you idiot, that's why."

"Do you mean to tell me you have *never* been unfaithful to your wife?" I said crossly.

He nodded seriously. "I wanted to," he said, "I really did." Suddenly his voice began to rise. "Oh yes. I committed infidelity in my heart many, many times."

"What, like Jimmy Carter you mean?"

"Er, quite. But then I turned forty, and then forty-one, and I thought, why not? Why should I carry on playing my part in this loveless charade? That's why I put in my ad. Because I wanted to find someone warm and kind and funny to love me. Why shouldn't I be loved?" His voice was rising. "I'm fed up with my marriage! I'm just *so* fed up with it!" he almost shouted. "I've been miserable for years. It's a *sham*."

"Well it's your fault, because you married for the wrong reasons," I said.

"Yes, I did," he replied quietly. "I married for money. Or rather, I let money come into the equation. I did love Olivia at the beginning," he explained. "In a way. It wasn't purely mercenary. But her father's cash was an enormous added incentive for a young, ambitious man. And I've paid the price," he said. "Over and over again. In loneliness. But you don't understand that Tiffany, because you're so *bloody* sanctimonious!"

"No I'm not!" I said.

"Yes you are—you're a prig, Tiffany." A prig! Imagine the impertinence!

"No I'm not," I said again primly.

"Yes you *are*," he countered. "You don't understand that things aren't simple, they're complex."

"I *do* understand that," I said, a sob rising to choke me. "But you've said you'll never get divorced, so it *is* simple, you see."

"But I can't leave my marriage because of my daughter. It would destroy her."

"Well that's fine. I understand that. But in that case please don't mess about with me!"

"But look Tiffany, the fact that I am technically still married is less important than the fact that you and I feel exactly the same way about each other, and the feeling is very, very strong."

"Don't go jumping to conclusions," I lied.

"That provocative postcard you sent me!"

"I was pissed. I regretted it profoundly."

"In vino veritas," he countered.

"But I'm drunk now," I pointed out. "And I'm *still* saying no."

He picked up the copy of the newspaper and then tossed it aside. "You've been driving me mad, Tiffany—you're so . . . so . . ." What on earth was the matter with him? He was staring at the coffee table. Then I saw him pick up the *Your Baby and Child* by Penelope Leach, and the book underneath it, *Protecting Your Baby-to-Be* by Margaret Profet. He turned them over in his hands. Then he replaced them and picked up Miriam Stoppard's *Complete Baby and Child Care* book, and beneath that was Sheila Kitzinger's *Natural Pregnancy Handbook*. He stared at me. Then he glanced at my middle, and suddenly jumping to his feet.

"Tiffany?"

"Yes?"

"Tiffany—*of course*," he said. He went and leaned against the mantelpiece. "I now see," he said quietly. "I understand. The *real* reason why you wouldn't see me. This shiny patina of high-mindedness you've been putting on everything, when the simple fact is that you've been involved with someone else and now you're . . . you're . . . pregnant. Oh God I feel such a *fool*," he went on. "That's the real reason, isn't it? You're expecting a baby, Tiffany. Aren't you?"

"Um, yes," I said. "I am."

"Whose is it?" he asked.

"What do you mean?"

"That spineless drip I saw you with in the Ritz?"

"Oh *no*. No. Not him," I said. *Credit me with a little taste, will you?*

"Or that man I saw you with in the restaurant?"

"Um, well . . ." I murmured guiltily. I stared at the floor.

"I see," said Seriously Successful quietly. Then he emitted a short, mirthless laugh. "I've been barking up the wrong tree with you Tiffany. How very ironic. It wasn't sanctimony I should have accused you of—but infidelity."

"Infidelity?"

"Yes. To me."

"What do you mean, infidelity? I wasn't even going out with you."

"Well, you should have been. I know you wanted to. And we belong together, you and I, and you know that too. Oh God, I feel such an idiot," he said, shaking his head. "But now it all makes sense. Of course you're pregnant—it's very obvious, that tired look you've got. Your pasty complexion. The lankness of your hair. That thickening around your middle. The bloatedness."

"Yes," I said. "It's really starting to show now."

"And that's why you were doing those breathing exercises."

"Yes. I've been going to ante-natal classes."

"But you shouldn't have drunk so much," he added crossly.

"No. You're right. I shouldn't."

"When's it due?" he asked with a bitter sigh.

"May."

"So you've been pregnant since . . . August," he said. I just looked at him blankly. "And so all the time I've been pursuing you, Tiffany, and thinking about you, and dreaming of the things we might do together, and the happy times we'd have— you've been expecting another man's child," he said.

"Well . . ." I began. "I didn't know for sure until December."

He stood up again and faced me full on. I could see a small muscle flexing rhythmically at the corner of his mouth. "Well, I'm sorry to have bothered you Tiffany," he said with cordial contempt. "I must say I thought you were my ideal kind of woman," he added. "My soulmate. My spiritual twin. The Snap to my Crackle and Pop. I only needed to meet you once, to know that. But I've clearly made a mistake. Well." He picked up his jacket. "Good luck with the baby. I don't think we'll meet again." Then he gave me a funny little smile and walked out of the house, shutting the door behind him with a quiet, definitive click.

February Continued

As I say, I'm really not one for rows, and so my last encounter with Seriously Successful left me Seriously Shaken. I was really, really disturbed, and terribly upset. Traumatized in fact. What did he *mean*—"pasty complexion"? I've been scrutinizing my face very closely since then, with the aid of a magnifying mirror, and I simply can't agree. However, I may get some more Elizabeth Lauderstein alpha hydroxy resin with serum derived from tropical fruit acids in order to enhance luminosity. Just in case. But then . . . what's the point? Because I know I'll never see him again. Or hear his lovely voice, because he won't ring me now, or send me flowers or make me laugh or anything like that ever, ever, again. In fact he'll probably never even *think* of me except, I suppose, with distaste, because he was really, really angry about my "pregnancy." I can't say I blame him. But that little deception of mine was necessary because it got me out of a very sticky situation; because if I hadn't lied about the baby I think Seriously Successful would have done more than hold my hand. He might have put his arm around me, which would have been dreadful, obviously. And then he might have kissed me, which would have been terrible too, and then he might have . . . we might have . . . and that would have been absolutely *appalling,* because, underneath my six layers of Shetland wool and my laddered leggings, I was wearing Big Knickers. Granny pants. Thermal ones, actually. They're perfect for this cold weather, you see. And also, let me not forget that Seriously Successful is, of course, still Seriously Married. But I felt dreadful after he left, *dreadful,* because I knew that this time, that was *it.* Bye Bye. Not even *au revoir* or *auf Wiedersehen,* pet. Just good . . . bye. Well, it was quite a bad bye actually. Very bad. So to cheer myself up I decanted the thirty-six roses into about five different vases, then I sat down and drew up the following list:

SERIOUSLY SUCCESSFUL — PROS AND CONS

Pros	*Cons*
Good looking (well I think so)	Is married
Clever	
Funny	
Kindhearted	
Lovely voice	
Likes fat girls	
Does not like golf	
Sends flowers	
Is generous	
And honorable	
Has impeccable taste in ties	
And suits	
Yet is not shallow	
For example, helps the homeless	
Yet is not sanctimonious	
For example, would quite like to have an affair	
Is musical	
And sensitive	
Yet is not perfect, far from it in fact.	

Now, you might well think that when it came to the bottom line, nineteen pros would easily cancel out one con. But it's not a simple matter of profit and loss, because when you're working these things out, well, some things weigh more heavily in the balance than others, don't they? So if, for example, Seriously Successful was Seriously Selfish, then that might counteract, say, his sensitivity, musicality, and natty neckwear because, in my book, selfishness is a very big con indeed. And being married—at least to someone else—is an even bigger one. In fact it's so big that it outweighs all the positive things, at least as far as I'm concerned. Cancels them out completely. Now, others might take a different view and go ahead and take the plunge—and the consequences. But I'm not going to do that, because I may be dim, but I'm not stupid, and he's told me for a fact that he's going to stay married because of his daughter, so I'm *not* going to get involved. And that's that. And when I read my list, I felt better immediately because it confirmed what I absolutely knew to be right; although when I looked at all the pros and cons again, and thought of Seriously Successful standing at my front door behind that vast bouquet, and then making me coffee, and sitting on the sofa with me, holding my hand, and looking so attractive—well *I* think so—and saying such nice things to me, I got very, very upset, and before I knew it my eyes had filled and I was bawling. Howling. I was having a really lovely, economy-sized cry—and then just as I was really getting into it, my eyelids swelling beautifully, tears seeping into the corner of my mouth and snot dribbling down over my upper lip and everything, and my breath coming in childish little gasps, this incredibly annoying thing happened. The phone rang. And it was Patrick. And that made me feel happy. So I was unable to carry on crying. And that really pissed me off, because there's nothing more irritating than someone cheering you up when you're having a lovely big cry.

"Tiffany, is this a good time to chat?" said Patrick politely.

"No it isn't, actually," I said. "In fact it's rather inconvenient. You've interrupted my weeping just when it was going

really well." Actually, I didn't say that at all. I said, "Oh yes,
Patrick. It's absolutely fine. Really. Hello!"

"You sound as though you've got a cold," he said.

"Er, yes, I do," I replied. "Not much of one, just a runny
nose, really." And in order to make this sound plausible I blew
it loudly, and theatrically, very close to the mouthpiece. Because I think that if he'd known that I was in fact crying over
another man, with whom I was, in fact, madly in love, well, he
might have been a bit put off. I thought he sounded very nice,
and we chatted for a few minutes about this and that, including
tennis—and he must be a really brilliant player because he told
me that he played in Junior Wimbledon in 1972! And then we
chatted a bit more and decided that yes, we did want to meet,
and so we arranged a rendezvous at Frederick's, in Islington,
on the twenty-eighth of February.

I thought I'd better mug up on Patrick's details before I went to
meet him, and so on the twenty-eighth I took his profile out of
the Potential Life Partners section of my index file and studied
it carefully for a couple of hours. In the Person Behind the Face
section, he said he had a "zest for life"—that sounded really
good—and that he enjoyed "socializing and eating out, accompanied by wit and sparkling conversation"! I'll see what I
can do, Patrick! Maybe I could tell him my joke about the unemployed talking pig, I thought to myself as I got ready. I
really hoped he would be as good-looking in three dimensions
as he appeared to be in two.

I got the number 73 to the Angel, feeling extremely optimistic and yet more than a little nervous. After all, this was my
debut with the Introduction Agency Male. Male order, I suppose you could call it. At a quarter to seven I walked into Frederick's in Camden Passage, passed the semi-circular bar, and
looked around expectantly.

"Is Mr. Miller here, yet?" I asked the maitre d'. He looked in
the book, nodded, and led me through to the large conservatory

dining room at the back. As we walked down the steps beneath the enormous chandelier, I saw a man seated at a far table get to his feet. It was Patrick. And he was even *better*-looking in the flesh than he had been in the photo! Really, very, very dishy. Matinée idolish, in fact. This was wonderful. It was a good job it wasn't February the twenty-ninth, otherwise I might have proposed to him on the spot! He was wearing a very smart suit, in a subtle gray check, with a pink stripy shirt and a teal-blue silk tie. Silver cufflinks. I glanced at his shoes. They were all polished—that's a good sign—and lace-ups, of course, not plebby slip-ons.

"Hello, Tiffany," he said. But then he did this funny thing. He didn't extend his hand, he tried to kiss me. Kiss me! This was *extremely* forward behavior. It took me by surprise and I must say I did not offer my cheek up to his lips.

"Don't I get a kiss?" he asked with an offended air.

"No," I said flatly. "I don't even know you."

He laughed. "Well, can we shake hands, then?"

"Yes, of course." So we did. And then we sat down, and he smiled at me. But I was feeling quite shocked, so I just gave him a frigid stare.

"Well, Miss Arctic Ice Queen, it's very nice to meet you," he said with a smile. Ice Queen! The cheek! I hoped that such impertinence was not a common characteristic of blokes on Caroline Clarke's register. I made a mental note not to tell him my joke about the talking pig. Despite my high hopes, the evening was not starting well. In fact it was clearly going to be a disaster.

"Let's have a drink," he said. He ordered a bottle of rather good Pouilly-Fuissé and before I knew what was happening the bottle was empty, conversation was flowing and I had melted like a choc-ice in July.

"So, tell me about Junior Wimbledon," I said, genuinely impressed. "How far did you get?"

"Well," he said. "I made it to the quarter finals."

"The quarter finals!" I exclaimed. "Wow!"

"Yes. And I was heading for the semis, when my opponent made an unexpected comeback and I narrowly lost it in the tie-break."

"Oh, *no*," I said. "But you did *terribly* well to get that far. Anyway, take me through the match, point by point."

So he did. And I found that I was really enjoying myself. And then we ordered something to eat, and had another bottle of wine, and we talked nonstop for about three and a half hours. And then I told him my joke about the pig and I was just about to hit him with the punchline, which is frankly *hilarious*, when he said, ". . . and the pig said, 'But I'm a *plumber.*' "

"Oh, you know it already," I said tipsily. "Damn. There I was thinking how funny it was, and how you were going to roar with laughter when I got to the end—and you knew it all along. You led me up the garden path there. God, I feel such a fool."

"But I was enjoying the way you were telling it," he said. And then he gave me a really dazzling smile, which made me feel a bit butteryfluttery, to be frank.

And then we got the bill and I said, "Can I contribute?" because it's nice to offer, though it's *not* nice when they accept. But Patrick looked shocked.

"Of course not," he said. He didn't say, "Yes. Let's go Dutch," like Paul from Eat 'n' Greet. And he didn't touch me for fifteen quid like Mungo Brown. He just got out his gold American Express card and paid. And then I looked at my watch, and it was midnight, and Patrick had to get back to Hammersmith and I had to get home.

"I've had a lovely evening," I said truthfully. "Thank you."

And I waited for him to say, "I'll call you," or "Let's get together again *really* soon," or "Let's go line-dancing," or something like that. But he didn't. He just said, "Well, good-bye," and I felt *so* disappointed because I thought that despite the unpromising start to the evening, we'd got on terribly well. As I sat in the back of the cab I wondered about having a little cry.

but decided against it; after all I might meet someone nice at Jonathan's wedding.

Early the following morning, at ten, the phone rang. I was still in bed.

"Yes?" I said.

"Tiffany?"

"Yes?"

"It's Patrick here."

"HELLO!" I said happily.

"Are you up, Tiffany?"

"Oh *yes*," I said. "Been up for. . ."—ten seconds— ". . . ages."

"Now, I know I'm not supposed to do this," he said. "I know I'm meant to be cool and leave it at least a week before ringing you again, but I can't be bothered with all that baloney. I just called to say . . ."

". . . yes?"

". . . how much I enjoyed meeting you." Wow! "And I wondered whether you'd like to come to the theater with me."

"Yes!" I said. "Yes! Yes! Yes! Any time. How about today?" Actually, I didn't say that. I simply said, "Oh, well, um, yes, that would be rather nice."

"Are you free on Saturday?"

"Oh, I'm afraid not," I said. "I'm going up to Yorkshire for a wedding."

"Next Wednesday, then?"

"I think so. Let me look in my diary. Yes, Wednesday would be fine."

"You can choose the play."

"OK," I said happily. "I'd like to see *The School for Wives*."

March

"Aren't the daffodils wonderful!" I said to Nick as we sat on the nine-thirty from King's Cross on our way up to Jonathan's wedding.

"Yes," he agreed as he gazed out the window. They lined the railroad banks, nodding and dancing with Wordsworthian *élan* as we swished through the Hertfordshire countryside. We had set off in good time, allowing almost three hours for the journey up to York.

"I hope Jonathan remembers his lines," said Nick with a grin.

"Sarah will prompt him at the slightest hesitation," I said as the train drew into Stevenage, our first stop.

"Did you bring the directions to the church?" Nick asked.

"No I didn't. Did you?"

"No. All I've got with me is the invitation."

"Same here. But it'll be fine," I said reassuringly, as the doors banged shut and we pulled away toward Peterborough. "It's St. Mary's, Westow, which is obviously very near to the city because the postal address is York. So it probably won't take more than about ten minutes in a cab. The wedding starts at twelve, the train gets in at eleven-thirty, and so we'll be in our pew by—ooh—eleven forty-five latest," I said.

"Perfect," he said. "I like your dress, Tiffany."

"Thanks. You look pretty good yourself." Nick, you see, was in morning dress. The full monty. This was going to be a smart affair. No New Labour lounge suits, thank you—coattails and stripy trousers only.

I fingered the viridian Swiss jersey of my Jasper Conran dress—it was very fitted, slinky almost, and totally unforgiving of the slightest bump or curve. I'd starved myself for a week to ensure that I'd be able to carry it off. And I accessorized it carefully with a big navy straw hat by Phillip Treacy and a velvet shawl in turquoise and lime. And as I sat there, happily daydreaming about Patrick, Nick reminisced, yet again, about our happy days in Downingham.

"Do you remember when Stuyvesant blew up the science lab?" he said with a sentimental sigh.

"Yes," I said dreamily, "I do."

"Bloody funny. And wasn't it amusing when Jack Benson got hold of a Kalashnikov and held up the Midland Ban—oh! Why aren't we moving?"

The train had ground to a halt. In fact it had been stationary for quite a while. Nick looked at his watch. "We've been stuck here for fifteen minutes," he said anxiously.

We were somewhere outside Doncaster—I looked at my watch, ten-fifty A.M. Suddenly the public address system crackled into life, and we heard the guard apologize for the "short delay."

"It's probably daffodils on the line," said Nick. "Just our luck."

"Don't worry," I said, "it'll be fine." Though to be honest, I was rather worried too. It's so embarrassing arriving late for a wedding—unforgivable, in fact—we'd have to get a wiggle on when we got to York. Twenty minutes later we were still sitting on the track and my anxiety levels were almost Himalayan. I got out my antique roses tapestry kit and stabbed away at the canvas to calm myself down. I had just completed a small leaf when we felt the train squeak and grind into life, and then slowly shunt forward again. It was eleven-fifteen. We were now cutting it fine. Very fine.

"We'll be fine," said Nick. At eleven forty-two we pulled into York. By now we should have been calmly sitting in our pew, studying our psalters! We flung open the doors, ran across the platform, out of the station, and found the taxi rank. Oh God, oh God, a long queue! There was only one thing for it—we'd have to push in!

"Look," I pleaded to the woman who was first in line, "I'm really really really sorry but you see, we're going to a wedding and we're terribly *terribly* late and I wondered *would* you mind, I know it's really rude of us and everything, and I know this probably confirms *all* your prejudices about appalling Southerners with *no* manners, but you see the service starts at twelve and, oh thank you thank you *thank you* that's *so* kind of you," I said.

"St. Mary's church, please," said Nick breathlessly.

"Which one?" said the driver.

"The one at Westow," he responded.

The driver rolled his eyes. "Westow? That's a bi' of a way."

"A bi' of a way?"

"It's twenty-five miles," he said as we drove off at speed. Twenty-five miles! That would take at least half an hour. Probably more.

"Well, *please* hurry," I said. "But safely, of course, and within the national speed limit. We're late for a wedding you see."

"I didn't know it was so far away," said Nick.

"Nor did I."

"This is entirely my fault, Tiffany," he said gallantly. "I should have brought the directions. I take full responsibility."

"No, no, no, let me share the blame!" I exclaimed. "I should have been more organized myself." And then I remembered something else I hadn't been very organized about. I hadn't wrapped my present. It was in my basket—an alabaster lamp from Heal's. I got it out and tried to start wrapping it, but it was impossible in the moving car. I'd have to do it in the church.

We hurtled through the countryside, only half taking in the green, lamb-filled fields, cross-hatched by dry stone walls, and the thick clusters of primroses along the winding road. And then we came to Westow, screeching to a halt outside the church, just in time to see Sarah stepping into the porch with her father, her veil lifting in the breeze.

"Oh God oh God, there she is! Quick!" We paid the driver, then dashed up to the church door. The congregation were all standing for the Entrance of the Bride. Nick and I waited until she'd made her stately progress toward the altar, and then snuck into an emptyish-looking pew halfway up the aisle.

"Sorry!" we said in hoarse whispers as four beautifully be-suited bottoms shuffled along the burnished wooden bench. "So sorry!"

"Dearly Beloved," said the vicar, ". . . gathered here . . . sight of God . . . Holy Matrimony . . . honorable estate . . ."

I looked around the church. It was full. And everyone was really well turned out. There was an abundance of frock coats and expensive suits—and the millinery—my God, the women's hats were so sharp you could have cut yourself on them. The organ suddenly sounded and we stood for the first hymn—"I Vow to Thee, My Country"—which we all sang with lusty enthusiasm, and this gave me the chance to inspect Sarah's dress. It was of ivory shantung silk, with long sleeves, a high neck, and a ski run of covered buttons all the way down the back. It had a dropped waist and a wide, flaring skirt, with a huge, soft bow at the base of her spine. It was lovely. Maybe I'd have something like that myself, I thought, when I marry Patrick, whose face, naturally, I substituted for Jonathan's.

"I take thee, Patrick," I mumbled happily to myself. "To be my wedded husband . . . for richer for poorer . . . in sickness and in wealth . . ."

Then we sat down for the first reading, which was from *The Prophet,* by Kahlil Gibran. My God! The present! I'd completely forgotten. I took the lamp out of my basket with the sheaf of wrapping paper and the Scotch tape, and surreptitiously started to wrap it.

" 'Then Almitra spoke again and said, And what of Marriage, master?' "

"Nick, could you just put your finger there?" I whispered.

" 'And he answered saying: You were born together, and together you shall be for evermore.' "

"No, not there. *There*. God, this sticky tape isn't very sticky."

"Shhhhhh!" said someone behind me.

" 'You shall be together when the white wings of death scatter your days.' "

"Oh God, I've lost the end . . ."

" 'Aye, you shall be together even in the silent memory of God.'"

"Have you got sharp nails, Nick?"

" 'But let there be spaces in your togetherness.' "

"OK Nick, just hold that there, will you, just there, now *don't* move your finger otherwise it'll all come undone."

" 'And let the winds of the heavens dance between you.' "

"Oh God, where are the scissors? I want to curl the ribbon." Eventually the deed was done—lamp and shade both wrapped. I stuck a shiny red bow on top, scribbled on the gift tag, and then returned the present to my basket. What a lovely wedding that was, I thought happily. I was really enjoying it. Jonathan and Sarah looked radiant, and the sun obligingly shone down on them through the stained-glass windows, flooding their faces with light. And then came the heavy bit.

"What God has joined together let no man put asunder," boomed the vicar.

Or woman, I thought to myself, thinking of Seriously Successful.

"I now pronounce you—Man and Wife." Oh, I always want to clap at that point. And then Jonathan and Sarah went to sign the register and someone sang "Ave Maria" and suddenly, that was it—they were hitched, and they were walking toward us down the aisle together, arm in arm, smiling and occasionally nodding as they recognized faces in the congregation, and Sarah looked so happy and so, well, *relieved*. Now she was Mrs. de Beauvoir. Mrs. Jonathan de Beauvoir. What a lovely name, I thought. Mrs. Patrick Miller, I reflected, wasn't quite as nice as that, but at least it wasn't an awful name. I mean I could never marry someone with a really hideous one, I thought to myself, like Cocup, Suett, Frogg or Shufflebottom. Tiffany Shufflebottom? Oh no. I really didn't think so. And then I looked at the bridesmaids following in Sarah's wake, and they were so adorable in their pale mint-green silk frocks, with winter jasmine and daffodil buds in their posies and celandines and primulas woven into their ivy headbands. They looked sweet, all except for the tallest girl, who was about eleven, and her hair—well it was terribly short, almost shaven, and were those Doc Martens I could see peeping out from under her dress? And her complexion—it was powdered a pristine white, with rings of black kohl around her eyes and—horror of horrors—there was a silver ring in her nose. Who the hell *was* she? She looked a sight! How could her parents let her go around looking like that? What a stark contrast she made to the angelic little girls and the cherubic pages in their dinky little breeches and bow ties. Widor's "Toccata" thundered as we all trooped out of the church into the sharp, spring sunshine and made our way down a tree-lined path to the Old Vicarage, Sarah's home.

"Wasn't that lovely?" I said to Nick.

"Yeah, it was a great show," he said.

And then we followed everyone into the yellow-striped marquee, where forty or so tables were laid with the whitest linen, shining silver and sparkling lead crystal and centerpieces of tumbling spring flowers. An English country wedding. It was perfect. Everyone looked happy as they sipped champagne and stood in line to greet the happy couple. I decided to find the loo before the wedding breakfast began. As I went into the bath-room, I could see someone was already in there, fiddling about in front of the mirror. It was the punky bridesmaid, and she was in trouble.

"Oh gawd," she said. "Oowww!" Her nose ring had caught on the lace edging of her dress. "Oooohh!" She was pulling at it, trying to release it, but having very little luck.

"Oh gaaaawd!" she said again. It looked terribly painful.

"Can I help you?" She nodded, as far as she was able, given that her head was attached to her dress. I got hold of the lace and gently worked it around until the silver nose ring was released.

"Oh fanks," she said gratefully. "I fought I was going to rip my nostril in two there and bleed all over me frock."

"Well, it's fine now," I said, looking at her. She was a mess. A complete and utter mess. In fact she looked as if she had been in a fight. But beneath the skinhead coiffure and nuclear holo-caust makeup there was an extremely pretty face.

"Your dress is lovely," I said truthfully.

"I feel a bit of an idiot in it," she said. "I didn't even *want* to be a bridesmaid, but my mum made me."

"Why didn't you want to be a bridesmaid?" I said.

"Because I think marriage is a load of bollocks?" Good Lord! Such cynicism in one so young. "I'm never going to get married," she announced as she washed her hands. I glanced at her nails. They were painted black. "I mean my parents—they're married," she went on, "and they're miserable. They argue all the time."

"Oh dear," I said.

"Lots of my friends' parents are divorced and it's brilliant, because they get loads of presents," she continued, "because their mums and dads are always trying to outdo each other. I wish my parents would split up," she said ruefully as she opened the door. "They don't even *like* each other."

"Oh dear," I said again, completely lost for words at this un-looked-for confidence. "Well, see you later."

I washed my hands and reapplied my concealer—the early start had left a pale penumbra under each eye. Then I went back downstairs, where lunch was about to begin. Nick and I were on different tables; he went to his, which looked large, and rather lively, and I found my way to mine. And sitting there already was the punky bridesmaid. She gave me a welcoming smile. And seated on her right was a rather thin, crisp-looking woman whom I took to be the mother. And on the other side was—*keep calm Tiffany, keep calm*—oooooooh! Mmmmmmm-mmm! Ooooooooh!

"Hallo Tiffany," said Seriously Successful calmly. "I noticed you in church. Quite an entrance. Did you manage to wrap your present? Darling, this is Tiffany Trott," he said. "Tiffany, this is my wife, Olivia, and my daughter, Saskia."

"Saskia and I have just met, actually," I said. "Upstairs."

"Tiffany's in advertising, darling," he said to his wife. "That's how we met."

"Yes. That's right," I said. "Through advertising." This explanation seemed to satisfy Olivia. She smiled at me in a reasonably friendly fashion, then spread her napkin over the lap of her black Issy Miyake tunic. She looked austere and detached, but also tired and strained as we all made awkward conversation over the lobster salad.

"More wine, Olivia?" said Seriously Successful coldly.

"Yes please darling," she replied in an equally frigid fashion. What *was* his name, anyway? I still didn't know, and she just called him "darling" all the time, in this acidulous tone of voice.

"I'd like some wine too, please," I said holding out my glass. *I'm sure it's beautifully chilled by now in this frosty atmosphere.*

"Well, I really don't think you should, Tiffany," he said, "in your condition." Bastard.

"You see Olivia, Tiffany is expecting a baby," said Seriously Successful. "Aren't you, Tiffany?"

"Well, I really don't want to disc—"

"She's going to be a single mother," he added.

"Oh, what a good idea," said Olivia, to my utter surprise.

"So, she can't drink, of course, which is a pity as this is a particularly good Sauvignon and I happen to know that Tiffany is rather partial to Sauvignon."

"Yes. Yes I am," I said as he placed the bottle beyond my reach.

"And I certainly don't think you should be eating seafood, Tiffany," he continued as he whisked away my starter and handed it to a passing waiter. "It would be very irresponsible of you to risk it," he added seriously. "Wouldn't it?" Bastard. "Though I must say," he went on smoothly as he poured me some mineral water, "you really don't *look* pregnant at all. What a very discreet little bump you've got there Tiffany. In fact—I do hope you won't mind my saying this—it's the discreetest I've ever seen. So much so that when I saw you in the church I said to myself, 'Well, Is She Or Isn't She?' " *Bastard.* "When's it due?" he continued.

"I really don't want to talk ab—"

"May, isn't it?" he inquired, giving me a penetrating stare. "Isn't that what you said, Tiffany? May?" Right. That was it. I know I'd misled him and everything, but this was simply going *too far.* He'd made his point. And I couldn't answer back in front of the family. I decided to ignore him completely and talk to his wife instead. That would really get up his nose.

"Olivia, what's your connection with Jonathan and Sarah?" I asked.

"I'm Sarah's first cousin," she replied. But then why weren't they at the engagement bash?

"What a pity you missed their party," I said to her. "It was rather good. It was at the East India Club."

"We missed it because Olivia opened the invitation and then forgot to tell me about it, didn't you Olivia?" said Seriously Successful. His wife glared at him. "You always 'forget' to tell me when there's something going on which I might possibly enjoy," he added.

"Oh, look I hope you're not going to start arguing *again,* you two," said Saskia wearily. She looked at me and rolled her eyes heavenward. "They bickered all the way up here in the car," she whispered. "For four and a half hours nonstop! I had to tell them to shut up." Oh dear.

"Saskia, I do wish you'd take off all that horrible makeup," said Seriously Successful suddenly. "You look awful."

"No I don't, Dad," said Saskia.

"Darling, I'm afraid you do," he replied. "You look as though someone's punched you in the face. And your accent— it's terrible. What's the point of sending you to Benenden if you're going to come out sounding like Barbara Windsor?"

"At least she doesn't sound like *Elizabeth* Windsor," said his wife acidly. "And as for her makeup—Saskia must be free to express herself in whichever way she chooses."

"My wife has very progressive views about children's education, deportment, behavior and appearance," said Seriously Successful to me, "whereas I'm . . ."

"Stuffy, uptight and old-fashioned," said his wife sharply. My head was swinging from left to right as if I were on Wimbledon Center Court.

"I am not old-fashioned," said Seriously Successful.

"Yes you are," said his wife.

"No I'm not."

"I'm afraid you are."

He is, you know," whispered Saskia. "He'd like me to wear"—she'd pulled a face—"Laura Ashley. And—yeeeuch!— Liberty. And the pictures he likes are dead boring, whereas Mum likes really modern stuff. She ought to run a gallery— she'd be good at that." This observation presented me with a good opportunity to change the subject, while simultaneously annoying Seriously Successful again.

"What sort of art interests you?" I asked Olivia.

"Abstract, Expressionist, post-modern, and of course conceptual," she said. "I think it's thrilling. I've never shared my husband's taste for dreary landscapes, sporting prints, and self-indulgent Rococo and Baroque—I like art that is contemporary, vivid and relevant to today."

"I really can't see how bits of dead animal are relevant to anything," said Seriously Successful as he cut into his lamb.

"I love Tracey Emin's work," said Olivia, ignoring him. "And Rachel Whiteread's installations are extremely haunting and thought-provoking. And I'm very interested in video art as well." Her husband was groaning audibly.

"Do you ever go to the Oscar Reeds gallery?" I asked her as a waitress spooned tiny new potatoes onto our plates. "The owner's a bit of a bore, but I think you'd like the work."

"Oh yes," she said cryptically as she picked up her knife and fork. "I know *all* about Oscar Reeds." Now what did *that* mean? It probably meant that Oscar Reeds had insulted her as well.

"How are your ante-natal classes going, Tiffany?" said Seriously Successful with a hefty sip of Bordeaux. "Are the breathing exercises going well?"

"Yes. *Very* well," I said truthfully.

"Would you like to demonstrate?" he inquired.

"No. No, I wouldn't." God, he was knocking back the booze.

"Well, just lay off the soft cheese, OK?" he hissed tipsily, as the dessert course arrived. "I don't want to see you touch that dolcelatte."

"And I don't want to see you drink and drive," I countered.

"I'm not," he retorted indignantly, "I *never* do. We're staying in the village tonight."

Oh. And then the champagne came around, our glasses were filled and Jonathan and Sarah cut the cake, and then speeches were made and they were short and funny, just as they should be, and it was all so, well, perfect, really. And I thought, this is how it's going to be when Patrick and I tie the knot. Just like this. And then the band struck up, and Sarah and Jonathan took to the dance floor while we all watched and clapped, and then, gradually, everyone else joined in. Fathers dancing with daughters, mothers with sons, grandparents with teenage grandchildren, husbands with wives, and then Saskia dashed off and found herself a young boy to twirl around with and . . . oh God. My heart sank. Pamela Roach! In a fetching, low-cut wigwam in bubble-gum pink. She was on the dance floor, gyrating furiously with a hideous-looking man of about fifty-five. She looked gloriously happy as she wobbled around with him, twisting and shaking her expansive frame to the tune of "Do You Think I'm Sexy?" by Rod Stewart. I lowered my head then hid my face behind my right hand. I didn't want to be spotted.

"What's the matter, Tiffany?" said Seriously Successful suddenly. "Toothache? Or is it indigestion? You mothers-to-be should be careful about your diet. Here," he said, passing me some grapes. "The Snack You Can Eat Between Meals." I gave him a withering look: *drop dead, gorgeous.* "Or would you like a little top-up?" he went on, offering me the cafetière. "There's An Awful Lot of Coffee in Brazil you know, Tiffany. Or perhaps, ooh, no, of course not—you should be drinking herbal tea instead, shouldn't you?"

Olivia was looking at her husband, then at me, nonplussed. "You're behaving even more strangely than usual," she said to Seriously Successful disapprovingly, as she popped a bright blue capsule into her mouth.

"Not at all," he said. "It's All Because the Lady Loves . . . oh, who's this?"

"Tiffany! Tiffany," barked Pamela. "You must be blind! Didn't you see me? I've been waving at you from the dance floor!"

"Pamela, hasn't anyone ever told you that redheads should never, ever, ever, even on pain of death, wear pink?" I said. Actually I didn't say that. I said, "Oh sorry. Didn't see you. Fancy bumping into you again."

"Well, after the engagement party I did a bit of research at

Somerset House," she began breathlessly. "And I discovered that I'm related to Jonathan by marriage. And when I told Sarah that I am in fact a second cousin of his, three times removed, on my mother's father's side, she very kindly sent me an invitation."

"Oh, I'm a cousin too," said Olivia with sudden interest. "Now which side are you on—the Fitzroys or the McCallums?"

Pamela looked blankly at her. And then a blush the color of sunburn spread from her throat up to her face. "Oh, er, er . . . the er, Fitzroys," she offered.

"Oh, they're a very interesting family," said Olivia. "Do sit down and I'll tell you all about them. I've done a very detailed family history, actually . . ."

"Well . . . I really don't want to bother you," said Pamela, suddenly retreating. "I only came over to say hello to Tiffany, and in fact my partner's waiting for me over there." She rushed off again and was soon swallowed up in the colorful shoal of shuffling dancers.

"How odd," said Olivia. "Well, excuse me while I powder my nose."

"Tiffany," said Seriously Successful with sudden quietness when she'd gone.

"Yes?"

"Why did you tell me you were pregnant?"

"I didn't," I said truthfully.

"But, I don't understand," he said with an inebriated sigh. "All those childcare books."

"My friend Sally's having a baby," I explained. "In May. I'm her birthing partner."

"Oh," he said. "Oh, I see. I made a mistake, then."

"Yes. You did."

"It was a bit mean of you, not to put me right," he said resentfully.

"I don't think so," I replied. "In the circumstances."

Seriously Successful glanced wistfully at the dancers, and then he looked at me and said, "Tiffany . . ."

"Yes?"

"I wonder. Would you . . . would you like to . . . ?"

"Trotters!" Suddenly Nick was standing next to me, extending his hand. "Come on, Trotters. Come and have a dance." He smiled at Seriously Successful, and at Olivia, who'd just returned. "Nick Walker," he said politely. "Do excuse us."

"Oh. Oh. Yes, Nick," I said as he led me onto the dance floor. And to be honest I was glad to have a break from Seriously Successful's domestic disharmony. Frankly it was a bit of a strain. I glanced at him from time to time as Nick gently whirled me around. He remained at the table, sitting there, silently, with his wife. And he looked miserable. Quite miserable. And I felt for him. I really did. But Seriously Successful's problems were not my business, his unhappy marriage none of my affair. Though at least he hadn't lied about his circumstances, as many men do. He and his wife seemed completely different, their incompatibility clear for all to see. And Olivia was obviously unhappy, too. Very unhappy. Was that why she wore black to weddings?

March Continued

ARNOLPHE: My grasp of conjugal cunning is complete.
               I'm an expert on uxorial deceit.
               I've taken steps, moreover, to prevent
               My cuckolding. She's wholly innocent
               Is *my* bride. Yes, a clot . . .

  "Want one?" I whispered to Patrick.
  "No thanks," he said.

CHRYSALDE: I can't quite see.
ARNOLPHE: I'm marrying a fool. No flies on me.

  "Have a Continental Truffle?" I said, offering him the box again.
  "Er, no thanks, Tiffany," he whispered back.
  "How about a Lemon Dream?"
  "No, no really." I looked at the leaflet in the box, I could just make out what it said in the half-light.
  "It says it's a *'light, lemon fondant cream draped in rich dark chocolate.'* "
  "No thanks. Not for me."
  "How about a Nut Swirl?"
  "Er, no."

ARNOLPHE: I'm sure your wife's as virtuous as can be.
                But one with brains is not a good idea.
                And certain husbands I could name pay dear
                For taking on the intellectual type.

"Isn't Peter Bowles marvelous," I said.

"Yes."

"He's one of my *favorite* actors."

"Good."

"Did you see him in *To the Manor Born*?"

"No."

"He was fantastic."

"Shhhhhh!" said someone, very noisily, behind us.

ARNOLPHE: The sort of wife I want is one, in short,
                Who wouldn't think a single, knowing thought.
                As for her pastimes, I'll allow her three:
                Sewing; churchgoing; loving me.

CHRYSALDE: You want a total imbecile. I see.

ARNOLPHE: I'd rather someone stupid and quite plain
                Than absolutely gorgeous with a brain.

"*Bloody* funny," I said, as the curtain came down for the interval in a shower of applause. "Bloody funny. God, I love Sheridan."

"It's Molière actually," Patrick pointed out.

"Oh, so it is," I said as we made our way into the bar. "Silly me. Are you enjoying it, Patrick?" I asked him when he came back with our drinks.

"Oh, yes," he said. "It's very amusing." Amusing? It was hilarious.

"Do you want a Black Magic now?" I said, offering him the box.

"Oh, OK then," he said. "Can I have a Hazelnut Cluster?"

Christ, I'd eaten those. In fact I'd eaten most of the others as well. All except . . .

"Why don't you have a Raspberry Roulade?"

"What?"

"A light and luscious fondant cream draped in rich, dark chocolate."

"Oh, right," and then I had another sip of red wine and suddenly the five-minute bell sounded and we trooped back into the dress circle.

The second half flew by in a flash, although it was quite hard concentrating on the play when my knees were nearly touching Patrick's. And it was so romantic, sitting there in the warm darkness on our red velvet seats, laughing at the witty translation and giggling at Arnolphe, this narrow-minded merchant who wants to marry his young ward, but is obsessed with the fear of being made a cuckold. And the whole point of the play is that Arnolphe's elaborate plans to preserve her chastity serve only to drive her into the arms of his handsome young rival. I thought it was a scream—deeply and richly ironic—but to be honest Patrick didn't find it as funny as I did. And I think I know the reason why. Because afterward, when we went to dinner, I asked him why he had got divorced.

"My wife had an affair," he said as he tore a piece off his bread roll.

"Oh. Oh." I wasn't quite sure what else to say, so I just said, *"Bad luck,"* and tried to change the subject. We talked a bit more about the play. And about the fact that Arnolphe is looking for someone thick, because he's too scared to marry an intelligent woman in case she deceives him.

"There are lots of men like Arnolphe," I said.

"What do you mean?"

"Well, men who don't want clever women. They find them threatening. Not so much because they're worried they'll have affairs, but because they feel they'll be put in the shade. Take my friend Frances, for example. She's got an intellect the size of several planets. She got a double first at Oxford and is head of family law at a top London practice. But men just don't seem very interested in her."

"Is she good-looking?" he asked.

"Oh, yes, she is. But it's the big brain, you see. They don't like it. I keep telling her to dumb down a bit, you know, go back to school, retake her O levels and *fail* them, but she just won't listen. She says men are boring, but that's only because she's too clever for most of them. Luckily, I don't have that problem."

Patrick didn't contradict me. "Well, I think intelligence is *extremely* attractive," he said.

"But lots of men don't take the same view."

"On the Continent it's considered very chic for a man to have a clever wife or mistress," he added, "as long as they're attractive too, of course. And I'm the same. To me, the woman's brain is her most important organ."

"I got quite a high 2:2," I offered.

"In fact, intelligence is the most attractive asset a woman can have."

"And two C grades at A level."

"In fact," he went on purposefully as he cut into his steak, "it's the *only* thing that really *matters*."

"One of them was nearly a B."

"Yes," he concluded comprehensively, "nothing makes a woman more appealing than a fine intellect. Well," he said as we got the bill. "Another lovely evening, Tiffany. How about a game of tennis on Saturday?"

"Oh yes, let's," I said happily. "That would be great. And afterward we can play Serious Pursuit."

"What do you think?" said Sally, as she showed me the Aquababe Birthing Pool standing at the ready in her vast sitting room.

"Er, it looks very interesting . . . but isn't it a bit premature?" I said. "I mean, the baby isn't due for another six weeks."

"I know, but I wanted to be well prepared," she said. "And to get used to the pool in advance."

"Where did you get it?" I asked.

"I hired it. The company assembled it for me, and then all we have to do when the time comes is to fill it up from the bath tap with this hose."

"Has it got a Jacuzzi?" I asked, fingering the blue fiberglass.

"Don't be silly, Tiff—of course not."

"Where's the springboard?"

"Tiffany!"

"And will you need a snorkel?"

"Tiffany—please be serious."

"OK. How much water does it hold?"

"200 gallons. And once it's filled up we cover it with this plastic lid to conserve the heat. And then when I'm ready, I just strip off and pop in."

"And then the baby pops out?" I said.

"Yes," she said happily. "Assisted by the calm atmosphere, the low lighting—I'm having some downlighters installed by the way—and of course the gentle, warm water. The baby just passes from one aquatic environment to another. I've heard that babies born like this are born smiling. Did you know that there's a tribe of South Sea islanders who give birth in the sea?" she added.

"In the shallow end, I hope."

"And that, according to legend, priests in ancient Egypt were born in water."

"Gosh. Well, that's very interesting," I said. Though I couldn't help feeling that if we were meant to give birth in water we'd probably have fins.

"It's going to be a wonderful experience," she went on with a beatific smile. "I'm really looking forward to it, Tiffany, aren't you?"

"Oh yes," I lied. "Can't wait." But to be honest I still find Sally's determination to give birth at home, without drugs, in an ad hoc pond, slightly alarming. No, I really don't hold with New Labour.

"What if it leaks?" I said. "There'd be a flood. It would really piss off the downstairs neighbors."

"It isn't going to leak," Sally said confidently. "But what we do is to put this large plastic sheet underneath the pool before we fill it up, just in case."

"You know, the Chelsea and Westminster hospital do have a couple of birthing pools," I said. "Lots of NHS hospitals have them now. That's what all the baby books say. Why don't you have a water birth, but have it in the hospital? I still don't see the advantage of doing it at home."

"I just hate the idea of all those faceless people intervening and giving me drugs and telling me what to do and when to push," she said adamantly. "I want to give birth actively, not passively, and I want this life-changing event to happen in the seclusion and intimacy of my own home, with just the midwife, and me and the baby—and of course you, Tiffany. And you'd be in the pool, too."

"I would?" Oh God, I hadn't bargained on *that*.

"Of course. You can wear a swimsuit, but a nice gentle color please, not that electric purple one you've got—it might traumatize the baby if that's the first thing she sees. And you see, if I had Leila in hospital," she continued, "I might hear other women screaming in labor, or see them being rushed around on gurneys. And I want Leda to come into the world in as calm and relaxed and unstressful a way as possible—so that means a home delivery. You see, what happened to Rosie happened because she had the baby in hospital."

"But you can still have a bad birth at home," I pointed out. "Giving birth is painful wherever you do it, isn't it?" But Sally didn't seem to hear. She lay back on the white leather sofa, pulled up her sweatshirt, and attached her Babyplus Fetal Sonic Stimulation device to her bare middle.

"I love this little gadget," she said happily. "And I'm sure it's doing the baby good. After all, it's been known for a long time that babies can hear from the womb. And by the time they're in their third trimester, like Libby is, not only can they hear noises, they can also react to them—and therefore the educational process can begin." She turned up the volume on the white Walkman-sized unit and had another sip of fennel tea.

"What's Lettice listening to now?" I said. "Italian lessons, beginners' biochemistry, or advanced differential calculus?" Because, you see, I don't really approve of all this "better babies" business, and ambitious pre-natal teaching.

"It's simply informational nourishment," Sally pointed out with a smile, "early learning, I suppose you call it. And I'm sure the baby's enjoying it because whenever I put the unit on I can feet her fluttering about and kicking."

"She's probably saying 'Turn that bloody noise off!' " I said. "Or ringing the council to complain."

"Oh Tiffany, you're so old-fashioned," said Sally with a sigh. "There's one baby I know of whose mother used this device and he was walking at *seven months*!"

"Yes, but I bet no one could *prove* that it's because of that . . . gizmo," I said dismissively. But then I thought I'd better shut up. Because it's Sally's baby, not mine. Although to be honest I thought the £200 she'd spent on the gadget would be better spent on nappies.

"Have you put her down for Eton yet?" I asked. Because of course by the time Lara is thirteen, Eton will probably be co-ed.

"No. But the minute she pops out, she'll be on the list for Winchester, Radley, Rugby, Gordonstoun, Charterhouse, Marlborough and Stowe."

"And what sort of career is she going to have?" Is that all mapped out, too?

"Oh don't be silly, Tiffany," said Sally happily. "How could I possibly know the answer to that now? And I'm certainly not going to be one of those awful pushy, ambitious mothers. Hav-

ing said which she'll probably run a global bank, or be a celebrated artist, or quite possibly become Prime Minister. Oh I
wish you'd have a baby too, Tiffany, a little friend for Lysette."

"Well, maybe I will," I said. "Maybe I will, because, actually, it's getting pretty serious with Patrick."

"It is? Oh *good*. Tell me."

"We went to the theater last Thursday, and this Saturday
we're going to play tennis. In fact, Sally, don't spread this
around," I added, "but I think he might be my boyfriend."

On Friday I took the morning off from writing brochure copy
for Waitrose to go shopping for some new tennis gear—I
wanted to look my best when I played Patrick. I wanted him to
take one look at me on the other side of the net and think to
himself, "Wow, what a woman!" And I didn't think that was
likely if I was wearing my graying old tracksuit. So I popped
down to Lillywhites to get some lily-white whites, or perhaps
that should be expressed as "whites to the power of two," or
"whites squared." And despite the fact that I was close to Piccadilly, I didn't give Seriously Successful a thought because,
just as I predicted, I *have* fallen in love with someone from the
introduction agency and therefore Seriously Successful has re-
ceded from my mind. And in fact I know that Patrick feels exactly the same way, because he told me not to bother meeting
anyone else from the agency, despite the fact that I've had lots
of requests actually, and so I'm not going to because, well,
what's the point because, to be quite frank, I believe it's only a
matter of time before Patrick seeks my hand in marriage.

Anyway, I went up to the second floor, and all the summer
stock had already arrived: white minidresses and frothy little
skirts and tops spread out before me, on rail after rail. I must
have tried on about, oh, thirty-five different outfits. And I decided not to get another tracksuit because I wanted to show off
my legs—N.B., do not forget to shave them. And so I tried on
skirts and T-shirts and polo shirts and halter-neck tops and

cropped tops—all in the whitest Swiss jersey or cotton or aer-tex, and all terribly feminine and sexy. But the one I liked the most—a very pretty dress by Fred Perry with navy trim at the arms and hem—was, of course, the most expensive. But what the hell? I was feeling happy. And I looked good in it—it was worth every penny, so why should I grudge myself a measly ninety quid? And then I thought I'd better get a cardigan to match it, as it's still not very warm, and there was a very pretty Sergio Tacchini one for seventy-five quid, and then I thought I'd better get some new Wilson tennis shoes, and they were eighty quid, and then, what with the new socks and the head-band and the three pairs of appliquéd panties and one of those natty little plastic things for storing your balls in, the bill came to £255. But then, when you're in love, no expense is too great, is it? And I handed over my credit card with a glad smile as the assistant bagged up my new gear. And then—dear reader, imagine my rapture!—Saturday arrived.

Now, I had told Patrick that I'd meet him at the club and I'd given him clear directions. And I'd booked a court for two hours, because I thought we'd need at least half an hour to warm up and then an hour and a half to play a couple of sets—unless he totally demolished me, which I thought he probably would, given his success at Junior Wimbledon in the early sev-enties. Anyway, when I arrived I noticed that there was a new coach—very attractive actually. And so I went upstairs to change, and when I came down I couldn't help noticing that two-headed Alan was talking to this new coach and in fact seemed to be on rather friendly terms with her. They were gig-gling about something and she was looking at him in an inter-ested, intimate kind of way as she gave him some advice about his forehand and I thought—that's great! That's really great, Alan. Because personally I find you about as attractive as a ba-boon's bottom, but she obviously has no objections to you, and *chacun à son goût,* as they say. And anyway, I was in love and feeling generous, overflowing with human kindness and understanding in fact, because, well, Patrick is a really gorgeous-looking bloke. And nice. Incredibly nice. And very successful.

Anyway, we'd arranged to meet at the club at two-thirty, and it was a wonderful spring afternoon. The trees were just coming into leaf, there were tulips and hyacinth nodding in every flowerbed, and the birds were twittering joyfully as I sat outside, on the terrace, waiting. And by two forty-five Patrick still hadn't showed up, which was odd, because he's normally *very* reliable. So I had a cup of coffee, and watched the players batting the balls back and forth with varying degrees of energy and skill. And then I picked up the *Telegraph*. And then, when I'd finished reading the news and features, I scrutinized the stock market report, and then I perused the sports pages, and after that I turned to the back page and looked at the crossword. And then I found that I'd done three quarters of the crossword, and Patrick still hadn't arrived. And it was *three* forty-five. And I must say my anxiety levels were really quite high by now. Somewhere just below the summit of K2. So I read *The Times,* just glancing, only out of curiosity of course, at the personal ads in the Rendezvous section. And then I started to do *The Times* crossword, and I'd got halfway through that, and was just struggling with fourteen down, when I thought, where the *hell* is he? Because I knew there could be no confusion about the day, or the time, or the venue, because I'd written it all down on a piece of paper when I'd given him directions to the club. "Oh, Patrick, please, please, please arrive soon," I said to myself. "Please." And the sun had gone in by now, and the clouds were massing, battleship gray, and *still* he hadn't arrived and I thought, what the *hell* is going on here? Suddenly I heard the phone ring, and through the window I saw the new coach pick it up. Then she came out onto the terrace and said, "Tiffany?" I nodded. "Hello," she said. "I'm Julia. I'm new here. Someone called Patrick Miller just phoned for you."

Patrick! Thank *God*! Everything was going to be all right. "I forgive you Patrick, don't worry, I really don't mind that you're almost two hours late," I said to myself. "Just hurry up and get here in one piece."

"He was just calling to say—"

"That he'd be arriving shortly?" I interjected.

"No. To say that he had to cancel."

"What?"

"Cancel," she said. "He sends his apologies."

"Cancel?"

"Yes."

"Oh. Did he give a reason?" I added.

"No," she said, shaking her tobacco-brown curls.

"He just phoned to cancel?" Julia nodded. "As in—not coming?"

"Yes," she said.

"Are you sure?" I said.

"Yes."

"Did he *definitely* use the word 'cancel'?" I asked.

"Definitely," she said.

"You couldn't possibly—sorry, I know you're new and everything—but you couldn't possibly have made a mistake, could you, or misheard?"

"No," she said. "He said 'cancel.' He said, 'Please could you tell Tiffany Trott that I'm afraid I'm going to have to cancel.' Those are the very words he used."

"Cancel, as in, not turn up?" I said. "Look, Julia, can I just clarify this again? He said 'cancel'? Is that right? Spelt, C.A.N.C.E.L.?"

"Yes. Cancel. As in no show. Cancel."

"And you're absolutely *sure* about that?" I said again.

"One hundred percent," she said.

"I see," I said, fingering the fabric of my new tennis dress. "So he's not coming, then."

"No," she said. "He isn't."

"I understand," I said. "He's canceled?"

"Yes. Yes. He has."

Then Alan appeared. "Hello Tiffany," he said. "Great new tennis dress you've got on there!"

"Thanks," I said absently.

"Have you got anyone to play with?" he asked.

"No," I said dismally.

"Why don't you two have a game?" said Julia. "You'd like to play again, wouldn't you, Alan? And you need lots of practice for the tournament."

"Sure," he said. "Come on, Tiffany."

"Er, it's OK," I said. "I think I'll just . . . to be honest I don't really feel like playing that much today. Wasn't *really* in the mood for it, anyway," I said as I put my new headband back in my bag. "Got a bit of a dodgy ankle, to be honest. Didn't really feel . . . and it looks like rain. Look Julia, can I just get this absolutely straight, once and for all, to clear up any possible misunderstanding. Patrick's not coming. Is that right?"

"That's right," she said.

"He said, 'I'm canceling.' Correct?"

"Correct."

"And it was definitely the same Patrick Miller, was it?" I said.

"Well, do you know two?" she inquired. Good point. Very good point.

"No," I said bleakly. "I don't."

I went upstairs to the changing room, a knife revolving slowly in my heart. I removed the Sergio Tacchini cardigan, my Fred Perry dress, my new Wilson shoes and Lillywhites socks, and got dressed again. And then I made my way home. And when I opened the front door my answer phone wasn't winking at me—cheering me up with the promise of some plausible explanation from Patrick. It was just staring at me, blankly. It had absolutely nothing to say. And then another thing struck me—he'd spoken to Julia, so why could he not have asked to speak to *me*, to explain his nonappearance, or at least to apologize in person? I didn't understand that at all.

Then I sat at the kitchen table, put my head in my hands, and cried. I really, really cried. The tears were streaming down my face, and I had a quick look in the hall mirror and I was a complete mess—my face segmented by wet streaks of smeary, brown mascara. And the whites of my eyes were red and veined, and my usually smooth brow was furrowed and corrugated with disappointment and distress and . . . *ring ring! Ring ring!*

"Yes?"

"Tiffany. It's Patrick."

"Yes?"

"Look, I'm sorry about the tennis . . ."

"Yes."

"But you see I got myself a bit tied up . . ." Tied up? "Did you wait there long?"

"Yes."

"I suppose you're a bit cross with me?"

"Er, well, yes. Yes. I am."

"I'm really sorry, but, you know how it is . . ."

"No. No, I don't."

"I just didn't realize the time and I . . ."

"Look," I said, "I'm not interested in your pathetic excuses. All I know is that you stood me up."

"Well, I wouldn't say I stood you up; you could have played with someone else."

"I didn't *want* to play with anyone else. I wanted to play with you. And you let me sit there, waiting, for almost two hours."

"Well, I'm sorry, Tiffany."

"And then you don't even bother to speak to me personally . . ."

"But it was tricky, I was on a mobile phone." Mobile phone? He didn't *have* a mobile phone as far as I knew.

"You just buggered me about—like all the rest."

"What do you mean, buggered you about?"

"You're buggering me about."

"No I'm not," he said.

"Yes you are, Patrick. And the fact is that I paid £700 to join Caroline Clark."

"Look, I said I'm sorry."

"And I didn't pay that kind of money to be buggered about."

"I really don't know what you're talking about, Tiffany."

"Because why would I pay £700 to be buggered about in an introduction agency when I know several men out there in the real world, who, I'm confident, would do it free of charge?"

"Tiffany, I *am* sorry . . ."

"Sorry? Ha!"

"How can I make it up to you?"

"I'm sick of men behaving like this . . ."

"Would you let me buy you dinner?"

"Just sick of it . . ."

"There's a very nice restaurant I know . . ."

"Treating me like dirt . . ."

"It's got a really nice menu . . ."

"As though I'm just no one. Someone to be trifled with . . ."

"They do lovely desserts . . ."

"And then discarded . . . I mean I'm sick of it. Sick. To. Death. Of. It. I just feel like . . ."

"Tiffany?"

". . . doing something *desperate* . . ."

"Would you let me . . ."

". . . like jumping off a tall building."

". . . get a word in edgeway . . ."

". . . or entering a Carmelite convent . . ."

". . . because I really would like to . . ."

". . . or moving to Milton Keynes!"

". . . see you."

"All men are *bastards*. All of them. Bastards. Even the nice ones. And I'm afraid that's all there is . . ."

"TIFFANY—"

". . . to it."

"... WILL YOU HAVE DINNER WITH ME ON TUESDAY?"

"Oh. OK. Yes. All right."

April

What a difference a date makes. Patrick poured me another glass of champagne and gave me a dazzling smile. I was in Bertorelli's in Charlotte Street, and I was in heaven. I was feeling happy and looking good. I had had a full leg wax. And I had completely accepted Patrick's apology for not turning up at the tennis club. He said he had "got delayed," and well, getting delayed can happen to anyone, can't it? Especially when you're a very busy and successful person like Patrick. And when you've had a lot on your mind recently, like the enormous size of your wife's divorce settlement. And, goodness me, I'm not going to start pressurizing the guy—after all, I haven't known him that long. I now realize that I had no right to get upset with him when he was unfortunately delayed last Saturday, thereby preventing him from keeping his rendezvous with me at the tennis club. Oh no—I'm not one of these mad women who start making demands on a bloke within half an hour of meeting them. I'm not one of those "bunny-boilers," I think the expression is (cf Glenn Close in *Fatal Attraction*), who think the bloke's dead keen when he isn't, or when he just needs a little more time before he feels he can commit—like twenty years or so. Because I know from my own experience that it's a mistake to say "OK, where, exactly, is this relationship going?" when you've only been seeing the guy for about—ooh—three years, and who can blame a bloke for turning round and saying, "Well, I don't think it's going anywhere," like Phil Anderer did

to me? Because I asked for it, didn't I? By asking. Yes. And so
I'm really into giving men space at the moment. Lots of space.
And after all I've only known Patrick for three weeks, and OK,
he did tell me to go "on hold" at the agency, which meant that I
haven't been meeting any other blokes. But I just don't agree
with Lizzie that it would be sensible to meet as many chaps as
possible to begin with and then see what happens with Patrick.
Because the fact is that Patrick is The One. I know that he's
very, *very* keen on me, and doesn't want other men to meet me,
which is why he told me to go on hold. He's being very possessive, which is really rather flattering, actually. And so I *have*
been on hold ever since I met him. And there we were, sitting
in Bertorelli's—such a perfect venue for a romantic dinner
tête-à-tête—and he'd ordered champagne and we were sharing
some foie gras, followed by brain-friendly steak and the crispi-
est French fries. And I was looking pretty damn good I can tell
you, and I was feeling very, very confident, and laughing just
the right amount. And I was on the point of telling Patrick that
I had put him on my BT Friends and Family list, when he suddenly gave me a meaningful look. Very meaningful. And deep. It
thrilled me to my core. And then he made an announcement.

"We're going to the South of France," he said with a
smile. "That's what I really wanted to tell you. That's why I
wanted to have dinner with you tonight, Tiffany." The South of
France—*wow*!

"How *fantastic*," I said. "When?"

"Well, I don't know. Probably the week after next. For a
fortnight . . ."

A fortnight. What heaven. We could go to Antibes, and Cap
Ferrat, and do a little gambling in Monte Carlo, and maybe we'd
get to see Princess Caroline, and of course Nice would be nice.

"I've still got to work out the best date for us both . . ."

"Well, I'm really flexible about work," I said.

"And I've got to look at exactly how much leave I've got
left."

"Of course," I said.

"And on the availability of accommodation."

"Quite."

"The weather should be lovely."

"Oh, *yes*."

"But obviously it all depends on when she can get away."

"Sorry?"

"Oh yes, didn't I tell you? I've met someone. We're going on hold together."

"Met someone?" I said. *What do you mean "met someone"— you've just met me.*

"Yes," he replied. "I've met someone. And I'm going on hold. With her."

"I see," I said. And then I thought, I had my legs waxed for this man.

"But—I thought *I* was on hold with you," I pointed out.

"Oh, I don't know why you thought that," he said, casually spearing a chip.

"Because you told me, after our first date, when you phoned me up the very next morning, that I ought to put myself 'on hold' and not meet any other blokes," I said. "That's why!"

"Oh, I was only joking, Tiffany! I didn't mean it."

"So you weren't on hold yourself?" I said.

"No."

"But *I* was."

"So it seems."

"And so you've been meeting other women? All this time?"

"Yes," he said. "I have. Why not?"

"How many?" I asked, fiddling with my serrated knife.

"Oooh," he started counting on two hands, then three, then four, "seventeen," he said.

"Seventeen?" He was seventeen-timing me?

"And now I have met someone I want to go on hold with," he said with another sip of sparkling wine. "And so we are. Going on hold. And then we're going on holiday. But I wanted to have dinner with you because I did feel bad about not turning up for tennis, but you see Sarah Jane asked me to go shopping with her, and that's why I got delayed. We were stuck in a traffic jam on the King's Road and that's why I couldn't make it, but I did *try* to let you know and luckily her Mercedes has a car phone. Tiffany . . . Tiffany, where are you *going*?"

"I'm going to get my GUN!"

"Why do men do this to me?" I asked Lizzie, again, as we walked around the National Gallery the following Sunday. "Why, why, why, why, *why*?"

"Because they're bastards," she said calmly as she stopped to light another cigarette in front of a rather gaudy Gauguin.

"Madam. No smoking!" said a guard crossly.

"Yes, but why do I *allow* them to treat me like this?" I said as she stubbed out her Marlboro Light in a fire bucket. "Why do I let them get away with it?"

"Because you're so stupid," she said. "Next question?"

"What should I do?"

"Complain."

"To whom?"

"To the introduction agency, of course," she replied as we wandered past a group of Italian tourists into the adjacent room.

"But how can I reasonably complain about the fact that Patrick Miller prefers someone else to me?" I said as we studied a serene-looking pastoral by Poussin.

"Well *I* would," she said simply. And so I did. I phoned Caroline Clarke up at ten o'clock the next morning.

"Well, it is rather unfortunate," she said sympathetically. "There seems to have been a communication failure here. But I must say I was a bit surprised when you said you wanted to go on hold at such an early stage."

"Now, this *other woman*," I spat. "Sarah Jane. Horrible name, incidentally . . ."

"Ye-es," said Caroline cautiously.

"Well, I know she's a client of yours and so you can't really say very much . . ."

"No, I'm afraid I can't."

"But just tell me *everything* about her," I said. "Tell me, for example, what she's got that I haven't."

"I really *can't* tell you anything, Tiffany. I'm sorry."

"I mean, is she stunningly attractive?" Silence. "Is she?" I persisted. "I can take it, you know."

"Well, well, no," said Caroline reluctantly. "She's, well, average, I'd say." Average! Ha!

"And is she incredibly intelligent, by any chance?"

"Well Tiffany, I really don't want to say . . ."

"I mean, are we talking Mensa here? Are we?"

"Er, well no. I don't think we are."

"And is she . . ." I braced myself, ". . . *younger* than me?"

"No, no. She's about the same age." Mmmm. No advantage there then. "And is she richer than I am?" I inquired. There was an awkward silence. "By which I mean," I continued, "has she got more money than me?"

"Well Tiffany, I really don't think it would make you feel any better if I were to answer that *particular* question, and in fact I've already said more than I'd have chosen to do, but you've been so terribly pressing. And in any case, this conversation just isn't going to help you very much."

But now I knew what I needed to know. Patrick was interested only in money, because he was going out with this physically repulsive, ageing woman who was also as thick as two short planks—and *why*? Because she had cash. Shallow, hypocritical bastard. Going on about how a woman's most appealing asset is her intellect when what he really had in mind was her bank balance. Right.

"Well, there are certain things I'd like to tell you about Patrick Miller," I said. "Now, I'm not sneaking on him or anything," I added, "but I feel you should know that he stood me up—at my tennis club. I waited there for two hours."

"Oh dear."

"And then there was another time when he said he'd ring me and he *didn't,*" I said. "And I had to ring *him.*"

"Oh."

"And then—now I'm not telling tales or anything—but there was another time when . . ."

"Look Tiffany, just *forget* Patrick," said Caroline calmly. "There's no point in thinking about him anymore. I'll find you someone *much* nicer."

And so that's what she's been doing—and the profiles just keep on coming. And every day there's some bloke or other ringing up wanting to meet me—which is balm to my battered ego. But it can be a bit confusing. For example, this morning the phone rang, and this voice said, "Oh hello, Tiffany, this is John here. From *Hertford.*" That's the codified way of saying they're from the Caroline Clarke Introduction Agency rather than from, say, the gas board, or MI5. Anyway, he said, "This is John"—and I didn't know who the hell it was because I've received the profiles of several men called John.

So I said, "Are you John the surgeon, John the sales executive, John the ophthalmologist, John the businessman or John the Baptist, ha ha ha!" And he said that he was John the surgeon, and so we chatted, and arranged to meet at a wine bar in Soho. And he was perfectly-OK-looking-bordering-on-the-almost-acceptable, except that he made one fundamental mistake.

We'd had a couple of drinks and we were getting on reasonably well when he said, "And what do you like to do in your spare time, Stephanie?"

"Tiffany," I said. "It's Tiffany."

"Oh sorry," he said, "of course it is. Anyway, do tell me about your leisure interests—do you like country walks, Stephanie, or stamp collecting?"

"It's Tiffany," I said again, with a little more emphasis this time.

"Oh Stephanie, I'm so sorry," he said. "You must think me really rather crass."

"Yes," I suddenly said, "I do. *Why* do you deep calling me Stephanie?" I inquired as I picked up my bag.

"Because that's my ex-wife's name," he said with a mournful look in his eye.

After that I met a banker called Anthony. He sounded OK over the phone and his photo was quite attractive. I met him at the Waldorf, in the Palm Court. And he was fatter in real life than he was in the photo—much fatter. And he didn't smile. Or laugh. In fact he seemed to have had a triple humor bypass and was completely immune to my jokes. Didn't get them at all. Not even the one about the farmer and the trailer-load of penguins. Nor did he ask me anything about myself. Not one thing. He just talked about the ERM. Nonstop. For an hour and forty-five minutes. "Gorden Brown . . ." I heard him say. "Interest rates still far too high . . . Single European Currency . . . fluctuating Deutschmark . . . " And as one narcoleptic gem after another dropped from his lips, I thought, I wonder whether he'd actually notice if I put my head down on the table and had a little sleep? "Convergence criteria . . . all depends on the Swiss franc of course . . ." No. I'm sure he wouldn't notice a thing. "The lire's been given a very easy ride . . ." But I decided against it—it was much easier just to leave.

"Tell me," I said as I stood up, "have you met many women from the Caroline Clarke Introduction Agency?" He blanched visibly, and looked quite shocked, as though I had just said something unspeakably vulgar. Because, you see, some people don't like to refer to the fact that that is how they met. In fact Anthony looked at me as though I had just said, "Have you always had hemorrhoids?"

"Er, well, yes," he blurted out, as a red stain spread from his neck up to his ears. "Quite a few, actually."

"Didn't you like any of them?" I inquired. I was curious, you see.

"No," he said flatly. "I didn't."

"Why not?"

"Well," he said with an involuntary shrug, "I thought they were all very boring."

Shortly after that I met a cardiologist called Chris, and a theater director called Hugo, but he was six foot six and he gave me vertigo. And then there was Andrew, an estate agent, and Joe, a restaurateur, and Ray, a solicitor, whose specialty, unfortunately, was defending pedophiles and this would *not* have gone down terribly well at the tennis club. And there was a Scottish architect called Hamish and an industrial chemist called Mark, but he was as camp as a convention of scoutmasters and had a badly pockmarked face. And then there was a charming chartered surveyor called Shaun, but he lived too far away, and then there was Wayne. I rather liked Wayne, who was a computer salesman, but when we met he kept saying that he was very worried about "gold diggers." Gold diggers?

"Well, did you bring your bank statements?" I said. Actually, I didn't say that, I just sat there wondering what on earth he could mean. After all, he was hardly in the Wall Street league. Gold diggers?

"You see, I do have a very comfortable lifestyle," he explained. What was I supposed to say to that? "Congratulations!"? "And so obviously I have to be very careful," he added. In fact, he said it twice. And we'd met at the Atlantic Bar, and all we'd had was a bottle of house wine costing eleven quid. But when the bill came he fumbled about awkwardly and then he looked at me inquiringly, and he said, "Well, how should we do this then?" And so I just handed the waiter the cash. Because, you see, I'd understood that Wayne has to be "very careful."

And then there was Dave, the orthodontist surgeon, and Angus, an electronics engineer, and there was a university professor called Bob, and frankly, it was all becoming too much. From having had practically no dates a week, I was now having fifteen dates a week and I just couldn't cope. Having to listen to all these men talking about their divorces, their jobs, their love of sailing, their love of golf; going on about their children, their careers, their ex-wives, their ex-girlfriends, their pension arrangements, their preference for Emmy Lou Harris over Bette Midler or their preference for Beethoven over Brahms. And OK, OK, I know it was only conversation, and I really couldn't complain. But it was just all getting too much. It was really getting me down. And then the phone rang *again*. "Oh, not another *bloody* man asking me out!" I said to myself as I picked it up, and it was yet another bloke from Caroline Clarke's agency, and so I went into the usual preliminary rigmarole about how much I like tennis, and how much I don't like golf, and how I'm not really that keen on action movies, but yes, I do like Harrison Ford. Oh *why* didn't I marry Kit? I thought for the umpteenth time as I put the phone down on my latest date. Or Seriously Successful, for that matter. Because I wasn't used to having all this choice—having choice is very tiring. No wonder the French call it *embarras de richesses* . . .

And then it happened. It just all fell into place. With Mr. Right. I found him. I actually found him. And there I was floating up the aisle on Dad's arm in my incredibly expensive wedding dress in ivory silk satin, and with the prettiest little bouquet—lilies of the valley and stephanotis—with small white roses in my hair. And I was feeling so relieved, because at last—phew!—IT had happened. I had met someone. And I had liked him. And he had liked me, and he had sought my hand in marriage. And I had accepted. And there I was at the church door, with Dad, and the organ was playing "Jesu Joy of Man's Desiring" which always has me in floods. And we walked slowly up the aisle, and I felt *so* emotional, there were tears standing in my eyes. And I could feel Dad's arm on mine, steadying me for what lay ahead. But I could hear people tittering and sniggering. And they were saying, "Oh yes . . . Tiffany's finally getting hitched . . . yes incredible, isn't it . . .

no, I never thought it'd happen either . . . well exactly, who'd have guessed?" But I didn't care. Their negative and bitchy comments didn't bother me at all, because it had all turned out right at last. I had met the man of my dreams, and he had proposed, and now here I was walking toward him as he stood with his back to me at the altar. I started mentally to rehearse my lines as I gradually drew nearer and nearer. "I take thee . . . I take thee . . ." Who the hell *was* I taking? Suddenly I hadn't a clue. Was it Tipsy Terry from Eat 'n' Greet? No. Was it Alex? Surely not. Or Tall Athletic? Hardly. Well, it certainly wasn't two-headed Alan from the tennis club, because he was fixed up now, with Julia. Maybe it was Patrick—or, God forbid, Peter Fitz-Harrod! No. No. It wasn't him. He definitely hadn't proposed. Perhaps it was Kit—oh that *would* be nice—or maybe that young bloke from the Ministry of Sound. Or was it Todd from Club Med . . . or José? *Who was it?* God, how embarrassing. Couldn't remember. Completely gone! I'd just have to busk it. That was all there was for it. I'd have to improvise. And then, as we proceeded further and further up the aisle—the flowers *did* look nice—I saw something leaning against the front right-hand pew. It was a bag of golf clubs. How *odd*! And then I drew level with the groom and he turned and looked at me, and it was Phil Anderer. What on *earth* was *he* doing here? I sure as hell didn't want to marry *him*. And then he looked me up and down, with this funny, yet familiar expression on his face, and he said, "Look, Tiffany, I'm sorry, but that dress, well, I just don't like it. It doesn't do *anything* for you. The cut's completely wrong. And the detail on the train is appalling. It's just awful—not stylish at all—I'm afraid you look a sight. Look, would you go and change?" And then I heard the phone ringing in the front pew. But no one was answering it. I went to pick it up, aware that my palms were wet with sweat.

"Tiffany! Tiffany!" It was Kit. "We're getting married!" he shouted.

"No we're *not*," I said.

"No—not you. Portia. And me. We're getting married!" he shouted again. I glanced at the alarm clock—it was seven a.m.

"I'm sorry to ring so early, Tiff, but I just had to tell you as soon as I could. Last night she told me . . . she told me . . . oh Tiffany, Portia's having a *baby*," he said. "And we're getting married. On Saturday. And Tiffany?"

"Yes," I said, through my tears.

"Will you be our best man?"

April Continued

"Come in you two! Come in!" boomed Pat. "The little woman's upstairs, feeding the baby. We'll take some nice herbal tea up there," she added as she ushered us into their Victorian house, just off Holloway Road. It was lovely, with blond wooden flooring, dado rails, high ceilings and elaborate coving.

"Nice house," said Sally admiringly as Pat put on the kettle.

"Did it all myself," she said, folding her beefy arms across her broad chest. "The place was a wreck when we bought it. Trees growing through the roof. But I'm a devil for DIY—I love my Black and Decker! Are you the same, Tiffany?"

"Er—yes," I said. "Well, actually, no. Not really."

"Now, if you wouldn't mind being very quiet with Lesley," said Pat as she led us upstairs with the tray. "I don't want her getting over-excited. She's still recovering from the labor."

"Don't worry, we'll whisper," said Sally reassuringly, pulling herself up wearily by the hand rail, stopping to catch her breath halfway. She looked tired and strained, but I suppose that's normal when you're more than eight months gone and look as though you just swallowed a Spacehopper. We followed Pat into the master bedroom at the front of the house, and there was Lesley, sitting up in the double bed in a white lace-trimmed nightie, smiling dreamily at the downy-headed infant feeding in her arms. The room was semidark and almost silent, except for the snuffling of the baby and the swish of an occasional car. Lesley looked up at us, and smiled delightedly.

"Oh, thank you!" she whispered, as Sally put a large brown teddy bear on the bed. We peered at little Freddie.

"Oh, he's gorgeous!" said Sally. "Is he feeding well?" Lesley nodded.

"He's lovely," I murmured. "Rather big though, isn't he? I mean, how much did he weigh?"

Lesley inhaled sharply through gritted teeth, and then she said, "Ten pounds."

"Ten pounds?" Sally repeated. Her face expressed a mixture of incredulity and fear. "Gosh. Well, I'm jolly glad I'm having a girl," she added with a burst of relieved laughter. "I don't think girls ever weigh as much as that." Pat pulled up a couple of chairs for us, and we all sat down around the bed.

"Have you had a lot of visitors?" Sally asked.

"Well, no. Not really," Lesley replied quietly. "Apart from our immediate families. You're the only ones from the antenatal group who've bothered to come and see us."

"Oh. That's odd," I said. "Well, I'm sure they *will* come." Though I wasn't sure at all. Lesley and Pat seemed to have made few friends at the class. The women had largely ignored them, while the men had been subtly hostile. Particularly toward Pat. I suppose they didn't like her beating them at their own game, which, in a way, she was.

"Yes, no one apart from you has even phoned," added Lesley, with a palpably disappointed air.

"Oh. Oh, well, that's a bit rotten," said Sally. "Perhaps they're too busy to come at the moment. But, well, we couldn't *wait* to see you," she added diplomatically. Then, becoming a little flushed as she tried to change the subject, she accidentally asked this terribly awkward question, "So who does Freddie look like?" she inquired, peering at him again. *Ah.* Get out of *that* one, Sally, I thought to myself as I casually studied a copy of *Autocar.*

"Well, Lesley swears he's like her," said Pat quick as a flash, "but I think he's got my chin."

"Er, yes," said Sally. "I can see the resemblance." She looked at Pat, and then looked at the baby again. "Oh, yes. Definitely. It's just like yours. Anyway, he's very sweet," she added brightly. "Lovely."

"Were you there?" I asked Pat. "For the birth?"

"Of *course,*" she said, rolling down the sleeves of her checked shirt. "Nothing would have kept me away, would it, Lesley?" Lesley gave her an affectionate smile. "It was the best moment of my life," Pat went on as she rearranged the tiny cellular blanket in the bunny-covered cot. "The *best moment of my life.* Seeing my little boy come into the world. It was even better than watching Arsenal blast Liverpool two–nil to win the title in 1989. I cried like a baby," she added. "You'll probably be the same, Tiffany. But don't feel ashamed of it," she said, putting a paternalistic arm around my shoulder. "Just let the tears come. We should, you know, from time to time. It's OK for us, you know, us . . . chaps . . . to cry."

"I quite agree," I replied. I'd long since given up trying to convince Pat that a) I was a woman and b) I was simply Sally's friend.

"Now, when's *your* little one due?" she went on.

"In three weeks," said Sally. "I'm feeling incredibly tired, to tell the truth. I can't wait for Lara to be born. These last few weeks are hell."

Lesley nodded sympathetically. "They're absolutely awful," she agreed. "You get to the stage where you're fed up with it—you're just fed up with being so big and so exhausted and so bloody uncomfortable. Never mind, Sally. Not long now. Which hospital are you going to?" she added as she swapped Freddie over onto her other breast.

"Oh, I'm having the baby at home," Sally explained. "I'm going to have a nice, quiet, calm, water birth in my apartment."

"You'll have a midwife, of course?" said Pat with a concerned air.

"Oh yes. From the Chelsea and Westminster," she replied.

"She's called Joan. I've been seeing her at the health center at World's End, so I've already got to know her a bit—and of course Tiffany's going to be there too."

I nodded with as much enthusiasm as I could muster.

"Well, we had Freddie in the Royal Free," said Lesley. "And it was fabulous. Five-star treatment all the way. But I'm sure a home birth is really nice too," she added encouragingly.

I'm sure it isn't, I thought.

"Tell me, was the labor awful?" Sally asked Lesley suddenly. Lesley shrugged noncommittally, but tactfully said nothing. *Of course it was awful, Sally—the baby weighed two tons.*

"How long did it take?" she persisted.

"Well, not that long," Lesley replied casually. "Really. Um. Not that long at all. Would you like some more fennel tea?"

"Not that long!" said Pat, with a great harrumphing laugh. "It was thirty-six hours! And it was thirty-six hours of sheer bloody *hell*! Rosie wasn't joking, you know."

Thirty-six hours! Oh no. Please no. I stared at Sally's bump, mentally willing the baby to try and make it in thirty-six minutes. "I'll get you anything you like," I told Ludmilla telepathically. "You can have the Teletubbies, Barbie dolls, Tiny Tears, Pocahontas, Polly Pocket, My Little Pony and any number of fluffy toys—anything, you can name your price. But just make it snappy on the Big Day, OK?" And then we said our goodbyes to Pat and Lesley and left.

Sally waddled slowly along beside me, stopping occasionally for a rest. Poor thing. She was so tired. We walked a little further, and then she suddenly stopped again and leaned against a garden wall.

"Sally, are you all right?"

She didn't reply. She'd gone completely quiet.

"Sally?"

Suddenly she put her left hand up to her eyes, and I saw her shoulders being to shake. And then her body was suddenly convulsed by huge, great, racking sobs. God, poor Sal. It must have been because of Pat's terrible tactlessness about Lesley's thirty-six-hour ordeal.

"Don't worry Sal," I said, putting my arm around her. "It really won't be that bad. Please don't cry. It'll be OK. Pat really should have kept quiet about Lesley's *hideous* labor," I added crossly. "Tactlessly going on and on about it—about how *protracted* and *painful* it was, and about how Lesley was in total *agony* for the best part of a day and a half. Yours will be *much* easier than that," I added reassuringly. "Honestly, I bet it's really quick and hardly hurts at all."

"Oh it's not that!" Sally wailed, tears now pouring down her pale cheeks. "It's not the pain. I'm not afraid of the pain."

"Well, what is it then?" I asked, nonplussed, handing her a tissue from my bag.

"Well . . ." She dried her eyes. "Well . . ." Tears continued to snake down her face.

"Sally, please tell me. Whatever it is, I'm sure I can help."

"Well . . ."

"Yes."

"Well . . ."

"Well, I went to the delicatessen this morning," she said, dabbing her eyes, "to get some bread."

"Yes," I said, intrigued.

"And you know I like that brown bread, with the nice pine kernels on the top?" *No.*

"Er. Yes," I said.

"That really nice, chewy, brown bread that I like so much?" she reiterated with a loud, wet sniff.

"Um. *Yes,"* I said again uncertainly. What on *earth* was she talking about?

"Well . . . well . . ." She started crying again, and then covered her face with both hands.

"What? Sally! What? What *happened*? For God's sake, tell me!"

"They'd . . . they'd *run out of it*!" she wailed. And now she was sobbing again, loudly, and uncontrollably, to the consternation of passersby.

"Oh. Oh dear," I said, not knowing *what* to say.

"And I really—uh-uh—*like* it," she sobbed again. "And they didn't—uh-uh—*have* any. So I had to have *white* bread," she concluded in a hoarse, falsetto squeak. She looked at me pleadingly. Her upper lip was slimy with snot. Her mouth was contorted with grief, her chin ridged and puckered in distress. I didn't know what to say. And then I remembered. It all came back to me from some of the baby books. It's the hormones. Toward the end of the pregnancy, a woman's hormones can go barking mad. Thank God, I thought—there's a rational explanation for this. Her hormones had run amok.

"I'm sorry, Sally, but I'm afraid your hormones will have to be sectioned under the 1983 Mental Health Act," I said. Actually I didn't say that at all. I just listened as she continued her tearfest.

"That bread's my *favorite* sort," she wailed. "I really, really love it. And they'd run out of it, Tiffany. And so I've been *terribly* upset all morning." Oh God oh God oh God. What should I do?

"There's a nice bakery in Upper Street," I said. "I'm sure we can get some there."

She shook her head violently, from side to side. It won't taste the *same*," she wailed. "It just won't . . ."

"Well, it might."

"No, it won't, it won't, it WON'T!" she almost screamed. She started crying again, making gasping little "uh, uh, uh" noises between each sob.

"But it's not just the bread," Sally suddenly added in a quiet croak, dabbing at her eyes again. Ah.

"Well, what else is it?" I asked. "Tell me." She plucked a couple of tiny pink cherry blossom buds from an overhanging branch, and rotated them thoughtfully in her hands.

"It's me," she said miserably. She wasn't crying now. "It's

what I'm doing." She looked at me bleakly. "Tiffany," she announced, "I'm having a baby on my own."

"But Sally, you big wuss, you've known that for eight months!" I pointed out. Actually, I didn't. I just listened.

"And seeing little Freddie with two parents made me feel awful," Sally continued, dabbing at her eyes. "Even if the father is a woman. Because, they've got each other, Lesley and Pat. And the baby's got them both." Her lower lip trembled, and then her face collapsed with grief again. "They're a *family*," she sobbed. "And I'm not going to be a family. And Lucretia isn't going to have a nice father like Pat," she added tearfully. "Who'll play football with her or take her fishing or whatever fathers do. I'm going to be a single parent, Tiffany. I'm going to be on my own. All on my own. Forever. And ever."

Ah. Men. So that's what this was really about. Sally's lack of a bloke. A bit late to start worrying about that now.

"Well, Sally, you're not on your own," I said briskly, "you're just not," though I was fighting back the tears myself, because I find crying, like vomiting, catching. "Lots of people love you," I added, aware of a lemon-sized lump in my throat, "and lots of people will help you, and you're very lucky because you don't have to worry about money like most single mothers do. And once Louella's born you'll be feeling happy again, and you'll love her, and then you'll probably meet some really nice chap who'll be a wonderful stepfather to her and so you'll be in a family with him, and then you'll live happily ever after." This seemed to cheer her up. She gave me a watery smile, then thoughtfully licked the slime off her lip. "You're just very tired and run down," I said wearily. "And you're probably a bit scared at the thought of giving birth."

"I'm not scared of *that*!" she said defiantly. And she looked so shocked at my preposterous presumption that she immediately stopped crying, and went off down the road again, at a brisk waddle.

"I'm not scared of childbirth *at all,* Tiffany," she said again firmly. "The thought of being in pain really doesn't bother me a bit. But you're right, though," she conceded as she stopped to blow her nose again. "I am tired. That's true. I'm tired of being pregnant. I can't wait for it all to happen. I can't wait to meet my little Lavender!" She clasped her bump with both hands and gave me a radiant smile. "I can't wait, Tiffany! I can't wait! I can't wait!" It was like a sudden burst of bright sunshine after torrential rains; and as we walked toward Highbury Corner Sally talked nonstop about the water pool, and her deep breathing, and the toys she'd bought for the baby the day before. And then she got in a taxi, waved cheerfully at me out of the open window, and was gone.

I decided to walk home—my nerves were too strung out to enable me to wait patiently for the bus. And as I walked down Canonbury Road, past houses swathed in yellow forsythia, with birds twittering in the blossoming cherry trees, Pat's words kept ringing in my ears: *It's OK for us chaps to cry you know, Tiffany, It's OK for us chaps* . . . Chaps! I mean, really. How *ridiculous.* It was mad! I mean, do I *look* like a bloke? I thought indignantly as I unlocked the front door. Then I went into my study, sat down at my desk and wrote my best man speech.

Sad ugly git, married obviously, said the lonely hearts ad in *Private Eye. Public School Chap seeks Hermès scarf-wearing woman,* said another. *You? 25. Me? Old enough to be your father, but still with plenty of go,* said a third. Fascinating. Absolutely fascinating. I always read them. Even when I'm not, you know, looking. Though I suppose I will have to start looking again. But not until May, because until then I've just got too much on my mind. I smoothed my pink cashmere tunic, flicked a speck of dust from my large straw hat and looked out the window as the number 19 crawled down the King's Road. Though it was Easter Sunday, most of the shops were open,

their beribboned windows full of painted eggs and fluffy yellow chicks and fat bunnies and bright spring flowers. The
emphasis on birth and youth and renewal provoked a sharp in-
ternal pang which took me by surprise. And then the Chelsea
Town Hall came into view and there was Kit, on the steps,
waiting. I glanced at my watch—eleven-thirty. We had an hour
to go. I'd consulted a book on wedding etiquette and I knew the
drill, though it wasn't easy boning up on the duties of best man
with only six days' notice. Most best men get six months. At
least I'd been spared the organization of the stag night, complete with ribald pranks, stripograms, epic amounts of alcohol,
recreational drugs and amusing adventures with plaster casts.
Kit had eschewed all that, in favor of a civilized dinner for both
families and selected friends at Langan's, two nights before.

And now here he was, in a new cream linen suit, with a silk
waistcoat in pale gold and a soft, pale yellow cravat. He looked
so happy as he greeted me that I felt ashamed of my momentary jealous twinge. It could have been me, I thought as I
pinned a buttonhole onto his lapel. But it wasn't. It was her.
But then if it was *meant* to be me, then it *would* have been me,
I added to myself. And that's all there is to it. This incisive
piece of analysis cheered me up. And then Portia arrived,
jumping out of a hired pink Cadillac and running up the town
hall steps, accompanied by her bridesmaid, Boris, who's been
her hairdresser for ten years. He was in a tartan suit and yellow
bow tie. Portia was wearing a Vivienne Westwood dark gray
fitted frock coat which had a huge, heart-shaped velvet collar
and a jaunty, matching hat. She was holding a small bouquet
of apricot-colored roses, and she looked lovely. She couldn't
stop laughing as she and Kit stood on the pavement together,
drawing curious glances from passersby.

"Yes, we're terribly famous!" Kit told some bemused Japa-
nese tourists who wanted to know who they were. "I'm Hugh
Grant," he said, "and this is my fiancée, Elizabeth Hurley."
The Japanese people seemed sufficiently impressed to want to

take their photo. "Of course, this is going to be a very *traditional* English wedding," Kit explained seriously as they snapped away. Of course it is, I thought. The bridegroom is in white, the bride is in dark gray, the best man is a woman, and the bridesmaid is a bloke. All we needed now was a talking dog to conduct the service.

Gradually, both sets of parents and Portia's two younger brothers arrived, and the ten of us went inside. No grating for the wedding ring to fall down, I thought to myself happily as we entered the register office; and no ushers to instruct, either. The room was tastefully furnished in soft gold and green, with heavy, fringed curtains in cream silk dupion, and elegant art nouveau chairs. Two sparkling chandeliers hung overhead, and the mahogany woodwork gleamed. And as the registrar asked Kit and Portia to sit in the two "thrones" in front of the desk, I thought of all the famous people who had plighted their troth there before—Judy Garland, D. H. Lawrence, David Niven, Wallis Simpson, Edward Elger, Des O'Connor. "I take thee Des . . ." or would she have said, "Desmond," I wondered, whoever she was. And then I stopped wondering about it because the service was about to start. I took my place in the front row, next to Boris, and then the registrar began.

"I would like to welcome you all here today," she said, "to celebrate the marriage of Kit and Portia." Portia smiled at Kit and squeezed his hand.

"Marriage, according to the law of this country," continued the registrar, "is the union of one man with one woman, voluntarily entered into for life, to the exclusion of all others." Seriously Successful didn't want to exclude all others, I thought ruefully. He wanted to *include* me.

"It is my duty to remind you of the solemn and binding vows you are about to take," she went on. I looked at Kit and Portia; they *did* look solemn at that point. And then Boris stood up and read *How Do I Love Thee? Let Me Count the Ways,* in a lilting, sonorous voice. Then came the marriage itself. It was a quick affair—just a matter of a few contractual sentences. And though it may have lacked the drama of a church wedding, it didn't lack romance. "I do solemnly declare that I know not of any lawful impediment why I, Kit, may not be joined in matrimony to you, Portia . . ."

". . . I call upon these persons here present to witness that I, Portia, do take you, Kit, to be my lawful wedded husband," she said with a smile.

"Who has the ring?" asked the registrar. I stepped forward and placed it on the tiny velvet cushion on the desk. And then Kit slipped the ring on Portia's finger, they both signed the register, and Boris and I signed it too.

"Kit. Portia. Congratulations!" said the registrar, smiling at them both. "I am very happy to tell you that you are now man and wife."

And we all clapped. It seemed the most natural thing to do. And Portia and Kit both burst into tears. And, as I say, crying's contagious, and so we were all dabbing our eyes as we made our way out of the town hall. We paused to take photos of them both on the steps, and showered them with confetti, and Portia just wouldn't stop kissing Kit. And then we all walked down Old Church Street toward the Chelsea Arts Club, laughing and chatting in the surprisingly warm spring sunshine. We stopped outside number 143, a long, low white building, knocked on the wooden door and were admitted into the shabbily genteel interior. A list of former club chairmen hung in the hall—Sir John Lavery, F. M. Lutyens, Roger McGough, Patrick Hughes. This was where Whistler had hung out, and John Singer Sargent, and all their painter pals. And we could see that it was business as usual in the bar, where a game of billiards was in progress. Then we turned left, down the parquet-floored corridor, opened the paneled dining room door and. . .

"CONGRATULATIONS!!!" All the guests were there, standing behind their chairs, waiting for Kit and Portia. And every third chair had a white and silver helium balloon tied to

its back, and the oil paintings that filled the dark green walls
were festooned with curling white streamers. And Kit and Portia took their seats in the middle of the central table, along with
their families, Boris and me. And then the champagne corks
went off like popguns. Glasses were quickly filled, and chinked,
and filled again, as the couple moved round the dining room,
happily greeting their guests.

"Hallo, Catherine," said Kit. "Hallo, Hugh. Frances—hi!"

"Congratulations, Portia," said Lizzie. "You look *lovely*."

"Well done, old boy," said Martin, standing up and giving
Kit a manly hug.

It was a big crowd and there were lots of people I didn't
know, model friends of Portia's, two sets of relations, and a
few colleagues of Kit's from TV. And outside, in the garden, a
traditional brass band was playing on the lawn. Kit loves brass
bands, though they tend to make him cry. But he'd always said
that he'd have a brass band at his wedding—preferably the
Grimethorpe Colliery Band. But I couldn't fix that up in six
days, so I booked the Hendon Brass Band instead. And as the
waiters brought in the first course the soft, plangent tones of
the tubas and trombones filtered through the open windows.
Earlier they'd played the Easter Hymn. Now, they were playing "Can't Help Lovin' Dat Man of Mine," from *Showboat*.
Portia was happily crooning the words to Kit: *Fish gotta
swim, birds gotta fly, I'm gonna love dat man 'til I die. Ca-an't
help, lovin' dat man of mine.*

What a lovely thing to play at a wedding, I thought, and noticed Boris quietly singing along to it too. I looked at the band
again; they were in dark uniforms, the thick strip of gold braid
at collar and cuff catching in the light. There were six or seven
cornets, three tenor horns, two tubas, two trombones and two
euphoniums, the sun glittering and flashing on their honey-
colored tubes and stops. There was euphony inside, too. There
was the merry rattle of cutlery on china, the chinking of cut
glass, and the sound of sixty people laughing and chatting and

bubbling with contented good will. I looked around at the decor—bottle-green baize on the walls, a selection of rickety tables, and the oddest assortment of wooden chairs. None of them matched, I realized. They were all quite different, but somehow they came together to produce a harmonious effect. And though it was lunchtime, there were white, lighted candles on every table—the bright tongues of flame bending and flickering in the breeze.

During dessert, I found Alice standing next to me. I knew she what she was going to say.

"Tiffany."

"Yes."

"Have you got a . . ."

"No, I haven't," I said as she picked some heart-shaped confetti out of my hair. I glanced at Kit and Portia, gazing rapturously at each other.

"Well, will you *please* get one," she said. "Soon."

"Yes. OK. I will," I said, with another spoonful of lemon syllabub.

"I mean, I've got one and I'm only seven," she said.

"I'll try."

"Because you know I haven't been anyone's bridesmaid yet. Ever. But Sarah Potts in my class has been one *four* times. Why didn't Portia ask *me* to be her bridesmaid?" she added, suddenly crestfallen.

"Because she doesn't know you very well, that's why."

"Oh." This seemed to satisfy her.

"But I know you *very* well, so I would definitely ask you." This cheered her up.

"Who was Portia's bridesmaid?" Alice asked.

"I was," said Boris from across the table.

Alice then went around and talked to him in a very serious manner about his duties as bridesmaid and what he'd had to do. And the fact that he was a thirty-five-year-old man in a three-piece tartan suit didn't seem strange to her at all.

"You have to look after the bride," Boris explained seriously. "And make sure she's happy on the big day. You have to make sure her dress is looking nice, and her hair, and her flowers. And you might have to hold her train, if she's got one. That's your duty."

And then I remembered my duty. As best man. Oh Lord. I'd never made a speech in public before. My stomach was churning violently. I thought I was going to be sick. But at least I'd got my notes in my pocket. As the coffee was poured, and tiny Easter eggs were passed round, I got to my feet and announced the cutting of the cake. Glasses were filled with champagne, and Kit and Portia cut into the three-tiered cake, pausing for the flash of the photographer.

Then I chinked the side of my glass with a knife and said, "I'd like to call on the bride's father to propose the toast to the health and happiness of the bride and groom."

Portia's father, Reg, got to his feet. "The 'ealth and 'appiness of the bride and groom," he said.

"The 'ealth and 'appiness of the bride and groom," we all repeated automatically, as though it were a responsorial psalm. And then we sat down to hear his speech. He was a distinguished-looking man of sixty-five or so, slightly shorter than Portia. He was a gas-fitter, recently retired. He beamed with pride as he enumerated Portia's many accomplishments on the netball court at school, where she was Streatham High's most feared striker.

"The 'arlem Globe Trotters had nothing on 'er," he said. "Now she wasn't too hot on the old ABC," he added. "Couldn't really get the hang of it at all. But she did show remarkable promise with cigarettes from an early age and proved herself a talented smoker." I looked at Portia; she was in hysterics. So were her brothers, and her mother, Trish.

"And at the age of nine, Portia could already mix a mean Martini," he said. "Of course we didn't actually let her *drink* them," he added. "No. She 'ad to wait until she was ten for that.

But we never thought when we looked at our little girl growing up, and up, and up . . ." More loud giggling. ". . . and up, that such a glittering future lay ahead. And we're very proud of what she's done, and that she's been such a professional and that she's got to work with so many talented people in the fashion industry—even if we did think they were a bunch of fairies. And although I suppose we would have preferred to see Portia float up the aisle in church today, Trish and I reckon we've seen her go up enough catwalks, in enough designer wedding frocks, to more than make up for it." More laughter. Then he looked at Kit. "And I'd just like to finish up by saying how proud and happy we are to have Kit as our son-in-law and to welcome him into our family. And we know that he'll look after Portia, and love her in sickness and in 'ealth, et cetera, et cetera, and, well . . ." His voice faltered suddenly. "We think the world of him."

Everyone clapped loudly and stamped their feet on the floor.

"Um, please, pray silence for the bridegroom," I said as the noise subsided.

Kit stood up, and thanked Reg warmly for his kind words, and for granting him Portia's hand. And he thanked his parents, Monty and Ruth, for his happy childhood. And then he thanked Monty, who's a wall paper designer, for arranging the reception at the Chelsea Arts Club—which wouldn't have been possible without his membership. And then Kit thanked Reg and Trish for providing such a splendid reception, even though I knew that he and Portia were footing most of the bill themselves. And he thanked everyone for coming, and for their generous gifts. And then he paid tribute to Portia herself.

"We may look like the proverbial Odd Couple," he said, "and in some ways we are—just look at the difference in our heights! And I was worried, when we first met, that I might not measure up to her. And indeed," he went on, "Portia did have to stoop to conquer . . ." Loud laughter. ". . . but I can only say that though I may not reach her Olympian level, I'm very long on love and devotion, and it is my firm intention to make my beautiful, my wonderful, indeed, my *model* wife as happy as I possibly can." He sat down, more than a little overcome, to thunderous applause, loud whistles, and a warm hug from Portia. And then he quickly stood up again. Because he'd forgotten. "I'm sorry," he said. "I'm neglecting my duties. I would like to propose a toast to the bridesmaid, and to thank Boris for doing such a wonderful job this morning." Boris blushed, and fiddled self-consciously with his bow tie. "Now, my wedding etiquette book advises the groom to praise the attractiveness of the bridesmaids," Kit added, with a smile. "And to warn them that they are like to be inundated with male admirers after the wedding. But believe me, this particular bridesmaid already *is*." Boris roared with laughter as we all stood and drank his health. And then it was my turn. Oh God oh God oh God. I did a few discreet deep breathing exercises as the noise subsided once again.

"Well, this my debut as best man," I began. "I've never been asked before. I can't think why. Because I'm obviously the best man for the job." I was gratified to hear a loud chuckle sweep round the room. "But anyway," I continued, "I thought I'd better get myself a wedding etiquette book too. In fact I have it right here." I held it up. "It's called *The Best Man's Duties,* um, published by Right Way at £3.99 if you're interested. And it says that one of my jobs is to thank the groom on behalf of the bridesmaid, and to present the bridesmaid with a small gift from the bride and groom, so here it is." I reached under the table and handed Boris an enormous, gift-wrapped box topped with an extravagant silver bow. "Don't bother to open it," I said to him. "It's a pair of cufflinks." Boris emitted a burst of surprised laughter, then Alice started to help him unwrap it.

"Now, unfortunately for me." I went on, "this book also says that the best man's speech should be funny. And that in fact it should be the 'high-spot' of the reception, so I feel under a certain amount of pressure here. And it also points out that weddings are a family occasion, and therefore wider issues should not be introduced, so I certainly don't intend to mention the Single Currency. Although I do happen to think the Chief Economic Adviser to the Central European Bank is quite misguided when he claims that fiscal conditions throughout the fifteen member states are like to be sufficiently harmonized by . . . oops! Ha ha! Er, sorry everyone, Sorry!"

"It's a dressing gown!" Alice suddenly exclaimed.

"Now, my book also says that three minutes' speaking time is quite enough," I continued.

"It's made of *velvet*!"

"And I've already been on my feet for . . ." I glanced at my watch. "One minute and twelve seconds."

"But it belongs to someone called Georgina," said Alice. "It's got her name in—Georgina von Etz . . . Etz . . ."

"So I'll press on," I continued, "with a few thoughts about marriage. Not that I've got any experience of it myself you understand—ha ha! Unfortunately. And frankly, rather surprisingly. In my view. Now, some people are very cynical about marriage," I continued seriously. "Groucho Marx, for example. He said, 'Marriage is an institution, but who wants to live in an institution?' Well, personally, I wouldn't mind at all, but I've never been able to find a decent bloke—apart from Kit that is. But that's another story. Though do, please, feel free to ask me about it afterward. Or him. It's perfectly OK. We're not embarrassed about it at all. And Portia knows everything. Everything. *Anyway*," I continued, "I know that Kit and Portia are going to be blissfully happy in *their* marriage. Kit has been besotted with Portia from the day he first met her two and half years ago. I remember it well. In fact I remember it with some bitterness, because he was churning out totally useless artwork for a fortnight afterward and we subsequently lost the Wagon Wheels pitch. But he'd been pierced by Cupid's arrow. Skewered, in fact. It really was love at first sight. Well, it was for Kit. As for Portia . . . well, I think it's fair to say she didn't feel the

same at all." More chuckling. "Well, not at first, that is." Oh
God, why was Kit rolling his eyes at me like that? "Anyway,"
I pressed on. "That's *all* in the past now. That bad patch they
had. In fact it really was *very* bad. They weren't getting on at
all. It went on for ages and ages actually. About a year. And
some of us wondered *why* they were bothering, frankly. But
then, finally, they got it together. In the end. And now they
couldn't be more harmonious. As you can see. Yes, they're going to be terribly happy, I know they are. And even though the
vast majority of people who pledge undying love and devotion
on their wedding day unerringly end up in court, I believe that
Kit and Portia are destined for domestic bliss. And if not, I'm
sure that Frances, who's sitting at the back there, will give
them a *very* good rate."

"It's free for friends!" she called out cheerfully.

"But Kit and Portia will be fine," I continued. "They've got
a tremendous amount in common. For example, they're both
very family-minded. In fact they're *so* family-minded that
they've decided not to hang about and I'm sure Portia and Kit
won't mind if I share with you the fact that—"

"Tiffany!"

"Portia is . . ."

". . . Tiffany, *don't!*"

". . . three months *pregnant!*"

This drew gasps, and then a round of applause.

"Not that this is one of those undignified shotgun weddings,
you understand," I added. "No. Far from it. But it's nice to
know that we're celebrating not just Kit and Portia's wedding
today, but the beginning of their happy, family life. And Kit,
I'm really sorry I told you to sell the Discovery, because you're
going to need it after all."

"He certainly IS," shouted Portia. "I'm 'aving TWINS!"

"What?" said Kit. "WHAT?" And then everyone clapped
and cheered and whistled again, and I decided that this was a
high note on which to end. I sat down. I'd done it. Phew. And it

seemed to have gone down rather well—the applause was still ringing sweetly in my ears. I should do this more often, I thought, as I went to the window and signaled to the band to start playing again.

"I only found out yesterday, darlin'," I heard Portia say as she divided an Easter egg in half. "I 'aven't 'ad a moment to tell you."

Kit looked at her and just kept shaking his head and smiling. He wasn't just over the moon—he was over the entire solar system. He was bliss incarnate. What a day. I looked at Alice; she had put on Boris's new dressing gown and had taken the irises out of the vase on the table and stuck them in her hair. Amy was petitioning Boris to let her try it on too.

"No, you're too small for it," said Alice, tripping over. "You'll get it dirty."

"No I WON'T," Amy shouted crossly.

"You can hold it for me, Amy, like a train. Tiffany, when I'm your bridesmaid, can I have one like this?" said Alice.

"Er . . ."

"Please."

"Yes. All right," I said as we all scraped back our chairs and moved into the bar. And as I passed Catherine and Hugh I heard them animatedly discussing the paintings.

"That's John Singer Sargent," said Hugh. "And I think this one's a Sickert."

"Wow, this is a Brough!" Catherine exclaimed. "He was the foremost British post-impressionist of his day," she explained. "He was considered superior to Whistler in many ways, but he died at thirty-three. He was killed in a railway accident. Isn't that sad? No one remembers him now."

"I think this one's a Brockhurst," said Hugh, peering at the adjacent canvas. "He outdid Augustus John as a portrait painter, but he's been completely forgotten as well."

And as they stood there, studying the paintings in their elaborate gilded frames, I thought, we'll all be forgotten too.

We'll die, one day, and leave not a wrack behind. But for the time being, I thought, we're alive. And I looked at Catherine again—good heavens, she was wearing a dress!—and at the solitaire diamond on her left hand. Then we went through to the bar, where the regular members of the club were sitting around in the battered armchairs, reading the papers or gossiping, apparently unresentful of our noisy and numerous intrusion. The French windows were open onto the garden, and I went outside and sat on a wooden bench on the terrace, under the sycamore tree. It was as hot and bright as midsummer, and the wallflowers and lilac were in full bloom; and the clematis which covered the pergola was already starred with pink flowers. The band were playing "Linden Lea," in the arrangement by Ralph Vaughan Williams.

. . . *I be free, to go abroad, Or take again, my homeward road.* Oh lovely. Lovely. *To where for me, the apple tree do lean down low in Linden Lea.*

Kit was right, I thought, as I sat and listened. There's something about the mournful muted tones of a brass band that brings tears to the eyes. Why is that? Is it the dignified eloquence of high passion expressed in low notes? Or just the soft, reticent timbre of the instruments themselves? The band wiped their mouthpieces, and then turned over the sheets on their stands.

Abide with me, fast fades the eventide . . . Oh no. Surely that's for funerals, not weddings. Not that one, please.

The darkness deepens, Lord with me Abide . . .

I felt my throat constrict. Not that one, please not that one. But it was too late.

Change and decay, in all around I see . . .

I heard shrieks of laughter from the bar. "No, Kit, it's *my* turn!"

Oh thou, who changest not, Abide with me.

I glanced inside. Portia and Kit were playing billiards with Lizzie and Martin, while Frances kept the score. I heard the sharp click of the cue and then saw the balls scatter like blobs of mercury.

Who, like Thyself, my guide and stay can be.

Through cloud and sunshine Lord, Abide with me.

God, I wish I *could* get someone to abide with me, I thought bitterly.

Sitting underneath the huge Victorian billiard table were Alice and Amy playing cards. "SNAP!" I heard Amy shout. "SNAP! They're the SAME," she added with triumphant fortissimo. "They go TOGETHER. They're PARTNERS. SNAP! SNAP! SNAP."

. . . and earth's vain shadows flee.

In life, in death, O Lord, Abide with me.

And, as I sat outside, looking in, I wondered whether I would always live my life like this, experiencing things at one remove, through my friends. Kit hitched; Sally's baby almost due; Portia pregnant with twins; Kate now living with Mike; Emma firmly ensconced with Lawrence; Catherine engaged to Hugh; Jonathan and Sarah happily married; Lizzie and Martin ditto. And Nick has a girlfriend now, someone he met at work. I was pleased about that, but it did make me wonder whether Tiffany Trott will always be giving these things a Miss. Standing in attendance, off-stage, in the wings, watching, and waiting on others. Waiting, I thought ruefully as the band played on. Waiting. Waiting. Waiting.

May

"I can't stand the waiting!" wailed Sally. "I just can't *stand* it. I don't know what Lena's doing in there, but frankly it's getting me down. She was supposed to be here by May the first—what on earth's going on?"

"Er, I don't know," I said. "I really can't help you with this one. You'll just have to wait for Dame Nature to deliver." But I felt for Sally. Terribly frustrating. And it's not even as though you can complain. I mean, if trains are late you can ring up the relevant authority, or fill in a form at the station, and if you're lucky you'll probably get some sort of compensation in the form of an off-peak day return to Crewe. But if a baby's late, you wait. "Two weeks overdue really is a bit much," I agreed. "Perhaps we should fine her."

"She's not a library book, Tiffany," Sally replied as she tied on an apron. "She's a baby." Then she put on a pair of yellow rubber gloves and produced a red bucket from under the sink.

"Sally, what are you doing?"

"Well I might as well do a bit of cleaning while I'm waiting," she said briskly. "This place is a complete *mess*." It isn't. It never is. Sally's cleaner comes in twice a week, and her apartment is always pristine, every inch of it sparkling, hermetic, and utterly devoid of dust.

"Sally, let me do that!" I intervened as she began to swab the floor. "I really don't think you should be exerting yourself . . ."

I just stopped myself from adding, "in your condition," aware that I was sounding depressingly like Pat.

"I'm OK," she said irritably, as the yellow sponge shot back and forth across the marble tiles. "But I just don't understand what's holding her up!" she added crossly as she pulled down the lever on the squeegee mop. "By the time she's born she'll be practically old enough to walk."

"Well, the Expected Date of Delivery is often approximate," I pointed out.

"Yes, but that's only because women often don't know the date of conception," she countered. "Whereas I do. I know it exactly. Because it only happened once." She paused, straightened up, then put her left hand on the small of her back. "It was Friday the first of August, at the Lake Palace of Udaipur in Rajasthan, India. Do you want the time as well?"

"Um, no thanks," I said. But what a lucky shot. It was like winning the lottery with a single ticket. You have sex, once, with someone you hardly know, and bingo! Full House. A baby.

"Does it really matter if she's late?" I asked.

"Not really," Sally conceded wearily. "It's just that it's no fun being nine and half months pregnant. She's kicking me to bits—it's like *Saturday Night Fever* in there. I daren't go out in case my waters break," she continued, "and my indigestion's dreadful—my intestines are so squashed up now, they're practically coming out of my ears. God, I could murder a piece of coal!" she added, with a hungry look in her eyes.

"Why don't you have her induced?" I suggested. Sally looked at me as though I had just said, "Why don't you have her adopted?"

"Nothing would induce me to induce her," she said emphatically as she mopped away again. "Because if I do, that means a hospital birth, and I'm going to have her naturally, at home. But I just wish she'd bloody well *hurry up*," she added in a peevish whine. She went to a cupboard, rummaged around, then triumphantly held up an old toothbrush.

"Sally, what on earth are you doing now?" I asked faintly. She was down on her knees, attacking the skirting board with the tiny brush.

"I can't stand the thought of all the dust lurking in these corners," she explained as she brushed away imaginary specks with violent, jabbing movements. "I don't want Leonie being exposed to unnecessary germs or allergens. Look, thanks for coming over, Tiff, but why don't you do something else? This must be quite boring for you . . ."

"Oh no no no no no," I said. "Well, yes. OK, I'll go and watch some tennis at the club then," I said, grateful for the chance to get away. "It's the finals of the men's tournament and I would quite like to see it. But I'll have my mobile phone on me," I added, "so at the first twinge, you just ring and I'll be here."

"OK," she said happily as she brushed away obsessively at the shining white woodwork. "I'll call you if I need you. Have fun."

I walked up to Fulham Broadway and got the tube. It would only take twenty-five minutes or so to get to the club, and I really wanted to see the match. Two-headed Alan was in it, which was amazing, as he'd never got further than the third round before. But he'd been playing like a demon recently. Not that he stood a chance against Ed Brooks, I thought, as I changed onto the Northern Line at Embankment; in fact Ed would wipe the floor with him, having won the title for the past four years. But it should be interesting to watch. As I went through the gate I could hear the thwock of tennis balls on catgut, and the occasional burst of applause. On the far grass court, a crowd of about fifty had assembled on wooden benches; everyone was watching with quiet intensity, heads swinging back and forth with each hit. I approached quietly and identified a spare place, halfway along the front row. They were midway through the second set. Ed must be thrashing Alan, I thought as I sat down. And then I looked at the score board. Ed had indeed taken the first set, but he hadn't won it six-love or six-two as I had expected, but seven-five. Alan was clearly holding his own. He was serving now, three games to four down. He threw the ball up high with his left hand, simultane- ously dropping his racket right the way down his back, and then—bang!

"Fifteen-love," called the umpire calmly. What an ace! Ed hadn't had time to blink, let alone move. Then Alan went to the other side of the serving mark and threw the ball up again, this time sending it deep into the right-hand corner of the service box. Ed returned it straight into the net.

"Thirty-love." Gosh. Alan looked so determined. I stole a glance at Julia; she looked nervous, but her eyes were shining as Alan power-served his way to forty-fifteen. Then—thwock! he put Ed's return away with a flying forehand volley.

"Game, Hensher," called the umpire. "Four games all. Brooks to serve."

This time, with Ed serving, much the same thing happened, but in reverse. Alan got in a couple of good returns but then lobbed the ball too high, giving Ed the chance to rush to the net and smash it with the velocity of an Exocet. Alan, would you please stop doing that, I found myself thinking. Would you please *stop* giving points away? And I was surprised at how much I was rooting for him to win. Not just because he was the under- dog, but because I felt bad at having been so dismissive of him before. Not that he could have cared less, I thought as I looked at Julia again. She was attractive, and she looked happy, clasp- ing her hands together with almost religious fervor every time her boyfriend hit the ball. And her imprecations seemed to be working—Alan was playing wonderfully well.

"Game, Hensher," called out the umpire. "Hensher leads five games to four."

Alan was in business now. He was serving for the set. His serve secured the first two points, but Ed came back with sev- eral cunningly placed lobs. Because Alan kept leaving himsel exposed at the net, while the ball sailed high over his head, landing neatly on the baseline and then bouncing out of the court. Ed's placing of the ball was quite brilliant. Forensic, almost. Alan was playing a hard game, but he didn't possess a fraction of his opponent's strategic skill. There was no way he could win this—tennis was about brain as much as brawn.

"Deuce," called the umpire.

Alan was perspiring heavily, frequently wiping his forehead with his white toweling wristband. He caught Julia's eye as he did so, and she flashed him an encouraging smile. Then he served again, this time putting a topspin on it which sent the ball curving away at a crazy angle. Then he did it again. It was completely unreturnable. Changing his service in mid-match was a high-risk strategy, but it seemed to work.

"Advantage Hensher."

Ed was looking irritated. God, I hope he's not going to do a McEnroe, I thought, as he bounced his racket down onto the grass.

"Racket abuse. Warning," called the umpire. Alan waited calmly, probably grateful for a moment's rest, and then he served again. Thwock! This time Ed returned it; Alan sent it spinning back low and fast over the net, Ed lobbed it up, but this time Alan was there, ready and waiting. He seemed to reach up for the ball with his left hand as it plummeted toward him, then he took it on the full volley and sent it cannoning across the court.

"Game and second set Hensher. Six games to four. One set all."

Gosh, this match is hot stuff, I thought as we all clapped appreciatively. Both players retired to the side of the court for lemonade and a quick sit-down. It was just like Wimbledon, without the hamburger stands. Ed was now looking distinctly rattled, while Alan appeared calm, but apprehensive. This was a three-set match, not five, so this last set would decide it.

"Time please," said the umpire, as though he were calling last orders at the Dog and Duck.

Ed served, and easily won the first game, though Alan came back with some strong returns which drew gasps of surprise from the crowd. At times the ball seemed to ricochet off both men's rackets like a bullet. This was fine play, though the rallies were short, but the ball just flew off the grass, skimming it with an almost audible "whooosh!" And now, within a mere fifty minutes or so, they were level pegging, five games all, and Ed was serving again. The audience was gripped. None of us moved a muscle as he threw the ball up high, and smashed it down—thwock!—straight into the tramlines. Palpably irritated, he threw the ball up again, and exactly the same thing happened. His first double fault. He was tiring. Even though he was ten years younger than Alan. But Alan was just doggedly hanging in there.

"Love-fifteen."

Ed served again, with a stertorous grunt, this time to Alan's backhand. But Alan just stepped into it beautifully with his racket swung right back, and powered it across the court. Ed returned it on *his* backhand, hard and low, but Alan kept up the pressure, driving forward toward the net with each successive hit. He was really playing an aggressive, turbo-charged game here, but by this stage Ed's accuracy was beginning to slip. Seeing that Alan was close to the net, Ed lobbed the ball up high, behind him, and our heads described a circular movement as we followed its trajectory down. Suddenly, the linesman's hand went up.

"Out!" called the umpire.

"It was not out!" Ed retorted, furious.

The umpire conferred with the linesman. "Out," she reiterated firmly, while we all whispered our agreement with her decision. It *was* out.

"—definitely out."

"—I couldn't really see."

"—just over the line."

"—I saw the chalk fly up."

"—he is naughty to argue."

"—yep, definitely, just over."

"Quiet please, ladies and gentlemen. Love-thirty."

Ed stamped back to the baseline and angrily picked up two balls. He served again, and Alan returned it hard. Then Ed sent it back and Alan clipped it upward in a high, looping lob. And now Ed was running backward as the ball sailed toward him, straining to catch it full on with the face of his racket and punch it down hard again. But as he ran back, keeping one eye on the descending ball, and one eye on the ground, he suddenly skidded, and fell. He quickly pushed himself back onto his feet with his left hand, but Alan's lob had already landed, just beyond Ed's desperate, outstretched reach. Ed picked himself up, cussing audibly, as he brushed the grass off his shorts.

"Love-forty," said the umpire. If Alan won this game, the score would be six-five, with his serve next. He could win it. This was a decisive point. If he could just hang on in there and break Ed's serve. Alan stood behind the baseline, bouncing on the balls of his feet, in readiness for the ballistic shock of the ball on his racket. Ed threw the ball up, we watched it rise above his upturned face . . . suddenly a high-pitched warble rang out across the court, then the ball smashed into the net. Ed stopped and looked accusingly in my direction. Oh God, where *was* it—I groped around inside my bag for my mobile phone, but still it was ringing relentlessly with shrill and unembarrassed abandon. My face was suffused with heat—oh God, what a mess in this bag, where *is* the bloody thing, I thought angrily, I can never lay my hands right on it.

"That put me off!" Ed shouted furiously, pointing at me. Everyone was tut-tutting disapprovingly, and the umpire was looking daggers in my direction.

"I stated quite clearly at the start of this match that all mobile phones should be switched off," she said crossly. "Play will *not* be resumed until they are." At last—got it.

"Yes, hello!" I said breathlessly as I struggled out of my seat, smiling apologetically at the watching crowd.

"Sally! Is it happening? It is? Oh don't worry, Sally," I said, trying to quell my feelings of rising hysteria. "I'm on my way. Sorry everyone!" I called out. "It's an emergency! Have you called the midwife? And you're sure they're contractions? OK, OK, of course you're sure they're bloody contractions. How far apart? Well, time them. I'll be right there," I said, feeling panic piling up in my chest. In the distance, as I ran out of the club, I could hear the ball thwacking back and forth as play resumed. Then there was a burst of applause.

"Six games to five," I heard the umpire say. "Hensher leads, final set. Hensher to serve." Two-headed Alan was prevailing. He was striking a blow for ageing underdogs everywhere. And it had all been done, I realized, with a pang, through the transforming power of love. I flagged down a passing cab.

"Chelsea Harbour, please, and as quick as you can, I'm having a baby!" I said.

"Not in my cab you're not, darlin'," he said, suddenly screeching to a halt. "I'm not having that 'orrible mess in 'ere."

"No, not me, I'm not having one—my friend Sally is, any minute now, so please get there quickly."

The driver raced down south to Fulham Broadway, thankfully avoiding the crowded King's Road. Within half an hour we were drawing up outside Chelsea Harbour and I shot up in the lift to Sally's flat. Joan the midwife opened the door. I felt instantly reassured. Here was someone who knew what she was doing. Thank God, because despite five months' preparation and seventeen books on childbirth, I didn't really feel I had a clue. It would be like trying to land a plane having only received training on the ground.

"Where is she, where is she?"

"I'm here, you idiot," Sally called out calmly. She was sitting on the sofa, watching television, methodically working her way through a box of Quality Street.

"What about your contractions?" I asked, surprised.

"Well, I've only had one so far," she said. "Or maybe it was just cramp. I don't know. I was just painting the bathroom when I felt this awful twinge. But that was three quarters of an hour ago, and nothing's really happened since. I think I may have brought you back under false pretenses, Tiffany, I'm really sorry, because I know you wanted to see the tennis, but you see it *was* rather painful but now it's completely stopp—" Suddenly she gasped, squeezed her eyes shut, opened her mouth, and emitted a startling noise, like the whine of a jump jet taking off. She held it for ten seconds and then, as the agony eased, her body relaxed again. She looked at me, then blinked, shock shining in her eyes.

"Actually, I think it *is* starting now," she whispered.

The midwife nodded. "It's the first stage," she said calmly as she took Sally's blood pressure. "Don't worry—you've got a long way to go yet."

"Tiffany," said Sally quietly, "please would you fill up the pool?"

Joan and I ran the hose from the bathroom and into the birthing pool, taking care to make sure the water was quite hot. It took about half an hour to fill, then we put on the lid to conserve the heat.

"Oh God, oh God," said Sally as she convulsed again. "Uuuuuuuhhhhh! Oh, noooooooooooooo!"

"Breathe deeply," I urged her as she gripped the sides of the coffee table. "Come on. In through the nose—that's it."

"Ooooooohhh! . . . hummmmmmmm! . . . Ooooooh! . . . ooooOOOWWWWW!" she cried out in pain again. It lasted for about twenty seconds. And then it stopped and she smiled in relief, then turned her gaze back to *Songs of Praise*. "It's from Southwark Cathedral," she explained, as the chords of "He

Who Would Valiant Be" struck up. I got out my cross-stitch to
calm myself down.

. . . *gainst all disaster.*

And I realized with a pang that I had had the antique roses
kit for almost a year, and had done less than half.

. . . *there's no discouragement, shall make him once relent . . .*

I'll just do a little bit now, I thought to myself, just a thorn or
two, and then suddenly Sally was groaning and bellowing
again—"Oh God, oh God! This is awful!"

. . . *his first avowed intent . . .*

"Why don't you get in the pool now, Sally," Joan suggested.
"You'll find the water comforting and supportive and that will
help with the pain."

Sally undressed, slowly and painfully, clutching her enormous abdomen. We helped her off with her things, checked the
temperature of the water, and then held her hands as she gin-
gerly stepped in and gently lowered herself down. She was so
slim and lithe, but with this bizarre bump in front. She looked
like a snake which has just swallowed a medium-sized pig. She
lay back, gripped the sides of the pool, and tried to relax, twisting and turning her body to try and find the most comfortable
position. I put on a CD of some Native American Indian
music—but Sally didn't like it.

"Too bloody depressing—all those wailing voices. Give me
the Bach solo cello suites, will you?" she groaned. "I just want
to follow one note. It's in the CD rack, about halfway down."
And as the almost human voice of the solo cello began to fill
the room, she closed her eyes and inhaled, snorting the air into
her lungs, before expelling it calmly through her mouth. I
looked at my watch. It was almost eight P.M. She'd been in labor for about three hours—only another thirty-three to go then,
I thought grimly. For a while nothing much happened, Sally
just lay back, with her head resting on the side. Sometimes she
let herself drop right under the water, which I found slightly

alarming. And then she'd surface again, like a mermaid, her hair in streaming rat-tails.

"Ooooooooooow! Aaaaaaaaaaaah! OOOOOOOOWWWW-WWW!"

I held an ice-pack against her perspiration-beaded brow as her knuckles went white with the pain. The contractions were longer now, lasting up to a minute, during which she bellowed and ululated as if it were death she were encountering, not life.

"Are you OK, Sally?" I asked her uselessly as her jaws clenched together violently. *Are you sure you don't want any drugs?*

"I'm fine," she said, through bared, gritted teeth. "I'm fine, I'm fine, I'm—uuuuuuuuuuuuhhhh! Ooooooooooooohhhhhh!! AAAAAIIIIEEEEEEEE! Oh God, I want it to *stop*." Stop? It had hardly started.

At nine P.M., the midwife put a hand-held electronic monitor under the water and listened to the baby's heartbeat. "I think we may have a problem," she said quietly. My heart nearly stopped, but Sally was in the searing spasm of another contraction and hadn't heard what Joan said. "Sally," said Joan, when the pain subsided. "You're doing OK, you're almost fully dilated, and the baby's head is well down. But I think there may be a slight problem with the heartbeat, and a chance of fetal distress. Now, I can get you a consultant," she added calmly, "though I think it would be easier if we went to hospital. But it's entirely up to you."

"Oh God, get me to hospital!" Sally groaned. "Just get me to hospital. I want to go to hospital—oooooooooohhhh! Uh, uhh, uuhh, uuhhh, UUUHHH, UUUUUUHHHHH! I *like* hospitals!" she almost shouted, as we helped her to stand up. "I like them! I never said I didn't."

Joan phoned the hospital and told them that we were coming in. "Have you got a taxi firm lined up?" she asked me.

"No. No. Oh God, oh God, I'm sorry, I should have had a number at the ready."

"There are some . . . cab cards in the . . . drawer by the phone," Sally said between spasms as Joan helped her to dress.

I phoned the first one. "My friend's in labor," I began, but he just said, "Sorry, we're not a delivery room," and replaced the receiver. I rang another, but they refused too. "Look, my friend's in labor," I said, to a third.

"Oh gawd!" he began reluctantly.

"And the baby's in distress, you see . . ."

"What's the address, luv? Give me five minutes."

Sally was ready now, though her voluminous Nicole Farhi dress was damp from her dripping hair. We got into the lift, supporting her on each side, and stood outside, in front of the marina. One or two of her "neighbors" tut-tutted disapprovingly as Sally stood there, like a *Titanic* survivor, groaning loudly and shivering, despite the cashmere pashmina which we'd wrapped around her shoulders.

Suddenly a brown Montego screeched to a halt on the forecourt to our left and honked twice. It was as close as he could get. We helped Sally up the steps, Joan spread a contingent towel on the backseat, and sat there with Sally, while I got in the front with the driver.

"Chelsea and Wesminster?" he asked. I nodded. We sped through the backstreets of Chelsea and up the Fulham Road, while Sally groaned and whimpered in the back. Ten minutes later we pulled up outside the white awnings of the hospital and Joan and I helped her inside, through the Tesco-style revolving doors. A stretcher was waiting for her, and as we almost ran through the corridors, trying not to look like extras in *ER*, I quickly took in the airy, white interior with its high walkways and expanses of glass, and enormous colorful sculptures. The lift took us to the third floor, to the Anne Stewart ward, where Sally was whizzed into a delivery suite and quickly transferred to a bed. I waited outside while a consultant obstetrician examined her, and distracted myself by studying a poster promoting the benefits of breast-feeding. After a few minutes the doctor emerged, and I heard Sally's voice.

"Tiffaneee . . ." I heard her shout. "Tiffanneee." I parted the floral curtain and went in. Sally was lying on the bed, in the semi-darkened room, wearing a green cotton hospital gown. Great, fat tears coursed down her face.

"He says the baby's—uh-uh—fine," she sobbed. "He says she's going to be all right. Joan just wanted to be on the safe side and I'm glad about that, but oh it *huuuurrrrts,* Tiffany. It—uh-uh—huuuuurts!" She turned her face to the wall; her neck was distended and veined with pain. What on earth could I do to help? It was awful. I felt as redundant as a vegetarian in a bacon factory. I handed her a wad of tissues and drew up a chair beside her.

"Oh I'm so hot," she said as she dabbed at her face. "I'm so hot." I turned on the fan, directed it toward her, and then poured her some juice. While she drank it through a straw I looked around at the birthing suite. It was painted in a restful, pale green, with a stenciled border of purple grapes; it was pleasant, though the occasional Sam Peckinpah splash of dried blood on the curtains engendered feelings of mild alarm. But there was no aroma of antiseptic, no anesthetic tang, and if there were other women screaming in childbirth, we certainly couldn't hear them. There was a clock on the wall, the second hand calmly ticking away with an audible click. It was eleven p.m.—Sally had been in labor for about six hours.

Suddenly she stood up and staggered around, clutching her belly and groaning. Then she went back to the bed and leaned forward on it. Joan raised it up, so that Sally could rest her weight on her elbows without having to bend down.

"AAaaaaaaggh! Oooooooooohhhh!" she grunted as the contractions began again. "Uuuuuuuuuggghhhhh!" she groaned.

"What can I do, Sally? Tell me."

"Could you—oooooooooohhhhh!—massage the base of my spine—hard." Joan passed me some aromatherapy oil, and I pressed the heel of my palm into Sally's lower back as she groaned with each baby-expelling spasm.

"Ooooooohhh! Could you . . . press harder . . . that's it. Really hard. That helps . . . ooooooowwww! I don't know why." Joan put an Enya cassette in the music center, but Sally was too possessed by pain to find it soothing.

"Do you want an epidural?" said Joan.

"No no no!" she cried.

"Well, have some gas and air, I don't think you've got long to go now." Joan pulled the air supply down and Sally perched on the edge of the bed, inhaling deeply, almost greedily, into the transparent mask. It seemed to help for a few seconds, before the next wave of pain knocked her down.

"I don't want to be on the bed!" she wailed. "I don't want to be on the bed!"

Joan and I spread out two mattresses on the floor, and Sally lay on one, clutching a beanbag to her swollen belly, cradling it like a child.

"Tiffany," she said weakly. "Tiffany."

"Yes," I said, holding a cold flannel against her brow.

"It hurts—oooooOOOOOWWWWWWWWWWW!!! It hurts."

"I know, but it's not long now, Sally," I said. "You're being really brave."

"I'm not being brave. I'm not. It's horrible. I, I . . ." Suddenly she began to flail about as though she were literally crazed. Her eyes revolved in her head, while guttural, animal noises issued from her throat. "Tiffany, I want you to go away!" she suddenly barked. "I want to be on my own. I want you to get lost. Do you hear me? Get lost!" What? *Now?*

"Do you want me to go?" I asked.

"Yes. Yes. I want you to get lost. Just fuck off, will you. Fuck off! Fuck off! Fuck. Right. Off—UUUUUUUHHHHHHH!"

"OK, OK, I'm fucking off," I said as I retreated, aware that it was the first time I had ever heard her swear. "Look, I'm going."

She wanted to be on her own. She wanted to encounter the pain by herself. I had read about that in one of the books. I parted the curtain and prepared to leave.

"TIFFANY, COME BACK!" she shouted. "Where are you GOING? Don't leave me on my OWN!" she wailed. "Come BACK! Come back RIGHT NOW!" *What?*

"Here I am," I said, "it's OK." Oh God, she was behaving so oddly. It was weird. I didn't know what to do. I looked at Joan, but she just smiled at me reassuringly and put her forefinger to her lips.

"I don't want to be on my own, Tiffany," Sally moaned as the pain subsided, giving her a moment's relief. Then it began again, the contractions coming every few seconds now, engulfing her in wave after wave of pain.

"OooooOOOOOOWWWWWWW!   AaaaAAAAARRRR-GGGGHHHH!!! . . . HELP ME SOMEBODY! HELP Me! Oh GOD! Oh GOD! OOOOOOOOOOOWWWWWW!!!"

Suddenly she got up, grabbed me by the shoulders, leaned her head on my collarbone, and held me in a viselike grip. Joan pushed a mattress under her and got down on her hands and knees.

"The baby's coming," she said, "I can see the head. It's crowning. Now push again, Sally. Push. That's it! Go on! You're doing really well." I held Sally under the arms as she bore down with her whole weight, groaning with a violence to match each spasm.

"AAAAAAAAAARRRGGGGGHHHHHH!!!!"

"It's coming," said Joan.

"OH GOD, OH GOD, OH GOD!!!"

"The head's almost through, not long now."

"OOOOOOOOWWWWWWW!!!"

"That's it, Sally," said Joan again. "Good girl! Good girl! Push again. Breathe through the pain."

"OOOOOOOOOOOOWWWWW!!!!!! OOOOOOOHHH-HHHHH!!"

"That's it! Just one more push now!"

"AAAAAAAAARRRGGGGHHHH!!!"

"Well done, Sally! Just a bit more. Baby's coming, she's almost here . . ."

"AAAAIIIIIEEEEEEEEEEEEEEEEEEE!!!!!!"

"Here come the shoulders. Just one more pu—"

Suddenly I heard a membranous squelch, and then a whoosh! and a splash! and, out of the corner of my eye, I saw Joan's white-gloved hands catch Sally's baby. It was over. Sally collapsed onto the mattress, whimpering, legs splayed, her face and mine both streaming with tears. Then Joan snipped the umbilical cord, quickly wiped off the pearly sac, then placed the bloodied infant in its mother's arms. And as she cradled her child for the first time, clasping it to her breast, a look of total astonishment crossed Sally's tearstained face. Then she looked at the baby, looked at me, and threw back her head and laughed.

May Continued

"Lancelot," said Sally, shifting slightly against the pillows.

"Leo," I replied.

"Louis," she suggested. "I like foreign names."

"How about Ludwig, then?"

She gently shifted the feeding baby, and brushed his tiny cheek with her thumb.

"Llewellyn," she suddenly said, with a smile.

"What about Laurie?" I offered. "As in Lee. Or you could just have Lee on its own."

"Oh, I don't know, Tiffany," she said, stifling a yawn. "I've got ages to think about it. But how incredible!" she exclaimed yet again. "The nurse who did my ultrasound said I was *definitely* having a *girl*!"

"Well, there are limits to technology," I said. "Because Leroy is clearly a bloke."

"Yes," she said, hugging him to her with an ecstatic smile, "he's a lovely little bloke. I'll have to repaint the nursery," she added with a giggle, "and I don't think he'll want to wear all those little pink dresses, will you, darling?" And was it my imagination or did the baby appear to roll his eyes in horrified agreement?

I looked at the brightly painted sheep gamboling along the wall, then lifted my gaze to the clock. It was four a.m.—an hour since we had left the birthing suite. Suddenly the baby let go of Sally's bruised-looking nipple. He had had enough for now.

"Tiffany," said Sally suddenly. "Do you want a cuddle?"

"Sorry?"

"A cuddle. Do you want one?"

"Well, Sal, I didn't realize you felt this way . . ."

"Not me, you twit—the *baby*!"

"Oh. Oh. Sorry. Yes. Of course I'd love one." I stood up and Sally gently transferred him to my arms, where he lay, eyes closed in blissful sleep. I inhaled the caramel fragrance of his velvety head.

"He's lovely," I said. "He's just gorgeous."

"And Tiffany," Sally whispered, careful not to disturb the other women.

"Yes?"

"I wondered—would you be his godmother?"

I nodded. Then I nodded again. "Thanks," I just managed to mumble as his tiny features began to blur. I felt shattered and drained, as though I were the survivor of some dreadful accident. It had been an extraordinary ten hours—or was it ten days? I felt I couldn't be sure.

"Why don't you go home now?" Sally said as I handed him back. "Come again tomorrow evening."

"OK," I said softly. "I think I will." I stood up, aching all over. "Time for bed, said Zebedee."

"Time for Tubby bye byes!" she quipped. And then she said, "Which is the yellow one?"

"What?"

"The yellow Teletubby. What's it called?"

"Oh. Laa-Laa," I replied knowledgeably.

"Perhaps I'll call *you* Laa-Laa," she crooned to the baby. He emitted what sounded suspiciously like a groan.

"Well done, Sally," I whispered as I parted the flower-sprigged curtains around her bed. "You were really brave."

"I wasn't.

"You were—you did it without an epidural."

"Well, if it had gone on for much longer, I don't think I

would have held out," she acknowledged with a grim little smile. Then I gave her a little wave, and left. The hospital was still busy, despite the lateness of the hour. As the lift doors opened onto the ground floor, I saw a man with a bloody bandage round his face being taken to Casualty. On the other side of the corridor, a weeping woman was being led away, her shoulders enfolded by a protective arm. What was her story, I wondered, and why was she crying? What had happened to her that night? As I passed the front reception, I stopped for a moment to read the granite plaque on the wall: *The Chelsea and Westminster Hospital was opened by Her Majesty the Queen, on 13th May, 1993,* it stated. The thirteenth of May. That was today. This was the hospital's birthday. And Sally's baby's, and, I suddenly remembered, my own. I stepped onto the Fulham Road, where I flagged down a solitary cab.

"To Islington, please," I said. The driver said nothing, but looked at me oddly. And then I realized why. My white cotton dress was spattered with Sally's blood.

"I've been to an all-night chainsaw massacre," I said airily. Actually, I didn't say that. I just managed to murmur, "Baby . . . born." Then I got into the cab, sped home through the silent streets, and slept.

I woke at eleven and sat outside in my dressing gown, thinking. The storm had passed, and I felt safe again. In my own little house. *Dolce Domum,* I thought happily; Home Sweet Home. Then I opened my mail. There were birthday cards from Lizzie, Kit and Kate, and to my great joy, a postcard from São Paulo. *Hola! Teeffanee,* it read. *I happy. I coming to London. I stay with you isn't it? We go salsa! I see you very soon Teefanee. Adios! José.* I smiled and sipped my coffee, surveying my little garden. The ceanothus was just coming into bloom, producing small pom-poms of a startling blue. There were tight green round buds on the peonies, showing just a tantalizing sliver of red. And the white bells on the lilies of the valley were

newly opened, like tiny parasols. Everything was about to
bloom, I reflected as I inhaled their sweet scent. Everything
was coming up roses, and delphiniums and sweet williams and
stocks. What should I do? I wondered. I knew I couldn't
work—I needed to go somewhere calm. Perhaps I should go to
church, I thought as I dressed, to give thanks for Sally's safe
deliverance. I decided to go the Royal Academy instead, to see
the Art of Holy Russia. I walked onto Essex Road and got the
number 38. I sat there, grasping my newspaper, but not even
registering, let alone reading its contents. I just stared blankly
out of the window, not noticing a thing, seeing only the events
of the previous night. Sally's agonized cries still rang in my
ears, and I was aware of a dull ache in my upper arms from the
fierce downward pressure of her body. I alighted outside the
Ritz in bright sunshine, and crossed the road. The Academy's
elegant courtyard was deserted. This was clearly a quiet time
to go. A good time.

I stepped inside, bypassing the wide, wrought-iron staircase,
and slipped straight through to the back. I was too weary to
walk up the frosted-glass staircase, so I called the lift. The
curved glass doors drew back, and I floated silently upward, as
if in a bubble, to the Sackler Wing on the second floor. It was
almost empty, apart from a small knot of students earnestly
studying the walls. I wandered slowly, from picture to picture,
my feet shuffling over the blond wooden floor. Serene, flat-
looking faces with ovoid eyes and deep-gold haloes gazed
down from the walls. I didn't feel as though I was looking at
them, rather that they seemed to be studying me. They were all
in tempera and gesso and painted on wood—the Virgin of
Vladimir clutching the infant Jesus, a long-haired John the
Baptist holding a baptismal chalice, the prophet Elijah, as-
cending into heaven. Then an array of saints passed before my
eyes—St. Matthew, St. Nicholas, St. Peter and St. Paul, and St.
George on a wonderful white charger. I stopped to read the ex-
planatory notes on the wall: *Russia's greatest master, Andrei*

Rublev, was active in and around Moscow between 1390 and 1430. Medieval Russia! What wild images that conjured, but the icons were emblems of serenity, created by monks who offered up their prayers in paint. I stood before an image of the Madonna and Child, her face alabaster white, tinged with carmine, the infant Christ clutching at her magenta gown. As I stood before her, she seemed to hold me in an intimate, personal gaze which filled me with peace. This was the right place to have come, I reflected. It was restorative. I needed it. I made my way outside, then sat on the steps in a wedge of sunlight. I leaned against a pillar, closed my eyes, and breathed in deeply through my nose, oblivious even to the loud, monotonous rumble of the buses and cars. Suddenly my tranquillity was shattered by the shrill warble of my mobile phone. Oh God. Not again. Why hadn't I turned it off? I pressed the button.

"Hello," I said. "Yes. Yes it is. Oh *hello. Thank you,*" I added, with a burst of surprised laughter. "How did you know? Did I? I'd completely forgotten that. How are you? Good. Yes, I'm fine. Mmm—the baby's fine too. He arrived last night, actually. Yes, Sally's fine too. It went pretty well really. Ten hours. Not too bad. Yes, I am rather shattered. No. No stitches. No, no epidural either. Yes, very brave wasn't it? And I didn't faint. Chelsea and Westminster. *Very* nice. Five star. Yes, I do prefer hospital births. Well, Top Breeders Recommend It. Erm, about eight pounds. Oh, no firm ideas yet. Something beginning with 'L,' I think. Ludovic? Well, that's certainly a possibility. Leonardo? Mmm, maybe. Where am I now? I'm at the RA. I've been to see the icons. I'm sitting outside. Well why not? I need a bit of a break after that. How about you? Packing? You're *packing*? What now? Why are you packing? Where are you going? You're not leaving London, are you? What, come round now? But I don't know how to get to you. You will?" I stood up, my heart beating wildly, my mobile phone clamped to my left ear.

"OK. OK. I'm listening," I told him. "Keep talking . . . right,

I'm leaving the Academy now, I'm turning left out of the courtyard . . . I'm walking along Piccadilly and now I can see Fortnum and Mason opposite, and I'm passing the Alliance and
Leicester building society on my left and I can see Hatchards
on the other side of the road. What? Oh hang on a sec, I can't
hear you anymore, I think we're breaking up . . . OK, now I'm
going past . . . what? I go left here?"

I stopped in front of a sign which said, ALBANY COURT YARD
W I. Set right back from the road was a Regency mansion
house in brown brick, with tall arched windows and a white,
porticoed entrance. I must have passed it countless times and
scarcely noticed it. I entered the building, crossed the scallop-
tiled floor, passed the Porter's Lodge and entered Albany. It
was like another world—here, incredibly, was cloistered calm
in the middle of Piccadilly. As my feet tapped across the floor,
I passed marble plaques which proclaimed that Bulwer-Lytton,
Lord Byron and Gladstone had once been residents. Then I
walked along the white canopied ropewalk, taking in the
heady, collegiate atmosphere. I half expected to see magiste-
rial dons rush by in flowing gowns. To left and right were narrow staircases, alphabetically numbered.

"Which one are you in?" I whispered into my phone. "P2?
Well, I'm just passing D . . ." I carried on walking toward the
end, and then turned sharp right. "I'm coming up now," I said
as my footsteps echoed up the long flight of worn, stone stairs.
On the first landing was a single blue door, with a brass dolphin door knocker, and a white painted "2." I didn't need to
knock.

"Hello, Seriously Successful."

"Hallo, Tiffany Trott—how lovely to see you. Come in. And
Tiffany . . ."

"Yes."

"Happy birthday again."

"Thank you. How did you know?"

"You told me. When we first met. Don't you remember? We

talked about birth signs. Among other things." He ushered me into his sitting room—I gasped. It was huge, with a ceiling at least twenty feet high, and a vast bow window which entirely filled the far wall.

"What a place!" I said faintly, taking in the fine furniture and the Aubusson rug on the floor, and the paintings in elaborate gilded frames.

"It is rather special," he said. "It's had some quite famous residents too—Stamford Raffles lived here for a while, and Tennessee Williams had the set across the way."

There were cardboard boxes and packing cases everywhere. Seriously Successful was clearly in the middle of a major operation. He unhooked paintings from the wall as he talked.

"Now, this is a James Baker Pyne," he said, removing a large landscape from its place above the gigantic granite mantelpiece. "It's Coniston Water," he explained as he leaned it against the sofa, and I surveyed the calm lake and cloud-capped mountains. "And this," he added excitedly, "is a Huber." I looked at the brightly painted panel, covered in clouds and pudgy *putti*. "It's a *modello*," he explained, "a sketch for a ceiling painting in a Rococo Bavarian church. I love it. But they've all got to go into storage."

"Why?" I asked as I sank into an adjacent chair.

"Because I'm moving," he said as he placed his amber-colored cello in its fiberglass case.

"Why are you moving?" I asked him as he folded up his music stand.

"Because all good things must come to an end, Tiffany. And bad things, too."

"What are you talking about?"

"This isn't my flat, Tiffany. It belongs to Olivia. Well, to be accurate, it belongs to a trust controlled by her family."

"But why are you leaving?"

"Because I have to."

"Why?"

"Because she wants to live here now."

"I don't understand. Surely she can live here if she wants to—after all, she's your wife."

"Not for much longer, Tiffany."

"Good God."

"Yes, right now, I do think God *is* good."

"You've left her," I said.

"No," he said firmly. "She's left *me*." He smiled.

"Why?"

"I have been betrayed," he said melodramatically. "She loves . . . *another*!"

"She *does*?"

"Yes," he said as he began to stick bubble-wrap around the frames. " 'Frailty, thy name is woman!' " he added theatrically. *"Hamlet,"* he explained as he pulled another piece of Scotch tape off the roll. "Act One, scene two."

"She's gone off, then?"

"By George, she's got it! Yes, Tiffany, Olivia has fallen for someone. She has fallen for a fat fellow—Tiffany, just put your finger here, will you?—who shares her interest in—and now here, that's it, a bit tighter please—contemporary and conceptual art. Just once more, please, I don't want the gold leaf to get damaged. That's it. Good!" He stood up with the picture, and then carefully placed it in a crate. "In fact she's going to open a gallery with him," he went on. "It's what she's always wanted to do. Or to be more accurate, she's bailing *his* gallery out. He's in big trouble. In fact I suspect that Oscar Reeds' main interest in Olivia is remunerative rather than romantic," he added as he brushed down his jeans. "But I don't want to rain on her parade by telling her that. And maybe he'll make her happy. I know I couldn't. Perhaps he'll even get her off the Prozac."

"Oscar Reeds?"

He nodded, then shrugged his shoulders happily. "None other," he replied.

"How did they meet?"

"She used to drop in at his gallery from time to time, and she fell for his obvious charms," he said with a sardonic little laugh. "I've met him myself once and I can't quite see the appeal, but then I'm not a woman. Olivia says they talk the same language," he went on as he removed a small late eighteenth-century portrait from the wall. "They like the same things. And so they're going to open a new gallery in their joint names, and leave me to my Claude Lorrains. And so it makes sense for them to live here, near the new gallery, so she's asked me to give up the flat." He shrugged his shoulders, then laughed. "Goodbye, Piccadilly," he said with a smile.

"You seem rather happy about it all," I said.

"I am. I'm delighted. God, I'd like to shake that man by the hand. He's done me one hell of a favor."

"Where will you live?" I asked as I went to the window and looked down onto Savile Row. A cortège of taxis crawled down the street, like a procession of shiny black beetles.

"Oh I don't know," he said. "I'll go back to the farmhouse for a while and then find somewhere in town. I've liked it here, but I can be perfectly happy anywhere else."

"So it's all been taken out of your hands," I said. "She's left *you*."

"Yes," he replied with a grin. "Aren't I lucky? Now, would you like to come for a walk?"

We wandered down Piccadilly, past Hatchards, then crossed Duke Street, passed a shop selling expensive bags, walked through the Ritz's colonnade where gaudy mohair jumpers and gleaming leather jackets seemed to jostle for attention in the windows. Then we came to the gates of Green Park and turned in. There were couples everywhere, sprawled on the shining grass, lolling in stripy deck chairs, or strolling under the trees. A distant plane passed high overhead with a ripping, tearing sound. Glossy crows waddled around awkwardly, picking quarrels with the pigeons or lifting lazily up and down with a single flap of their huge black wings. We ambled down toward an avenue of plane trees, dressed in the glorious lime green of early summer, and found a bench which was half in shade.

"Let's sit here," he said.

Seriously Successful drew me to him and we sat there, side by side, smiling into the sunlight, our thighs touching. Then he took my right hand in his right hand, and slipped his left arm around my shoulder. A wave of heat rose up, like mercury in a thermometer, from my toes to the crown of my head.

"Well, Tiffany, here we are," said Seriously Successful simply.

"Yes," I said. "Here we are." And then his face drew nearer and nearer, and I felt his lips on mine, dry and soft, and I could smell the Givenchy on his neck, and I thought, if I were to die, right now, this instant, then I wouldn't mind at all, because I'd die feeling incredibly happy. And the roar of the traffic was masked by the blood pumping in my ears, and the urgent, rhythmic banging of my heart. Then Seriously Successful kissed me again, and then he just kept hold of my hand, fiddling with my fingers, as though they were a puzzle he was trying to solve.

"Oh Tiffany," he said quietly. "You're so lovely and . . ." he cast his eyes to the sky, ". . . odd."

"Thank you," I said.

"That's why I like you so much," he said. "Because I find you so . . . peculiar."

"Singular?" I suggested.

"Yes," he said. "That's it. Singular. And you're so well informed, Tiffany. I mean, the things you know." He looked at me quizzically. "137?" he said.

"Um, Crystal Palace to Oxford Circus."

"Via?"

"Oh. Um. Clapham Common and Hyde Park Corner."

"Very good. 271?"

"Liverpool Street to Highgate."

"Stopping at?"

"Essex Road and Holloway."

"Yes. OK, the . . . 249?"

"Waterloo to White Hart Lane, via Seven Sisters."

"Excellent. And what about the number 65?"

"Oh . . . er . . . er . . ."

"Come on."

"Um . . . oh . . ."

"I'm sorry. I'll have to hurry you."

"Er, Ealing Broadway!" I said suddenly.

"Going to?"

"Oh God, um, um, Kingston. Yes, Kingston, via Kew Bridge and Richmond."

"Excellent. The number 48?"

"London Bridge to Walthamstow via . . . Shoreditch and Hackney Central."

"Very impressive. And finally," he said, "the 68a."

"Oh I know that one. Um . . . Elephant and Castle to South Croydon via Camberwell and Herne Hill," I concluded happily.

"Oh Tiffany," said Seriously Successful. "You're so clever." And then he kissed me again. "And Tiffany?"

"Yes?" I looked up into his brown eyes, and then he reached again for my hand, my left hand, and started fiddling with my fingers again.

"You know, Tiffany, a Double Diamond Works Wonders . . ."

"Does it?" I said faintly.

"Yes. And I was just wondering whether . . . later on . . . my circumstances having unexpectedly changed, I might be able to interest you in a . . . in a . . . full-time position?"

"Oh. Oh . . . well . . . I don't . . . I don't . . ."

"Because you see, Tiffany"—he looked down at me—"it's the Real Thing, isn't it?"

I laughed. "Well, I don't know . . ."

"We're Getting There, aren't we?" he added with an inquiring smile.

"Well, yes . . . yes . . . maybe," I conceded. "Possibly . . . I . . ."

"Yes," he said. "I really think we are. And I feel we should be together, Tiffany, you and I, Because Life's Complicated Enough."

To our left, a little way off, was a very young woman with a small boy. And she was reading to him from *The Wind in the Willows*. I glanced at them out of the corner of my eye as they sat cross-legged on the grass. She looked like his nanny, rather than his mother, and the little boy was listening to her, entranced, and occasionally peering at the pictures.

" 'Rat was walking a little way ahead . . . ,' " I heard her say, " '. . . as his habit was, his shoulders humped, his eyes fixed on the straight gray road in front of him; so he did not notice poor Mole when suddenly the summons reached him, and took him like an electric shock.' "

"Why did your father-in-law impose that condition on you all those years ago?" I asked. "About never leaving Olivia."

"Because of what happened to him."

"What did happen?"

"He left Olivia's mother, for another woman, just before their silver wedding anniversary. A month later Olivia's mother killed herself, and he's been racked with guilt ever since. And so he tried to ensure that that would never happen to his daughter. I suppose he was trying to rewrite his own emotional history, and I was ambitious enough to accept his terms and you see, Tiffany . . ."

"Yes?"

"I do keep my promises, you know. And I really *was* worried about how it would affect Saskia. But I think she'll be OK. We've talked about it and she seems to understand far more than I thought. And there certainly won't be any problems about access. And you'll be such a lovely stepmother, Tiffany."

"Oh."

"You got on so well with Saskia at the wedding. She told me afterward how much she liked you."

"Well, I liked her too . . ."

"And we could have such a nice life, Tiffany. Of course you'll have to sell your house," he added.

"Oh."

" ' *"Please,* stop, Ratty!" pleaded the poor Mole, in anguish of heart. "You don't understand! It's my home, my old home! I've just come across the smell of it, and . . . I *must* go to it, I must, I must!" ' "

"But we could have a lovely flat somewhere. Maybe in Belgravia."

" ' "O, come back, Ratty! Please, please come back!" ' "

"Or perhaps Knightsbridge."

" 'The Rat was by this time very far ahead, too far to hear clearly what the Mole was calling, too far to catch the sharp note of painful appeal in his voice.' "

"And of course you wouldn't have to work anymore." My euphoria dipped, and died.

" 'Poor Mole stood alone in the road, his heart torn asunder, and a big sob gathering, gathering, somewhere low down inside him, to leap up to the surface presently, he knew, in passionate escape.' "

"Now," said Seriously Successful, "are you enjoying your birthday, Tiffany?"

"Oh, oh, yes," I said. "I mean so far, it's been, very, well, memorable," I said truthfully.

"And have you had any presents yet?"

"No. No I haven't. My parents will give me something when I see them," I added. "But I've had some cards." In fact I was carrying that day's mail about with me in my bag. I removed Lizzie's birthday card and showed it to him. "She's my best friend," I explained, as a boy on roller-blades whizzed by with a spaniel barking at his heels. I reread Lizzie's postscript: *Alice is ecstatic,* she wrote. *Catherine has asked the girls to officiate. So you're off the hook—for now!*

"Can *I* give you a present, Tiffany?" said Seriously Successful suddenly.

"Gosh! Well . . ."

"I'd really like to."

"Well, yes. OK. Thank you. That would be lovely."

"Right then. Let's go shopping." He held my hand as we walked out of the park, crossed the road and went up the steps of the Burlington Arcade. We stood outside N. Peal cashmere.

"Made to Make Your Mouth Water," he quipped. Then we strolled through the glass-ceilinged arcade, looking at Georgina von Etzdorf's velvet scarves, and Mont Blanc pens, and fine leather bags in Franchetti Bond, and then Seriously Successful stopped outside the Burlington Jewelers, and suddenly my heart seemed to sink. "I think we might find something in here," he said.

"Oh no, far too expensive," I said.

"Rubbish. In fact," he said, peering through the glass, "they're Surprisingly Ordinary Prices."

"No, but Seriously . . ."

"Come on!"

"Well, as long it's very, very small," I said, suddenly filled with misgivings.

We sat at a glass counter, while Seriously Successful went through the merchandise, rejecting brooches, watches, earrings, dress rings, and strings of cultured pearls. I sat there, silently. Now he was looking at gold chains. The manager put about ten in front of us, on a red velvet tray. Seriously Successful looked at them all, and held them up against my throat. Finally he selected one that he seemed to like, and he put it round my neck. It was very, very heavy, with thick eighteen-carat links.

"Oh Tiffany, it's lovely," he said. "Can I give you this one? I'd love you to have it." What could I say?

"Well, if you're sure, I mean it's really beautiful, but it's so . . ."

"It's just you," said Seriously Successful.

"Well, thank you. Thank you very much," I said, as Seriously

Successful got out his credit card. I looked at myself in the hand mirror. It *was* beautiful, but it was so big, and so heavy, and the links were just . . . enormous. And the metal appeared warm, but against my skin it was cold, and although I could see that it *looked* good, somehow it just didn't *feel* right. Seriously Successful signed his name on the slip with a flourish.

"Thank you, Mr. Clutterbuck," said the jeweler with an ingratiating smile. I looked at Seriously Successful.

"Clutterbuck?" I said. He nodded. I glanced at his sprawling signature. "D. W. Clutterbuck," it said.

"What does the 'D' stand for?"

He gave a little cough. "Damian."

"Oh. And the 'W'?"

"Warren."

"Damian Clutterbuck?" He nodded.

"Damian Warren Clutterbuck." I smiled at him. "Now I know!"

"Yes. My dreadful secret is out, Tiffany," he said with an embarrassed grin. "Do you still feel the same about me?"

"What? Oh yes. Yes, of course I do," I said truthfully. "Don't be silly . . . Damian." *Honestly, your truly awful name makes absolutely no difference to how I feel.* And, gentle reader, it didn't. Because when he secured the gold clasp round my neck, I realized then, in that instant, exactly how I felt. Something that I knew to be there, but had not yet been able to see, now, suddenly, became clear—like a photo gradually emerging in a tray of developing fluid, it had shape, and form, and depth. And what it was, was doubt. That was it. I felt doubtful. Very, very doubtful. I felt things closing around me, Seriously Suffocating, and the ceiling begin to descend. I didn't really want to be tied down, I realized. It felt all wrong. Anyway, I was too young, I said to myself. Far too young. I had my whole life before me. There were so many people I still wanted to meet, places I wanted to go, and things I needed to do before I could possibly take such a momentous step. In my mind's eye

I could see myself Seriously Settled, and suddenly I was Seriously Scared. Did I really want what Seriously Successful was offering? And did I really want to be full-time? I wasn't sure that I did. And did I really want to live in Belgravia? No. In fact, did I *want* to say I do? No. I didn't. I really didn't. And in any case, I thought, as I picked up my bag, José is coming to London! But . . . then . . . on the other hand . . . I thought wearily as we left the shop, Seriously Successful is *so* nice. He's the answer to a maiden's prayer. With him I could be "we" instead of "me," and familiarity would probably breed content. And he does have *such* a comprehensive knowledge of advertising slogans, and *such* good taste in ties . . . and oh God, I thought as we strolled down Piccadilly together—oh God, what on earth should I *do*?